ADRIAN LAING

KOSMOS

This is a **FLAME TREE PRESS** book

FLAME TREE PRESS
6 Melbray Mews, London, SW6 3NS, UK
flametreepress.com

Distribution and warehouse:
Marston Book Services Ltd
160 Eastern Avenue, Milton Park, Abingdon, Oxon, OX14 4SB
www.marston.co.uk

Publisher's Note: This is a work of fiction. Names, characters, places, and
incidents are a product of the author's imagination. Locales and public names
are sometimes used for atmospheric purposes. Any resemblance to actual
people, living or dead, or to businesses, companies, events, institutions, or
locales is completely coincidental.

Thanks to the Flame Tree Press team, including:
Taylor Bentley, Frances Bodiam, Federica Ciaravella, Don D'Auria,
Chris Herbert, Matteo Middlemiss, Josie Mitchell, Mike Spender,
Cat Taylor, Maria Tissot, Nick Wells, Gillian Whitaker.

The cover is created by Flame Tree Studio with
thanks to Nik Keevil and Shutterstock.com.
The font families in this book are Avenir and Bembo.

Flame Tree Press is an imprint of Flame Tree Publishing Ltd
flametreepublishing.com

A copy of the CIP data for this book is available from the British Library.

HB ISBN: 978-1-78758-053-4
PB ISBN: 978-1-78758-052-7
ebook ISBN: 978-1-78758-054-1
Also available in FLAME TREE AUDIO

Printed in the UK at Clays, Suffolk

ADRIAN LAING

KOSMOS

FLAME TREE PRESS
London & New York

Dedicated to my wife, Deborah

PART ONE
THE AWAKENING

'Souls never die, but always on quitting one abode pass to another. All things change, nothing perishes. The soul passes hither and thither, occupying now this body, now that.... As a wax is stamped with certain figures, then melted, then stamped anew with others, yet it is always the same wax. So, the Soul being always the same, yet wears at different times different forms.'
Attributed to Pythagoras of Samos c. 570 – 495 B.C.

CHAPTER ONE
Disturbance

20th September 2000, Hampstead Heath, North London.

"Is he dead? Oh God, that's all we need," muttered Fred, one of the dog patrollers, as he drove past the high mound of earth where the Iceni Queen, Boudicca, was once thought to have been buried.

Hampstead Heath had seen its fair share of strange events over the years. The sight of a corpse, lying facedown in the dew-fresh grass, decomposing and returning to Mother Earth, was not that exceptional. Once, maybe twice, a year a body would be found, half hiding in some quiet corner of the once-wild expanse of woodland now dominated by dog-walkers, seriously committed joggers, female middle-aged American power walkers, celebrities puffing behind their personal trainers, and liberal North London types attracted by the life-enhancing experience of a dip in the freezing-cold, open-air bathing ponds. It was just past six o'clock in the morning.

Fred and Kevin had been working together as a dog patrol team for nearly two years. Their job was to maintain a watch over the Heath and respond to calls concerning problems with dogs, which were many.

Fred came to a slow halt in his little patrol van and decamped from the vehicle. He and Kevin walked slowly closer to the body. This was not so easy, as the mound was covered with a fairly dense and irregular circle of high Norwegian fir trees, which itself was surrounded by two concentric railings, the inner one of metal and the outer of wood, to keep the notoriously inquisitive public at a safe distance.

Fred, being both Kevin's boss and older by many years, naturally asked Kevin to go first. "Maybe we should just call the police and let them deal with it," suggested Kevin, fearing the worst as he ungracefully clambered over the railings. "If it's a drugs case, I don't want to know."

From the safe distance of the car, there appeared to be a large, highly decorated object lying almost upright against one of the trees – perhaps a piece of wood or maybe a stick.

As Kevin inched closer it looked more elaborate, like a walking stick lovingly carved and covered in all manner of trinkets, charms, and coloured ribbons. On closer inspection it was clearly a hiking staff, the head of which looked unusual, perhaps a bone from a small animal, probably an antler, thought Kevin.

As Kevin approached ever nearer to the scene, he was struck by the appearance of an elderly man, who was curled into a near-foetal position at the very top of the rising, in the centre of the trees. His hair was long, but thin, grey, and tightly matted. His clothes looked almost theatrical, a baggy dark blue cloak half covered a faded pair of crimson velvet-looking trousers. The shoes looked handmade and basic, like medieval leather slippers. More than that was difficult to see.

"Is he dead or what?" old Fred whispered as he leaned over the railings, now worried that a stray walker with an inquisitive dog would become entangled in the events. "I bet he's a leftover from last night's concert at Kenwood. I told them *The Sound of Music* would do their heads in."

Edging closer through surprisingly thick growth, Kevin lost his nerve completely. "I don't know and I don't wanna know. It don't feel right, Fred. Let's get out of here."

Fred decided that he would have to show Kevin why Fred was the boss. If they reported a rotting corpse to the police, only to be informed later that it was a sleeping drunk who had crashed out for a few hours on his way back from a fancy-dress party, he and Kevin would be the butt of jokes back at the sheds for the foreseeable future. Fred did his best to climb over the railings without making it look like the effort it was, and boldly moved closer to the body.

The staff was irresistible to Fred, who, without hesitation, picked it up and held it outstretched. "Jesus, it's got some weight to it, Kevin," he said, and quite instinctively decided to prod the old sod who was threatening to ruin his day.

Fred dug the staff into the rib cage of the still-quiet body, and again, and yet again. The combined effect of all the bits and pieces on the body of the staff made a cheap-sounding trinkety noise.

Kevin had already resigned himself to a tedious day of interviews with the police, paperwork, and sitting around, when a soft muted sound came from the body.

"Shit, he's alive!" squealed Kevin.

Fred acquired the posture fully befitting his hard-earned status of Senior Dog Patroller, standing upright, leaning with his two hands on the staff like a farmer commanding his dogs. "Get up, you old beggar. You frightened the shit out of us, and now it's going-home time. Come on, it's a new moon, you silly old dip-hip."

The old boy stirred and moved his head towards Kevin, his tired but clear blue eyes indicating more fear and disorientation than menace while they sought to focus upon the outside world. He began patting his body as if seeking reassurance that everything was where it was supposed to be. But he looked so old and dirty it was difficult to tell where the bits of dirt and twigs ended and the frail-looking body began.

Fred reacted by appearing relaxed and stood back, sounding pleased with himself. "Take your stick and move it, old boy. Try Bishop's Avenue. This party's over."

After rising ever so slowly to his feet, the slight figure moved sheepishly towards Fred with an outstretched hand, gesturing for the return of the staff. Once the hand of the old man had made contact with the staff, Fred felt a keen and determined pull, which surprised and annoyed him. He pulled the staff back with a smile and a sneer, despite the sudden realisation of his disadvantage of being on lower ground. Without any words being exchanged, but with many grunts, groans, and mean eye-to-eye contact, Fred and the old boy engaged in a spontaneous tug-of-war over the staff.

Quite suddenly, while still holding his grasp on the staff, the old man became completely motionless, and then without warning swung the staff with a compelling force. Fred, according to Kevin's statement to police later that day, was lifted right off his feet and was flung into the air, landing awkwardly against the inner railings in a thick growth of nettles.

Fred groaned in pain and humiliation while Kevin ran to his aid.

"You just wait, you silly old bastard, you'll pay for that. You'll be paying over the odds for non-slippy soap before you know it! Oh, my back! I'll be off for weeks with this. Stay away from me, you old devil. Kevin, help me up, we're getting the police all right."

CHAPTER TWO
Chambers

Three Harcourt Square was a home away from home for George Winsome. Situated in a quiet courtyard in the very heart of the Temple on the northern banks of the River Thames, sheltered from the public gaze by the high mock-Tudor facades of the modern world of banks, clothes shops and cafés, near the ancient Inner Temple Church, where effigies of the Knights Templar lay in glorious and respectful silence, chambers were a haven of peace despite being no more than a couple of hundred yards from the bustle of Fleet Street and Chancery Lane.

Thirty-three barristers worked from these chambers, comprised of twelve rooms spread over two floors. Barristers-in-training – pupils – came and went; once taken on by a set of chambers, a pupil became a tenant and was immediately immortalised with a hand-painted wooden slat bearing their name on the outside communal entrances.

George was still a pupil and therefore not a 'real' barrister, although that statement would raise eyebrows from those he represented in court. The first six months of his pupillage with his pupil master – a senior member of chambers – Laurence Trivoli, an extremely cultured middle-aged criminal hack of noble Italian extraction, had been successfully completed three months previously, and now he was entitled to accept instructions from those few solicitors who maintained miraculous faith in a clerk's judgement as to which pupil was right for any particular case. The clerks' power over pupils was awesome, like an experienced talent agent and a young actor. The system had worked for as long as anyone could remember, and worked well because the clerks acquired knowledge and skill over many years, often passed on from generation to generation.

Paul Styles, the senior clerk at Three Harcourt, had spent over thirty years developing his skills and while he felt every decision he made was a gamble, it was a calculated gamble, which invariably paid off. Paul belonged to the old school of senior clerks who dressed immaculately and was often mistaken for one of the barristers from his 'set'.

The names on the thin, narrow wooden boards outside the communal entrance changed slowly over the years, like a slow-motion film credit rolling slower than the growth of a blade of grass.

The older, predominately male barristers would usually retire or accept academic or judicial appointments. Some might fade from life following an illness or other catastrophe normally involving drink or women, or more often, drink *and* women. The name of a new member of chambers would be added to the bottom of the list on average once a year following a series of chambers' meetings culminating in the do-or-die 'tenancy meeting,' during which the future of a pupil would be reviewed and discussed and decided upon, every member acutely aware of the enormity of the consequences of the collective decision for the pupil. For every 'tenancy' awarded to a profoundly grateful pupil, there were at least five rejections each year.

The head of chambers, Michael Backawf QC ('M.B.' to his friends), aged fifty-eight, was considered by his peers to be enlightened and progressive. Though he had warmly embraced – 'in principle' – the new technology that many chambers were still managing to avoid, he had written a well-received article in the *Bar News*, which had argued passionately that 'email was the most dangerous threat to interpersonal communication since the television'. M.B. agreed with the Bar Council that every member of chambers should – 'in due course' – have a monitor on his or her desk. (Obviously it would take some time to agree what 'in due course' meant, and difficulties were envisaged over the fact that only fifteen members of chambers had a desk they could call their own.)

In September of 2000, George was one of five pupils. The competition for a place in chambers was fierce and frightening. George had no plan B if they did not take him on as a tenant – in effect a lifelong partnership with a guaranteed, ready-made practice. George had a lot in his favour: he was not too bright (Three Harcourt had never taken on a pupil with a first-class degree for fear that such an individual would walk in with too much of a career advantage over everyone else in chambers), he was good-looking and he had a sense of humour. George also knew, instinctively, that he should never – ever – bad-mouth the competition. So long as he fanned the egos of the tenants, embraced the wisdom of his esteemed pupil master, kept on the right side of the clerks, and worked hard he was in with a chance. The black-ball tradition of entrance to chambers sharpened the diplomatic skills of pupils to a standard required of a seasoned politician.

The first hurdle to overcome was not M.B. but Paul Styles. The senior clerk did not attend chambers' meetings, but his recommendation was the most influential ingredient for the application to be successful. If the senior clerk had 'put a word in,' and your pupil master was still on your side, you had a chance. So far, George was on track. But it could all go wrong in five minutes, at any point in time.

★   ★   ★

An invitation for a 'little, private chat' with the senior clerk was not to be turned down. Yes, it might be bad news, but then again it might not. "George," said Paul, talking loudly to overcome the well-bred voices in the background of the Fleet Street wine bar, "what are your ambitions at the Bar? Where do you see yourself in five years' time?"

George took a very small sip from the glass of white wine and collected his thoughts.

"My mother always joked that I would be knighted one day."

"So, you're aiming for the High Court?"

"Well, I don't know. There's nothing more satisfying than making a great speech. And there is no greater challenge than representing a man in front of his peers, with his liberty and reputation at stake. I can imagine no other life. I can't wait for my first jury trial."

"How did you get on today at Southend?"

"I was for John Smith, as you know. He was up for drink-driving and assault on the arresting officers."

"Did you win?"

"We won the assault charge and went down fighting on the drink driving."

"The client was happy with the result?"

"Sure, and the family. I'm sure Leggitt will hear favourable reports, in due course."

"That's good, George. Always remember who your client is."

Paul took a long gulp from his pint of cold lager and looked at George intensely.

"George. You know how important the Leggitt firm is to our chambers. That firm accounts for nearly sixty-five percent of our business. We do try and spread our bets but we always end up with Leggitt. Bernie Armour has been the main man there for nearly ten years, ever since old Leggitt – Ralph – God bless him – was killed in a car accident on his way to the Old Bailey. You've probably heard that story. Anyway, Bernie has confided in me that he's getting tired of this game and wants to retire pretty soon. He's been grooming Leggitt's boy – Sam – to take over the reins when he goes. Have you met Sam?"

"Er, can't say I have, Paul. Obviously, I've heard of him."

"Well, you will soon enough. The point is that a lot of briefs will be coming into chambers from Sam, and I want you to know that he's taken a shine to you – you're about the same age – and Sam wants to try you out with a trial. He knows it's your first. I just want you to know how important it is for chambers for you to keep Sam happy. The papers will be arriving tomorrow. The case has yet to be sent for trial, but that's where it's going. Nothing too heavy, just an assault case involving some old nutter. First thing is to get him bail and make sure the case ends up in the Crown Court. Right up your street, eh, George?"

"A real trial? I'm...I'm in heaven. Thanks, Paul, I won't let you down."

"I know you won't, George. I know a lot about you, it's my business. I know what happened to your dad. Laurence told me the story. I even know the counsel who represented your father. He was a very honourable guy, your dad."

George looked down, worried that tears might show in his eyes. George's dad had worked himself up from a lowly door-to-door insurance salesman to become chief executive of the company he had dedicated his life to for over thirty years. The company was bought out in a dawn raid. The new owners had insisted that his father sack half the workforce. When he refused he was dismissed on a false charge of claiming bogus expenses, cleared his name, but died of a heart attack days after the court decision that finally vindicated him, four years after he was sacked. George was thirteen years old when his father died. The press, at the time, sung his father's praises and portrayed him as an innocent victim of modern-day corporate thuggery.

George composed himself. "I can only try to live up to my father's name. He really was a good man, and the treatment he received motivated me to become a lawyer, a good lawyer."

At which point Paul's mobile phone rang with a surprisingly plausible rendition of 'Land of Hope and Glory,' and Paul made his way back to chambers, leaving George on cloud nine. George looked at his watch. Nearly seven o'clock. Time for a drink.

It was no surprise that the Middle Temple Bar was packed out. It always was at seven o'clock. Sitting in one of their usual spots was Heather Armstrong, a fellow pupil of George's, and David Palmer from a nearby rival set of chambers. It didn't take long before George was holding the floor among his brothers.

"So, this guy John Smith is so permanently pissed he can hardly speak, let alone take the oath. His entire family has been drunk for about three generations. Whenever he's asked a threatening question by the mags or the prosecution, he says 'pardon?' Well, exactly how much did you drink that afternoon? Pardon? Was PC Hyde telling the truth when he says that you literally fell out of the car? Pardon? Was your car veering across the road as suggested by the independent witness? Pardon? Are you suggesting that three police officers have fabricated their evidence against you? Pardon? How do you account for that fact that you smelt, as the officer put it, 'Like a brewery'? Pardon? Well, this goes on for about half an hour and the clerk is getting increasingly agitated. Eventually he explodes and yells at the defendant, 'This "pardon?" response is wearing a bit thin. Do you suffer from some sort of medical affliction affecting your hearing, in which case no doubt your counsel will produce some corroborative medical evidence, or is this merely a ruse to avoid saying anything that might be remotely damaging to your case? Well, Mr. Smith?' Long pause, followed by 'Pardon?'"

David nearly fell over in tears of laughter, as did three others who overheard the tale. Heather brushed away the fringe of her fiery red hair and merely sighed.

"That's a very typical Winsome case. I can imagine hearing that one in ten years' time as if it was yesterday. You're destined to represent the arseholes of the world, George. Why don't you grow up?"

"Your problem is that your cases are all so fucking heavy, Heather. No doubt you've been down the juvenile court pouring your heart out for some ten-year-old trainee psychopath who's been caught supplying crack cocaine to buy a new pair of trainers."

David chuckled. "How did you know, George?"

Heather looked very serious when she said, "George, you may think all of this is a bit of a lark, but do you think it will help you get taken on?"

"Rumour has it that Paul reckons you're dumb enough to accept a tenancy at Three Harcourt, eh George?" enquired David. "We heard about your tête-à-tête with Paul before you had finished your glass of chilled Sauvignon."

"It's all right for you, David. Your chambers will be in deep shit if it doesn't take on at least one person who isn't a privately educated, Oxbridge white boy this year. You're likely to take silk before you're thirty, hit the bench before you're forty and end up in the upper house while you've still got hair on your head. Hail positive discrimination, and the very best to you!"

"Less of your shit, George. I'm from the Caribbean not Botswana, you silly white mother. There's probably more upper-class blood in my DNA than there is in yours," David said before he roared with laughter.

George lowered his head. "I'm sorry, David. Don't know where that crap comes from. Guess I've still got some growing up to do."

"Excuse me, guys, but I've got work to do," interrupted Heather.

"See you later, Heather," said David.

"No sense of humour, that's her problem, eh David?"

"Needs a good man to put a smile on her face," David answered.

"You can go first."

"No, after you, George. The pipe and slippers can wait. I'm ready for another beer."

CHAPTER THREE
Merlin

By late September 2000, George Winsome had been playing the role of barrister, on his own feet, for nearly four months. He had been taught by his esteemed pupil master, and now knew instinctively to treat police officers 'like shit when defending and with contempt if prosecuting.' "Address the public as you would talk to your father's chauffeur," advised his pupil master.

At least George had developed a sartorial consciousness – it was critical to dress immaculately always, and especially if there was no wig and gown to hide behind.

Whether or not George was wearing 'the kit', as he called his court uniform, his thinly striped double-breasted suit would be freshly dry-cleaned, the usually cream-white shirt with a detachable collar crisply ironed, the not-too-loud stylish silk tie twisted and turned expertly into a sharp triangular Windsor knot, with a matching silk handkerchief casually stuffed into the left-hand jacket breast pocket, cuff-links mostly of gold and always expensive, amusing, and prominent; black leather brogues spit-polished, every one of his short jet-black hairs in its place, his sharp-featured face closely and lovingly shaved and gently washed over with his favourite Aramis aftershave lotion, regularly flossed white teeth almost shining and, of course, fingernails trimmed and clean. Every day he remembered the words of his pupil master on the subject of 'presentation of self in everyday life': "If you look like crap, you are crap. If you look great, you are great."

To complete the overall image, George carried around a large black leather case, sometimes referred to as a 'pilot's case'. The case was large but not large enough to be confused with the box of tricks carried by a travelling salesman. It was the home of his beloved kit: a large oval-shaped black-and-gold-coloured box bearing his full name in gold leaf on the outside that contained his embarrassingly white horsehair wig, three detachable wing collars (stiff), collar studs (cheap), and several (brand-new) bands. Wrapped around the box was a long black gown, impervious to creases. Stuffed in the farthest corner of the bag was the most recent edition of Archbold's textbook on criminal law and procedure.

As George was not able to afford a car, the tedious Underground journey and short walk to the courtroom threatened his immaculate image, but normally three or four minutes', quick work in the men's toilet would restore his perfection.

It was ten o'clock in the morning of a very cold and overcast day in Highgate, outside Highgate Magistrates' Court, which was adjacent to the police station. In thirty minutes the three magistrates' courts would open for business. Those thirty minutes were always a very tense time for the police officers who dealt with the lawyers of those who they kept in custody in the cells of the station.

George sniffed the still-cold morning air, put on his most serious barrister face, pulled open the door to the station, puffed himself out, and walked up to the officer in charge, bristling with confidence. "I trust my client is still in one piece, otherwise you'll be sweeping the streets like the rest of your family," George announced to everyone.

The duty sergeant had heard it all before and couldn't be bothered with the antics of yet another arrogant young member of the Bar. His time would come, eventually.

"Mr. Winsome. What a pleasure. Yes, old Merlin. He's in suite 101. Been waiting for you. Ring the bell for room service, won't you?"

"Suite 101? I hope the view is the same as in the brochure, otherwise I'll need to file a formal complaint."

"Watkins. Take Mr. Winsome to the executive suite on the lower floor."

"Sure, Sarge. This way, please, sir."

George always felt sick walking down into prison cells. Always. It wasn't the smell. It was just the feeling incarceration induced.

PC 2150, or Watkins as he was known, selected one key from the assorted bunch dangling from his trouser pocket and turned it this way and that, before pushing the cell door open to reveal a now-familiar image of a darkened room, eight feet by ten, one heavy wooden board covered in seditious graffiti underneath the small dirty window, and a lonely soul looking like a refugee from a fancy-dress party that had gone pear-shaped, sitting on the edge of the seat, which was often used for sleeping, his head in his hands.

George had been briefed, as promised, by Sam Leggitt. The few pieces of A4-size paper folded vertically in half and wrapped around with lashings of red tape hadn't taken long to read, and told a rather sad story of an old man who had been arrested at about six a.m., Wednesday, the 20th of September 2000, on Hampstead Heath following a fracas with two dog patrollers, one of whom had slightly injured his back and was now off work. The medical report had not yet been submitted.

The defendant had been interviewed by the police, who informed the duty solicitor – Sam Leggitt – who managed to spend five minutes or so with 'Merlin', the name given to the police by the old man, and had advised his client to say nothing. Little damage had been done. The old boy had said very little. On his charge sheet his name was simply recorded as 'Merlin'. Under the heading 'Reason for Arrest' it was stated that he had 'assaulted a dog patroller over Hampstead Heath causing actual bodily harm'.

The door slammed behind George and he sat down at the other end of the bench, carefully placing his case beside him and quietly taking out a fresh blue counsel's notebook with the conveniently serrated edges, and gently clicking the top of his favourite gold-plated Parker ballpoint pen. He opened the notebook and wrote in large capital letters: *Merlin: Highgate Mags, Wednesday, 20th September 2000, NISP* (the latter entry being George's shorthand for 'no instructing solicitor present').

George surveyed his immediate territory. Unusually peaceful. The client was quiet, perhaps too quiet. Sitting at one end of the bench with his head in his hands, his thin long grey hair protruding from his long grey fingers, he cut a sad and lonely figure. The white beard had almost turned into dreadlocks. There was only five feet or so between George and this old man, but George could hear nothing, until a soft and familiar sobbing sound came from Merlin's end of the bench. The old boy was definitely crying like a baby.

Although George had been through the crying routine before, this was the first time the crier was an adult male, and he felt deeply uncomfortable. Not knowing what to say, he said nothing and did nothing until the moment passed. George took the opportunity to have a good look at his new cellmate. He looked scruffy and dishevelled. His shoes, being no more than thin leather moccasins, must give little protection from cold concrete, thought George. He looked quickly at the charge sheet to confirm the only item that had been removed at the time of arrest was a wooden staff.

It was time to break the ice.

"Er, Mr. Merlin. Are you all right? My name is George Winsome. I am your counsel – your barrister, instructed by your solicitor, Sam Leggitt, who I understand you met on the day of your arrest. I will be representing you in court this morning. We only have a few minutes before we go upstairs to the magistrates' court. If you want me to make a bail application then I'll need some basic information. You told the police that your name is Merlin. Is that your real name? I need your help, please."

The sobbing recommenced with fresh vigour as the small flap on the cell door flipped open.

"Five minutes, Mr. Winsome," bawled PC 2150 in a surprisingly deep voice.

George heard himself say, "The audience will need to wait. First night nerves and all that. My tutu is too tight. Whatever. We'll need another half an hour."

"Your call, Mr. Winsome, sir."

This was new ground for George. Young barristers learnt the art of survival as quickly as front-line troops. To get in and out of a crowded magistrates' court it was essential to be ready. Counsel or solicitors who were unready were placed at the back of the long line of cases waiting to go on, and the next opportunity to stand up and say what had to be said and return to the sanctity of chambers might not occur until noon or later. Much later. And the pay – if it ever arrived – was the same whether it took ten minutes or four hours.

"As I was saying, Mr. Merlin, er, Merlin. May I call you Merlin? When we go upstairs to court there will be three people who will decide today whether to grant you bail or not. If they don't grant you bail today then you will wait for your trial in jail, perhaps until next year. Unless, of course, you wish to plead guilty, in which case there's a good chance you'll walk today. However, if you want to fight the case and want me to make an application for bail, then I'll need some basic information about you. Where you live, what you do, your age, your personal circumstances. Do you understand me, Merlin?"

George's patience had already been exhausted. He brought his face so close to Merlin's their noses were pressed against each other. He looked into the water-filled crystal-blue eyes in the midst of the tired, aged, well-worn face that reminded George of his grandfather shortly before his death at age ninety-one. George momentarily dropped his professional guard and saw the image of a man for whom he felt enormous sympathy. Ignoring the excess mucus dribbling down from the corners of Merlin's thin mouth, George said, "I need to know where you live, all right?"

Merlin moved his tear-stained face away from George's.

"You are on my side. I can tell. Praise the forces. You are here to fight my cause. Who sent you? St. Yves?"

"It doesn't matter who sent me, does it? I need to know where you live."

"Yes, yes, of course you do. I understand. I have been known by many names, but Merlin is the name I remember my name to be. If I am not Merlin, then who am I? I live under the stars. I have been asleep for a very long time. Some…" Merlin paused for a moment, looking distant and distracted. "Some force disturbed my peace. Two ruffians set upon me. I feared for my life. That is all. I am so tired."

George wrote down in his pad: *Name: Merlin. NFA* (being the common abbreviation for 'no fixed abode'), and *SD* for self-defence.

"The point, Merlin, is that we are to appear in front of the magistrates this morning for them to decide whether to grant you bail or remand you in custody pending your trial. Do you understand that?"

"I fear your language is not entirely familiar. I am to be tried? By what ordeal?"

"No, Merlin. There is no trial today. Today the magistrates decide whether you stay in jail before your trial or whether you are allowed out."

"These men have such power. Well, I should like to be free."

"Yes, that's what I'm here for. But in order for me to persuade them to let you out, I will need to let them know where you'll be staying."

"But my kind sir, this is a strange world and I have nowhere I call home. My powers have deserted me."

George realised that his best bet lay with the social services – try and find the old boy a bed for a few days while his background could be pieced together.

George stood up to push the large red button that would signal to the officers he was ready to come up for air.

"Merlin. Listen to me. I will try and find you somewhere to stay. The social services will need to do some ringing around. So I'll need to leave you just now. I'll see you in court later this morning."

Merlin pulled George towards him, and hugged him, and hugged him some more.

"Yeah, OK, Merlin. Nice. OK. See you later," George squeaked.

Merlin put his hands around George's face and pulled George towards him.

"The dungeons are not that bad, my friend. I have seen worse, much worse. I miss the moon, that's all."

★   ★   ★

"Bail refused."

"But sir, this man cannot be considered a risk to anyone. The police have no evidence that he has a criminal past. It's really a matter of finding the old boy a place to stay. The social services are on the case, trying very hard to find him somewhere to stay. The charges are relatively minor. Even if convicted he would not expect an immediate custodial sentence. To remand the defendant in custody is unnecessary and unjust, and a waste of public funds, with all due respect, sir."

The three lay magistrates informally conferred on one side and then the other.

"Mr. Winsome. Your client thinks he's Merlin, for goodness' sake. He is accused of a serious assault. He has no address. We think the police should check with the psychiatric wards of the nearest mental hospitals to see if one of their inmates, sorry, *service-users*, has escaped. Until we know who he is and where he stays we can't be expected to put the public at risk by letting him roam at large. Your application is refused, Mr. Winsome. Next case, please."

CHAPTER FOUR
Tenancy

Once a year the entire membership of Three Harcourt Square convenes to decide whether any of the current batch of pupils should be offered a place in chambers. A tenancy in a decent set of chambers is the Holy Grail to a would-be barrister. As they say in football circles, it's not a matter of life and death; it's far more important than that.

There were five candidates, including George Winsome and Heather Armstrong. The three others, Adrian Boswell, Stephen Hampshire and Roberta Baker, were non-runners for varied reasons. Adrian had been overheard saying to a fellow pupil that he thought M.B. was 'past his sell-by date'. That was the end of his chances, although he didn't know it. Stephen was 'too ambitious' and had come to view the criminal Bar as the dregs of the earth, and was known to be courting a number of 'real' chambers that only undertook specialist civil work. Roberta was considered 'too pushy' and 'lacking a sense of humour,' therefore her chances were nil. The fact that Roberta was American, raised in New York, and spoke with a pronounced American accent was not mentioned, as being so obviously irrelevant.

And so, the annual ritual began at six o'clock in the evening on a Friday. Not all members could attend, but by tradition they could inform the head of chambers of any veto card they wanted to play before the meeting. The decision-making process was entirely fluid. There were no written rules of any description. Precedent and tradition, as interpreted by M.B., was all. An informal pecking order prevailed, determined by one's year of call.

Thirty made it this time round, huddled uncomfortably in a room that could take ten without a push, and convened, without any fuss or complaint nor any token rearranging of the room, which was by any standards a shambles to start with.

The nervous chatting and coughing came to an abrupt halt when M.B. signalled with an exaggerated clearing of his throat that the proceedings were about to commence.

"Welcome, welcome, to you all. I am so pleased that so many of you could take the time out from your busy and profitable practices to be here tonight. Well, it's that time again. We have five applications for a tenancy to consider. I think we are all agreed that only one unfortunate soul will be made an offer?"

A collective murmuring and tittering indicated that M.B. was not to be challenged on that point.

"Now. Before the proceedings begin in earnest, let me say, *en passant* if you will, that we should – no *must* – not be distracted by issues of politics and Bar Council quotas. We have tried over the years to be more proactive in reaching targets of one kind or another, but you can't pick the right person for the wrong reasons. Or vice versa. Is that fair enough?"

Everyone nodded, not understanding a word.

"Well, I am glad we cleared the air on that score. OK. In no particular order, let's go through the list. I think it's up to the pupil master to propose the applicant." M.B. looked over to Mark Engels, the pupil master to Adrian Boswell. "Adrian Boswell – Mark, your views?"

"Adrian, I am afraid, lacks discretion. Perhaps a matter of maturity. Maybe next year."

All heads bowed in sympathy for Adrian. Clean bowled, first ball.

"Er, thank you for that, Mark. Shall we move onto Stephen? Strong candidate. Very able. Henry, what have you to say about young Stephen?"

Henry Younghusband shuffled himself into a space where M.B. could see him more easily.

"Stephen, I have reason to believe, has set his sights higher than Three Harcourt Square, M.B. Yes, he would be delighted to be offered a place, but only as a launchpad for a tenancy in a more commercially orientated set. He'll do very well without us, I must confess."

"Er, very helpful, Henry. Any further comments on Stephen? No. We'll move swiftly on, then. At this rate we might even make it to El Vino's before dark," which prompted most present to look at their watches.

"Now, Roberta Baker. Helen, you know more about Roberta than anyone else present. What do you make of her?"

Helen Boxhall-Smith was the most senior female barrister present and the first woman to be offered a place in chambers fifteen years previously. She looked like a retired GP, aged fifty-three going on eighty.

"Roberta is a star," yelled Helen, which everyone understood to be the worst start Roberta could have, given the everyday deployment of the 'delayed, deftly delivered shafting technique', of which everyone present was either a past master or master-in-training.

"But she's too loud," Helen continued, still yelling.

"I don't mean she's American, I mean, obviously she *is* an American, very sharp and quick, but she's just too loud – you know – over the top. The other day, in court, I heard that she threatened the magistrate 'with a whack on the backside from the High Court' – I mean in open court, for Christ's sake. She'll do well in commerce, but Three Harcourt Square is not her future."

"OK," said M.B., rubbing his hands with glee. "Straight to the playoff. George and Heather!" He looked at his watch again, smiled and licked his lips in anticipation of a very cold glass of Sancerre '83. "Let's have a vote and hit El Vino's."

*   *   *

Pupils were not supposed to know when chambers were meeting to convene to discuss matters of extreme importance, but of course they always did. On this occasion, the drinks were flowing ever more quickly at the Middle Temple Bar. In attendance on this evening were George, Heather, David, Patrick, and, unusually, Roberta.

"Why do women take so long to go to the toilet? I think this is something men should be told."

It wasn't intended to be Patrick's best line, but the atmosphere was very intense, and it was true that Heather had been away for some time.

After a sip from her glass of chilled sparkling water, Roberta cut to the chase.

"Let's stop pretending, can we? One of us will be offered a chance to join the club; the others will have to take their act elsewhere. If it helps, I can tell you that my mum's passing has put things into perspective for me. It's not that I don't care. I do. I really do. But I accept my fate, whatever."

Roberta lowered her head and spoke in barely a whisper.

"Life is just so…so precarious, so random. If, by some miracle, I'm offered a place I'll celebrate like there's no tomorrow. If I'm not, I'll take a junior position with my dad's firm of corporate lawyers in the Cayman Islands and celebrate like there's no today. I guess it's just that my mum would have been so proud. It's what she always dreamt of for me. But since she passed away, last year …she was so young."

George looked solemnly at Roberta with tears in his eyes. *She has a heart of gold,* he thought, and was moved at the depth of empathy everyone round the table felt for Roberta. Roberta started to sob, gently and with some dignity, and raised her head slightly.

"Do you think there is such a thing as a soul? Something that exists independently from the body, something that lasts for all time?" Roberta's question was obviously born from her suffering, but was clearly not rhetorical.

The group fell into a respectful and reflective silence. *Maybe Roberta would appreciate some light relief from the slings and arrows of outrageous fortune,* wondered George.

"Roberta, did I ever tell you about PC Butterworth?"

"This better be good, George," David warned.

"Well, there I am in full-flowing glory, on my feet at Inner London Crown Court in front of Recorder John Ryder when—"

At which point George's mobile phone rang, indicating it was from the clerk's room. George pressed the green answer button and held the phone close to his ear.

"Sure, I can be around in a couple of minutes," he said into the phone. "Er, been asked to pop round to chambers. Apparently, M.B. wants a word. Where the hell is Heather?"

"Does that mean you're in?" Roberta asked, her temporary lapse into metaphysics having been abandoned.

"Hell, I don't know," said George, feigning innocence.

"Of course it means you're in, old boy. Do you think they're asking you round to tell you that you've been rejected? Hurry up and put us all out of our misery, will you?" said Patrick, looking at his watch. "We're about to be thrown out. We'll be in the Mason's Arms. Time for the bubbly stuff. Gallons of it."

Roberta had had enough and already in her heart knew the outcome. Another life waited for her, and she was glad that her future lay in the Cayman Islands' sun-drenched shores. She had promised her father and herself that either it would be a career at the English Bar 'living the life of an English lady, married to an English gentleman' or it would be the slog of a corporate lawyer in the gilded cage of the Cayman Islands, earning a million dollars a year before her thirtieth birthday. What the hell. It might not have been the precise dream that her mother had for her, but it was closure, of a kind. On reflection, Roberta decided it was just a toss of a coin between one fantasy and another.

★   ★   ★

"I'm in! I'm fucking in! Hallelujah!" And George proceeded to hug everyone he knew or remotely knew in the Mason's Arms. It was such a great night, it would take George nearly twenty years to remember it in any detail.

What he would never forget, however, was waking up the next morning, in a small and tidy flat in Islington, in the arms of a smiling Heather Armstrong, with a splitting headache, both bodies eager for another round of energetic sex.

Later in the morning, over a cup of coffee, an embarrassing silence developed between George and Heather. On the rare occasions George did find himself in the den of a single female, early in the morning of a Saturday or Sunday, with only a fuzzy recollection of the night before, every part of him screamed to get out – quickly – before anything remotely close to a relationship might start.

With Heather Armstrong, things were different. They knew each other quite well to start with and – worse still – they would be seeing each other at work the next week. There was clearly no escape, and so a conversation was inevitable. Heather, being on home territory, felt slightly braver than George.

"Look, George, I know this is just as embarrassing for you as it is for me. It just happened. Just a good shag between friends. I was up for it and so were you, OK?" Heather smiled and brushed away her fringe. "God, we drank enough to sink a cruise liner last night. You were off yer head with excitement. I've never seen anything like it."

She giggled slightly and smiled at George. She looked so different, so more real, and quite lovely, considering all traces of makeup had long since been removed. Indeed, she looked as if she had been licked clean, a thought which began to stir George's imagination. *Snap out of it quick*, he thought.

"And besides, I won't be in chambers much longer, so you won't have to worry about any of that."

George looked puzzled, if not actively concerned.

"You really were pissed last night, George, weren't you? Shit, you don't remember, do you?"

"Er, remember what?" George asked timidly, fearing the worst.

"I told you several times, but the only thing on your mind was yer bloody tenancy. I'm leaving chambers; I'm leaving the Bar. I'm going to work for a publishing company called Pentheus, as a rights executive."

"A rights executive? What's that?"

"A rights executive, George, is a real job with real money. Hell, I was over ten grand in the red when I left uni. The Bar fees cost another ten, which I didn't have. My mum re-mortgaged her house to help, and Three Harcourt was generous in giving me a grant during pupillage, but I'm only in my early twenties and hopelessly in debt. I can't afford to play this game any more. I get a real sense of satisfaction from the Bar, but the figures don't add up for me. At this rate I won't be out of debt until I'm nearly forty years old, by which time a one-bedroom flat in Islington will cost a million pounds. The job at Pentheus gets me on the corporate ladder, and I'm not going to let it go. Their building is that new one on the south side of Blackfriars Bridge."

Heather paused for breath and looked sad, almost defeated. "It's not what I really wanted to do. I'd seen myself defending the poor and the disadvantaged – that's why I wanted to be a lawyer. But it was all a fantasy, a childish ideal. Slaving away is the real world. Guess I just had to grow up, like we all do at some stage. If we want to see each other, we can. If we don't, then so be it."

George didn't know whether to laugh or cry, he felt so many emotions simultaneously. He reached out to Heather and put his hand on her cheek.

"I'm going to miss you, Heather," he said, before he gently kissed her, not out of lust but friendship.

"Want to share a bath before you go, George?"

CHAPTER FIVE
Conference

October 2000.

Several days passed before George spoke again with Heather, and that was only to say goodbye and wish her well. Roberta was leaving for the Cayman Islands, and now Heather had decided to move on for a junior position in publishing. Times changed so quickly, it was hard to keep track. But there were still David and Patrick to share a pint with.

The phone on George's desk in chambers rarely rang for him. There was no direct line to George; all calls had to come through to the clerks' room. That's how everyone liked it. If he was alone in his room, as he was, the clerks would know, and if the phone rang then he knew a call was coming through for him.

"George, it's Sam Leggitt on the phone."

"Thanks. Hi, Sam, you there?"

Sam had yet to learn the art of small talk; he simply didn't have the time.

"Listen, George, we need to talk about this Merlin case. He's on remand, as you know, in Brixton Prison. I have a number of clients in Brixton. Anyway, I saw him for a few minutes, and I don't know what you've done to him but he thinks you're his saviour. Silly prick gives me a hard time because he thinks you've promised to get him a room with a 'moon view'. So, because he still can't see the fucking moon from his cell he thinks I'm some sort of devil. Look, I know he's off his head like most of our clients but you can't go raising expectations with people like that. It's me that deals with the fallout. D'you know what I'm getting at?"

"Merlin just happens to like me, Sam. Nothing more to it than that. It's easier to like your counsel than your solicitor. We see them less and we don't handle their money." George realised instantly that he sounded stupid and patronising. "The point is that we didn't discuss Merlin's accommodation in any detail. I had a bit of a banter with the boys in blue at Highgate cop shop and I imagine they've been winding him up." He swallowed hard. "Look, Sam, I'm sorry if you feel you've been put in a difficult position, and I'll make sure the next time I speak with Merlin he will think you're really Sir Lancelot. OK?"

"OK, George, OK. I don't mean to have a go at you, but you spend little of your time with clients. They talk. Your name is spread for good or bad. Brixton Prison is a big source of my clients. This old boy who everyone calls Merlin is very popular with the screws and the inmates. They ask him for horoscopes, they sit and talk about history, he listens to their problems, and he's in demand. Even the old lags sit at his feet, hanging on every word. If he badmouths me it'll take Leggitt a long time to recover. I need you to work with me. That's all I'm saying. I've spoken to Paul and I've arranged a conference at Brixton next week. We can get his story straight and get our act together for the trial."

"That's great news, Sam. I look forward to it," replied George in all sincerity, trying to hide the fact that the mere mention of the word 'trial' struck fear into his heart.

⋆   ⋆   ⋆

Inner city prisons depressed George more than others. But of those George had already visited – Brixton, Pentonville, Holloway (girls only), Wandsworth, and Wormwood Scrubs – Brixton depressed him the most. It was the most confined and the smelliest. It didn't feel so bad when the weather was cold and wet. But when it was hot it was a hell on earth. The collective nausea was etched on every inmate's face – black or white, young or old. It was like watching people rot alive. It was a slow death by piss ammonia.

The only occasion when George was sure that his instructing solicitor would be present was when there was a conference inside a prison. *They must be paid well*, thought George.

True to the arrangements, Sam Leggitt was waiting at the prison gates at precisely ten a.m. Sam looked exactly how George had imagined – young, untidy blond hair, two days' stubble, wafer-thin cheap suit, open-neck shirt with loose-fitting polyester tie, cheap scuffed black shoes, carrying an imitation-leather briefcase – the perfect disguise for a partner in a small law firm making a mint out of the legal aid system. The irony did not escape George that he himself looked like a million dollars and was worth nothing, whereas his solicitor looked like a student in his first job and was making a fortune.

George and Sam approached the barrier that marked the beginning of the private road leading into the prison complex. Being conscious of the fact that innumerable CCTVs and discreet recording devices were monitoring – and listening – to their every sound and move, from every angle, George and Sam merely shook hands, said 'hi' and proceeded straight towards the checkpoint and introduced themselves.

The security guard phoned through to the administration office to confirm that the legal representatives for Merlin were expected. George and Sam confidently set forward on the short walk past the high walls of the prison towards the visitors' entrance.

Feeling slightly more relaxed, Sam broke his silence. "Good to see you, George. On time. I'm impressed. Let's see what this Merlin character is all about, shall we?"

"Good to see you too, Sam." George took a long look at the imposing structure that was Brixton Prison. "Camelot has changed since my last visit."

"Well, it ain't utopia, that's for sure. I just hope this Merlin character is up to giving us a statement today. I fucking hate prisons. You end up smelling of piss, shit, and fear for days."

Once they had passed through no less than four further security points, through the large concrete courtyard and into the bowels of the prison, George and Sam were asked to wait for their client in a small, grey, tatty room, airless and windowless, while Merlin was escorted from his cell.

Merlin and a prison officer of menacing authority followed a token knock on the door.

"All yours, gentlemen. You've got two hours."

Merlin sat in the chair placed opposite George and Sam, bald as a coot and clean-shaven, the resulting image of which took them both by surprise.

While papers were placed on the table George and Sam took furtive looks at their client, who looked surprisingly alert, his theatrical outfit now replaced by a cheap-looking polyester blue tracksuit and matching blue plastic slippers. The absence of a single hair on his head or chin made Merlin look almost Asian, and strangely vulnerable. George had to stare down at his papers for a while to stop himself giggling. It was a childish reaction to baldness, but one he simply couldn't help.

Merlin sat motionless, gazing into George's eyes, and then suddenly spoke.

"I see love in your eyes, Sir George. May your heart remain as true as your spirit. Shall we pray for guidance?"

George blushed and faltered, completely taken aback by Merlin's indiscretion, but recovered before Sam could take the initiative.

"Less of the personal stuff, Merlin. We've got a lot to get through this morning," George said in his best barristerial voice.

"Forgive me, Sir George. But being in the presence of true love lifts my heart."

"I appreciate your comments, Merlin, but we're not here to discuss me. Shall we start at the beginning?"

For the first time George heard Merlin laugh: a deep, mischievous laugh of an old man, like a naughty little boy, which was quite infectious.

"I fear if we start at the beginning we may never get to the end."

"OK," said George, while Sam opened a notebook ready to take detailed notes of the old boy's mutterings.

"When and where were you born?"

Merlin closed his eyes and let his head flop backward in deep thought, his breathing slow and exaggerated.

Sam was about to interrupt, but George kicked him under the table.

Eventually Merlin lowered his head and opened his eyes.

"I'm not entirely sure of my entrance into the world. It was a very long time ago."

George and Sam sort of huffed in frustration, in unison.

"Who is your father? Your mother?" enquired George, trying a different tack.

"My father I never knew. Some say I was not born from an earthly father. I do not know. My mother? I haven't thought about my mother for so long."

There was another long silence during which George and Sam feared Merlin would retreat into a bout of sobbing, but he pulled himself back, obviously with some effort.

"My mother was a dear lady and a wonderful human being." Merlin gave George another piercing look. "I cannot bring myself to utter her name, it grieves me too much."

Sam looked at his watch and could contain himself no longer.

"You were arrested on the morning of the twentieth of September. I saw you later that day. Where had you been the night before?"

"The night before the morning of my captivity? I was asleep, under the stars."

George tried to regain control of the interview.

"Do you remember where you were sleeping?"

"Oh, yes," said Merlin innocently. "In a tree."

"OK, you were sleeping *in* a tree." George began to lose his patience slightly, but noticeably.

"I presume you have no documents which would help us, Merlin. You know – passport, driving licence, birth certificate – anything?"

Merlin sat in silence, looking puzzled.

Sam, by this time, was becoming annoyed.

"Is your name actually Merlin, or are you merely saying that you are Merlin?"

Merlin closed his eyes and lowered his head. After a few seconds he raised his head back up, and said to both of them with the first hint of anger, "My name is Merlin. I am Merlin. Others have called themselves by my name and have besmirched my reputation and character. I can do little about it. Perhaps you can help. A physician has already asked me these questions; must we go through all of this again? Are we not here to prepare for the great battle?"

"Yes," replied George quickly. "Let's get into the trial issues. We'll have more reports about Merlin's background than we know what to do with. There'll be a social services report, a medical report, a separate psychiatric report, and numerous searches made by the police through the centralised criminal records office. Let's move on."

Move on they all did, but little was gained other than the same story, over and over again. It was very simple, and amounted to an act of self-defence.

Before the two hours were up, Merlin suggested that they leave due to his tiredness.

"OK, Merlin," Sam said. "That's been, er, very helpful. Now, about bail and timing...."

"Bail?" said Merlin. "No, no. I don't want bail. It's very cosy here. They ask for no money. A bit noisy sometimes. There is mayhem, but no more than elsewhere. I have good companions and the chief was kind enough to move me to the west wing, so I can now see the moon out of my window. I am quite happy, you know. My fellow captives know who I am. I am content to wait here. I will need all my strength. I have much to learn."

"And the haircut?" asked Sam. "That was your choice?"

"I have no need for hair in this place. It will grow again in time. Sometimes we need a clean start, do we not?"

George ignored Merlin's rhetoric. "Is there anything you want us to do? Is there anybody you'd like us to contact on your behalf?"

Merlin laughed one of his loud infectious throaty laughs.

"Everybody knows where I am. That's why I would prefer to stay here, Sir George. And thank you, thank you kindly, but I have food, clothing, shelter, protection, and companionship. I feel safe. I am in need of nothing other than peace and time to strengthen my spirit. I have made friends with many of my fellow prisoners. Some of them study a great deal and enjoy discussing my past. The depth of their knowledge is of great comfort to me. They like to talk about gods, about powers and forces greater than themselves. And the smoke is good."

George and Sam pretended they didn't hear the smoke bit or the 'Sir George,' and said their goodbyes.

★　　★　　★

George and Sam walked towards the Underground station down the hill, away from the prison confines, before they started any conversation, and soon they found themselves having mugs of coffee in a workman's café.

"He's a silly old prick, taking the piss," said Sam. "Waste of taxpayers' money. Keeps me busy so I shouldn't complain, I suppose. Pay's not so bad. But look, George, are you going to defend him on the basis that he's Merlin, or what?"

"Let's keep our eyes on the ball, Sam. Whether he's Merlin or Mickey Mouse, he's facing a criminal charge to which he's entitled, on his version of events, to plead not guilty. End of story. If it's our case that he believes himself to be Merlin, then the issue will be his sanity, not his innocence."

"But insanity is a defence to a criminal charge?"

"Well, of course it is. But the consequences are draconian, with the Mental Health Act kicking in. All it would mean is that he would be detained in a secure psychiatric ward rather than a prison – win, lose, or draw. Do you understand, Sam? If the jury accepts that he's not guilty by reason of insanity, he doesn't walk out of the court. The judge can still detain him if there's evidence that he's suffering from a psychiatric disorder and he's a danger to the public – or himself. For a straightforward case of assault, it's not really in the client's interests to run insanity. For a very serious offence, it's a different kettle of fish. For murder, for example, you could weigh up the difference between the statutory life sentence – which means on average seven years in prison – against a detention order in a mental hospital without limitation of time – which means until a psychiatrist reckons it's not a threat to his career to let you out – depending on the public mood at the time, of course."

"OK, just thinking out loud. And that bit about love. What was that all about?"

"Nothing, Sam. Nothing at all."

CHAPTER SIX
Death

Heather Armstrong was having great difficulty in putting George Winsome out of her mind, despite all her efforts and the intensity of working for a high-powered commercial conglomerate. The change in her routine journey to work from her small, private sanctuary in Islington merely involved getting off one Tube stop earlier, at Blackfriars Underground instead of the Temple. The daily emotion of loss and change was at its height the moment she stepped off the Underground train, but she was surprised at the speed at which the intensity of such feelings diminished. Although the distance between the two points was only a one-mile stretch of the Embankment along the River Thames, after a few weeks, it felt like a million miles. From Heather's office window she could just make out the expansive garden grounds of Inner Temple, behind which George would no doubt be sitting at his desk, thinking about nothing in particular. Was George, Heather wondered, thinking of her?

★   ★   ★

George was indeed at this desk contemplating his life, as usual. Contemplating life was an occupation that involved great concentration and was not to be confused with daydreaming, which was an entirely different activity. George was deeply experienced in both.

George stared proudly at the bundles of papers wrapped in red tape, now sitting on what he called 'his desk'. Those three sets of papers represented his entire practice: the Merlin papers (a trial in the Crown Court), a guilty plea in the Crown Court, and a fight in the magistrates' – prosecuting. Not much, thought George, but a start. The briefs had his name typed on them. He was a tenant in a decent set – an achievement considering his grammar school education in Glasgow, followed by an undistinguished university degree at Exeter University. The death of his father while George was at school was something that he had still not come to terms with – he had not even discussed the events with anyone except a few old school friends who knew of the circumstances firsthand. The move from Glasgow to Exeter had allowed a lot of history to fall into a black hole.

The money involved at this stage of his career was embarrassingly low – his 'call-out' rate to a magistrates' court was lower than a plumber's, but cash was easy to borrow, particularly as a tenant, and the big money would roll in sometime in the not-too-distant future. He stared long and hard at the papers, trying to make an informed guess as to when they would be heard. The thought of conducting his own jury trial made George sweat with fear. But it was a fear that could be harnessed, in time. As long as he didn't faint, dry up, go blank, collapse at the knees, or whatever, he should be all right, he thought. Besides, there was nothing really serious about his cases – at this stage he thought of Merlin as a sort of training for the real challenges that he would face in the years to come. Just cutting his teeth.

And then the phone rang.

"Sure, Paul, put Sam through," George responded, as if George had any choice in the matter. Young Sam Leggitt was very agitated, and excited.

"George. Shit. You just won't believe what's happened. I've just taken a call from the Crown Prosecution's office. They've just cleared it with the Director of Public Prosecutions. You know the old boy who Merlin was supposed to have caused a bit of damage to? Well, he's only gone and died of an aneurysm. On the basis of an autopsy report that makes a direct link between the assault and the cause of death, they're amending the charge to manslaughter. Thought we'd like to know. On top of that someone's leaked the story to the press. The immediate question

– tell me if I'm wrong here, George – is whether you need a leader. Now that it's manslaughter, legal aid will cover us for a QC. I mean manslaughter, as a first trial, is a bit much for a rookie. No offence, but you know what I mean. Think about it. Er, speak with you later."

George didn't manage to say one word, not a single word. He stared again at the bundle of Merlin papers in a completely different light. Sam was right. Should he take a leader? Then another question came into his mind: did he have to take a leader? Without thinking, he dialled Sam's mobile number.

"Sam, arrange another conference with Merlin. I need to know what his views are, and I need to know right away. Got it? Great."

George put the phone down feeling ten years older and smiled. *It's my fucking case*, he thought. *It's my fucking case.*

*   *   *

Five thirty p.m. took a long time coming, that day. George needed a drink and sympathetic company. His mind was racing so fast, he felt almost dizzy.

A small crowd of diehards waited impatiently outside the door of Middle Temple Bar at five twenty-five p.m. looking at their watches. At five thirty sharp, the door was unlocked and the best seats taken immediately. George sat on his own, knowing someone would soon sit opposite him. Unexpectedly Heather arrived, looking every inch the corporate executive, her once unruly and wild red hair now a short-cut, tidy-looking affair. In her grey trouser suit Heather looked a real professional, almost too professional.

"Heather. You look great. I mean different. Er, different in a nice sense."

Neither of them knew what to do, resulting in a rather clumsy handshake, which turned into a double cheek-kissing ritual.

Heather sat down, plonked a packet of Silk Cut on the table and lit up a cigarette while George went to fetch a glass of wine.

"I think I may be joining you soon," said George.

"You leaving the Bar?" Heather asked mischievously.

"No, no, I mean smoking cigarettes." George looked long and

hard into Heather's wide emerald eyes and his heart raced even faster than before.

"Heather?"

"Yes, George?"

"About that night, you know when I was taken on, when we…."

"Yes?"

"Well. I—"

Before George had any time to say something he might regret, David Palmer pulled up a chair.

"Heather Armstrong! You look absolutely exquisite. Publishing must suit you. Pentheus keeping you busy? Missing the Bar? Tell all."

Heather took a long drag on her cigarette.

"You ever worked in an office, David?"

"An office? Don't be silly. I couldn't take it. It would bore me to death. I'd rather pull me teeth out."

"That's what I thought. It's not quite like that. I mean you don't have time to be bored. They pay me fifteen grand a year and I'm expected to give them my whole life, body and soul. For fifteen grand. God, it's hard work. The learning curve is about ninety degrees. But it is fascinating, believe me. Have you any idea what's involved in publishing a book? Have you any idea how many rights there are in a published work?"

George looked again at Heather and felt some relief that she was OK. Almost jealous.

George could contain himself no longer.

"I need guidance. Help me out here. You know my Merlin case? Well, the old boy who got a bit bruised in the fracas has bit the dust. Bastard. Apparently it was an aneurysm – you know, a blood clot – which exploded inside his head. Massive internal bleeding, death within minutes. The autopsy says it's a direct result of his injuries, so the charge is now manslaughter. Sam reckons I might need a leader. What d'you think?"

Heather was first in.

"From memory, there's no rule from any source which states that you must have a leader. Correct? So, you don't *have* to have a leader."

"Get real, Heather. Times are hard. Some silks at the criminal Bar are earning less than a hundred grand a year," David said.

"My heart bleeds," said Heather sarcastically, thinking about how few people at Pentheus earned more than one hundred thousand pounds a year. "What's your point, exactly?"

David continued, pleased with himself that he had brought Heather back to her old self so quickly.

"The point, my dear dragonette, is that a chap charged with manslaughter is entitled to the best legal representation the legal aid board will allow. And that includes leading counsel, a QC if preferred. So, the first question is: what is the fully informed view of the defendant? The second, more important question is whether our friend here will get past his instructing solicitor, his senior clerk and M.B., who hasn't had a decent case since he fucked up that fraud trial at Wood Green Crown Court. I'd say your chances of holding onto this case are about one over N plus one, my friend."

George pondered his options and realised that his instinctive reaction was right all along.

"I'm going to avoid Paul and M.B. until I see the client. It's his call."

"Heather," said David. "You haven't been sending our George any of those racy bestsellers, have you? You know the ones. I fear our friend here has moved into fantasyland. Let it go, George. Oh, and by the way. Did I tell you I've been offered a seat in Eight Grey's Inn? Moboto's chambers."

Heather smiled broadly and gave David an embarrassing and prolonged kiss on the cheek.

"Good for you, David, good for you!"

"Congratulations, David. Really. Well done. Champagne, anyone?"

Heather smiled and looked at George who returned the smile, accompanied by a rub of his leg against Heather's under the table.

David went to the bar to order a bottle or two of champagne.

"If it's Friday, I'm going to get fucked," quipped George.

"It *is* Friday, George," Heather purred.

★　　★　　★

"Morning, Mr. Winsome," said the private security guard at the entry gate. "No solicitor with you today?"

George flipped open his brand-new state-of-the-art, all-singing-and-dancing image-sending micro mobile phone, the type that made him feel like Captain Kirk asking Scotty to beam him up to the Starship *Enterprise* from some papier-mâché film set trying hard to look like some faraway planet. He pressed a button and shouted "Sam," which prompted Sam Leggitt's phone number to be rung.

"Yeah, hi, George. Look, I'm completely stuck in traffic. Fucking gridlocked. There's been an accident on the A31. I'm not going anywhere. You either postpone or get stuck in without me. Your call."

George smiled. "I'll just have to carry on without you, Sam. See you whenever."

"OK, I'll stick this out and call you in about an hour."

"Cheers, Sam."

This being George's second visit to Brixton, the wheels seemed to move more quickly and before he knew it, Merlin was once again sitting opposite him in another bland conference room.

"My good knight, Sir George. You bring me news?"

"Er, less of the 'Sir George' stuff, Merlin."

"Oh no, I insist, Sir George. I insist."

"OK, have it your way, if you must. Your solicitor is stuck in traffic. I have come a long way to see you, and so if it's all right with you we'll continue in Mr. Leggitt's absence."

"You are my advocate. Do we need two?"

"Well, that's one of the reasons I've come to see you. You recall the gentleman with whom you had a tussle on the day of your arrest? Well, he has died, Merlin. And the prosecution service has decided that you are responsible for his death. At your committal next week, you will be charged with manslaughter."

"*Man* slaughter? I am to be accused of being a murderer?"

"Well, manslaughter is very different from murder."

"How so, Sir George?"

"Well, in your case it amounts to having committed an unlawful act – assault – which was the cause of death. Murder is far more serious. It's when you cause death with the intention of taking life or intending to cause serious injury. If you're found guilty of manslaughter, the judge may sentence you in any way he sees fit. With murder, the only sentence is life imprisonment."

"Hmm. Sounds like 'deep shit', as they say in Brickstonia."

"Now you're talking my language. Yes, you're in deep shit."

"And you have travelled a long way to tell me this?"

"Yes. But other matters arise."

"Other matters?"

"Merlin. Listen to me. I have yet to defend someone on my own in front of a jury. You are likely to be my first jury trial. Because the offence is so serious you are entitled to be represented by a more senior lawyer – one with more experience."

"You are not to be my advocate? How so? I don't understand."

"Not quite. I still act for you, but you have the right to a more senior and experienced lawyer to speak on your behalf."

"I have the right, Sir George, to represent myself, do I not?"

"You've been reading your rights, Merlin?"

"Oh yes, Sir George. The Human Rights Act is the most widely read document in this prison. Human rights. What an interesting idea. Not entirely original but interesting, nonetheless."

"So, you're saying that you want to represent yourself. Is that what you're saying?"

"My word, no. What I am saying is that I have the right to defend myself if I so choose. If I have the right to be represented by a senior lawyer, I must also have the right *not* to be represented by a senior lawyer. Is that not correct?"

George smiled at Merlin, and said "Yes."

"Well, I have you and the boy, Leggitt, to represent me. In my heyday you know, at your age, you would be commanding an entire army. You are ready for battle, Sir George. I do not want a senior lawyer to be my advocate. You are my advocate, or I will represent myself."

George sighed deeply.

"Thank you, Merlin. Thank you."

"You are welcome, Sir George."

"Er, would you mind just signing my brief, just here. I've written: 'I am to be charged with manslaughter and I wish to be represented by George Winsome.'"

"Certainly, Sir George. But in return you must promise me two things."

"Go on."

"You must never betray the love of another."

"What?"

"And you must be aware of the movements of the moon. These are the only requests I make."

"I must never betray the love of another, and I must be aware of the movements of the moon?"

"That is all."

George paused and closed his eyes in thought. "It's a deal," he said, shaking Merlin's surprisingly strong hand. "OK, Merlin, you can let go now," he said, having to pull his hand away from Merlin's vise-like grip.

CHAPTER SEVEN
Politics

M.B. was in a serious mood. A very serious mood indeed, as was Paul Styles, who sat in a chair at the corner of M.B.'s desk, placed in a position to indicate clearly that he was on M.B.'s side, literally.

"I know you're potentially very sound, very sound indeed, Winsome. But you have a duty to your client. Consider his best interests. Surely you must agree that with a possible life sentence for the defendant, complicated issues of law, psychiatric, and medical evidence involved, it must be in the interest of the defendant to be represented by silk? Surely you agree with that proposition, don't you?"

"If that is the defendant's wish, of course," replied George, feeling increasingly angry.

"Don't spar with me, Winsome. You're avoiding the question. Paul, can you assist Winsome, please?"

Paul Styles leaned forward onto M.B.'s desk, managing to rest one elbow on the corner.

"George. Please listen to me. There's a lot more at stake than this case. You and I both know that the client here is Sam Leggitt. He wants to win this case. Have you ever been to an Arsenal match with Sam, George?"

"Er, can't say I have, Paul."

M.B. smiled as Paul went in for the kill.

"It's like this. You have never seen the joy on Sam's face when Arsenal score a great goal, or the agony when the opposition put one in the net. It's a total passion. Winning is all."

"I'm afraid you've lost me."

M.B. signed and shook his head. "It's no good being obtuse, Winsome. Go on, Paul."

"George. I have already spoken with Sam. He believes you're too junior for a manslaughter case. He thinks Merlin is a winnable case, a potentially high-profile one at that. But he doesn't think you'll win on your own. He wants you to have a leader. He's already cleared the appointment informally with the legal aid board."

"Only one problem, gentlemen," said George firmly.

"Which is?" enquired M.B..

"Merlin has endorsed my brief to the effect that he wants me to represent him. If we appoint a leader, he will sack us all and go it alone. Therefore, the question is: is it in Merlin's best interest to be represented by me or by himself? I defer to your senior judgement."

"And does Sam know of this?" Paul demanded impatiently.

"Not yet. I was going to ring him later today. He couldn't make the conference at Brixton."

"This is a very serious matter, Winsome. Am I to understand that you took instructions from the defendant in the absence of your instructing solicitor on such a weighty matter? I fear this may be a matter the Bar Council needs to hear about. Why can't you be sensible about this? I'll let you cross-examine the police officers, give you something to get your teeth into. What do you say, old boy? Eh?"

"Forgive me, M.B., but I find this exchange verging on the offensive. Merlin wants me to represent him. I have studied for many years to get this far and have successfully completed my pupillage. As a tenant in a very decent set of chambers I have every right and qualification to take this case on. There was no objection when it was a simple ABH charge. I see no real difference now the indictment has been amended, albeit to manslaughter. I will represent Merlin. But thank you for your advice, which is appreciated."

M.B. lowered and shook his head. "Spell it out, Paul."

"It's like this, George. We can't stop you going ahead with the Merlin case on your own. But you must remember that your work comes from your instructing solicitor, who in turn takes advice from me. I agreed with Sam that if you could not demonstrate the maturity expected of you in these particular circumstances, then there would be consequences." Paul looked particularly sinister.

"Consequences?" replied George, feeling slightly nauseous.

Paul continued while M.B. leaned back, staring intensely at George's reactions.

"Let me run at this again in language you might understand. Sam and I take the view that if you could not see reason on this occasion you obviously lack judgement. You'll be receiving no further instructions until this matter is resolved satisfactorily."

Whether George was lost for words or decided on some level that his best bet was to remain calm and silent, he wasn't sure. But silent he remained, his head bowed in a combination of shock and shame.

"Is that clear enough for you, Winsome? If you want to reconsider your views, we'll be here until six thirty this evening. By tomorrow it will be too late."

George looked at his watch. Five p.m. "No need to wait, gentlemen. I have expressed my views. So be it."

★   ★   ★

For the first time George could ever remember he walked straight past the doors of the Middle Temple library, which led to the doors of the Middle Temple Bar. Coming out of Middle Temple Lane, he crossed the busy Embankment to be closer to the Thames, passed the huge sailing ship that was permanently moored and used as a restaurant and conference centre, along farther to Blackfriars Bridge, where he turned south and stood in the centre of the bridge, from where he could look west along the swirling silver flow of the River Thames. From where he was standing he could see, at the end of the bridge looking south, the new building in which Heather worked. Across the Thames looking northward he could see the collection of ancient buildings in which his chambers were housed. Despite the noise of the grinding traffic behind him and the proximity of the pedestrians walking from one side of the bridge to the other, George placed his head in his hands and wept softly. At that moment he realised there was only one person in the world he wanted to share his feelings with, and that was Heather.

A half-baked idea had come into George's mind. He would arrive unannounced at Heather's workplace. Perhaps, by divine intervention, Heather would just be leaving and fall into George's arms. George wiped away his tears and walked halfheartedly towards the award-winning purpose-built Pentheus Tower, a bizarre six-story cylinder-like structure. Its reflective glass exterior provided no clues as to the activity inside.

With some trepidation George entered the building and approached the reception area.

"Er, I'd like to see Heather Armstrong. She's a rights executive," he said, almost with pride.

"Heather Armstrong? Oh yes, she left about fifteen minutes ago. Sorry. Do you want to leave a message or is there anyone else who can assist?" enquired the smartly dressed young lady, who could easily have passed for a teenage model.

George lowered his head and muttered something about catching her later. "No message, I'll give her a call. Thanks."

George realised that the only place in the world where he would feel at home at that point in time was the Middle Temple Bar, and he surrendered to its magnetic pull, loosened his tie, undid the top button of his shirt, and prepared himself for some hard drinking.

★　★　★

"So, you've had a chat with Paul?" Sam asked with a slightly high-pitched edge to his voice, betraying his nervousness.

"Yeah, we talked yesterday, with M.B.," replied George, trying hard to disguise his hangover.

"And what have you decided to do?"

George paused for a few seconds.

"Are you still there?"

"Yeah, I'm still here. I told M.B. and Paul yesterday. I will represent Merlin."

"George, listen to me. You're out of your depth. You need

a leader. I'm your instructing solicitor, I mean which bit of 'instructing' don't you get?"

George paused for breath and knew he was in deep, unchartered territory.

"Sam, have you ever felt that you *must* do something, no matter what?"

"Er, can't say I have. Pissed myself in court once, if that counts."

"Sam, listen. I'm going to represent Merlin. Without a leader. I know there are consequences, as Paul put it yesterday, but fuck it, I *will* do this, OK?"

"Shit, George, you're a stubborn bastard. OK. On your head be it. You can continue to represent Merlin – he's taken a shine to you – but you're off my list until further notice. That's what I've agreed with Paul. You understand that?"

George bit his lip to prevent his true feelings being exposed.

"I understand all right."

"Right, now we understand each other, the Merlin case. Did I tell you I've got a new girlfriend? Fiona Baker, she's the listing officer at Southwark Crown Court. I've got news for you. We've got a date for a pre-trial review at Southwark Crown Court on the first of November. We've to agree a list of witnesses and length of hearing. They'll give us a trial date, probably around Christmas if we can keep the trial to within five days. You might want to take a pot at a bail application. Merlin has already been assessed by the medical team at Brixton, including their psychiatrist. You have the reports, George, guess you'll need a bit of time to digest them. The initial view is that he's simply a confused old man, but time will tell. But I'll leave that to you to work out and how to play out before the jury. I've also been in touch with the CPS. They want to know if Merlin's fitness to plead is an issue. Can you bear another conference at Brixton?"

"Sure, Sam. Let's travel together this time."

"OK, we'll meet in chambers and then go together by cab. Have a chat on the way. Oh, and by the way, the CPS has appointed counsel for the prosecution. One of the chambers in Grey's Inn Square. Moboto. Everyone calls him Mobo. Have you heard of him?"

"Of course I've heard of him. David Palmer sings his praises daily. Juries love him. Did you know that David got a tenancy there?"

"I heard about his tenancy but didn't connect it with Moboto's set. Moboto will need a junior. Perhaps you could put your ear to the ground and find out who he's leading?"

"That won't be difficult," replied George.

"Perhaps it will be your mate, David. Then we could have some fun."

"Fun? Now that's a word I haven't heard in a long time. Yes, perhaps we could have some fun with this one, Sam."

★   ★   ★

The guard almost bowed as Merlin walked through the door. Merlin's demeanour was brimming with confidence, and despite his surroundings he appeared physically strong.

Sam and George were already sitting at a table, awaiting their star client.

"Sorry I couldn't make it last time, Merlin. The traffic was appalling," Sam said.

Merlin, still quite bald apart from a new small white goatee beard, did not look impressed or convinced by Sam's excuses, and simply made a sort of huffing sound.

"This is not the first time we have met here. You must enjoy the surroundings, gentlemen. What news, pray tell me. I have willed the man to come back to life. Is my magic working?"

Sam didn't know whether to laugh or cry. He was convinced the old codger was having them on, and felt not insulted but simply annoyed that Merlin wouldn't let them into his joke. Sam wanted to help with the script, and thought Merlin's act could be improved.

"Ah, I thought not. I can tell by your faces. You look sad, Sir George. You have had bad tidings?" George looked at Sam but did not reply.

"I have spoken to the spirit of the departed. I needed to say sorry. He was thinking about returning to these earthly shores.

But it's too late. I can see that. The trial, yes, the trial. That is why you are here."

"Yes, that's why we are here," George said. "Four issues are at stake: your fitness to plead, your state of mind at the time of the incident, the reasonableness of your actions, and the cause of death. The judge has to decide whether you are fit to plead even before the trial starts. That depends on whether it is thought you sufficiently understand the nature of the charges against you and the nature of the proceedings. If we cross that bridge, in order for you to be acquitted, we must put a defence to the jury. That can either be self-defence or insanity. If insanity, we need expert medical evidence, from at least one psychiatrist."

"Insanity. You wish to argue that I am mad?" enquired Merlin with some anger in his voice. "I have spoken at length to one of these mind doctors you call psychiatrists. Books are read and shared generously among the prisoners, I have heard of many works including the psychiatrists' book of magic, *DSM III*. It is written by the devil, of that I am sure. I am not mad, my friends. I am Merlin."

"Merlin, listen to me."

"Of course, I will listen to you, my good knight. You have moved from love to pain. It is natural. Your voice is strong. Speak, please."

George sighed but carried on.

"It is clear from the reports that you understand the charges and are capable of understanding the proceedings. Your fitness to plead is not going to be an issue unless we decide to fight on that ground. Personally, I don't see the point. The idea is to get you out of here a free man. If we argue successfully that you are unfit to plead you will remain in a psychiatric institution for a long time. Possibly longer than if you're found guilty. The other issue, your state of mind at the time of the incident, is another matter. The psychiatric report so far indicates that you might be in the process of recovering from some trauma or, possibly, that you have a split personality disorder and delusions of grandeur. You also seem to think that you are not just the Merlin of the court of King Arthur but that you have lived several lives as a Merlin figure going back to an earlier Merlin character born in Scotland. The theory is that you probably had an accident of some kind, after which you lost your memory and reinvented yourself in a sort of fragmented fashion, so to speak, as Merlin. I recall a passing reference in the report to a state of mind they call 'metempsychosis' – a belief that your soul has been transmitted in some fashion from one life to another. They also believe that in time the likelihood is that you'll 'come to your senses' and remember who you really are. However, if your delusions persist that's another matter. They expect your true identity will be revealed soon enough and then you'll soon be OK."

Merlin listened intensely.

"So, they say I am not Merlin. Who do they say I am?"

"Well, obviously they don't know. In the past five years, according to the figures from the police, over two thousand people in the UK have simply disappeared. Of those two thousand possibly as many as one hundred and eighty could be you. But they don't have the time or money to solve that problem. As far as the authorities are concerned you caused the death of the dog patroller and are deluded about your identity. The rest is up to the jury to decide. They don't really care."

"They are trying to make me lose my mind, that is what they are trying to do. This is a cruel game. We should make amends with the family of the deceased and put an end to the matter," suggested Merlin.

"I'm afraid that's not how it works," George said.

"How so, Sir George?"

"We want you to walk out of the courtroom into the fresh air, not into a mental hospital. To do that we must accept that you are fit to plead, persuade the jury that you are not mad, and break the causal link between your actions and the death of the deceased. We'll never be able to prove that you are Merlin, obviously."

"We could call King Arthur, if he's still around," Sam muttered before he could stop himself. "Make a great character witness."

"That's not very helpful, Sam," said George.

"Besides," Merlin said, "I fear your jury would have some difficulty taking Arthur seriously. He was no more than fifteen years of age when he was made king. I knew when we first met that he was a king, although I also knew others would need persuading. The allies he wanted to bring together needed to believe that he was chosen to be their king, not by them but by other-worldly forces. It wasn't easy, you know. He was a very strong and smart lad, he had a strength in his voice that was beyond his years; his self-belief gave him power, with a bit of help from me, of course. It was nothing to do with pulling a sword out of a stone, as some now believe. I asked him to make a rallying speech at a time I anticipated a great storm. It was spectacular. There was not much work for me to do. Battle-hardened men fell to their knees and praised the heavens for delivering a warrior to defeat our foes."

Merlin laughed his uncontrollable and infectious laugh until both Sam and George succumbed.

"No, seriously, Merlin," said George, pulling himself together and realising how impressed he was at Merlin's ability to spin a yarn with such conviction. "I won't fall into the trap of arguing that you are insane. The jury may find you odd – inconsistent, even – but fundamentally I think they will respond to your good nature. You have a sort of authenticity. Insanity is not the key that opens the door to your freedom. In days past it was a sound tactic to avoid the rope. The issue of insanity we will argue is irrelevant. We'll seek to persuade the jury that if you wish to be known as Merlin that is a defensible right. If you honestly believe you walked with King Arthur, that's good enough for me. We'll persuade the jury that there are solid historical grounds to form such a belief; most people have no difficulty in accepting a Merlin figure from the court of King Arthur. And if you also believe you've lived several lives as Merlin, I'll deal with that in my own way. I'm sure there is an answer to this; I'll do some research. The simple truth is that there was an incident, you reacted in self-defence, intended no harm, and therefore you are entitled to be acquitted and walk away a free man. That is our case."

"You are truly my knight in shining armour, Sir George. We go into battle with clear minds and strong spirit. I salute you."

CHAPTER EIGHT
Judge

November 2000.

Timothy Claude Watts had always wanted to be a judge; not any old judge but a Law Lord, just like his father, Lord Watts of Weybridge. Tim (as he was known to his friends and family) could rattle off the various types of judges from a precocious age. He knew the difference between a High Court judge as opposed to a circuit judge, a master, a Recorder, and a stipendiary by the time he was seven years old. Not much later he was capable of lecturing to his class the differences between a Law Lord (like Daddy), an Appeal judge (of the High Court) and a member of the Privy Council. He knew this not from dry textbooks or from the mouth of a teacher, but from the conversations he had overheard in his mock-Tudor house on the Thames in Surrey, where he grew up as an only child.

Tim felt he had always known the difference between the various wigs worn by members of the Bar and the judiciary. Once his father had been appointed to the High Court, he gave Tim the short horsehair wig he'd worn during his practice at the Bar, which Tim would secretly wear in his bedroom, looking in the mirror pretending to address the jury, always on the side of the prosecution.

Even in the sanctity of his bedroom, addressing the mirror, Tim was careful to make sure that the wig covered his fringe, knowing that an old-fashioned judge would take exception to the slightest show of real hair. It was a matter of form. Much to his parents' delight, Tim had even taken the smelly, itching 'periwig', as he called it, to show and tell at school.

Tim also knew the differences between the High Court and

a County Court, and between a Crown Court and a magistrates' court, because he had been taken along to see the courts in action from the earliest age. His father's social circle was made up almost entirely of barristers and judges, and he learnt their way of life almost as a second language.

Of course, Tim was very unpopular at school for this reason, not only among the teachers, whom he thought were rather stupid and 'second class', but also his peer group, who considered him boring. Others in his prep school might want to talk of football or rugby or racing, but Tim was happier talking about court cases. The law was his one and only vocation, and the thought of another life had never entered his mind.

Tim was now fifty-eight. He was a judge, but only a Recorder, empowered to preside over jury trials and other matters in the criminal Crown Courts. Tim had never really impressed his seniors in the civil courts, and his practice had never reached the heights he had anticipated from an early age. Perhaps he simply wasn't smart enough, or perhaps he understood the law better than he understood people. The sad fact for Tim was that he considered himself to be a failure. His applications to take silk were always ignored, and over the years he had come to the sorry conclusion that he would not make it to the High Court. Therefore the route to becoming a Law Lord – via the Court of Appeal – was cruelly closed off. The invitation to become a Recorder was a consolation prize that he knew he would have to live with. But the sharpness of the pain of defeat and failure softened over the years and Judge Watts now accepted his fate in the same way he expected those who came up before him to accept their sentences.

The real problem for Tim Watts was not his work, his peers, or his undistinguished reputation, but his family. His wife, Christina, once a flirty and effervescent woman, now seemed permanently depressed and was nearly three years into an open-ended course of psychoanalysis to help her deal with her severe condition, for which no medical cause could be found. To her few remaining friends, the reason for her debilitating angst was obviously attributable to her one and only offspring.

Simon Watts would be flattered to be introduced as a seventeen-year-old teenager from hell, having fled his expensive boarding school to return home as a born-again anti-hunting eco-warrior complete with a Mohawk and low grunge uniform.

Simon now insisted on being called Sihairly, a Celtic name long ago corrupted by the forces of post-pagan political correctness, Simon claimed. Accordingly, he flatly refused to acknowledge the name Simon, resulting in a deal being struck, after some hard bargaining, to the effect that his parents would call him Si.

The fact that Christina had married Tim in the expectation that he would become a Lord and she a Lady was not forgotten. No formal title came attached to 'Mrs. Recorder'.

And so, the three Wattses lived out their unhappy lives in the gilded cage known to them, a few friends, and their postman as Sunny Meadows, a quiet house inherited from Tim's father in a quiet hamlet tucked away in the stockbroking belt of Surrey.

The household had reached the point of perfect dysfunctionality, there being no happy relationship between husband and wife, father and son, nor son and mother. Indeed, as Christina's well-known and very expensive therapist, Robert Schilling, remarked, they lived in a perfectly balanced symmetrical loathing; the only pleasure left to each of them was the pain and humiliation they caused to one another.

The sole diplomat was Dayan, the ageing but deeply mischievous jet-black half-breed Labrador retriever who was loved by all, a fact that Dayan understood and exploited to the full.

Into this quiet little hell came news that Judge Watts was to preside over a forthcoming manslaughter trial. No matter what grief he was given at home, he could take comfort in the undeniable fact that while he sat high on the bench in Court 12 of Southwark Crown Court he was the judge, and was treated by the court staff accordingly. Tim therefore became quite attached to the title Judge Watts, as evidenced by the small, fiddly nametags sewed personally and lovingly by hand onto all his clothing, including his socks, pyjamas, and underwear.

The papers had arrived from Southwark Crown Court to Sunny Meadows by courier. Judging by the thickness of the tidy A4 sheets of paper, it appeared to be a short case, less than two inches thick.

Before Tim had opened the bundle, he was wondering why this would take a whole working week as indicated in his diary. He studied the indictment headed: The Crown v. Merlin. There were two charges: manslaughter and actual bodily harm. *Oh Christ!* he thought, *I'm on a hiding to nothing with this piece of nonsense.* He read further into the papers and noticed that 'the highly regarded and totally fearless if somewhat verbose Ojukwu Moboto' – was presenting the case for the prosecution. *Now I know why it's listed for a week*, Tim chuckled to himself. *Moboto will make the most of this one.*

The next surprise in the box was the realisation that the defence consisted of a recently called member of the Bar by the name of George Winsome. *That can't possibly be right,* was the thought that crossed the judge's mind. "You must have a leader for a case of manslaughter. You simply must," he muttered.

Judge Watts also noticed that the listing office had, of their own volition in accordance with Home Office issued guidelines, listed the case for a pre-trial review for early the following week.

★　★　★

Ojukwu Ibo Moboto was a highborn Nigerian whose hero was Mahatma Gandhi. Mobo, as he was affectionately known, had fought against prejudice at the English Bar for a lifetime. Mobo was better educated and smarter than most of his colleagues at the Bar, but it had been a long hard struggle to find a set of chambers willing to take him on, and an even greater struggle to establish a practice, particularly in the Sixties, when racism of every type was a way of life in each corner of the little island known as Great Britain or – as Mobo once notoriously described it in a Middle Temple debate on the subject of racism at the English Bar – "this mongrel island of bastard invaders, looters, robbers, rapists, and raiders; the land of blood and gory."

In a career-enhancing move in the early Seventies, Mobo set up his own chambers in Grey's Inn. The slow progress from pupil to head of 2 Grey's Inn Court had taken thirty-five years, every one of which was etched into Mobo's jet-black face and classic aristocratic features. Once the establishment, as represented by the Bar Council, realised that Mobo wasn't going to go away, they politely listened to his sorry tales of the difficulties faced by would-be barristers who weren't from English private schools, and educated at Oxbridge, and made many promises to address the situation.

Mobo had made many enemies along the way, but the friends acquired during the hard years were true allies. Two of his closest friends were Nancy and Washington Palmer, the husband and wife founders of Palmer & Co, Funeral Directors, based in Brixton.

David Palmer had not known that his father had spoken to Mobo about David's fight for a tenancy. But a call from Washington to Mobo had been made. It was a great relief to Mobo when he interviewed David Palmer and saw for himself the great potential the young man clearly had: good presentation, confidence, ambition, humour, and style. The fact that he had such an English-sounding name was not held against him, although it did seem incongruous on the boards outside Moboto's chambers.

★   ★   ★

Court 12 of Southwark Crown Court looked much the same as practically every other Crown Court built since the late Seventies. There were many old courtrooms, notably at the Old Bailey and others situated in ancient buildings around the country, that had remained unchanged for decades, but all modern courts looked as though the same builder had constructed them all at the same time, as if the whole legal process had become a business franchise. The wall panels were no longer old English oak, but an artificial shiny veneer as might be bought in the bargain bin of a local DIY store. The jury seating area was neat and tidy, the seats possibly designed by the same sadist who designed waiting chairs in airports; the witness stand might double as a presentation stand used at a marketing seminar; the décor intended for counsel's papers and books might be confused with a kitchen worktop and the clerk's area, situated below the judge's mini-throne, radiated an air of reluctant competence. Behind the four rows of seating designated for the lawyers, was the dock in which those charged would be expected to sit quietly, sometimes flanked by one or two burly prison officers.

The fact that the lawyers did not face the defendants, and that the clerk could not see the judge, meant that the only person who could see all the players, at the same time, was the judge, above whom hung a plastic-looking insignia of the Royal Garter, enshrined by the words: *Honi Soit Qui Mal Y Pense*. The overall impression was one of cost-effective functionality, as might be found on a hastily constructed, tightly budgeted, temporary film set.

For this reason, it was particularly important for the judge, clerk, and barristers to wear wigs, gowns, upturned stiff collars, and bands, without which there would be no sense of foreboding or regal-based formality, and the true banality of the whole legal process would be exposed.

Barristers opposing each other rarely meet for the first time in the actual courtroom. A telephone call might have been made the day before to confirm what was likely to be argued, and the length of time the hearing might take. There might even be discussions about how best to carve up the case. Even if no conversation had taken place over the phone, the barristers would inevitably meet in the robing room, the exclusive changing area for barristers, into which solicitors were never, ever allowed.

The atmosphere in the robing room, particularly in the minutes before ten thirty a.m., was tense, similar to the backstage scene prior to a first night opening of a fringe Shakespeare play. The odd layout of the room – segregated with thin partitions to create token privacy, like half-finished changing-room cubicles – unwittingly created schoolboy-level mischief. Barristers could play with the fact that they could be heard but not seen until they stood in front of the large communal mirror. There was usually a joker, trying to bring some light relief to an ever-increasing tension.

"David! David Palmer! I know you're here somewhere. You're in the Merlin case, aren't you?"

"Hi, George. Careful what you say to the prosecution, old boy."

David Palmer and George Winsome paired up to face the mirror, and laughed aloud like old school friends meeting up at a school reunion.

"I thought you might be on the Merlin case, but it was such a long shot, I mean, Mobo has about fifteen juniors to choose from. Well, well, who would have guessed it?"

David had already taken off the soft detachable collar from his shirt, and was struggling to attach the stud protruding from the back of his shirt to the new stiff-wing collar before he could put on his band.

"New collars are always a bugger, David. Do you want a hand?"

"No, thanks. I'm nearly there. That's it."

George and David stood side by side, looking at themselves in the large mirror while they put on their wigs and checked that the front stud, which attached the shirt to the two ends of the collar, was not exposed. Once the wig and bands were sorted, the heavy gown could be thrown over the shoulders, the weight of which encouraged the wearer to straighten up and broaden the shoulders. In the space of less than five minutes both George and David had made the transition to barristers, a double act of a routine that they both obviously enjoyed enormously.

For a moment or two they looked at themselves and each other in the mirror, the more or less identical costumes failing to obscure the stark contrast in height and colour.

"Wow. Don't we look the part. Feel a sequel to *The Defiant Ones* coming on, David. You remember, Sidney Poitier and Tony Curtis on the run together. Guess I know which part you'll get."

"Poitier's real challenge in that film, George, was being chained up to a guy with smaller legs and fewer brains."

George smiled at the thought of the images in front of him being spread across the silver screen. "Perhaps we're all slaves to something, David even if it's our own destiny."

"Slavery? Chains?" boomed a deep, confident, cultivated but slightly exaggerated upper-class English voice, its resonance and depth betraying more than a hint of Nigerian origin.

"Am I not allowed even to dress myself without having to hear echoes of the distant unforgivable past reverberating throughout the hallowed grounds of a robing room of Her Majesty's Crown Court?"

The voice rose even louder.

"Did my brothers and sisters sacrifice their very lives in order that the defenders of truth and justice themselves would perpetuate the language of apartheid and injustice?"

A silence fell among those present, until a voice rang out: "You're not in court now, Mobo, keep it for the jury."

Mobo let slip a small smile and recognised the voice of John Elmer, an old battle-weary foe and friend.

"Where are you hiding, John? And have you seen that useless junior of mine?"

"Which one, Mobo?" replied John, "all pupils look the same to me. Overworked and underpaid."

David came out of hiding.

"Morning, Mobo. I've been working on our opponent. He's going to plead guilty to all charges."

"He better not," said Mobo, giving a sly wink to his favoured pupil. "This is one for my memoirs. A plea would take all the fun out of it. No, no. This is to be a fight, a glorious battle decided by the closing speeches. May the best man win. Ah, Winsome, there you are. We should have a chat. We've still got twelve minutes. Lots of time."

"Er, chat, Mobo? I'm not sure what you've got in mind. Merlin will not be pleading guilty."

"Yes, yes, Winsome, I know that. About today. Can we agree the issues, the witnesses, the timescale? How many experts will you call?"

George hesitated, knowing that he was under no obligation to reveal his defence but was, nonetheless, required to disclose details of expert witnesses. Mobo was already fighting, even before he was robed.

"I'll be calling at least two witnesses, at least one of whom will be an expert," George heard himself say confidently.

"An expert in what?" Mobo took a long sideward look at George.

"I'll let you know in due course, Mobo. I think in the meantime, it's time to go."

*   *   *

"Court rise!" shouted the ageing but still-flirtatious court usher, Margaret, a few decibels too loudly. The numerous counsel in Court 12 of Southwark Crown Court, some for the immediate hearing, others waiting for their case, immediately stood up. Once the judge had reached his chair and just before he sat down, the ritual exchange of token bows was exchanged between His Honour Judge Watts and counsel. To bow with some conviction without the wig slipping was an acquired art.

George looked around nervously, wondering why on earth his instructing solicitor was not present.

The clerk of the court, also bewigged, stood up and bawled at no one in particular: "Be present all parties in the case of the Crown against Merlin."

Judge Watts looked at Mobo. "Mr. Moboto, I understand you represent the prosecution in this case?"

"Indeed, I do, Your Honour. My learned junior David Palmer is seated behind me, and my learned friend Mr. Winsome represents the defence."

George smiled nervously without rising to his feet and exchanged a token smile with the judge.

"Have you agreed the number of witnesses with the defence, Mr. Moboto?"

"We have not. My learned friend appears reluctant to disclose any element of the defence, despite the recent rulings, Your Honour," Mobo said with an exaggerated air of impatience.

"Mr. Winsome," said the judge.

George rose slowly to his feet, regretting deeply the half-cooked bacon sandwich that he had called breakfast, a feeling not helped by his gown having somehow managed to get stuck in the back of his flip-up chair, requiring George to pull and tug in order to stand up properly. An embarrassing silence took over the court while everyone watched George in his struggle with his gown, a battle only won following a piercing ripping sound, resulting in George nearly falling over sideways. Once the tittering had ended, the judge continued.

"You are ready, Mr. Winsome?" enquired the judge with a false sense of patience.

"Yes, Your Honour, may it please Your Honour, I represent the defence, Your Honour."

"We know that, Mr. Winsome. Mr. Moboto just told me. Before we agree witnesses and a date, can you inform me of the whereabouts of the defendant and your instructing solicitor, Mr. Winsome?" the judge asked, looking at the empty seat behind George where Sam Leggitt was supposed to be seated.

Mobo sat down, theatrically holding a hand over his eyes in feigned embarrassment. David, seated behind Mobo, was either crying, or more probably, had been overcome by an attack of giggles.

"My instructing solicitor, Your Honour," said George, looking around in a state of controlled panic, "has just arrived." He saw the grubby little figure rushing to a seat behind him in a cowered manner favoured by little boys trying to pretend they're invisible. "The defendant has indicated to my instructing solicitor that he does not wish to make an application for bail and therefore his attendance is not required." George at last found a hint of confidence in his court voice. "The defence intends at this stage to call at least two witnesses, including at least one expert."

"An expert in what, Mr. Winsome?" asked the judge innocently.

Mobo turned around and shared a joke with David.

"An expert, Your Honour, in history," said George. He felt his stomach starting to churn like the first slow wet rinse of a washing machine.

"An expert in history? In history?" the judge asked.

"Yes, Your Honour. And a psychologist, and perhaps a forensic scientist, as there is clearly a medical issue of causation in this case. It is my respectful submission, Your Honour, that I need disclose no further information. The relevance at this stage is merely to allow a realistic timescale to be indicated to the court, which will enable a date to be set."

"Mr. Winsome. Am I to understand that you intend to conduct this case without the benefit of a leader?" the judge asked threateningly.

"Indeed, Your Honour."

"And that you will be calling a history expert, a psychologist, and possibly a forensic scientist?"

"Er, yes, Your Honour."

"I make that three experts. Do you wish to challenge my arithmetic, Mr. Winsome?"

"No, of course not, Your Honour. Yes, three experts, three, maybe."

The judge stared at George, as if he was suppressing a deep rage.

"Mr. Winsome. Perhaps it is not for me to comment. But this is a very serious charge of manslaughter that carries a potential life sentence. I am giving you the opportunity, right now, if you wish, to make an application to this court for the appointment of a leader, and I will forward my recommendation to the legal aid board, if that is where the difficulty lies. Do you follow me, Mr. Winsome?"

"Indeed I do, Your Honour."

"Well, Mr. Winsome, do you wish to make such an application?"

"No, I do not, Your Honour."

"And that is your considered and professional view, bearing in mind the severity of the charges?"

This time it was Sam's turn to shield his eyes and shake his head.

"It is, Your Honour."

"And the view of your instructing solicitor, Mr. Winsome?"

Sam took his hand away from his eyes and stared intensely at a blank sheet of paper.

"Absolutely, Your Honour," said George without turning around.

"Very well, but I fear I may have to remind you of this conversation sometime in the future, Mr. Winsome. Now, Mr. Moboto, you have heard from the defence. Do you think we can get through this in five working days?"

Mobo rose slowly and theatrically to his feet.

"Oh, I should think so, Your Honour, comfortably."

"Very well, can we agree a date? In the defendant's interests I should like this heard before the end of the year."

The court clerk looked as if he had suddenly been startled and began flitting through a diary. Then he stood up and whispered something to the judge.

"If everyone is agreed we can fix a date for Monday, the eighteenth of December. Mr. Moboto? Mr. Winsome?"

George Winsome indicated that the date was convenient to the defence before Mobo had finished looking at his pocket diary.

"Yes, Your Honour, the week beginning the eighteenth is acceptable to the prosecution. We will only have five witnesses."

George turned around to Sam and whispered, just a touch too loudly, "Five fucking witnesses?"

Mobo continued. "We have the young surviving dog patroller, Your Honour. Two arresting officers. A further witness to the fracas who has only recently come forward, and an expert in rebuttal."

George instinctively rose to his feet, overcome with a controlled anger.

"Your Honour, this is the first time I've heard of this 'further witness to the fracas'. I understand that my learned friend might wish to call an expert in rebuttal. But I would urge the court to impress upon the prosecution the need to disclose all prosecution statements well before the trial."

The judge remained silent while he wrote something down in a notepad in front of him.

Then he announced, "I order as follows: the case of the Crown against Merlin will commence on Monday, the eighteenth of December. Within fourteen days from today the prosecution will serve on the defence all statements as to fact. Leave given for the prosecution to call one expert in rebuttal. Defence to serve any and all expert witnesses' statements within six weeks. Any other matters, gentlemen? That is all. Thank you, Mr. Moboto, you were very helpful." The judge looked over at George Winsome but could not think of anything to say. "The court will take a ten-minute break."

"Court rise!" bellowed Margaret the usher, even louder than before. "Court will reconvene in ten minutes." At which point the judge rose, bowed to counsel, and made a quick exit.

George remained standing, looking for some consolation from some quarter that his performance had been OK. Everyone seemed to look through him, apart from David, who patted him on the shoulder.

"Never mind, George. It can only get better."

"Don't bet on it," said Mobo as he headed towards the exit.

George lowered his head in shame, knowing that he had performed like the rookie he was. Sam rushed off, following Mobo. "Er, I'll give you a call, George, must rush."

George felt and looked completely dejected and shuffled wearily towards the door, the small tear in his gown not making him feel any better.

CHAPTER NINE
Love

6 p.m., Friday 15th December 2000, Middle Temple Bar.

"So, are you ready for the big one, George?" Brian Appleyard asked mischievously.

"I never feel ready before I go into court, Brian, you should know that by now," replied George, looking tense. "To be honest, I'm shitting myself."

George and Brian sat in unaccustomed silence, sipping their beers as if they were their last, and an hour passed before George noticed that it was past seven o'clock. Not wishing to talk much about his never-ending fraud case, which was still ongoing, Brian was in a nostalgic mood.

"I can't believe how much has changed in the past few months," he said, apropos of nothing. "David is nowhere to be seen now that he's Mobo's favourite junior. Patrick's doing well in Dublin, I hear. Roberta's making a mint in the Cayman Islands."

"And here we are, like Vladimir and Estragon, waiting for Godot," added George.

"And Heather, are you two...you know...still in touch, so to speak?" Brian asked, not quite sure whether he was walking into a minefield or not.

"Heather? I haven't seen Heather for ages," said George sadly. "Perhaps I should send her an email."

Brian's ability to put on a blank poker face, an art already developed during his years in the police force but sharpened greatly at the criminal Bar, was pushed to the limit as Heather entered the room, unseen by George, and stood behind him. She looked at Brian with a finger across her lips, not quite hiding a very playful look on her face.

George continued, in blissful ignorance of the fact that Heather was now right behind him.

"What is it with women, Brian? Can't live with them, can't live without them. I miss Heather a lot. Particularly on a Friday night." George paused, while Brian began to look slightly concerned. "And Saturday morning," George said, almost smiling.

Heather decided to quit the game while she was ahead, and placed her hands over George's eyes.

"Guess who?" said Brian.

George held the soft hands over his eyes, smiled from ear to ear, took her hands away from his eyes, placed them over his mouth, and kissed the inside of Heather's hand. Turning around, he saw what felt like the most beautiful sight in the world, and realised for the first time the depth of the feelings he had for Heather. He didn't notice her new hairstyle, or her designer clothes, only the brightness of her gorgeous green eyes. George didn't want to show affection in such a public arena, but try as he might, it didn't work, and he quickly jumped out of his chair, stood up and hugged Heather like the long-lost lover that she was, and whispered into her ear, "God I've missed you, Heather, I really have."

"Hmm," huffed Brian. "I feel like a spare prick at a wedding. I'll leave you two lovebirds to it."

"No, no, Brian," said Heather and George in perfect unison, both now inseparable and giggly.

"Please stay, let's have a drink," George said. "Then Heather and I can go out for a meal together."

★　　★　　★

Perhaps the cheap and cheerful curry house, the Indian Ocean in Holloway Road, wasn't the most romantic of places for George and Heather to share a meal, but it seemed a logical starting point, being halfway between George's hideaway in Highgate and Heather's pad in Islington. The slightly worn red carpet and cheap floral wallpaper passed George and Heather by as they spent most of their time staring into each other's eyes and smiling, following a fifteen-minute taxi ride, kissing slowly and passionately, hardly pausing for breath.

George and Heather were taken by the cockney-speaking Indian waiter to a quiet corner away from the group of lads competing as to how many lagers they could down.

"You really do look great," said George. "Given up smoking as well, I notice. How is Pentheus? What's it like in the real world?"

Heather looked slightly embarrassed.

"I've been promoted," she said as humbly as she could. "You remember I was a rights executive. Well, Pentheus created a legal department soon after I arrived, and the new Head of Legal was looking to recruit an assistant and heard I was a barrister. So, I'm now the formal Legal Assistant at Pentheus."

"That's great, I'm really pleased for you."

"And my salary went up – in one leap, from less than twenty to thirty-five grand a year. I get a car next year. A three series BMW."

"Thirty-five grand a year! Wow, I'm impressed. And a new BMW? I'm green with envy. That's wonderful, Heather, I'm really pleased for you."

"And what about yourself, George. Have you taken Three Harcourt Square by storm, or are you biding your time?"

George lowered his head and spoke softly, almost whispering.

"To be frank, Heather, I've blown it at Three Harcourt. I'll probably move chambers early next year. I had it all and blew it, I really did. The bastards wanted me to take a leader for the Merlin trial. I told them to stuff it. The trial starts on Monday. Can you believe it? I haven't had a good night's sleep for days. So, because I wouldn't play their game and let that idiot M.B. take over, I've been excommunicated by Sam Leggitt. I blame Paul, he's the mixer. The only work I've been doing for the last few weeks has been absolute rubbish. I was doing a plea this morning at Highbury Mags. My client – a sixteen-year-old recidivist – was up for nicking thirteen Curly Wurly bars from the newsagent next to his school. The magistrates put him on another supervision order and told him to go on a diet. And that's one of my better cases."

"Thirteen Curly Wurly bars? Greedy bastard," Heather joked. "Any mitigation?"

"Yeah. His dog had just died. Only friend he had in the world," said George, looking genuinely sad.

Heather leaned over and held George's hand; he seemed quite young to her in that moment.

"George, don't worry. You're still in there. No matter which way it goes with Merlin, you can still start afresh in another set, once this one is over. It's a lot easier, if I remember correctly, to move from one set of chambers to another than to get a tenancy in the first place."

"Sure, I know that. It's just that things haven't quite turned out the way I'd hoped."

"That's life, George."

Heather looked deep into George's eyes and held both his hands.

"One of the reasons I needed to be with you, is that I need to tell you something. Please don't be angry with me. In fact, don't say anything." Heather noticed a fear creep into George's eyes. "I'm pregnant, George. I'm pregnant." She tried unsuccessfully to hold back a flood of tears.

George's shocked expression lasted only a moment. "It's mine, isn't it, Heather?"

"Of course the baby's yours, yours and mine. There was never anyone else but you." Heather suddenly looked very young and vulnerable. "It's been a while. If there's someone else, I'll understand. Please tell me, George. Is there someone else?"

George felt something swell inside his heart and tears came into his eyes.

"There's no one else. Can't imagine anyone else in my life other than you, Heather. Ever. Let's have dessert at my place. You've never been there. I only have one real luxury – a Victorian rolltop bath."

CHAPTER TEN
Trial

9:45 a.m., Monday, 18th December 2000, the prison cells beneath Southwark Crown Court.

The cell of the prison door slammed shut with a loud bang that echoed in a manner now familiar to George. It was a sound that George heard in his sleep, an unmistakable and unforgiving sharp sound made when a steel door clangs against a steel frame, enclosing a small space designed to incarcerate humans against their will. George was already robed and carried only a blue counsel's notepad. George and Merlin sat next to each other on a wooden plank as they had done before. George had only half expected his solicitor to be present, and was therefore not surprised that Sam Leggitt had obviously forgotten their agreement to meet outside the cell at ten o'clock.

Merlin was quick to notice that George was ashen white, his hands trembling slightly, but noticeably.

"Those who are not afraid have the most to fear," Merlin said to George, a comment that George chose to ignore. "The first day of battle is always the worst. You will sleep better tonight, my friend."

Before George could think of anything to say, Merlin continued. "Do you approve of my appearance? I was told by my friends in Brickstonia that an English jury expects the prisoner to be well-presented. The garb was a present from the priest, who offers us his prayers."

George had hardly noticed that Merlin was dressed in an ill-fitting two-piece pinstriped suit, a clean white shirt and blue tie. Merlin's hair had grown to a short stubble on his head but he was clean-shaven, the goatee beard having disappeared, and looked quite dapper, apart from the dirty trainers which somewhat spoilt the overall image. George wondered what the first impression of the jury would be of this character. It was very difficult to anticipate. *Yes, that's it*, he thought. *A retired schoolteacher perhaps. Or maybe a man of the cloth. Perhaps a lecturer in philosophy from a small left-wing college.* Could have been worse.

Merlin, likewise, was sizing up his companion, paying particular attention to George's wig, which fascinated Merlin as it would a child.

"May I touch it, Sir George?"

George had been through this before and knew from experience it was best to play along. He took off his wig, handed it to Merlin, and said, "Go on, try it on."

Merlin examined the object slowly and methodically. He rolled his fingers over the tightly wound loops of horsehair, lifted the wig to his nose and breathed in deeply. "Ah!" he exclaimed joyfully. "Horses. How the nose can fire the memory." He ever--so-carefully placed the garment on his head. Then he lifted his head quite theatrically, looked around the cell as if he was about to make a speech. It frightened George that Merlin looked more barristerial than many of the barristers he knew.

Merlin took off the wig and handed it back to George as if he was holding a sacred object.

"It has great power. Be calm, Sir George. There is a popular saying in Brickstonia: 'nothing is to be feared except fear itself.' The outcome has already happened, but I will not spoil the story for you." Merlin closed his eyes. "Glory is for the few. Savour these moments, my friend, we are in good hands."

George looked at his watch, and needed to exercise great self-control over his bladder when he accepted the fact that it really was five past ten. In twenty-five minutes he would be expected in court for the commencement of his first jury trial. He had another rush of fear, and tried hard to control his breathing.

"Listen, Merlin, you won't have to say anything this morning other than to state your name and answer 'Not guilty' when the charges are read out. The jury will be sworn in, and that can take some time. The prosecution will outline their case to the jury and call their witnesses. You won't be called to the witness box today. I am allowed to cross-examine the prosecution witnesses. Sam Leggitt may come and ask you questions from time to time. Do you understand?"

"Yes, I understand, Sir George. My role is to remain silent until I take the oath and then I may tell my story. Is that correct?"

"Er, yes it is," said George. "I must go now. I'll see you upstairs in a few minutes."

Merlin put his arms up to embrace George.

"Not now, Merlin, please. I'm not a great one for hugs."

Merlin pulled himself back and smiled.

"You haven't changed, Sir George. Not one little bit. You were the same as a child, many years ago. Appearances can change like the weather, but the soul remains the same."

George looked at Merlin with some concern, wanting to dig deeper into Merlin's comments, but the moment passed and the cell door was opened.

"Are you ready, gentlemen? The judge wants to get going," said a deep voice from behind the door.

"We're ready, aren't we, Sir George?"

George intended to say "of course" but no words came out of his mouth.

*　　*　　*

George had taken the precaution of leaving his papers and textbooks on the front row nearest the court clerk on the right-hand side of the courtroom, the side farthest away from the jury.

George took one final look at his watch before he walked through the courtroom door. Ten twenty-nine. He realised that he wouldn't be able to go to the toilet until probably lunchtime, which usually meant one o'clock, a thought that made his bladder weak.

Knowing there was only one route forward and that was through the courtroom door, George walked into Court 12. He was beyond merely trying to control his nerves; his immediate struggle was to keep upright and not faint.

As he entered all eyes turned on him as if to say, "Where

the hell have you been?" The court clerk picked up his phone and said in a voice loud enough for all to hear, "Tell the judge wandering Winsome has been found, yes we're ready." Even the usher looked angry; according to the court's clock, George was late.

George noticed that Mobo was where George had been expecting to sit, and that his papers had been moved to the other side of the front row bench, causing George to blush as he remembered that as defence counsel he was expected to be closest to the jury. Mobo was studying some papers quite intensely and did not acknowledge his opponent. David Palmer, seated directly behind Mobo, looked round and smiled at his friend. George then noticed Sam, seated in the same row as David, who also turned around to smile sheepishly at his counsel.

George hardly managed to get to his seat before Margaret exclaimed, with her now-familiar booming tone, "All rise!" heralding in Judge Watts, who paused momentarily to bow to counsel before sitting in his large chair and ceremoniously putting on his gold half-rimmed glasses.

George's mind went completely blank; his only conscious thought was that he had no clue as to what was supposed to happen next.

Everyone sat down, including Mobo. George looked around in a panic and then realised that the judge was waiting for something. Everyone looked quite relaxed, almost excited, apart from George, who felt not only in dire need of a pee, but physically sick. Hearing some shuffling from the back of court, George turned around and saw Merlin being shown to a small seat in the dock. George turned around quickly before Merlin could catch his eye.

The usher stepped forward to announce: "Gather all ye in the case of the Crown against Merlin. Let the indictment be put to the defendant."

Don't remember that bit, thought George.

The clerk stood up and asked in a clear loud voice, "Are you Merlin?" The prison officer whispered something to the old boy, who immediately stood to attention, rigidly.

"That is my name, yes."

The clerk continued. "You are charged on count one of this indictment that you did unlawfully cause the death of one Frederick Owen Russell, contrary to the common law. To this charge do you plead guilty or not guilty?"

Merlin stood mute, as if transfixed by the whole affair.

A second or two passed before Merlin seemed to snap out of his trance and replied in a soft voice, "Oh yes. Not guilty. By the gods above us and below us, not guilty." George sighed with relief.

Merlin sat down, an act that prompted another little whisper from the prison officer, and Merlin stood up again.

The clerk waited. "You are further charged that on the twentieth day of September in the year of our Lord 2000 you did unlawfully cause actual bodily harm to Frederick Owen Russell contrary to the Offences Against the Persons Act 1861. To this charge, how do you plead?"

"Not guilty," answered Merlin, who remained standing even though the clerk had sat down.

"You may sit down, Mr. Merlin," said Judge Watts.

"You are a kind man, thank you, learned sir," Merlin said before resuming his seat. He looked rather pleased with himself, particularly when he noticed two members of the pubic taking copious notes of the proceedings, both rather attractive young ladies.

"Bring in the jury, please, usher," said Judge Watts.

"Now. Mr. Moboto, Mr. Winsome. I have one or two observations to make before the jury is sworn in."

Mobo and George rose to their feet.

"You are both aware, no doubt, of the Lord Chancellor's recent guidelines on wasting court time, are you not?"

Both Mobo and George instinctively said "Of course," though neither of them had the faintest idea what the judge was going on about.

"I want to place a marker from day one," the judge said firmly. "This trial concerns the guilt or innocence of the defendant by reference solely to the charges on the indictment. This is not a trial of the defendant's identity, which may have relevance in a different context. I do not want either of you—" the judge looked at George, "—sidetracking or confusing the jury into thinking that the issue is whether the defendant is or is not 'Merlin'. Is that clear?"

Both Mobo and George nodded furiously. "Indeed, Your Honour," said Mobo.

"Of course, Your Honour," said George.

"Good. I am glad we're agreed on that point. I am fully prepared to take whatever steps are necessary to ensure that valuable and expensive court time is not wasted on matters that are not central to the case. Now, I see the jury panel has arrived."

A panel of fifteen members of the public were ushered into the courtroom, like disorientated sheep unsure whether they were heading for fresh green pastures or the abattoir. The collective look of fear was palpable.

George turned around to Sam and whispered, "Great. Looks like their first day. Our chances of an acquittal have just risen by fifty percent." George knew from recent studies and anecdotal evidence that most jury members were required to attend court for an average of two weeks. In the first week they tended to acquit the defendant, but come the second week they were more likely to convict.

The process of swearing in a jury for a trial under English law had become relatively swift, even more so once the law was changed forbidding the defence to challenge a juror unless they had 'proper cause'. Without the complications that arose in a case involving national security, or a lengthy and complicated trial, the process was relatively quick and painless.

The usher called out a name from a list that she held out in front of her. George had been told by his pupil master not to make eye contact with the jury too soon and let the process unfold, keeping his head down.

Within an hour, six women and six men had taken an oath to deliver a just verdict, based solely on the evidence presented to them. Once the jury was in place, George scanned their faces and noticed that they were either very young or quite old. For what it was worth, George made a hastily scribbled note on his pad: *six men, six women. Two v. young, one Asian. One v. old Rasta. One Greek?*

Although less than two hours into his first jury trial, George now understood that a courtroom could lapse into an eerie void, like an old man who loses his train of thought and falls silent in mid-sentence. As long as nobody was looking expectantly in his direction, there was nothing to worry about, he thought. After the jury had been sworn in, the judge rather proudly flipped open a very thin and expensive-looking laptop and turned to the jury.

"Members of the jury. Welcome. For your convenience I can tell you that this case is expected to finish before the end of this week. May I remind you that we will convene at ten thirty sharp each morning and rise at four thirty in the afternoon, although that may vary somewhat. Luncheon is between one and two o'clock. You will notice, members of the jury, that I am using a computer, please do not let that distract you. It means I can type my notes straight into this machine and then edit the text, print it, and read out my summing-up to you much more efficiently than before. May I also remind you that if any of you have any special needs then please tell the usher. Don't be shy. Is that clear?" The jury collectively nodded. "Now, I think we are ready, Mr. Moboto."

A respectful silence overcame the court as if an invisible curtain had fallen and was about to rise before the start of a play in a small theatre. Mobo rose slowly, paused for dramatic effect, and looked solemnly towards the jury.

"Members of the jury. My name is Mr. Moboto. I represent the prosecution. Behind me is my learned junior, Mr. Palmer. To my right is my learned friend Mr. Winsome, who represents the defence. In the dock is the defendant, who goes by the name of Merlin." Moboto paused to let the ripple of laughter subside while David Palmer sat back as if basking in newfound fame.

"This trial is not about the identity of the defendant," said Moboto to an approving nod from the judge. "It is about the guilt or innocence of the defendant, who is charged with two counts on the indictment: one of manslaughter and the other of actual bodily harm. Before I set out the facts of this case, I must remind you that the prosecution must prove the case against the defendant; the defence need prove nothing."

Sly old bastard, thought George. *Only five minutes into his opening speech and the jury already has him down as Mister Nice Guy.*

Mobo quickly rattled over the sorry events of the morning of the 20th of September, paying attention to each member of the jury, particularly the older members.

Mobo took what felt like an eternity to explain the elements of manslaughter and summarised the medical evidence that would prove a direct link between the events of the 20th of September and the cause of death. Mobo came to an end by telling the jury, as if the prosecution had Merlin's interests in its heart, that he was not seeking to establish that the defendant had intended to take the life of the deceased nor had he intended to cause him really serious injury. "If that was our case, then this would be a murder trial, which it is not." The jury sat listening attentively throughout and nodded at every turn of Mobo's opening. The last point seemed to reinforce the impression that the prosecution felt rather sorry for the old boy and that he was being treated with the utmost courtesy and fairness. Mobo's tone was almost apologetic when he ended by requesting the jury to do their 'painful duty' and convict.

Mobo looked at his watch. Twelve fifteen.

"Your Honour. Shall I call my first witness or would the court rather rise for a few minutes?"

The jury looked at the judge, all of them hoping for a break. Four of them seemed to be suffering acute withdrawal symptoms of one kind or another, and one of them was clearly desperate for the toilet.

"Oh, I think we should carry on, Mr. Moboto. We should at least get through the first witness's evidence in chief before two. But very courteous of you to ask."

Nobody noticed one of the jury muttering 'bastard' under his breath, rubbing his nose furiously, except Merlin, who was also desperate for the loo. Merlin could hear the aged prison officer snoring behind him and noticed a small black rubbish bin by the man's chair. Merlin reached over to the bucket and placed it between his legs, pulled out his prick and started to pee, creating, just for the first couple of seconds, the unmistakable sound of running water against metal. Merlin tried to maintain an air of innocence while peering over the dock, but one jury member looked over towards Merlin, who now had the sublime look of a man relieving himself just before losing control of his bladder. A series of nods and winks passed through the jury like a wave until most of them were in a state of uncontrolled giggles, except for two of the female elders who shook their heads in disbelief and shock.

Perhaps the judge and the lawyers mistook the sound for the pouring of water into a paper cup, Merlin didn't care. The few members of the public situated at the back of the courtroom, behind the dock area for the accused in the well of the court, did not notice either. However, Merlin was left with the new problem of what to do with a bucket half-full of steaming piss. This thought preoccupied Merlin for a few moments, as it did the jury, who were now complicit in Merlin's dilemma. Merlin deftly placed the bucket next to the prison officer's legs.

Meanwhile Mobo had called his first witness, Kevin Arter, the eighteen-year-old assistant dog patroller, who was with Fred Russell on the morning of the 20th of September. The jury's giggles had subsided, and the judge and the lawyer and others had missed the drama.

"You say the defendant, quote, 'hurled Fred into the bushes with his staff'. Could you be more specific?" enquired Mobo.

"Er, what d'you mean?" responded the very nervous witness.

"Well, can you describe exactly the manner in which the defendant caused Fred to fall to the ground?"

"Not really, there was a bit of pulling on either side, then Fred went flying into the bushes. That's it, really." Kevin looked as if he was going to get into trouble for not being more helpful.

Mobo conceded, in his own mind, that it was not going to get any better.

"Yes, thank you, Mr. Arter. Wait there, please," said Mobo.

Mobo sat down and the judge looked with some concern at George, who was talking to Sam.

"Mr. Winsome. Do you intend to cross-examine the witness?"

George stood up. "Yes, Your Honour, I do."

"Well, you can do so at two o'clock. Court will rise."

Merlin heard one of the jury mutter, "Thank God for that."

The usher's loud announcement that followed woke the prison officer. He knocked over the bucket, spilling the deep yellow liquid onto the floor of the dock, and exclaimed, "What the fuck?"

His Honour Judge Watts looked sternly at the officer. "Any more of that and I'll have you in the cells for contempt, Officer. All you have to do is stay awake. If that's too much for you then we'll find a replacement. Is that clear?"

The red-faced officer mumbled an apology and looked at Merlin, who remained poker-faced, his eyes facing the floor.

Most of the jury was trying to stifle giggles, a fact now picked up by the judge.

"Members of the jury," said the judge in his sternest voice, "I appreciate that you are in very unfamiliar circumstances and that this is probably your first time in court." The judge's tone had the desired effect of creating an immediate sombre atmosphere. "But do please realise that you fulfil an important function in the criminal justice system. There is nothing wrong with the occasional light moment in a criminal trial but never forget that the defendant's liberty is in your hands. I should also remind you, at this early stage, that now you have been sworn in you must not, under any circumstances, discuss the case with anyone other than your fellow members of the jury. Not even your loved ones." The judge peered over his half-rimmed glasses and paused for theatrical effect.

"Is that absolutely clear, members of the jury?"

Sam and George made a hasty retreat to the cells, to pay a courtesy call upon their client, who had already been escorted down to the prisoners' cells. While they waited at the door of the cell, Sam peered through the small eye-level 'suicide flap' and noticed that Merlin was flat out on the wooden bench, fast asleep.

"Let's leave him, George. All this excitement has obviously worn him out, let him have a kip."

"I think you're right," said George. "Let's go across the road for a sandwich."

"What did the jury find so funny, George?"

"I don't know, they often start to laugh out of pure nervousness, it's quite common," said George, as if he had many years of experience in such matters.

"How far do you reckon we'll get by the end of today?"

"Well, I'm not going to be more than an hour with their first witness. Then it's the police evidence and the interview. I might not even get to cross-examine the police before tomorrow."

"Should be a quiet afternoon, then."

"Yeah, should be, Sam."

*   *   *

A full day in court has the same ebb and flow of a below-par fringe play: the first half being a battle to stay still; the second half being a struggle to stay awake, particularly if alcohol has been consumed during lunch.

But the jury had not been permitted outside the precincts of the courtroom during the brief break, and therefore as the court proceedings resumed there was no waft of alcohol following them into the jury box; this time the stale stench of cheap beer was coming from young Kevin Arter, who was looking the worse for wear as a result of a dangerously indulgent liquid lunch intended to calm his nerves, but that in fact had the opposite effect.

Kevin shuffled back into the witness box and the judge gave a discreet nod to counsel that the show was to continue. "May I remind you that you are still under oath, Mr. Arter?" Judge Watts sat back with an air of undisguised superiority.

George rose tentatively to his feet, having thought through what he wanted out of this witness, which was not a lot.

"Yes, Mr. Winsome, you may proceed," said the judge.

George Winsome gave a muffled "Thank you," conscious of the fact that he was too nervous to make eye contact with the jury.

"Mr. Arter, can you clarify whether the defendant was awake or not when you first saw him?"

"Oh, he was definitely asleep, we thought he was dead."

"And by the way he was dressed, you also thought he might have been to a fancy-dress party?"

"Well, as I said, his clothes were a bit strange, not the type of your usual down-and-out. I don't know how to put it – like he was dressed up for something."

"And it was early in the morning?"

"Very early."

"Was it bright or dark?"

"A bit of both, if you know what I mean."

George continued, gaining confidence. "Had the sun risen, yes or no?"

The witness looked hesitant. "The sun wasn't yet up, but the sky was real clear and there was a bit of a moon."

George remembered one of his pupil master's little tricks to get what you wanted out of a witness: the old 'CTB' routine, otherwise known as 'confuse the bastard'.

"So, you were really relying on the moonlight in order to see. Was it a full moon or merely a waxing gibbous?"

Judge Watts could take no more.

"Mr. Winsome, I have warned you about wasting court time. If your intention is to take us into the realm of waxing and waning moons, equinoxes and pagan rites of passage, I will lose my patience. What is your point?"

George feigned surprise at the judge's mini-outburst, feeling pleased that he had, so early on, managed to provoke the judge, a fact that might assist in developing some bond with the jury, a tactic advised by esteemed pupil masters. It was a dangerous game, but George felt a real need to try and put on a decent sort of show for the jury. They deserved it, he thought.

"I am merely trying to establish whether there was sufficient light for this witness to see all he says he saw, Your Honour."

Timothy Watts peered over his glasses, narrowing his eyes as he would to a cheeky schoolboy.

"Well, why don't you get on with it then, Mr. Winsome?"

"How well could you see the defendant, Mr. Arter?"

"Er, fairly well, not perfectly but—"

"Not perfectly. And there was a staff lying next to the defendant?"

"Yes, there was."

"And would it be fair to say that given the appearance of the defendant and the position of the staff, one could reasonably suppose that the staff belonged to the defendant?"

"How d'you mean?" asked Kevin, now regretting his third pint of beer.

"The staff or 'stick' as you called it in your statement, obviously belonged to Merlin, didn't it?"

"If you say so."

"Was it *yours*?"

"No."

"Was it *Fred's*?"

"No."

"So, if it wasn't yours or Fred's who else might it belong to?"

"Er, I don't know what you're getting at, I hadn't thought about it."

"Mr. Arter, let's try and make some progress, can we? The staff obviously belonged to the defendant. Are you seeking to challenge that proposition?"

"Er, no."

"So, your senior colleague takes it upon himself to pick up property that doesn't belong to him and starts to assault a peaceful, sleeping old man?"

"Assault? What are you talking about? It was him," shouted Kevin, pointing at Merlin, "who assaulted Fred, and now Fred's dead. Killed by the old boy. I bet he does Tae Kwondo or somethin'."

Mobo smiled a big Mobo smile and the judge smugly asked the stenographer to read back the exact words used by the witness.

George struggled hard to remember some words of wisdom from his esteemed pupil master for such circumstances. Ah, yes, as a hastily remembered thought passed through his mind: *If the witness gets the upper hand, hit him in the nuts.*

George leaned forward and stared into the eyes of the witness.

"Let me put my client's case to you, Mr. Arter. Your colleague took possession of property belonging to Merlin, and then proceeded to strike him in a completely unjustified manner. The defendant, quite reasonably and justifiably, tried to retrieve his staff and Fred simply lost his balance and fell over. That's what happened, wasn't it?"

"Bollocks," uttered Kevin, immediately placing his hand over his mouth in disbelief that he could use such a word in front of a judge.

"Careful, young man, or you'll end up spending the night in the cells for contempt," warned a stern-looking Judge Watts.

"Sorry, Judge, it just slipped out, sorry," Kevin whined before emitting a slight burp.

"Let's move on, shall we, Mr. Winsome?"

George felt that his undefined strategy of destabilising the witness had somehow worked and was suddenly consumed with an all-out desire to move in for the kill.

Kevin, however, looked as if he knew that the reality he was in was now so hostile, another burp, if audible, could land him in jail, a thought that made him even more nervous.

"You had been working with Fred for how long?"

"About two years. I joined straight from a government youth training scheme."

"And it would be fair to say that Fred could be a bit grumpy at times?"

Kevin seemed to lighten up and half smiled.

"Yeah, you could say that, yeah."

"And impatient?" enquired George on a hunch.

"Yeah, a bit."

"And used bad language?"

"It wasn't that bad...."

"And he could be provocative sometimes?"

"Well, I don't know about that."

George realised that he had no idea where he was heading, as if for some reason he had turned off the main road and was tearing along a rough track for no discernible reason. Before he could re-orientate himself a distinctive 'thud' was heard from the direction of the jury box. It appeared that the youngest-looking male had abruptly lost consciousness and whacked his head on the wooden ledge in front of him used by the jurors for resting their papers upon and making notes.

The jury collectively panicked, shouting for help, apart from the Rastafarian whose constant grin broadened slightly.

The judge had seen it all before, but normally the sudden loss-of-consciousness routine was performed by the defendant whose lies had become so entangled and contradictory that it was like watching an invisible noose slowly tighten around the liar's neck until no air could be breathed in or out. The colour would drain from the face rapidly, followed by total collapse sometimes forward, sometimes backward; never could tell.

"Ask Matron to come to court immediately, would you?" the judge ordered Margaret, who was busily undoing the man's shirt for no obvious purpose.

The young juror by now had been removed from the jury box and was lying flat out on the floor. He didn't look too good: his pimply face was ashen-white, almost marble-like. He was obviously still breathing but there was clear concern among the other jurors as to whether even that would continue. The jurors' collective concern was heightened by the judge's apparent indifference to the whole scene.

Margaret was now leaning over him, her long hair having spilled out of its tidy bun, covering her face, which was now on top of the young man's. No one was quite sure what first aid ritual Margaret was deploying but equally no one wanted to interrupt.

"Don't be too alarmed, members of the jury. Quite common, you know. I'm sure it's just the excitement of the day. Let's assess the situation in the morning. Ten o'clock, sharp," Judge Watts suggested as he rose to his feet for a quick exit in the direction of his private chambers before he witnessed anything he might regret. Many years on the bench had taught him that jurors were prone to all sorts of reactions to sitting still for hours on end without a break; invariably it was best to pretend all was well and what seemed as a crisis would tend to pass as abruptly as it had begun. The usher noticed the judge standing up and reacted as she always did in such circumstances. "Court rise!" she bellowed, and the judge made a sharp exit.

★   ★   ★

The prison officers felt unusually warm towards Merlin – he wasn't your average villain, and they felt he was owed a favour for keeping them in good cheer following the bucket episode, now classified as a minor courtroom classic.

Instead of Merlin being ushered down into the bowels of the courtroom into an airless cell, he was led into a relatively smart 'interview suite' outside the courtroom usually reserved for prosecution counsel and police solicitors.

"First day, and only one casualty. Poor lad. But we are doing quite well, I would say," Merlin commented to George and Sam.

An uneasy silence followed, confirming in George's mind that his performance so far was transparently that of a nervous wreck expected of a rookie.

"You were very good to enquire about the moon, Sir George. The full moon did not follow for several days. It is always the best moon of the year, at the time when the days and nights are in harmony. I am glad you kept to your word, I knew you would," said Merlin.

Sam twigged that there was some sort of private joke going on between Merlin and George and tried not to giggle. Sam's immediate concern was how he could excuse himself to flit away and flirt with his girlfriend, who was upstairs in the listings office.

"Er, do you mind if I leave the two of you to it? I've got some calls to make if you don't mind."

"Not at all, young sire, please attend your business," Merlin said as if excusing a stable lad.

Merlin and George let the peace and silence take over, each now relaxed in each other's company.

"I wonder what overcame the boy?" said Merlin, looking both perplexed and concerned. "There are so many forces at work, we must be on our guard, Sir George. At all times." He looked around as if unseen forces were in the ether.

"Yeah, I know what you mean," commented George. "I don't think that the judge is too fond of me, Merlin. I hope you don't feel that it's harming your case."

"Not at all, Sir George." Merlin paused as if to reinforce his observation. "My staff is heavy, very heavy, you know. Do you think the jury would care to see it?"

George turned white with panic. "The staff, of course! How on earth could I forget the staff? Yes, of course, the jury must see it. How could I let that slip my mind? I'll ask Mobo about it. Thanks, Merlin."

"That would be very helpful, Sir George. But be careful with it, it can be easily excited." Merlin looked mischievous.

George took no notice of Merlin's warning and continued to mutter on about how he could possibly forget such an important piece of evidence.

"Listen, Merlin. I'll speak with Mobo about the staff. I'm sure he should have got the arresting officer to produce it as evidence," George suggested, trying hard to sound convincing. "But anyway, the way things are going, you're not going to be in the witness box until Wednesday, I guess, perhaps even Thursday. I must go and speak to the prosecution about the staff."

"You are a good man, Sir George. God's speed, and rest well this nightfall."

CHAPTER ELEVEN
Magic

The Crown v. Merlin, Day 2, 9:40 a.m., Tuesday, 19th December 2000, Southwark Crown Court.

"Have you seen the papers, George? This case is beginning to take off. Look at this, in the *Sun*, it says that the City boys are offering three to one on a straight-run acquittal and the *Star*'s got a picture of 'How He Would Look as MERLIN' – full-page colour spread, a guy with the 'Full Monty Merlin' kit on, standing next to a topless wench handing Merlin a staff saying, 'Show me your magic, Merlin'. There's also a small piece in the gossip column of the *Guardian*. No mention of your name, George, but, you know, early days."

Now that the press was following the case, albeit as a running joke and only in a small way, Sam Leggitt had discovered a newfound enthusiasm for the trial and was sporting a brand-new silk tie, and his shoes were noticeably shiny.

George couldn't get worked up about a column or two in the newspapers, as he was preoccupied with other matters and had decided to arrive early enough to have a coffee with his instructing solicitor in the courtroom building's public café. George was robed for court but had placed his wig on a chair, which reduced considerably the number of prying eyes staring in his direction, as it wasn't often barristers sat in such vulnerable places where witnesses might be found or even a stray juror or two, even though the members of the jury were never supposed to venture outside their enclosed area.

George looked at his watch, having decided to be in court at nine forty-five to have enough time to clarify with Mobo the whereabouts of the staff. The realisation that he could have overlooked such a fundamental issue was eroding his confidence and he felt deep embarrassment at what he felt was total negligence. *Not something a QC would overlook*, was the painful thought that he could not get out of his mind.

"Wait until Merlin gives evidence, then we'll really get some quality coverage," Sam said. "Oh boy, and when the jury lets the old codger off, then we'll be front page. Fucking marvellous, don't you think, Sir George?"

George had already had enough of Sam and decided to put him to work. "Sam, why don't you pop down to the cells and say hello to Merlin. Tell him I'll see him later. I need to have a chat with Mobo."

Sam merrily scuttled off in the direction of the single lift that took officials down into the bowels of the buildings where the cells were situated, and George wearily placed his wig over his hair and headed for Court 12, feeling many years older than he did the previous day. The acute sense of fear that dominated him on the first day seemed to have been replaced with an incredibly overpowering sense of responsibility towards his client.

George approached the entrance to Court 12, surprised at the number of people waiting outside for the usher, who would decide who was allowed into the Court.

As George strolled confidently into the now-familiar room, he was relieved to see Mobo sitting studying papers and even more relieved to see the staff lying in front of the clerk's seat, obviously ready to be produced as an exhibit.

Mobo heard footsteps behind him, turned and saw his opponent, obviously in battle mood.

"Ah, good morning to you, my learned friend. What fun we're having. Glad to see you've retrieved the weapon of death. I had presumed the officers would bring it yesterday. I was getting worried about it, you know. Had a word behind my back with the police officers to save my ass? Well done. Wouldn't be the same without the murder – I mean manslaughter – weapon, would it?"

George paused and bit his lip to stop himself from disillusioning Mobo.

"Er, no it wouldn't, Mobo. Nothing wrong in me holding it, is there?"

"Not at all, but be careful you don't cast any loose spells. That would not be cricket, would it?"

George carefully picked up the staff by its centre, surprised at its weight. It had to be treated gently otherwise the bells, trinkets and charms would start to clink and rattle.

"Nice head," he commented. "What kind of wood do you think it is, Mobo?"

Mobo was still seated, studying his papers. "Not for me to say, old boy, something your client may assist the court with. Not of a type I've ever seen before."

George was examining the staff very closely, looking for some detail that he could use against the prosecution.

"You won't find any bloodstains on it, George. If it was our case that Merlin had actually *struck* the deceased, the charge would have been murder."

Before George could respond he realised that the court had been opened to the public and there was an undignified scramble by members of the public, including some ladies and gentlemen of the press, to bag the few seats at the back of the court available to those not directly involved in the case.

Within two minutes the courtroom was packed out and the players, minus the jury, but including David Palmer, Sam Leggitt, and Merlin, had taken their places for the day's entertainment.

The usher emerged from the side door from where the judge would majestically appear and let rip with her loudest "Court rise," heralding the theatrical entrance of His Honour Judge Timothy Watts, who sat down and whispered something into the ear of the clerk.

The judge set up his laptop while the jury was herded into their seats. Much to everyone's relief the young male juror was among them looking fine, if slightly self-conscious and clearly embarrassed.

The judge knew how to deal with these situations.

"Members of the jury, I am so glad you are all here today. One of your number took a bit of a turn yesterday but I understand all is well. These things do happen, you know. Nothing to worry about. If you do feel unwell, please do not hesitate to let us know. Is that quite clear?"

The judge then noticed the staff lying less than six feet away from him. "The staff. Good. I'm glad you remembered to have it in court today, Mr. Moboto, well done."

Mobo rose to his feet but George beat him to it.

"Your Honour, might I raise a small procedural issue at this stage?"

"You might, Mr. Winsome. The question is whether you will indeed raise a procedural issue or not," responded the judge smugly, looking in the direction of the jury. "Now, do you wish the jury to be absent, Mr. Winsome, or is this a matter we can safely deal with in the jury's presence?"

Mobo looked towards George with a concerned look on his face, while David Palmer tried to bury his head to hide the attack of giggles that had just overcome him.

"The jury can stay, Your Honour. It is only this: perhaps the jury might welcome a mid-morning break. To sit listening to evidence requires enormous concentration and the morning stretch can be a challenge, Your Honour."

George looked over to the jury and was sure he heard the Rastafarian gentleman say "Right on" or words to that effect. The jury all looked towards the judge. The lad who had fainted rubbed his head, the young lady rubbed her nose, and one of the older men crossed his legs. The judge smiled with a knowing smile and looked at the jury with the best concerned judge look he could muster.

"I was just going to suggest that we take a break each morning, members of the jury. Mr. Winsome helpfully raised the issue before I could," the judge said, not hearing the youngest female member of the jury mutter, "What shite is this?"

"Of course, we will take a break each day at eleven thirty for ten minutes." The jury collectively sighed. "But, of equal concern, we have a lot of ground to make up, so we'll sit every day until further notice at ten o'clock and maybe a few minutes later in the day." His Honour did not realise the havoc he had just caused to the jury's finely-balanced domestic arrangements, particularly for the young single mother. "Now, Mr. Moboto, can we proceed?"

"Indeed, we can, Your Honour. I call Xavier Feelgood."

Xavier Feelgood was already in the witness box, taking the oath, before George could think of anything further to say to His Honour.

George was suddenly reminded how misleading a witness statement can be when a real person turns up to deliver its contents; the document is unlikely to refer to the height and general appearance of the witness, for example. Xavier Feelgood was a strange-looking character indeed, and George felt instinctively that there was fun to be had with this one as he tried to guess whether Xavier was over seven feet tall or not. It was difficult to tell. George wasn't really listening to the evidence and neither was the jury. This man had a shock of grey hair that reminded George of an old black-and-white Hammer horror movie: the type of hairstyle when the mad professor receives an electric shock. It almost stood on end. Xavier's voice was deep, very deep. David Palmer was in an uncontrolled state of giggles, again. By the feel of the shaking going on behind him, it was likely that Sam had caught the bug as well. George dared not turn around in case he lost his control. He tried hard to concentrate on what Xavier Feelgood was saying, but the more he looked at him the more he saw a picture of Lurch from *The Addams Family* wearing a ridiculous wig.

Mobo was clearly struggling, as Xavier was not keeping to the script that was his witness statement. Xavier was supposed to say that he was walking with his girlfriend over Hampstead Heath 'one fine moonlit morning' when he came across a fracas involving the defendant and the two dog patrollers. He said in his statement he saw the deceased being 'flung into the air' and 'landing with a slow crunching thud on the ground'. But that was not what Xavier was saying now. The story now was that he had been 'moon bathing' with his lover on the banks of one of the swimming ponds nearby. Xavier was in a hurry to get home before sunrise. George was sure he heard one of the jury use the word *vampire,* but it was difficult to tell given the now-open but stifled laughter coming from the public area at the back of the court. Xavier certainly did not see Merlin fling anyone into the air and had heard no noise. Mobo asked Xavier with an angry tone, "Why are you here?" only to be told that Xavier was consulting his psychic inner self on that point.

A wry smile appeared on Mobo's face and he sat down to indicate he was finished with his witness.

The judge was keeping his head down, focused on his laptop as if all was well, as if this debasement of Her Majesty's court would suddenly pass. Mobo did a grand job in not losing his cool completely, thought George. Lesser barristers would have succumbed to the temptation to treat Xavier as a hostile witness, allowing him to cross-examine the witness on his own statement, a desperate last-minute tactic normally scoffed at by the jury. No, Mobo was obviously too experienced to fall into that trap. He simply sat down as if he had performed brilliantly.

George rose cautiously to his feet and turned around to see Merlin trying furiously to get his attention. George politely asked the judge for "a moment to take further instructions" and packed Sam off to talk with the client. The whole court watched Sam cock an ear to Merlin, who whispered something to Sam, who rushed back and whispered into George's ear.

Looking composed, George put on his best barrister voice and asked, "Do you recognise the defendant?" pointing to the small, well-dressed old boy in the dock.

"Oh yes," said Xavier, "he's Merlin."

"You know the defendant?"

"Merlin is an old friend of mine. I didn't recognise him at the time of the incident. He was too far away. I later heard it was Merlin and went to see him in prison."

The judge suddenly intervened. "Mr. Feelgood, as a prosecution witness surely you must have known it would be quite improper for you to see the defendant in prison."

"Well, I didn't actually go along to see him in person; it was more a spiritual visitation, in dream-time, if you know what I mean."

The judge shook his head and asked George to continue.

"How long have you known him?" enquired George innocently.

Xavier paused and looked to the stars. And looked around again and answered sincerely, "Ooh, about a thousand years, as of the last Great Count-Up."

His Honour Judge Timothy Watts could take no more, not one little bit of it. Not even Mobo had ever seen Tim Watts so angry. It was like a tidal wave of righteous indignation.

"Mr. Winsome, I will not have you turn this court into some sort of circus! This is a very serious matter, very serious indeed. If you think this tactic of challenging the dignity and reverence of Her Majesty's court will help overcome your obvious immaturity and lack of experience, then you are sorely mistaken. Do I make myself clear, Mr. Winsome?"

George, and he thought the jury, quite understood the judge's need to take his frustrations out on someone. George quite enjoyed the judge's little outburst and was content to reassure the judge that he was only asking questions, as was his duty, and could not be held responsible for the answers.

"Well, unless you have any further questions of this, this…Mr. Feelgood, I take it we may move on, Mr. Winsome?"

"Absolutely, Your Honour, I have no further questions to ask this witness. Thank you, Mr. Feelgood, you've been very helpful."

"Not at all, sir, I am always happy to help Merlin, he's been such a good friend—"

"Yes, yes, thank you, Mr. Feelgood, you can go now, please," said the judge. "Now, Mr. Moboto, are you ready to call your next witness?"

"Indeed I am, Your Honour. I call the arresting officer, PC Murphy."

The jury looked expectantly in the direction of the court entrance as the usher went outside and yelled, "PC Murphy!"

PC Murphy looked as if he had been through the routine a hundred times before as he confidently took the oath, his large beer belly and reddened face providing further evidence that he was of a certain age and experience.

The judge took a sideways look at the uniformed officer and

sighed with relief as if normal service had been resumed.

PC Murphy did not see the incident but had been called to the scene once the commotion had died down. The defendant was sitting quietly at the base of a tree on a mound, in the middle of Hampstead Heath, looking confused, dazed, disorientated, and grubby. Fred Russell was lying near some railings, obviously in some discomfort, complaining of a pain in his back. PC Murphy had spoken to Merlin, who did not seem to be making much sense, and the defendant had been arrested and taken to Highgate Police Station for questioning. The police officer read the statement from his notes, made shortly after the incident. Much of what Merlin had said was incoherent but it was clear that he was denying using any force with the intention of causing Fred Russell any serious harm, although he 'more or less' confirmed that the 'weapon' was his property and that there had been a struggle. Finally, PC Murphy confirmed that the staff in front of him was the object found at the scene.

Unlike with the previous witness, Mobo had a smooth ride and sat down wearing the now-familiar expression of the smug prosecutor.

George rose to his feet, feeling every inch the trial lawyer.

"Pass me your notebook, please, Officer."

Policemen hated this tactic but knew from experience the defence were perfectly entitled to examine their notebooks. George was fishing but the jury didn't know it. He took his time and slowly turned the pages, making feigned expressions of surprise as he did so.

"Yes, thank you, Officer," George said as he looked at the usher to indicate that the notebook could be returned. George did not find any point that he could make, but he knew the brief examination would unnerve the policeman, a trick learnt from his esteemed pupil master.

"The prosecution's case is that Merlin flung the deceased into the bushes, using the staff, is it not?" asked George, looking at the jury.

PC Murphy looked warily at Mobo, who nodded to him.

"Er, if you say so, sir, I wasn't there at the time, as I said."

"Usher," said George, "please hand the staff to the officer."

The usher looked quite pleased to be the centre of attention and hurriedly picked up the staff and handed it to PC Murphy, who held it by the handle, outstretched with one hand, as if the other end was covered in dog shit.

"Yes, Officer, just hold it like that, can you, please?"

The policeman looked rather concerned as the staff was light enough to pick up and walk with, but its weight seemed to increase dramatically as the seconds ticked by. The judge waited patiently while the officer's ability to hold out the stick clearly began to wane and eventually he let his arm drop, causing a light rattling sound.

"It's heavy, isn't it, Officer?" George asked.

"No, it's not. If you asked me to hold out a two-pound dumbbell my arm would get sore very quickly," responded PC Murphy as if he was dealing with a kid who was too smart for his own good.

"Your Honour, I think the jury should be permitted to examine the staff, with Your Honour's leave."

"Yes, yes, Mr. Winsome. They may indeed examine the weapon...I mean staff. Usher, if you wouldn't mind. Thank you."

The usher retrieved the staff from PC Murphy and held it in the palms of her two hands, as if walking with a ceremonial mace during a coronation, and placed it in front of the jury.

"Now, members of the jury, you may examine the staff, but with care, please," warned the judge. "I suggest you pass it along the front row first, then along the back row."

For once, it appeared that the entire jury was wide awake and fully engaged in the proceedings.

The first juror, a stern-looking Caribbean lady, picked it up; she handled it carefully, with obvious respect, looking at the intricate carvings on the wood, stared through her glasses at the bone handle and touched one or two of the dangling trinkets and then indicated to the usher that she was done.

For a few minutes the staff was passed from juror to juror, each in their own way at least giving the impression that they were deeply interested in the object.

The whole process of the examination of the staff by the jury had taken only a few minutes, but the judge was clearly running out of patience and sighed with obvious relief when the usher was handed back the item, signaling the jury had dutifully examined the exhibit.

"Thank you, members of the jury. Very good. Usher, please hand the exhibit to counsel," said the judge, knowing that Mobo and George were entitled to conduct their own examination. George was first to handle the staff and looked towards Merlin. He got the distinct feeling that all was not well as Merlin was passive, with his eyes closed.

"Your Honour, might I talk with the defendant? I will be brief."

The judge nodded, and George handed the staff to Mobo and approached Merlin, who was not entirely motionless; nobody else had seemed to notice that he was fast asleep. George leaned over and whispered, "Merlin, Merlin. Not a great time for a nap. Wake up."

Merlin stirred slightly, his eyes barely open. "I'm fine, my friend. Just need to rest. Later." And with that Merlin closed his eyes and returned to his nap.

George approached the Counsel's table and addressed the judge.

"Your Honour. No need for alarm. But I wonder if you have noticed that the defendant is fast asleep."

All eyes turned on Merlin, who was clearly out for the count, snoring and sniffling quite happily.

"Well, Mr. Winsome. Why don't you wake him up?

"Your Honour, I already have. He is clearly exhausted. I appreciate it's an indulgence, but we are making solid progress and with a fair wind the jury will be out in good time for this trial to close as intended, on Friday. Please, might we adjourn for the day? It is only fair to the defendant and I imagine the jury might welcome some unexpected free time."

The jury nodded in the judge's direction. Mobo was still entranced with the staff but looked at the judge without even rising to his feet. "The prosecution has no objections, Your Honour, none at all."

"Very well," the judge sighed. "But in return, counsel, I expect you both to be conscious of this lost time when it comes to closing speeches. Is that clear?"

Both Mobo and George understood the deal being made and muttered a synchronised "Yes, Your Honour."

"A bit too much for the old boy, all this excitement. Listen, George," said Sam, looking at his watch, "I know it's a bit early, but I could murder a pint. Wanna join me?"

George looked around the courtroom, which was now empty. It appeared everyone had immediate tasks to hand.

George looked at his watch – ten past twelve – and realised he hadn't had a morning beer for as long as he could remember.

Sam and George walked out of Southwark Crown Court in search of a pub in the nearby complex of shops and restaurants overlooking the Thames, on the Thameside pathway heading towards St Katharine's Docks. When the judge's secondhand battered green Volvo came screeching out of the underground car park, Judge Watts looked cross and bothered.

"Well, he's obviously decided to take the day off like the rest of us. Back to his mansion, wherever it is, to have an early glass of brandy and a quiet day tuned to Radio 4, no doubt," George said to Sam as they crossed the road in search of a beer.

"You never know what these judges get up to in their spare time, George. Probably off for a sauna and massage down the West End, if you ask me. We'll be able to tell tomorrow, I bet. Now let's find a decent pint. Only the one, mind."

CHAPTER TWELVE
Therapy

9 a.m., Tuesday, 19th December 2000, Wimpole Street, London.

Dr. Robert Schilling was generally recognised to be an effective, if somewhat unorthodox therapist. He was entitled to call himself 'doctor' by virtue of the letters 'PhD' after his name, though his patients – or 'clients' as they preferred to call themselves – naturally presumed he was a doctor of medicine, not of philosophy. But 'Dr. Bob' was a qualified psychoanalyst, having studied for four years at the Tavistock Clinic in Hampstead, and the distinction between one form of doctorate and another was never an issue. Professional analysts were expected to follow the methodology of either Carl Jung or Sigmund Freud, unless they chose an independent method of their choosing. Dr. Bob was known through his writings, teaching, television, and radio appearances, and practice as a 'leading independent', allowing him a free hand with his fee-paying clients, most of whom were married middle-aged women whose husbands had the money to fund their search for authenticity.

Dr. Bob saw his ageing female clients as lost hearts, whose identities had been neglected over many years in favour of their husbands and children. Almost without exception they were deeply depressed, usually for good reason. Christina Watts was almost a paradigm of Dr. Bob's very successful practice: late fifties, married to a successful but frustrated professional, a mother with deep feelings of failure, and an obvious but hidden desire to be recognised as someone in her own right. It was also true that Christina was a near-perfect client whose gullibility was only equalled by the reliability of her platinum American Express card.

Christina had been in therapy for over two years, but there was much work to be done. Dr. Bob was secretly concerned as to whether Christina would reach the end of the long road towards self-enlightenment within the remaining timescale. It was also a worry that if Christina saw the light too soon she would leave the cause of her woes behind her, abandon her husband and child and achieve the happiness and self-fulfilment she craved. This would be very good for Christina but very bad for the good doctor, as his bills would inevitably remain unpaid while the lawyers picked over the carcass of her marriage. It was tricky work, being a therapist.

Dr. Bob practiced from rooms in Wimpole Street, in the West End of London, parallel to but considerably cheaper than the more celebrated Harley Street practices. His small consulting room was relatively inexpensive, partly due to the fact that the costs of a receptionist and administrator were shared with two dentists on the ground floor and the consultant dermatologist on the top floor.

Christina knew the routine. She would turn up five minutes early and press Dr. Bob's buzzer, the door would open magically, and she would nervously stroll past the receptionist, uttering an almost silent "Hello," up the single flight of stairs and push open Dr. Bob's door, which would always be unlocked by the time she had arrived.

Dr. Bob was a tall, fit, and handsome professional in his late forties, although the half-rimmed glasses and greying hair made him look older. He spoke in the soft well-educated tone of a professional and was expert in unspoken communication.

Dr. Bob's consulting room was sparse but functional and deceptively arranged with thought and precision: three easy chairs and a chaise longue positioned around a wooden Victorian fireplace, which had several small logs placed in the wrought-iron grate. The fire was never actually lit but the impression that it might be seemed to have a calming effect on those who walked through the door.

"Where would you like to sit today, Christina?" Dr. Bob asked in his ever-so-friendly therapist voice. "Do you want to lie down, or shall we sit and face each other? Whichever you prefer."

Christina had already made up her mind to lie down on the chaise longue, which was Dr. Bob's cue to pull up one of the easy chairs and sit behind her, so he could see Christina but she could not see him.

"Things are getting worse, Doctor, a lot worse."

Dr. Bob quickly looked at his watch.

"In what way, Christina?"

Christina sighed, said nothing, and then let out a flood of tears. Dr. Bob remained silent.

"Tell me, Christina, has your husband made love to you recently?"

Christina's sobbing reached new heights.

"We haven't, you know, done anything like that...for a long time."

"Are you ready to talk about it? I mean right now? We've made great progress recently in that respect, but tell me now, when was the last time you and your husband made love?"

Christina managed to take control of the ebbing and flowing of her tearful floods and took a moment to respond. It had taken two years to get to this point.

"Remember I told you about the time in Cyprus? We walked along the beach in the moonlight, after a wonderful meal, went back to the hotel room, and made wonderful love."

"Er, yes, I do. From memory, that was eighteen years ago. Yes?"

"Yes, eighteen years ago."

"And since then...."

"Nothing. Since Simon's birth we've slept in separate beds."

Dr. Bob waited for what felt like a very long time, and then said, "Massage yourself, Christina. Between the legs. Do it... softly...gently. Do it now."

Christina paused only momentarily to hitch up her skirt and place her hand inside her tights. Within minutes she was writhing in long-forgotten pleasure, moaning without inhibition.

Dr. Bob looked again at his watch. Thirty minutes were left of this session, enough time for him to sketch out his thoughts for a radio interview due to take place later in the day, a few minutes' walk away at the BBC's Broadcasting House.

Twenty minutes passed and Christina was still going strong, groaning and moaning in ever-increasing cycles of ecstasy.

"Very good, Christina, very good."

The sound of Dr. Bob's voice had the intended effect of bringing Christina back into the real world and she quickly came back to earth. After three or four minutes the judge's wife was composing herself.

"Christina. Maybe your husband feels the same frustrations as you. Maybe he is longing for love from you." Dr. Bob stood, walked over to his briefcase and took out a small sachet of powder.

He sat down on the chaise longue, facing Christina, whose face was hidden behind her hands.

"Listen, Christina. In this sachet is powdered Viagra; the very latest. It is tasteless and colourless and very effective. You can take some yourself. You may consider giving some to your husband. He doesn't have to know. It takes about forty minutes to take effect, so timing is all. Take it, please."

Christina dried her eyes and straightened her hair, looked at the small packet and smiled.

"Maybe I will, Doctor. Maybe I will."

With that Dr. Bob looked at his watch. "It's that time again, Christina. I'll see you next week. Are you OK?"

"Oh yes, Doctor. I feel a lot better, thank you so much. I can't tell you how much better I feel. Thank you."

*　　*　　*

Seventeen-year-old Sihairly Watts lay in his bed, staring at his bedroom ceiling at Sunny Meadows, thinking of the top ten reasons why he hated his dad so much. First, he thought, he was an absolute hypocrite, although he would work on that one as that ground might be broken up into at least three separate reasons. Second, his dad treated his mother badly, and made her unhappy, although he had to think twice about that one too because Sihairly also disliked his mother so much; the fact that his father made his mother unhappy was, unfortunately, a point in his dad's favour. His dad had never paid him enough attention. The bastard had sent him to a cheap and nasty boarding school. Now *there* was a ground he could work on – the beatings and ritual humiliations, the cold, painful, long hours on the playing fields, the sadism of the teachers and the bullying of his peers. Sihairly moved onto fresher grounds of complaint. His friends weren't allowed into his room, he wasn't given enough spending money, his father didn't listen to him and treated him like a failure. The list grew and grew until Sihairly hated him even more. He tried to imagine his dad sitting in judgement on others, innocent people caught up in the unjust and punitive system and wondered by what method he could teach his father a lesson.

Sihairly got up and retrieved his secret small wooden box hidden in a secret little place, and had a look at what gear he had left. There was enough cannabis to roll a joint or two. Sihairly looked at his watch: nine thirty in the morning. *Good time to skin up*, he thought. Also in his box were three tabs of ecstasy and a very small piece of blotting paper carrying the mark of an eagle's head. *My last acid trip*, Sihairly remembered, *kept for a rainy day*. Sihairly placed the piece of paper to his lips. One lick and he would be on another planet for over seven hours. It was tempting, but another thought went through his mind, recalling the subversive writings of the Sixties guru Timothy Leary, compulsive reading among his radical friends.

Leary advocated that the world could be put right if only people could understand the glory and complexity of the universe, if they could rediscover universal love and empathy. If they could experience just one acid trip, they would come to their senses and shed the superficial veneer of normality and conformity. Was it not Aldous Huxley's medication of choice on his deathbed?

Yes, that's the answer! Sihairly was instantly ecstatic at the idea. *If only my dad took a tab of acid, he would see the light. Tomorrow's the day.* He took a long puff on his joint and smiled as he remembered that his dad always took with him to court a flask of lemon tea, which he enjoyed hot or cold. *I'll be doing the old bugger a favour. Best therapy he could ask for.* And with that thought fresh in his mind, Sihairly placed Mike Oldfield's *Tubular Bells* inside his CD player, fixed his tiny earbuds securely into his ears, and drifted off into the sanctuary of his own mind.

CHAPTER THIRTEEN
Trip

The Crown v. Merlin, Day 3, Wednesday, 20th December 2000, Southwark Crown Court.

Sam and George both managed, with considerable effort, as agreed over the third pint the previous day, to meet outside the lift that would take them to the cells at nine fifteen a.m., in good time to have a few words with Merlin before the trial recommenced. They had both stopped counting the beers after number three, and neither could remember exactly what time they left the Slug and Lettuce, nor agree upon how many drinks they eventually sank between them. But it was now nine fifteen in the morning of day three.

Much to their mutual surprise, the numerous prison officers, keys dangling from the outside of their trouser pockets, all seemed to be joking and laughing and in some state of excitement. "Merlin going into the box today, counsel?" said one almost affectionately. "I'm giving two to one on a straight acquittal, what d'you reckon? The bookies are down to even money."

George noticed a newspaper lying on a seat, and there was mention of Merlin on the front page, left-hand column: *Merlin on Trial for Manslaughter,* but George's eyes were too blurred to pick up any other detail. It was becoming quite clear that Merlin was the talking point of the day, and his lawyers were going to get the red-carpet treatment.

"No need to go into the cells, gentlemen, I've sorted the conference room for you outside Court 12. We'll bring Merlin up and keep an officer posted outside," one of the more senior officers said. George was taken aback at this gesture as the prosecution lawyers, police officers and their witnesses normally bagged the conference rooms immediately outside the court, but the room was now reserved for Merlin as and when the need arose. This was new ground for George, and he smiled at the thought of the wave of indignation that would overcome Mobo when he realised that the defence had taken over his territory, with a guard to boot.

Sam and George contentedly retreated to the conference room and within minutes a prison officer showed Merlin in, as if he was royalty. "Any coffees or teas?" asked the officer politely.

Merlin looked splendid. His soft blue two-piece pinstriped suit looked as if it had just come back from the dry cleaners. His dirty trainers had been replaced with well-polished black leather shoes, and a very expensive-looking and equally new deep blue silk tie offset his new crisp white shirt. His head and face were completely shaven, and his eyes were clear and sparkling. He no longer looked like the retired professor or tired pastor: his appearance now was more that of a chief executive of a successful business or the head of a large public service conglomerate.

"Good morning to you, good morning. I feel in such good spirits this morning. Everyone has been so kind. Do you like my apparel? I left Brickstonia this morning to the chant of 'Merlin, Merlin, Merlin!' coming from every cell. Today will be a great day, my friends. A truly great day."

Sam and George looked at each other in pleasant disbelief that the man in front of them was the same as the Merlin of the past few days and weeks. Indeed, he looked considerably sharper than his solicitor and barrister, both of whom were nursing severe hangovers.

"OK, Merlin, OK. You look great. But the statement we took from you some time ago looks a bit thin. Can we run through it, please? We don't have much time," George asked, sounding unusually officious.

"Oh, there's no need for that, my good knight. You know what happened on the day I was imprisoned. It is very simple. What is there to concern you?"

George tried hard to dispel the fuzziness that was dominating his mind. Sam couldn't help but interrupt, as if to help George.

"Listen, Merlin. How far are you intending to go with the

Merlin stuff? That's the point. I mean we were discussing this yesterday for some time, and both feel that you can keep all the Merlin business to a minimum and concentrate on the facts of the day."

Merlin looked at George with a degree of sadness and disappointment.

"My dear Sir George. You must not lose faith. I am Merlin. I am on trial. I understand what they will try and do to me today. I am prepared. My mind has been returning, slowly. I now remember many things that I could not before. I slept not one wink last night, and feel mightily refreshed. Do not doubt me, my friends, otherwise we are lost. You must remember who I am."

George and Sam looked at each other with some concern. It was now nine fifty a.m.

The officer outside abruptly interrupted the cosy threesome.

"Er, sorry to disturb you, Merlin. Apparently, the judge wants to see counsel in his chambers. Right away."

George shot up and checked that his wig was on straight. He felt the now-familiar feeling of impending doom and headed straight for Court 12, where he knew the clerk would show him to the judge's chambers via the door at the back of the courtroom, where Judge Watts made his daily entrance.

"I'll see you later, Merlin. Sam, perhaps you wouldn't mind taking over."

The court clerk greeted George as soon as he entered the courtroom. "Hurry, Mr. Winsome, Mr. Moboto is already with the judge. They are waiting for you."

George tried to control his breathing as he followed the clerk out of the courtroom, along a corridor seen only by judges and high ranking and trusted court officials, and into a small cosy room not unlike his own chambers but more expensively furnished, with a complete set of *All England Law Reports*, shelves upon shelves of the tomes, which dominated the judge's quarters.

Mobo and the judge were having a quiet tête-à-tête about the old days, exchanging names of common acquaintances.

"Come, George, please come in," said the judge with disarming familiarity. "Please, sit down next to Mobo."

Without his wig the judge looked alarmingly ordinary. Just like one of the boys, one of the old boys, and George suddenly realised that he was being given the old boys' welcome. This was new territory to George. Usually when counsel was called in to see the judge, training barristers, pupils, were told to wait outside. George had always wondered what went on behind closed doors. And now he was there, wishing to God that he had left Sam after one beer the night before, as he had intended.

Judge Watts looked very relaxed and happy. He put his hands together behind his head and stretched his arms upwards.

"Ah, I can tell today is going to be a great day. You know, sometimes I do wonder whether it's all worth it, you know. I gave up quite a lucrative practice to sit on the bench and often wondered whether I did the right thing or not. But sometimes a trial comes along and lifts your heart. Hope you don't think I've been too beastly to you, George, but the jury will love you for it. I'm doing you a favour really." The last comment caused Mobo and the judge to have a small conspiratorial chuckle together.

The judge leaned over to his pilot-style leather briefcase that he kept from his days practising at the Bar and took out a flask, unscrewed the top that doubled as a cup, and poured himself a small cup of still-hot tea. Timothy Watts looked over at George and Mobo. "Anybody for tea? Or perhaps you'd prefer a coffee?"

George and Mobo looked at each other, and said, "No, thanks."

"Very kind of you, Judge, but a glass of water would be fine, thank you," said George.

"And me," added Mobo. The judge went over to his drinks cabinet and poured both George and Mobo a glass of water.

The judge slowly sipped his tea from his little plastic cup, holding the little plastic handle delicately. George glanced at his watch.

"Don't worry about the time, old boy. The jury isn't going anywhere. I was thinking of having a couple of paramedics on the sidelines today, just in case we have any more casualties. This is for my memoirs, this one." Again the judge chuckled.

George was still perplexed as to the reason for his and Mobo's presence in the judge's chambers, but felt the best course of action was to remain silent and wait for the judge to initiate the serious stuff, which he felt was just about to be sprung upon him. But no, the judge rambled on about his 'stupid reconstructed hippy of a son' and informed Mobo and George that he was very surprised that Simon had agreed to watch the proceedings today, the first time ever. "A different day, my friends, a different day."

Judge Watts emptied the cup with a final swig, ceremoniously placed his long wig over his head, said, "It's showtime, folks!" and continued his little chuckles, which Mobo found quite infectious.

George and Mobo slipped back into court ahead of the judge, the court clerk allowing a few moments to pass before announcing the appearance of His Honour Judge Watts.

Merlin was chatting in an animated and friendly fashion with his guard, and the jury was sitting, waiting impatiently.

"Good morning, members of the jury." Judge Watts settled down. "Now, Mr. Moboto, where were we?" The judge fired up his laptop and looked at his last entry. "We have finished with the police evidence, have we not? Is that right, Mr. Winsome?"

George looked at Mobo, who informed the judge that both police officers had been involved in a near-riot in South London the night previously and were unable to be in court. But he hoped that his learned friend would agree that the case could proceed without further evidence from the police, as the second officer was only going to corroborate evidence that had already been given. George decided quickly that he shouldn't complain – the less evidence the better, he thought.

"There is only one other witness to call for the prosecution, Dr. Stoppard, Your Honour," indicated Mobo, "who will give evidence as to the cause of death."

Dr. Stoppard looked very relaxed and doctorial and took the oath with a degree of confidence and authority that indicated he had done this many, many times before.

Mobo didn't take long to get to the real issue and, within minutes, posed the killer question.

"So, can you say with any certainty whether the injuries sustained by the deceased on the twentieth of September 2000 were or were not a direct cause of his death some days later?"

"It is my considered and professional opinion that, in all

likelihood, and with reasonable certainty, the injuries sustained by the deceased were the cause of his death. Without those injuries, death would not have occurred. That is my firm view."

"Thank you, Doctor," said Mobo as he sat down to a welcoming smile from his junior.

George rose to his feet, wondering again why he had drunk so much the day before.

"Doctor, how many people each year, in the UK, die of aneurysms of the type which took the life of Fred Russell?"

"I don't know exactly. A few hundred, at a guess," replied the doctor, immediately wrong-footed.

"Is it a hereditary condition?"

"Not necessarily."

"But if your father or mother died of an aneurysm, then might it not be more likely that you would die in the same manner?"

"Well, on the evidence that there is available, and given there are so many factors involved, I am not convinced of the hereditary theory."

"You are avoiding the question, Doctor. Answer this one: You state that there are 'so many factors', Doctor. How many, exactly?"

"I couldn't say, exactly. It depends on one's lifestyle, one's physical fitness and strengths. But I can say—"

"How many factors, was the question, Doctor. How many?"

"I can't say with any precision."

"In other words, you don't know."

"That's not what I am saying. It's not that I don't know, it's just that there are several causes depending on an individual's personal circumstances and background."

"Did the deceased's mother or father die of an aneurysm?"

"Er, I don't know."

"How many cigarettes did the deceased smoke a day?"

"I don't know."

"How much alcohol did the deceased consume in a week, on average?"

"I don't know."

George found himself sobering up rapidly and decided to go for the jugular.

"You don't seem to know very much about the deceased, do you, Doctor? The fact is that without knowing the detail of the deceased's family background and history, and without knowing such important details as to his smoking and drinking habits, you surely cannot say more than the injuries might, I repeat, *might*, have contributed to his death. Is that not correct, Doctor?"

Dr. Stoppard looked defeated and knew when to retire gracefully. "It is my opinion that the injuries caused his death. But I accept other factors may influence the precise timing. That is as far as I will go."

"Thank you, Doctor. You have been very helpful, very helpful indeed."

George sat down and felt a heart-warming pat on the back from Sam, the hungover feeling having magically disappeared.

Mobo stood and indicated to the judge that the prosecution case was over.

George stood to announce that he would call Merlin, and the public gallery whispered loudly among themselves, and the numerous reporters sharpened their pencils.

As George watched Merlin stride confidently towards the witness box, he failed to notice that the judge hadn't moved for a few minutes. Indeed, had he looked carefully, he would have noticed that the judge was completely still, his pupils wildly dilated, staring vacantly into his computer. He also might have noticed that a rather scruffy young lad by the name of Sihairly, sitting at the back of the court, was trying hard to stifle his giggles as he looked at his watch. Sihairly had worked out that the acid wouldn't kick in for about twenty minutes, maybe half an hour. The time was now ten twenty-five a.m. and Sihairly was staring intently at his mute father, waiting for the fireworks to begin.

Merlin strode to the witness box, brimming with confidence.

The usher asked Merlin his religion, the answer to which would determine whether he took the oath on the Bible or whether he would affirm.

"My religion?" said Merlin thoughtfully and cautiously. "I know of all the gods, and your Christian god is a fair one. I am content to take the oath on the Christian Bible."

Sam and George heaved a sigh of relief and Merlin took the oath.

George was now on his feet, ready to take Merlin through his evidence, with a feeling in his stomach as if he was about to canoe through swirling white-water rapids.

"Please give the court your name."

"My name is Merlin."

"And where do you live, Merlin?"

"I am a guest in the fort of Brickstonia," Merlin replied seriously.

"That would be Brixton Prison?"

"Yes, some call the fort by that name."

"Do you recall the morning of the twentieth of September of this year, the day you were arrested?"

"I do."

"What happened?" enquired George, wondering for how long his luck would hold out.

"I was asleep among a grove of tall fir trees, in a place I now know to be Hampstead Heath. Two ruffians trying to steal my staff awakened me. The elder of the two men would not let go and we struggled. He lost his grip and fell among the bushes. Later two men in uniform took me to a prison cell and asked me many questions."

Mobo was expecting George to continue his examination-in-chief for at least another half hour. But George suddenly sat down.

"I have no further questions, Your Honour."

Mobo shook himself in disbelief at the brevity of Merlin's evidence and rose to cross-examine the old boy. Having been taken somewhat by surprise, Mobo felt he needed a little time to focus on how best to deal with the defendant.

"Perhaps Your Honour might consider this to be a convenient time to take a short mid-morning break?"

His Honour Judge Timothy Watts sat transfixed in front of his laptop, as if he had looked into the face of Medusa.

"Your Honour, might we take a break?" asked Mobo again, his voice two levels higher than before. But the judge remained silent and still, causing a wave of concern to circulate throughout the courtroom. Sihairly could hardly contain his glee and rubbed his hands in anticipation.

Unknown to everyone in the courtroom, except of course

the judge's son, His Honour Judge Timothy Watts was now fully under the influence of a particularly strong form of lysergic acid diethylamide twenty-five, recognised by connoisseurs of such matters, as being of vintage stock.

The judge could hear the words coming out of Mobo's mouth. That wasn't the problem. The problem, as recorded in his memoirs many years later, was that the judge was under the deep and very real impression that his laptop was some kind of mystical device that enabled the judge to peer into the inner workings of the universe. He was not in a fishlike sleep, far from it; his mind had not been so busy for many years. He stared wide-eyed in wonder at the screen in front of him quite convinced he was looking at the inside of a machine that held the secrets to the origins of creation, the natural order of all life, fascinated to the point of losing all sense of time. Mobo's voice was a distant whisper in the wind.

Mobo thought that maybe the judge had a secret hearing aid that had broken down; perhaps the batteries had gone flat. Or something.

Mobo raised his voice another level, and bellowed, "Shall we rise, Your Honour?"

This time Mobo's voice did manage to penetrate the judge's defences and the judge looked in Mobo's direction, much to everyone's relief.

The judge looked at Mobo and saw not a big man in courtroom dress, but a huge elephant wearing a funny little white wig. This caused the judge to let loose a very clear scream, of the scared-shitless variety. Mobo clutched his chest in surprise, which in turn caused everyone else to laugh.

George sensed something was seriously out of kilter, and thought it might help if he also asked the judge if the court might rise. When he did so, the judge turned his head towards George.

The judge stared at George as if he wasn't there, for unknown to George, the judge was looking at a tiny mouse, wearing a tiny little white wig, the whole theatre of the courtroom having been transformed into an unworldly three-dimensional cartoon.

It was at this point, recalled after many months of subsequent counselling, that the judge realised that he was under the influence of some drug. He also realised that with enormous effort, he could control, to some extent, the constantly moving visions in front of him, at least to the point where he regained a basic trust in what was real and what was illusionary. Sounds came from every quarter and angle. Colours moved and shifted. Patterns of light danced around the courtroom. Tiny gestures played out in slow motion, assuming enormous significance.

The judge looked over towards the public seating area and zoomed into the eyes of his son and the penny dropped. He felt himself say to his son, in a telepathic way, *It's you, it's you, you put something in my tea.* As if to confirm the judge's intuition, Sihairly could no longer hold his father's gaze and ran out of the courtroom, tripping on a loose shoelace on his way out. *Tripping*, thought the judge, who suddenly remembered overhearing a conversation between his son and his wayward friends. He remembered hearing the word 'tripping'. The judge suddenly realised, in a flash, *That's it. That's it. I'm tripping, tripping. That's what they called it.*

Judge Watts shook his head in soul-felt sorrow at the sight of his only son scampering out of the court. He was not angry, but deeply, deeply saddened to his core.

Mobo and George interpreted the shaking of the judge's head as a negative answer to their common question, but Mobo wanted to make sure.

"Is Your Honour all right? Shall we rise?"

There was no question of the judge going anywhere. Judge Watts was at the stage where he could connect to the real world – just – but the idea of moving, let alone standing up and walking, seemed too ambitious at that point in time. He had no choice but to continue, and feared for the worst as he said to Mobo the Elephant, "Thank you, counsel. Very kind of you. Everything's fine." At which point Mobo morphed back into his more usual form, as did George.

"Er, very well, Your Honour, I shall proceed with my cross-examination of the defendant," Mobo said, keeping a close eye on the judge.

Timothy Watts suddenly felt as if he were the sole pilot of a fighter jet travelling at enormous speed just above ground level. He was getting used to the controls. He could see problems ahead. He knew where the horizon began, and the sky ended. Provided he didn't panic, he felt he could come through this unharmed. He tried to lift a finger, a thought that caused him to feel as if he was about to crash, so he let go of the idea, and the plane he felt he was in steadied itself.

Mobo took his time before asking Merlin a question. He straightened his wig, looked at his notes, turned around to have a word with David, theatrically cleared his throat and held onto the lapels of his gown, looking at the jury.

"You were sleeping on Hampstead Heath when you were disturbed by 'two ruffians' as you put it, who you thought were intent upon stealing your staff. Is that correct?"

"Yes, it is."

Mobo had thought of a lever for him to tear the old boy apart, quickly.

"Perhaps you could tell the jury how and when you acquired this object?"

Merlin looked unshaken as he asked, "Could I hold it, please?"

"Of course," said Mobo, nodding to the usher to hand Merlin the staff.

Merlin held the staff in a careful and almost loving manner, examining it closely as if inspecting it for any damage.

"It has many parts to it, and each part has its own story. I shall begin with the wood, which is very old oak, grown on these very shores on which we now stand. It is many thousands of years old," said Merlin as though he was an expert from the *Antiques Roadshow*. "The head is carved from the remains – the left tibia if I recall correctly – of my dear friend Myfedd, who asked if I would carry his soul along my journeys through life. The 'trinkets' as you call them—"

"I beg your pardon, Merlin," said Mobo with genuine astonishment. "Are you telling this court that the head of this staff is made of human bones?"

"Oh yes, indeed. If I can tell you about the—"

Merlin was obviously very keen to tell the jury about all the other bits and pieces, but the collective gasps of disgust and disbelief from the jury drowned him out.

His Honour Judge Watts had already been, very quietly, to his own hell and back and felt compelled to stretch out his hand, indicating that the staff should be passed to him. This time he felt sufficiently confident that he could stay in control of his mind as he did so.

The usher pulled out a handkerchief from her skirt pocket and placed it around the staff, holding it as far away from her face as she could, with her other hand over her mouth as if she might catch something. The object was placed into the hands of the clerk and then handed to the judge, who was at last showing some real signs of life.

As the judge held the staff he felt such a wave of energy he momentarily thought of himself as Thor wielding his hammer. Then he felt as if he were Moses himself carrying the tablets of stone from Mount Sinai. Coming swiftly back to his senses, he handed the staff back to the clerk. "Amazing, absolutely amazing," said the judge.

"Now, Merlin, you were going to tell us about the trinkety things, I believe. Take your time, please," said the judge, looking at Merlin, who he now saw as a giant white-robed druid.

"Thank you, yes, I would like to tell you about the trinkets. The casings are silver, from the old mountains on the west coast of these isles. Inside the casings are the teeth of small animals who, in days gone by, were friends of mine. The ribbons, as you call them, are the hairs of both man and animal dyed in my favourite colours. It is a very special and powerful object."

"Fascinating, fascinating," the judge commented.

Mobo realised that his original idea of catching Merlin out on the issue of the staff had seriously backfired. It was time to up the stakes, he thought.

"Enough of the staff. You are asking this jury to believe you are Merlin. Would that be the same Merlin from the court of King Arthur, or perhaps you are some other Merlin? Please, enlighten us." Mobo looked at the jury as if the whole charade would be broken down with one question.

"There was a King Arthur, yes. I was very close to him, a fine, brave young man. A warrior and a scholar. We were very close in heart and mind. My knowledge of the natural forces of the world were well known and much valued in conflict. He sought me out, you know. But I don't think the King Arthur I knew is the same person you see in your mind. You probably see a young boy who took a sword out of a stone and was proclaimed king. That is not the true story. Arthur lived in the place you call Cornwall. He became a good soldier, loved by his brothers-in-arms. His father was a very talented blacksmith and sword maker who created a new method for the making of very strong sword blades. Arthur soon learnt the skills of his father and was known as the man who could make swords out of stone."

Merlin turned to the judge. "I think that is how the myth of Arthur taking the sword out of the stone started, Your Honour. I have lived several times on this earth. I have spoken to many scholars in Brickstonia to be assured that matters of the soul are familiar to all wise men and women."

Merlin paused for a moment and continued solemnly, the jury clearly entranced.

"I first came into the world in the very northern part of these islands. I was born into a group of very fine, learned men who were called the Picts, or painted ones. I am originally from where you call Scotland, born many years ago. I became very knowledgeable in matters concerning the stars and the sky and my opinion was much valued in warfare, as I could anticipate the movements of the rains, the winds, the strength and timings of the sun and the moon. I have had several lives but I cannot recall all the details yet, but I remember once falling in love with a beautiful lady who was jealous of my powers, and I remember feeling great sorrow, but I am unclear of its source."

"Yes, yes," said Mobo, trying too late to create an impression in the jury's collective mind that they were dealing with a very sophisticated con man. "But the fact is that you deliberately tried to cause the deceased some harm, and, as a result Mr. Russell is no longer with us, is that not true?" he asked desperately.

"Not true at all, sir. Not true at all. We could summon Mr.

Russell and ask him for the truth."

"No need for that, Merlin." Mobo could not resist a gratuitous piece of sarcasm. "You don't sound very Scottish for a Scotsman, Mr. Merlin."

Merlin smiled and replied, "Kind sir, you sound none too African to me."

Mobo decided to cut his losses, and sat down looking and feeling heavily defeated.

Judge Watts stared at Merlin in awe.

"So, the spell has worn off, eh, Merlin?" he asked.

"That is what I believe, Your Honour, but I have yet to fully comprehend why I awoke where and when I did. I have come to accept and understand that this is not my first awakening. You teach that Merlin was one man who lived one life, a sorcerer who was close to a King Arthur. History and myths become intertwined. Sometimes stories tell of a Merlin from the north, sometimes the south. Merlin is remembered all over these islands. Many places claim to be the spiritual home of Merlin and they may all be truthful. What I know is that I am the one called Merlin. I believe I have been on this earth several times and have learnt about many gods and beliefs that might explain my presence. I live and die yet my eternal spirit returns for reasons I do not yet understand; I fear I may never find the answers that I seek. In truth I do not really know or understand why I am here. Do any of us? There have been many events since my spirit was last disturbed.... It might be that something else caused my awakening, something more...." Merlin looked skywards, his voice trailing off into an awkward silence. "Something connected to the kosmos, perhaps even with the timing of a passing comet or the alignment of the stars that breathes life into me and awakens my spirit with its passing. Yes, that's it, I think."

Merlin let his head fall and appeared to fall into a deep reflection.

The judge allowed a sympathetic moment or two to pass. "Yes, yes. Indeed, indeed," he said sympathetically. The remark caused Mobo to have a court tantrum, the first in many years.

"Your Honour. Your Honour, I must protest. You have quite rightly indicated to myself and my learned friend that we should not waste court time or indulge this silly old man in his fantasies and now it appears it is Your Honour who falls into this trap and undermines the prosecution by giving credence to this nonsense. In all my years at the Bar—"

The judge looked intensely at Mobo, who was snarling like a raging bewigged hippopotamus, running at full flight towards His Honour, teeth bared in unbridled aggression, the enormous head swinging from side to side, the wild look in the animal's bulging eyes signaling a clear intention to cause immediate death to its intended victim. This last drug-induced psychotic episode was too much for the judge, being in the delicate state of mind that he was. He placed his arms in front of his face to protect himself, shouting, "Take him away, take him away!"

And so Mobo was led to the cells, yelling all manner of obscenities and protestations. The judge, now in control of a sufficient number of his faculties to stand up and utter the magic words, "Court rise," sped off to his private chambers, where he tried to compose himself to the best of his ability. His nightmarish episodes became less frequent and less intense, although there were the occasional sudden shockers just when he thought the worst was over.

His Honour Judge Watts lay flat on his back, on the floor of his chambers, his hands clasped tightly over his eyes when, soon enough, the clerk gently knocked on his door.

"Er, pardon me, Judge. Shall we be reconvening after lunch? Counsel and the jury are not quite sure. Are you unwell? Shall I call Matron?"

"No, no, please, not Matron," said the judge, holding back the image of a giant nurse brandishing a three-foot syringe.

"I'm fine, just tired, very tired. Get me a car to take me home. Tell counsel and the jury we start again tomorrow at ten o'clock."

"Very good, Judge. And Mr. Moboto, Your Honour. I understand the most senior silk in the building, Michael Oldfield, will be making an application for bail on Mr. Moboto's behalf as soon as you are ready, Your Honour."

Judge Watts thought he could hear the growling of a caged bear roaring in his ears.

"No need for that. Inform the officers that I have ordered Mr.

Moboto to be released immediately. Er, pass onto Mr. Moboto 'No hard feelings and sincere regrets.'"

"Certainly, Your Honour, as you wish. Perhaps a cup of tea, Your Honour?"

"No, thank you. Just a car to take me home."

CHAPTER FOURTEEN
Experts

The Crown v. Merlin, Day 4, 21st December, 2000, counsels' robing room, Southwark Crown Court.

Mobo and David Palmer were sitting in a small anteroom inside counsels' robing room, designed to give some privacy to counsel from their colleagues. George looked through the glass panel to catch Mobo's attention. Mobo immediately beckoned George inside.

"Survived the experience of incarceration?" George asked mischievously.

"Indeed I have, my friend. The prison officers understood that the judge had gone quite mad and I sat and had tea with them for a few minutes before word came through that he was dreadfully sorry about his mistake. I will test the temperature of the water this morning before deciding whether to take the outrage any further," said Mobo, while David Palmer bit his lip. "Do you think the jury will retire today, George?" Mobo knew this was an old trick designed to elicit details of the defence.

"Well," replied George cautiously, "I did indicate that the defence would call a historian, a psychologist, and perhaps a forensic scientist."

"Yes, you did, my friend. The question is whether you are actually going to do so. Well, are you?"

"Er, I'm not sure, Mobo."

"You're not sure. When will you be sure? It's nine forty-five. We're on in fifteen minutes."

"Shit. Is that the time? I'll see you downstairs, Mobo. Must run." And George scurried out the door.

★   ★   ★

George was surprised as to how familiar the court environment had become in just a few days. It was day four and the players now knew each other's roles, cues, functions, and peculiarities. George felt greatly relieved that a determination to see the job done now replaced the acute sense of fear.

The arrival of the jury and Merlin signalled the imminent presence of the judge, who entered and sat down, looking ten years older and softer, somehow.

"Counsel. Members of the jury. Yesterday I was not very well. But I feel much better today. I must have eaten or drunk something that disagreed with me. Looking back on the events of yesterday, I feel I owe an apology to Mr. Moboto. I do understand, with hindsight, why Mr. Moboto felt compelled to challenge me in the manner he did, and I fear I overreacted enormously. Mr. Moboto, do you accept my apology? I will understand if you wish to answer in the negative." The judge looked at Mobo with deep concern in his bleary eyes.

Mobo paused for a moment before saying, "Your Honour. I have a precondition to accepting Your Honour's apology. It is this: I must ask that Your Honour accepts *my* apology for the unforgivable outburst of mine, and the undignified tone of my challenge."

The judge smiled broadly and indicated that he was indeed happy to accept Mobo's apology.

"We can therefore draw a line under yesterday's unfortunate events, Your Honour," said Mobo, as if talking to an old friend.

"Indeed we can, Mr. Moboto. I am very grateful."

Sam leaned forward to make some childish remark to George, which George did not want to hear. He had other matters on his mind.

"Now, Mr. Winsome," said the judge, "where are we?"

"Your Honour, there are three defence witnesses waiting to be called. But before I call my first witness, I have an application to make to the court."

"Yes, Mr. Winsome, please proceed," the judge said politely.

"Your Honour. I do appreciate that it is more usual for a submission of 'no case to answer' to be made immediately following the prosecution's case. But there is ample authority that the defence may make such a submission at any time during the trial, if the prosecution intends to call no further evidence."

The judge looked at Mobo and asked whether, solely as a matter of law, he agreed with the proposition of the defence.

Mobo took the view that it was highly irregular, and was entirely a matter for the trial judge, but in principle, his learned friend was correct.

"Members of the jury. Learned counsel for the defence wishes to raise a matter of law that need not trouble you. It is a matter for me to decide upon. You may therefore leave and we will let you know when we are ready for you to return. Thank you."

The jury was about to file out of the jury box, but stopped abruptly when Merlin stood up and shouted, "No! No. The jury must remain. The jury must decide my fate. Please, kind sirs, I want the jury to stay."

George looked deeply embarrassed, asked for the judge's forgiveness for the defendant's behaviour, and asked if the judge would give him a moment to talk to the defendant.

"Yes, of course. Please explain to the defendant the nature of your application. I imagine he is rather confused," the judge said in an overtly friendly tone. "You should however remind Mr. Merlin that it is bad form to make utterances from the back of the court, however pertinent such observations may be, if you could be so kind, Mr. Winsome."

"Of course, Your Honour," replied George.

The jury sat back down while George leaned over the dock to engage Merlin in conversation, trying not to be overheard.

"Listen, Merlin. The judge is in such a good mood I might just persuade him to call a halt to this trial here and now. Don't you understand, the judge has the power to direct the jury to acquit you on all charges right now if he thinks there is not enough evidence to go to the jury. It's worth a shot."

"No, my friend, no. It must not end like this. The jury alone must decide my fate. That's the way it is. It can be no other way.

If I have any say in the matter, I wish the jury to remain. Is it my decision or yours?"

George lowered his head like a football striker walking back to his mates, having just missed a penalty. "You're quite right, Merlin. It is your choice, not mine. I should have discussed the matter with you beforehand."

George walked back to his flip-top chair in the front row of counsels' seating area and addressed the judge solemnly. "Your Honour. The defendant does not wish me to pursue my application. He wishes to be judged by the jury. My apologies for wasting the court's time."

The judge looked at George with some affection. "Most commendable, Mr. Winsome. Tell your client I respect this noble gesture. Now, does the defence wish to call any further evidence?"

George looked at his notes, having momentarily forgotten the plot completely.

"The defence calls Dr. Philips."

The usher put her head outside the door and bellowed, "Dr. Philips," ignoring the young, studious-looking individual sitting right outside the court.

Dr. Philips took the oath, his voice faltering nervously.

Within a few minutes George had established that Dr. Philips was a twenty-six-year-old with a Bachelor of Arts degree in theology and humanities followed by a doctorate in philosophy, obtained from the Open University. His post-graduate thesis was concerned with the historical basis of British medieval mythology. Dr. Philips, it transpired, was well versed in ancient English literature, particularly the Latin texts which made reference to the Arthurian legend and the figure of Merlin, the subject matter of a book he was currently writing.

"And do you, in broad terms, understand the nature of these proceedings, Dr. Philips?"

"Oh, yes. Of course," said the young man, looking around nervously.

Mobo rose to his feet with exaggerated weariness.

"Your Honour. Please. I cannot fathom what this boy, sorry,

expert, will tell us about events many hundreds of years ago that could possibly have any relevance to the guilt or innocence of the defendant. This is a total abuse of the court's time, surely Your Honour must agree?"

Before the judge could respond, the usher handed a note to the clerk who read it, smiled, and passed it to the judge.

Timothy Watts looked at the note, written by one of the jury. *WE WANTS TO HEER IM*, it read, and the judge placed the note by his side.

"It seems to me, Mr. Moboto, that I would have some difficulty in deciding whether the evidence is relevant before it is given. Do you not agree, Mr. Winsome?"

"Indeed, Your Honour. Very sound," said George, who almost felt the warm breeze of a favourable change of wind.

"Please proceed, Mr. Winsome."

"Briefly, Dr. Philips, can you inform this court, from your lengthy studies, whether there was or was not a real Merlin character?"

Dr. Philips blushed and cleared his throat. "There are several written legends surrounding Merlin. The earliest dates to the early tenth century – 'The Prophesies of Briton', or more formally: 'Armes Prydien, Y Gododdin,' in which a Merlin figure is referred to, initially as a prophet, and then as a magician and counsellor to King Arthur. His name in this poem is 'Myddin', but later texts refer to the Latinised 'Merlin' because 'Myddin' sounded too similar to the Roman word for 'shit'."

Dr. Philips seemed to relax enormously when he heard the titters around the courtroom. The judge and jury listened like five-year-olds sitting attentively on a mat, being read a story by their favourite teacher on a Friday afternoon.

"It is thought that Geoffrey of Monmouth, writing in the twelfth century, was responsible for that invention, among others."

Mobo threw down his pen, quite theatrically, clearly indicating his feelings about the history lesson.

Dr. Philips continued: "This Merlin, the one associated with King Arthur, was the illegitimate son of a princess and his father an angel."

Mobo could hardly contain himself. Knowing he was on a hiding to nothing with the judge, he assumed the role of heckler-in-chief, and mouthed the word "Blasphemy" quite loudly.

Dr. Philips was hitting his stride. "Some people, of course, thought that Merlin was the son of the devil, but once he had solved the riddle of the collapsing fort built by Vortigern to protect the Britons from the marauding Saxons—"

"I'm sorry, Dr. Philips, you're going rather fast. Who is Vor-ti-gern?" enquired the judge.

"Sorry, Your Honour. Vortigern might best be described as the High King of the Britons at the time. According to one tradition, Vortigern's fortress, built in the immediate anticipation of a merciless Saxon attack, kept collapsing and he was advised that he needed to sacrifice a fatherless child to remedy the situation. The child Merlin was to be sacrificed but used his visionary powers to explain that the cause of the building's constant collapse was due to two fighting dragons – one white, one red – living in a subterranean pool."

Mobo was definitely heard to say "Bloody dragons!" but Dr. Philips continued.

"Anyway, Merlin explained that the white dragon represented the Saxons and the red dragon the Britons. The white dragon won, and thus Merlin foresaw the downfall of the Britons. Vortigern was slain by the Saxon leader Ambrosius Aurelianus. Merlin's reputation was firmly established and he later became close advisor to King Arthur—"

George interrupted the witness, as if this point in the evidence was anticipated.

"Yes, thank you Dr. Philips. Now, is there another myth?"

"Oh yes."

"Oh no," said Mobo.

Dr. Philips looked at Mobo and felt his luck might have run out. "Some scholars now believe that there was more than one Merlin, because the texts referring to Merlin span nearly two hundred years, roughly between 420 AD and 580 AD."

"Tell us briefly about this other Merlin, Dr. Philips."

"Well, even Geoffrey of Monmouth in his *Vita Merlini* refers to a period in Merlin's life when he travelled to Scotland and became known as 'Myrddin Wylt' or 'Merlin the Wild', having been driven to despair and madness after the slaughter of his closest friends at the Battle of Arfderyd."

"And what is your theory, Dr. Philips?" asked George, looking to see if the jury was taking it all in.

"My theory is that there was a completely distinct and real person from Scotland whose extraordinary life inspired the myths, who was later mixed up and confused with the Arthurian Merlin. Some refer to him as 'Merlin Caledonius,' a born-and-bred Scotsman, or more precisely a Picti, from the north-eastern part of present-day Scotland, who had great spiritual gifts, but whose life was marred by extreme tragedy."

At which point the entire courtroom looked round to Merlin, who was sobbing, loudly but with considerable dignity.

George took a deep breath and knew if there was a time to spell out Merlin's story to the jury, this was it.

"Finally, Dr. Philips. One more question. Your Honour, in anticipation of my learned friend seeking to persuade the court that the next issue is completely irrelevant, might I ask the court to allow the witness to answer before making any intervention?"

"That's a bit optimistic, Mr. Winsome. We'll see. Go ahead and ask your *final* question."

"Dr. Philips. You understand Merlin's own theory that he was originally born in Scotland and has since been 're-born', so to speak, at least twice since. Does that idea have any resonance with your extensive studies?"

Dr. Philips looked at the judge, who indicated with a soft smile that he should answer.

"Well, obviously the idea of being 'born again', so to speak, is a widely held belief in many cultures, though obviously in very different types and forms. The resurrection of Christ Our Lord is not the same as the concept of reincarnation or indeed baptism. But the idea of the soul of a human being coming back to life in another body is not that uncommon. The phenomena has several names: palingenesis, transmigration, metempsychosis, reincarnation. So the answer to your question is yes."

"That is all, Dr. Philips. Thank you."

Mobo rose quickly to his feet. "I have no questions of this witness, Your Honour. I submit the jury should be invited to disregard everything he has said on the grounds it is completely otiose to these proceedings and an affront to the dignity of the court."

The judge smiled and said, "That's a matter for the jury to decide, in due course. I think we could all do with a break. I suggest thirty minutes."

★   ★   ★

George knew that the time had come for him and Sam to spend a few minutes together with Merlin, and the prison officer indicated that the three of them could convene, as was now their habit, in the consulting room outside the court.

Merlin composed himself, looking rather embarrassed at his emotional outburst.

"Forgive me, my friends. Your expert brought back too many memories too suddenly. I fear he is on the right track, and I was overcome by feelings of great loss, feelings that I have been harbouring for many years. So many years."

Sam wanted to lighten the meeting with the numerous press reports of the previous day, but George shuffled the papers away.

"We understand, Merlin. We really do. There is obviously a very dark history to your life, which these proceedings are starting to unravel, but we must, if you can bear to do so, concentrate on the remains of the day."

"Indeed, Sir George. No purpose is served by dwelling on the past; we must concentrate on the present. You advise well, my friend. What is your strategy?"

"We have two witnesses ready to give further evidence on your behalf. The first is a psychologist, the second a medical expert. Mobo will think that the evidence of the psychologist is intended to lay the ground for a defence of insanity, but that is a trap. You know him, Merlin, he saw you twice in Brixton on our behalf. He shall say that you are a harmless character, that's the real point of his evidence. I have already planted the thought in the jury's mind that there is some historical basis for your beliefs, which lays the ground for you being thought of as an honest person whether you are deluded or not; hope that makes sense. Trust me on this one, Merlin. The last witness will have a report with him that will hopefully break, once and for all, the causal link between the events of the twentieth of September and the death of Fred Russell. Do you understand?"

"Yes, I think I do. Deluded? That word confuses me, but yes, I do trust your judgement."

Sam interjected: "I'm pleased to hear you're now sharing your game plan with us, George. I see where you're coming from with the psychologist, but haven't we already broken 'the causal link' as you put it?"

"I don't think so, Sam, not from my recollection of the evidence of the prosecution. I think there's still work to be done on that one."

"If you say so, counsel," said Sam, clearly not convinced.

George could see the concern in Sam's eyes.

"Look, the forensic scientist, Professor Morton, will have with him an updated report. I'll review the decision to call him once I've seen the papers, OK?"

"Sure, George, you're the boss," said Sam sarcastically. "But this isn't a one-man show, counsel. Sure, take all the risks you want, but remember your client's interests come before yours. I'm not convinced Morton will deliver the goods, but, hey, it's your party."

George felt the sharp pain of the truth in Sam's sarcasm; it wasn't all about him. He looked to the ground in acceptance of the point Sam had made. A small period of silence descended upon the three of them, which Sam took to be his cue for another attempt at looking at the newspapers.

"It might not be the best time, George, but the papers really are full of all of this. Look at the *Mail* and the *Express*—"

"Not now," said George, rubbing his jaw. He looked at a very sad and solemn Merlin. "Not now, Sam."

★   ★   ★

"Your Honour, I call Dr. Eisner."

"Very good, Mr. Winsome," said the judge. He looked slightly more alive than he did at the beginning of the day's proceedings.

Dr. Eisner was a very relaxed-looking individual, partly due to his tight-fitting black polo-neck sweater, which overrode the effect of his sharp black suit, but mainly due to his long greying ponytail dangling down his back. George thought the jury might see him as a musician or other creative animal, which was not too bad a start, all in all.

Dr. Eisner provided some impressive qualifications and had been working with extremely disturbed individuals over many years, although his core work was with adolescents.

"Have you interviewed the defendant, Doctor?"

"You mean Merlin? Oh yes, a couple of times, but in the confines of Brixton prison, not the best environment."

"Have you seen enough of Merlin to form a professional view as to his character?" George asked carefully.

"Yes, I have." The witness responded as if everyone, George included, needed to be treated with extreme caution. "He truly believes himself to be a person called Merlin, a figure from the distant past, although not the traditional Merlin mythical figure, as I understand. I am not here to comment upon that issue."

Mobo rose to the bait, stood up and asked the judge to seek clarification from his learned friend as to the precise relevance of this witness.

"Perhaps he might confirm that this courtroom is actually situated somewhere in Avalon or Camelot or perhaps Picti-land. I fear I am becoming rather confused, Your Honour."

Only David Palmer could muster a halfhearted titter. The others in the courtroom didn't seem to share Mobo's sense of humour.

"I am sure Mr. Winsome has good reason to place Dr. Eisner in the witness box, Mr. Moboto. If you please."

The witness looked around for some sense of bearing, as if he had walked onto a stage not knowing what part he was supposed to play.

George continued. "Thank you, your Honour. Dr. Eisner, you have come across many varied individuals, disturbed in some form or another. Your expertise, if I may be so bold, is to assess the behavioural patterns of such people. Can you please give the court your professional opinion as to Merlin's psychological profile? What type of person he is?"

Dr. Eisner looked at George as if a penny had just dropped.

"Oh yes. Sorry. My view is that Merlin is a well-bred and cultivated individual, although obviously disorientated at present. He has no propensity towards evil or violence and is almost a monastic character with an impressive knowledge and understanding of a wide range of beliefs and gods. Fundamentally, to answer your question more directly, in my view, he is a good man with a peaceful disposition."

"Thank you." George sat down, feeling as if he had just walked another tightrope.

Dr. Eisner walked away from the witness box looking deeply perplexed, a look that turned to fear when Mobo boomed, "Stay where you are, sir. I have some questions for you on behalf of the prosecution."

Mobo stared at the witness in silence, each second that ticked past making the doctor feel increasingly unsettled.

"Dr. Eisner. Isn't the defendant completely mad?"

George rose to his feet to object but the judge waved his hand, signaling that George should not pursue the objection.

Taken aback, Dr. Eisner explained that he was a psychologist, not a psychiatrist, and was not qualified to make such a judgement.

"Not qualified?" bellowed Mobo. "This old boy has the audacity to tell this court, under oath, with a straight face, that he's a figure from the Dark Ages who was imprisoned by force of magic in a tree, hailing from bonny Scotland of all places. Not to be confused of course with the 'real' mythical Merlin who advised the 'real' mythical King Arthur."

Mobo was doing quite well rehearsing his closing speech but ended his tirade with one question too many: "Are you saying that he's as sane as you or I, or the judge, or the jury?"

George rose to his feet, having decided that he would not be shut down by an unrecorded gesture from the judge; he had to object.

"Your Honour, my learned friend is merely baiting this witness. Merlin at no stage said that he is a figure from the Dark Ages," a point which would have had some credence had Merlin at that point not stood up and shouted, "But I am, I am."

The judge looked very calm and collected, and even managed to raise a smile.

"Mr. Moboto, I think what your learned friend wishes to state is that if the witness is of the view that he is not qualified to judge the sanity of the defendant whom he examined, then – *a fortiori* – how can he be qualified to make the same judgement upon myself or the jury. Is that not your point, Mr. Winsome?"

Whatever tactic Mobo was employing had the effect of causing George's mind to go blank, not sure whether the judge was trying to help or leading him into a trap. Needing some time, George turned around to Sam and whispered, "What the fuck is he going on about?"

"Just say yes George, just say yes."

"Yes, Your Honour," said George, not really knowing what was going on. But as if to confirm Sam's take on the world, Mobo sat down and the judge indicated that the witness could go on his way, which he did, muttering under his breath as he walked past the jury, "They're all fucking mad if you ask me."

George looked at his watch with some concern. He wanted some time to collect his thoughts. He began to doubt whether he was winning the mind game with Mobo or not. Perhaps Mobo was out-foxing him and would ask the jury to acquit on the grounds of insanity? It was a very unnerving feeling.

"Mr. Winsome," said the judge in his spanking-new soft, relaxed voice, perhaps slightly overstated in an ever-so-friendly-and-helpful pitch. "Could we please proceed with your last witness, and then we can all take a long lunch before closing speeches?"

The sly old bastard was up to his tricks again, thought George. He wanted a break but did not want to appear to be depriving the jury of a long lunch if he didn't get on with it.

"My last witness. Oh yes. Er, might Your Honour indulge me with a five-minute break to make a final decision on that matter?"

"Five minutes, Mr. Winsome? Or fifteen?"

"Five, Your Honour, five."

"Very well, the court will rise for ten minutes."

The aged, short and stocky, white-haired Professor Morton was waiting impatiently outside the courtroom. George introduced himself with breakneck speed and asked if the professor had an updated written report. Opening up his brown leather briefcase, which looked as if it had accompanied the professor throughout medical school, he handed a slim folder of A4 papers to George, who walked over to a quiet corner and read the document, shaking his head. Then he returned to the professor, who was quietly fuming at the treatment he was receiving.

"There have been some developments, professor. Having looked through your report, I believe your evidence will not be needed. I am dreadfully sorry, but there it is. Your bill will be met, but I am afraid I have put you through this inconvenience. Sorry."

And with that last apology George made a hasty retreat to the courtroom before the professor could make his feelings known.

The usher was waiting for George to return and the court reconvened within ten minutes, a first for many in the courtroom. Few wanted to give up their seats unless they really needed the toilet, a smoke, or some other hit and most of the jury was quite content to sit, chatting among themselves for a few minutes.

"Mr. Winsome. Will you be calling any further witnesses, or have you concluded the case for the defence?" asked the judge.

"I have no further witnesses to call, Your Honour. The defence rests." George bowed his head towards the judge, wondering whether he came across as if he had been watching too many American courtroom trials.

"Very well, I suggest that we adjourn until two thirty this afternoon, at which time we will hear counsel's closing speeches. I intend to sum up the case to the jury tomorrow and the jury should retire mid-morning."

George looked at his watch – twelve fifteen.

The usher knew her cue and with a solid "Court rise" the judge retired to his chambers, leaving George to explain to his instructing solicitor what had transpired outside the courtroom.

"I think he forgot who was paying his bill," said George unconvincingly. "OK, Sam, on that issue you were spot on. His final report was the opposite of what I thought he'd say. You were quite right to express reservations about that one. Sorry."

Sam smiled at George, realising that this was the first time he could ever remember counsel treating him with some respect, let alone uttering the *S* word.

"Shall we nip over to the pub, George?"

George looked again at his watch and it occurred to him that before the end of the day he would have made his first closing speech to a jury, and he suddenly felt quite nauseous.

"I think I'd better work on my speech, Sam. Could you pop down to the cells and say hello to Merlin? A bit of PR, eh?"

"Sure. Look forward to your speech. I'm sure it will be great."

★   ★   ★

Mobo rose confidently to address the jury. The thought did not cross his mind as to how many times he had embarked upon this task in his career; it was too many times to remember.

Mobo knew that juries couldn't take long speeches, no matter how passionately delivered. Forty minutes was the maximum, after which they turned off. It was also a time for some theatrics, as the stenographer never recorded the speeches, and few notes would be made by the judge or his opponent unless the speech strayed into unacceptable territory, such as introducing new evidence or misleading the jury on a point of law. Other than those few guidelines, a closing speech was a golden opportunity to turn a difficult case around with some good, old-fashioned oratory.

"Members of the jury. What a thankless and difficult job you have. We, the lawyers in this trial, have it easy; we do not have to navigate a path through the minefield of conflicting evidence presented to the court and come to a view as to the truth of the matter. That is your job, by no means an easy one, particularly when the stakes are high, as they are in this case. Let us not forget that at the heart of this trial is the death of an innocent and elderly man, Fred Russell, who was, according to his young colleague, simply doing his job.

"You are aware of the charges laid against the defendant. The first question you must ask yourselves is this: 'What does the prosecution need to prove for you to return a guilty verdict?' Remember there are two charges on the indictment. They are alternative charges, so if you find the defendant guilty of one, there is no need to consider the other. You will return a guilty verdict on the lesser charge if you come to the view that Merlin intended to cause Mr. Russell some harm, and guilty on the second, more serious charge of manslaughter, if you are sure beyond a reasonable doubt that the injuries suffered by Mr. Russell on the morning of the twentieth of September were the cause of his death."

Before Mobo could turn on the histrionics, he needed to wade through the formalities, as quickly as possible.

"Bear in mind at all times that the defence need prove nothing; the prosecution has brought this case and they must prove it, to your satisfaction."

Mobo could now have some fun.

"The issue of the defendant's identity has been troubling me, members of the jury, as I am sure it has you. What relevance has all this stuff about Vortigern, Arthur, magic spells, and stories from our ancient past? I tell you what I think. I want you all to take a good look at the defendant, and ask yourselves, what do you see? Does the defendant impress you as a silly old man, whose identity has been lost in the foggy mist of time? Perhaps you see a man who really is Merlin, born in Scotland, let's say fifteen hundred years ago, who was suddenly awakened, having been asleep since medieval times, by two dog patrollers on a moonlit morning on Hampstead Heath? And then, just to add some spice, a touch of reincarnation? Really? Is that what you believe? Or perhaps the truth is a lot simpler. Perhaps this rather engaging man is really in full control of his faculties and knows exactly who he is. I suggest that he is a con man, members of the jury, make no mistake about it. A clever, sophisticated con man who is trying very skilfully to pull the wool over your eyes. And why would he want to do that? What would he achieve? The answer is obvious: he knows full well that he is guilty, he knows better than anyone that he flung Fred Russell to the ground, intending to cause him injury. What defence could there be to such a charge? Why, you might have thought the best way out of his predicament would be to say, simply, 'I meant him no harm, it was simply an accident'. But no, this defendant goes further and concocts a complete self-serving mirage of deceit, designed to throw you off balance, take your eye off the ball, play to your sympathies, confuse you, obfuscate, throw sand in your eyes – all for the intended purpose of walking out of this court a free man, freed by your verdict obtained by treating all of you as gullible fools."

As Mobo hit his stride George closed his eyes, imagining himself to be on the jury. Was he persuasive? Were the jury following him along his path towards a guilty verdict? As Mobo continued, George felt increasingly unsure.

Mobo indeed carried on for forty minutes – and the rest. But, come the end, George wasn't listening. He was staring at his notes, which seemed very thin, only signposts along the way, a very sketchy map. His stomach muscles tightened to the point that he felt real pain, his throat felt unusually dry, his legs drained of energy, his sweaty hands visibly shaking. He wished Mobo would stop so he could get his speech over with. He also wished, at the same time, that Mobo would go on forever, so the moment he stood up to address the jury for the first time would never arrive.

Mobo's voice suddenly reached a crescendo, followed by a long pause. "Therefore, members of the jury, whether the defendant has won your affection or not, I respectfully submit that it is your duty to return a guilty verdict to the charge of manslaughter. Thank you."

Mobo sat down and was patted heartily by David Palmer, beaming with pride and admiration. .

"Mr. Winsome, you may address the jury, if you are ready."

George sort of pushed himself to his feet, whatever thoughts he had to get him going having disappeared; his mind completely blank. He looked over to the sea of faces around the court and felt as if he was going to throw up. His eye caught Merlin's, who discreetly pointed to the staff, and George instinctively held out his hand, a gesture that the usher took as a request that the object be given to George.

George held the staff with his right hand.

"It's heavy, isn't it, members of the jury?"

The jury laughed nervously as if they all were sharing a common experience from a party the night before. Merlin smiled. The judge sat up, looking at George with a fatherly respect.

George forgot about his notes and was suddenly filled with such confidence as he'd never known before; he felt strong, and angry, and placed the staff down on the ledge in front of him.

"I wonder what you were all expecting before you came into this courtroom on Monday morning. A murder trial? An armed robbery? A rape?" George scanned the eyes of the jury, gauging their attention levels, and searching for any clues, however small, that might indicate whether he was talking to the converted or the sceptic. He wanted desperately to know who to focus upon, who he needed to turn around and decided that the oldest-looking lady, in the back row, was the most sensible-looking, and therefore the most dangerous to his cause.

George's tactic from the beginning had been to play down the 'Merlin factor', but he was now singing a different tune.

"What harm is there in asking yourselves: who is this man? Might he be the real Merlin? The prosecution told you on more than one occasion that the defence need prove nothing. This man has gone into the witness box and told you who he is. Has the prosecution proved to you that he is not who he says he is? And consider this, are we all not entitled to hold beliefs close to our heart concerning matters of the spirit and the soul? Are we to be judged as mad or dishonest because we believe in such matters?"

George paused and scanned the jury.

"Would the prosecution seek to challenge every person who held a spiritual or religious belief?"

Mobo shifted around, looking up at the judge, wondering whether he could take this line of attack, which he thought was quite improper, but the judge was listening politely and attentively, as was everyone else in the packed courtroom.

George noticed that the officious-looking, middle-aged male juror was frowning, fidgeting with his Windsor-knotted tie in disbelief, and George held his gaze.

"Perhaps you have some difficulty in believing Merlin's story, members of the jury. I do. I am sure the learned judge does also. We know what my learned friend for the prosecution believes. But ask yourself, what does the defendant believe? Does he believe himself to be the Merlin he has explained to you? Yes or no? If the answer is yes, then I put it to you that you must acquit him on both charges. Why? Because you will have come to the view that he is an honest man, telling you the truth as he sees it. He may be mistaken, but is he *honestly* mistaken?"

George took a pause and turned his back to the jury to drink some water without them seeing a tremble in his hands. But his hand remained steady so he turned back around, confidently holding the glass, and lifted the glass to his mouth while looking at the jury.

George could now return to his notes and listed ten reasons why the jury should have doubts about the guilt of the accused, from the poor lighting at the time the accident occurred to the 'Grand Canyon of doubt' surrounding the actual cause of death. He felt himself rise and fall through a spirited speech as if, at times, he was listening to someone else. It was another white-water rapid ride, but this time he felt fully in control and realised when he felt it was time to wind down, how much he was enjoying himself.

"Members of the jury. We have shared, together, something very special over the last few days. We have all had our ups and downs, and have the wounds to prove it. This is no ordinary trial, no ordinary defendant. I am not seeking to appeal to your emotions; the sanctity of your heart is not my domain, and I would not dare trespass into such hallowed ground. I ask you to acquit Merlin solely on the ground that the prosecution have not delivered their promise to prove to you beyond a reasonable doubt that Merlin is guilty. Therefore you should acquit this troubled old man who some may think has already been punished enough for being in the wrong place at the wrong time. Thank you. Thank you all."

George sat down to the traditional and respectful silence, hearing only in his own head, whoops and cheers and loud applause. George did however notice Merlin, who stood up and bowed theatrically to his counsel.

CHAPTER FIFTEEN
Verdict

Out of the depths of the Underground station on London Bridge, in the midst of a tight throng of City workers, George walked into the piercing early morning sunlight of a cold winter's day and made his way by foot across the Thames to Southwark Crown Court. He rarely took much notice of the outside world, but today felt like a new dawn. The worst was over, the speeches made, and now it was time for the judge to earn his crust and then for the jury to do their work. George stood in the middle of the bridge, ignoring the crawling traffic, took in a breath of cold air and looked eastwards over the dark grey waters of the Thames, down towards the court buildings on the south bank. He allowed himself a moment or two to reflect on what the day had in store: the judge to sum up, jury to retire, come back and say 'Not guilty.' George imagined the taste of vintage champagne on his lips, which might become a reality, he thought, before noon. But he was indulging himself with a fantasy, and felt that he was tempting fate. The reality was that it was just past nine o'clock in the morning of Friday the 22nd of December, the fifth and presumably the last day of the Crown versus Merlin.

Within a few minutes George approached the steps to the main entrance of the courtroom. Outside, much to his surprise, were at least two television crews setting up their gear and a small number of people – mainly student types but some considerably older – waving placards bearing the message: *Free Merlin*. They looked as if they could well muster a hearty chant, but it was early and the main activity was centering round the mugs of hot drinks and bacon sandwiches being ferried from one of the nearby cafés.

George breezed through the small crowd, past the security

guards into the main foyer and reception area of the court complex, where Sam was waiting for him in eager anticipation.

"Today's the day, George. Today's the day," enthused Sam, dressed with surprising attention to such details as polished shoes, neatly arranged tie, and a well-pressed grey suit.

Sam walked with George to the lifts, though he probably knew that George would not permit him to enter the counsels' robing rooms with him, leaving his company on the second floor, on which Court 12 was situated.

"See you in a few minutes, George. I'll go and say morning to our star client."

Everything seemed to be happening in slow motion; the realisation that there would never be another day like this was a thought that George could not banish from his racing mind. Entering the robing room felt quite surreal, a feeling that quickly disappeared when he caught sight of David Palmer, already grooming himself in front of one of the many full-length mirrors, fully robed, making the final adjustments to his wig.

"Mobo's already in court, George. Maybe he's worried that you're going to take his seat," David said, still looking into the mirror and addressing George's reflection. "I'm glad you cut out early last night. This is a day I want to remember without a hangover. Brian was still going strong when I left, shortly after you did. How are you feeling this bright morning?"

"You know when you've got the flu, and everything seems a bit disconnected?"

"Don't know what you're talking about," joked David. "You look OK, that's all that matters today. What d'you reckon, jury out before twelve?"

"Probably," said George, still in a bit of a daze. "Why don't you go to your leader. I'll see you downstairs."

* * *

George was taken aback by the mob of people outside Court 12. Angry words were being exchanged with court officials, who seemed to be out in force. The card-holding press believed they had priority over ordinary members of the public and there were clearly going to be many disappointed people. The egalitarian 'first come, first served' rule was not going to be easily enforced on this day, thought George as he pushed his way through the scrum into the courtroom, which was empty apart from Mobo, David Palmer, the usher, the stenographer, and the court clerk.

Within seven minutes the whole scene had completely changed: the jury was settled, Merlin was in the dock, Sam was sitting behind George, the judge was seated and clearing his throat. The public area was fully occupied, and the press was spilling over into whatever seats they could find without being moved.

George turned around to smile at Merlin, who was once again dressed immaculately and looked fresh and alert.

The judge looked up from his notes and a familiar silence swept over the courtroom.

"Members of the jury, as learned counsel for the defence, Mr. Winsome, said to you yesterday in his closing speech, we have shared something very special over the last few days. That much is true. You have listened very patiently to the evidence and I must ask you to listen with equal patience to me. You will judge this case on fact, not emotion. You will judge the case on the law, which I shall explain to you in some detail in a few moments, and you will reach your own opinion – collectively, as a jury without interference from any third party. Are you all with me?"

The judge paused for a few seconds while he scoured each member of the jury assembled before him.

George looked round to make sure that Sam was making a full note of what the judge was saying. George wanted to study the jury.

After what felt like an eternity, the judge continued: "And so, members of the jury, you must be satisfied so that you are sure of the defendant's guilt. Nothing less will do. As I said earlier, your verdicts must relate to the specific charges on the indictment and to no other matter. Did the defendant intend to injure the deceased? Has the prosecution proved that the injuries caused the death of the deceased? If you come to the view that the defendant was acting in self-defence, was the force he used reasonable in all the circumstances? It is entirely a matter for you, members of the jury. So, I now invite you to retire and consider your verdicts. At this stage I must have a unanimous decision. If you have not already done so, I strongly recommend you appoint a foreman as your spokesperson. Thank you. The court usher will look after you from now on."

Margaret, the usher, sprung into life, belted out an oath to keep the jury in 'some quiet and convenient place, and let no man interfere with the jury's true verdict', and proudly herded the jury out of the courtroom into one of the enclosed jury deliberating areas, designed for the specific purpose of arranging twelve people around an oval table for them to come to a decision.

"Right, all your mobile phones in here, please," commanded Margaret, placing a large plastic tray into the middle of the table. "Turn them off now and you'll get them back when you leave for the day, but while you're deliberating there can be no contact with anyone except yourselves. And me, of course. That's what I have to do – look after you lot. The toilet's over there. If you need anything, press that button on the wall. OK?"

The jury fiddled with their mobile phones' on/off buttons, then surrendered their mobiles like gunslingers handing in their weapons upon entering a Wild West saloon. They slowly took their places to play out the last act in their part in the trial as Margaret slipped out of the room.

"What a fucking bore that judge is. I thought I was being hypnotised," was the first comment, coming from one of the younger female jurors, bristling with sassiness.

"I think we should agree to converse in a civilised manner. It costs nothing to speak without using bad language," retorted a middle-aged female juror, sounding like a schoolteacher scolding a naughty kid.

"Let's get one thing straight, shall we? You're no judge of whether my language is good or fucking bad. We're not in school and you're not my teacher. OK?"

The eldest male had other thoughts on his mind. "Can I remind everybody that the judge asked us to appoint a foreman. Can we get on with that, please? Perhaps we could introduce ourselves? That might help us proceed in a calmer manner. My name is Henry." Henry looked around expecting everyone to follow suit, but instead there was an awkward silence.

"Er...hello everyone. I am Hilda, Hilda Breakspear. I think Henry is quite right, the appointment of a foreman is our first task. I suggest you," looking at the very calm Caribbean lady, who responded quickly. "Why thank you, Hilda. My name is Martha."

"Yes, I agree. I'm Sanjit Patel." Sanjit placed his hands together in front of his heart, closed his eyes and bowed to the group. "Namaste. Let us start with the appointment of a foreman, or should I say 'foreperson', as the judge suggested. Let us all write down the name of the person we want to be in charge, and see if we have a clear majority on that issue. Shall we agree that no one is allowed to vote for themselves?"

Each of the jury had been given a notepad and a pencil, and each of them wrote down the name of one person, and then the names were read out loud. There were four votes for Henry, six for Martha, and one each for Sanjit and Hilda.

Henry was clearly not happy with the result, but being the old soldier that he was, he knew when he was beaten and smiled.

Martha seemed to immediately grow in stature, and puffed out her chest. "My, my. This is a big responsibility. So, I'm in charge. OK. Why don't we listen to one of the 'Guilty's and see how far we get."

"Very good idea, Mrs. Foreman," said Sanjit.

The sassy young girl was straight in. "Hi, I'm Cherie. Look, his smarmy lawyer said it all. It's spit or swallow, isn't it? You either swallow his shit or you don't. I don't. I agree with the prosecution. The old boy's taking the piss. He knows he's not Merlin, for fuck's sake. He's guilty, all right. I can't believe you're all so stupid not to see through him. Wake up, the lot of you, let's convict and get back to our lives."

All concerned listened to Cherie's plea attentively, and, for the first time since they retired to consider their verdicts, there was a momentary silence.

The Rastafarian, seemed to spring to life. "I'm telling you, that old boy is the son of the devil. We heard it in court. He's the fucking anti-Christ, man, you gotta get real. That stick of his has the power of darkness. He meant to fling the old boy from Hampstead to Tottenham. He had just woken up, so his powers weren't what he thought they were, so the Fred guy just gets lifted off the ground a bit. He wanted to kill him, all right. I am Rufus, by the way. Rufus Christian, that's the name. Some people call me Christian Rufus, but I'm cool with Rufus."

"What a load of shite. I can't believe we're listening to this crap. It's fucking unreal," Cherie commented.

Henry was beginning to enjoy himself. "But you agree with Rufus, don't you, I mean that Merlin should be convicted?"

"Well, yeah, and on the manslaughter one as well, but not for the same reasons." Cherie realised that she was now on the side of the anti-Christ camp as represented by 'Christian Rufus'.

"Hello, everyone. My name is Amelia. I think he did mean to hurt the old boy, but I think he was perfectly entitled to use, you know, reasonable force. He had just woken up and thought that his stick was being stolen and that he was being attacked, so he lashes out trying to protect himself, so he's not guilty on the small charge, so he's not guilty on the more serious allegation. It's quite simple."

Amelia sat back as if she had just made a closing speech for the defence, but the hitherto silent Greek Cypriot-born gentleman decided he should make his presence known. "Yassas, my friends. I am Andreus." Andreus launched into a spirited mini-speech, the gist of which was that Merlin was a sharp old character who would be 'well-pleased to get off with a guilty on just the assault charge.'

Henry sighed. "Mrs. Chairman, I mean Foreman, I mean Martha. Let's take a vote and see if we've made any progress."

"Very good idea, Henry," Sanjit said, "shall we ask the question 'Who wishes to convict on the lesser charge?'"

Henry nodded at Martha, who suggested that they all write down either 'guilty' or 'not guilty' to the charge of actual bodily harm, an exercise that resulted in nine votes for guilty and three votes for not guilty.

"Oh shit," exclaimed Cherie, "we're gonna be here till fucking Christmas. I'm starving. Don't they even feed you in this dump?"

"Cherie, it is 'Cherie' isn't it?" said Martha almost too politely. "We've only just started our deliberations. We should treat Merlin with as much respect and concern as we would want our loved ones to be treated. As we would expect to be treated. It is a great responsibility. I feel as if I'm part of a wonderful system, one that's taken many, many years to arrive at this point. At great cost. The system is as fair and just as we are. We are the system. So, we must take our time, listen to each other, respectfully. Is that all OK? Right, let's go around the table and hear what we think and do so with an open mind. That's the way we're going to do it. That may take a little time."

Martha looked at the young lad who had taken a turn on the first day. "Are you feeling all right? We all felt for you when you fainted."

"Sure, I'm OK. Guess I get dehydrated quite easily. Nothing to worry about. My name is Rupert, by the way."

"That's reassuring, Rupert. OK, round the table – one by one – take your time and try not to interrupt, let's just say it as we see it and listen to each other."

Martha's suggestion resulted in exactly what was asked and eventually everyone had had their say.

Rupert was by now struggling to stay awake and in dire need of a drink, or two. "I feel knackered, Martha. Is it too much for you to ask for some food and drink? Maybe a beer? It ain't right for them to keep us in here like this. It's Friday, for fuck's sake, I'm due a beer, that's my verdict."

Henry looked at Martha. "This should be a duty for the foreman, but I can assume that responsibility if the foreman so chooses."

"Why, thank you, Henry. You're a real gentleman, aren't you?"

All eyes were on Henry as he stood up and pressed the button, feeling very important indeed. For some reason he thought there would be some kind of buzz or bell-like noise, but there was nothing to hear and Henry quickly sat down as if he had successfully completed a very complicated challenge.

Margaret duly appeared with all due haste, and Henry peered round the door as if Margaret was a bellboy in a five-star hotel.

"I'm speaking on behalf of the foreman, Margaret," Henry said, suddenly noticing the bright name badge on the lapel of Margaret's well-worn black gown. "We want some food, please." He heard shouts from inside the room as if Margaret was a fast-food waiter.

"Look, I'm not standing here taking bloody orders. No doubt everyone wants something different. Here's the menu card from the restaurant and a card for you all to fill in with your orders. Anything over £2.32 will be deducted from your expenses. Let me know when you're sorted." Margaret handed him a single form on which all the orders were to be written down and shut the door.

"Jesus, what an uptight cow that one is. I wonder what her fucking problem is," Cherie said just loud enough to let Margaret hear.

Before any comments could be made in reaction to Cherie's indiscretion, the door opened again and Margaret popped her head round.

"The judge wants you all in court, *now*," she said firmly, looking at Cherie with daggers in her eyes.

The time was now one thirty, two and a half hours having passed since the jury first retired. The court quickly reconvened, some observers not having left their seats in the first place.

Mobo was used to the vagaries of the jury; George was not. He had hotfooted the short journey from the robing room to the court, having spent no more than a few minutes with Sam and Merlin after the jury had first retired.

Judge Watts looked quite excited. "Well, members of the jury, I'm glad you have surfaced for some air. Perhaps you could do the honours," he said to the clerk, who launched himself into his 'verdict routine'.

"Members of the jury, have you reached a verdict upon which you are all agreed?"

Martha stood up nervously. "Er, no we have not. We're hungry and want something to eat."

Before the collective sniggering could die down, Rupert managed to throw out the words, "And drink!"

Judge Watts looked down on the jury sympathetically. "Yes, members of the jury, we do understand how difficult your task is. Of course, we will make sure that you are brought refreshments as soon as you return to your room. Now, I would like to enquire whether you believe any progress is being made?"

Judge Watts soon picked up how dire the situation was, when not a single member of the jury said a word, not even Martha.

"Er, very well, members of the jury. It is a bit premature perhaps, but I am legally entitled to take a verdict from you at this stage if at least ten of you can agree. Do you think that will help progress matters?"

Martha nodded, looking around at her fellow members, not quite sure whether she was doing the right thing.

"OK, members of the jury, please return and try to come to a unanimous verdict, but failing unanimity, I will, as I have indicated, accept a verdict of at least ten of you."

The jury shuffled back to their place of deliberation, handed the list of their demands to the usher, and waited patiently for their food and drink to arrive.

Rufus slowly and reluctantly emptied his large pockets to reveal a bag of biscuits, about twenty in number.

"Now we're talking," said Rupert. "Let's tuck into the biccies."

"Right, where were we?" Henry asked Martha.

"Nowhere, fucking nowhere," Cherie interjected.

"OK, let's write down guilty or not guilty on the manslaughter charge," said Martha wearily.

Henry collected twelve crumpled bits of paper and handed them to Martha.

"Well, heavens be praised. Twelve 'not guilty's," said Martha.

"Now we're talking," said Cherie, "let's do the same for the assault charge and get the fuck out of here."

The jury repeated the process and Martha did a little count-up while the others looked around anxiously.

"Nine 'guilty's, three 'not guilty's," said Martha.

"Right," said Cherie impatiently, "let the three 'not guilty's declare themselves, and let's have this out."

"I know," said Martha, asserting her authority, "let the nine who wish Merlin to be convicted say who they are."

"OK," said Henry, "put your hand up if you want to convict Merlin of the assault charge."

Nine hands duly rose, leaving Sanjit, Henry, and Amelia with their hands firmly by their sides.

Before another debate kicked off, the door opened, and the usher brought in trays of sandwiches, crisps, fruit, tea, coffee, water, and orange juice, ending the discussion temporarily while an undignified scramble commenced for the tastiest-looking food.

The group held an informal truce while paper plates were stacked high, including, for most of the group, at least one of the biscuits supplied by Rufus.

A few minutes went by while the jury stuffed themselves, as if the case had been forgotten. Rupert was heard to mutter some obscenities about the lack of alcohol, and now seemed quite content scarfing as many of the biscuits as he could and making faces at Rufus.

"Right," said Henry, "let's go around the houses one more time."

This caused Cherie to start giggling for some unknown reason, and soon the giggles started to spread like a yawning wave.

"I know," suggested Rupert, "let's tell the judge that we find the prosecution guilty of being a fat ugly bastard and the defence of being a snooty-faced twat."

Henry stood up. "Members of the jury. I ask you to acquit the defendant on the grounds that he's been dead for five hundred years."

"Not bad," said Cherie, "but I want to know whether that staff takes double A batteries or whether it runs on solar power."

Even Amelia was reduced to tears and was beyond any serious discussion.

Rufus was the first to come to his senses. "The man is Merlin, as I told you."

There was another round of hoots and laughter before Martha managed to regain some order.

"It seems fair enough to let him off the manslaughter and convict on the assault," she said, trying to stifle her laughter. "Look, if one of the three 'guilty's can change their mind, then we can all go home."

This latter comment seemed to deflate the conversation, and a moment of almost silent reflection overcame the group.

"OK," volunteered Henry. "I'll go turncoat, just for you, Martha."

★   ★   ★

"Would all parties in the case of the Crown versus Merlin please return to Court twelve immediately."

Sam and George had decided to stick together in the public cafeteria, feeling quite sure that the jury would return any minute following the judge's majority direction.

"They're going to convict, I can feel it, Sam," George said nervously as he placed his wig back on his head, rushing towards the court.

"Nah, I don't see it, George, straight acquittal, bet you two pints and a packet of crisps."

George and Sam, now in a small group that included Mobo and David, pushed themselves through the courtroom door into Court 12, where the judge and jury were already in place.

Judge Watts was looking quite severe. He nodded to the clerk and told Merlin to stand up.

Sam leaned forward to George and whispered into his ear, "Make that four pints and some good nuts. I've never seen such a happy-looking jury."

Martha stood up, now familiar with the routine.

"Members of the jury, have you reached a unanimous verdict on count one of the indictment?"

"Yes, we have," said Martha proudly.

"Members of the jury, have you reached a unanimous verdict on count two of the indictment?"

"No, we have not," said Martha apologetically.

"Members of the jury," the clerk continued, "have you reached a verdict on count two of the indictment in respect of which at least ten of you have agreed?"

"Yes, we have."

"With respect to count one on the indictment, to the charge of manslaughter, what is your verdict?"

"Not guilty."

Once the whooping and cheering from the back of the court died down, the clerk continued.

"Is that a unanimous verdict of the jury?"

"Sure is, I mean yes sir, Your Honour," Martha said confidently.

The clerk continued. "And what is your verdict with respect to the charge of actual bodily harm?"

"Guilty," said Martha to a loud chorus of moans and groans.

"And is that the verdict of the entire jury or of a majority?"

"It was ten to two," Martha said, not enjoying her moment of fame.

George sat rooted to his seat, completely at a loss as to what was supposed to happen next.

"Mr. Winsome," said the judge. "How long has the defendant been in custody?"

George shook his head as if he was struggling with some difficult arithmetic.

"If I can assist the court," said Mobo. "The defendant was arrested on the morning of the twentieth of September and has been in custody ever since, some fourteen weeks or so."

"Thank you, Mr. Moboto. I take it that there are no previous convictions to put before the court? I thought not," said the judge with half a smile. "Mr. Winsome, your client has been found guilty of a serious assault. Do you wish me to consider any mitigating factors before I pass sentence?"

George realised that this was no time for any mistakes.

"Your Honour, I do appreciate that the offence is serious but, with respect, Your Honour should proceed on the basis that the defendant caused a relatively minor injury, in no way connected to the death of Mr. Russell."

"Of course, Mr. Winsome, I fully acknowledge the verdicts of the jury."

"And I respectfully submit that the defendant should be sentenced on the basis that he is a man of good character."

"Indeed, Mr. Winsome, I fully agree," said the judge.

"Furthermore, Your Honour, I would urge the court not to delay the release of the defendant a moment longer. Your Honour will have before him no fewer than three formal reports, and there was the evidence of Dr. Eisner."

"Mr. Winsome," Judge Watts said, trying to keep a straight face, "I can, of course, remand Merlin in custody pending further reports, but the nub of the matter, to me, is whether your client poses a further risk to the public. I recall the evidence of Dr. Eisner, who stated on oath, in his professional opinion, that the defendant was not a dangerous character. I have also had the opportunity to form my own opinion during the course of this trial, and if it helps you, Mr. Winsome, I share that opinion."

George looked at the judge, not sure whether to keep going or keep quiet. He recalled the advice of his esteemed pupil master: "When in doubt, say nowt," and remained quiet, allowing the judge to continue.

"Stand up, Merlin," said the judge firmly. "I have been through many trials, but none as trying as this one. You might have pleaded guilty to the charge of assault, but you chose not to. That is a very serious matter. However, you have been in custody for many weeks and I see no further purpose being served in detaining you any longer. I hereby sentence you to three months' imprisonment, which has now been served. Merlin, you are free to go. Please, take your staff with you, and good luck."

★   ★   ★

For many years, George could hardly remember the moments following the utterance of the words "you are free to go". Pandemonium broke out in the courtroom; the prison guard hugged and kissed Merlin and almost pushed him out of the dock into the sea of strangers all vying to be the first to wish him well. The judge slipped out without further ceremony to allow the celebrations to continue without judicial interference. Sam even hugged and kissed George, whose back was sore for days from the number of hearty slaps on the back he received within the first few minutes following the judge's sentence. George retrieved the staff from the usher and passed it to Merlin, who lifted and shook it like a trophy, much to the delight and cheers from the courtroom crowd.

"I live!" shouted Merlin. "And I am free!" George could not tell, exactly, for how long Merlin hugged him: somewhere between a moment and an eternity.

PART TWO
FREEDOM

'Educating the mind without educating the
heart is no education at all.'
Attributed to Aristotle of Stagira

384 – 322 B.C.

CHAPTER SIXTEEN
Money

11 a.m., Saturday, 23rd December 2000, 118a Huddleston Road, Tufnell Park, North London.

George Winsome did not have the courage to open his eyes. His head pounded, his mouth was dry, and his eyes were not yet ready to confront daylight. His mind was swirling with the still-vivid dream that seemed as real as it was implausible: Merlin was a free man, George Winsome was the hero of the hour. But the future seemed so uncertain; how was this story to unfold? The question bounced around the inside of George's mind relentlessly: who was Merlin, and what was the relevance of Merlin's life to his – and Heather's?

George tried to steady his mind and breathe, consciously. He rolled his tongue, which felt enormous, inside his mouth to feel slightly more alive, and tasted the dry, bitter taste of yesterday's alcohol. He took as deep a breath as he dared, and guessed, correctly, that he had made it home, a theory confirmed once he sniffed the unique odour of his duvet cover. Yes, he was home, definitely. He remembered it was Saturday, probably sometime late in the morning, and moved his arms around cautiously to ascertain whether there was another life-form in his bed. Thankfully, there was not, and George made the decision that it was time to look the world in the eye.

He peeked through a half-open eye and saw the blurred evidence of his North London basement flat: empty wine and beer bottles, compact discs out of their containers strewn everywhere, remnants of a half-cooked, half-eaten pizza and then the sight he had been dreading: someone asleep on his floor, still comatose from the night before.

He closed his eyes again and tried to trace his movements from the time he was being hugged by Merlin inside the courtroom. He remembered the 'Free Merlin' crowd outside the building, and the television crews crowding around Merlin. He suddenly recalled the suggestion by a wild-looking youth called Sihairly to go for a drink in the Slug and Lettuce. The judge's son! George tried to remember where he went afterwards but it was clearly too early for such an ambitious task.

Now that George felt relatively safe, he asked himself, *Now, what did I do last night, what on earth did I do?* and was trying hard to answer, but the throbbing inside his head distracted him completely from the challenge.

The time had come to sit upright and go for the full two-eyes-wide-open approach. Rubbing his eyes, he realised that the body on the floor was that of Merlin, sleeping like a baby, cradling his staff like a cuddly toy.

"Oh fuck, oh fuck, oh fuck," said George aloud, causing Merlin to begin stirring back into life.

George had, over the years, developed his very own 'Saturday Morning Recovery Programme' and knew exactly what he needed to do: Step One – take at least two heavy-duty painkillers, Step Two – drink a pint of water, Step Three – swelter in a steaming hot bath, Step Four – go back to bed, Step Five – wake up and have another drink. Unfortunately, George realised that Step Four was not going to happen so he went straight to Step Five, retrieved a cold can of beer from the fridge, and pulled the ring-top impatiently, making what sounded like a very loud noise as the compressed gas escaped. He was a great believer in the hair-of-the-dog theory, knowing the real reason behind having a drink was to postpone the inevitable hangover for another few hours. Sunday was the day for suffering, not Saturday.

George sat on the edge of his tiny sofa bed and looked at Merlin on the floor, wondering what he was to do next.

"Did you call her?" asked Merlin without moving.

"Call who?"

"Your lady, Heather. Did you call her?"

Something stirred inside George and he almost vomited. *Heather,* he thought, *I was going to call Heather.* He managed to find his mobile phone and noticed that there were ten unanswered messages. Before he could play them back, he realised that his answer phone was blinking a red light, indicating un-played messages.

Within two or three minutes he had listened to all the messages, mainly from the press, who had somehow obtained his home telephone and personal mobile numbers. But there were two messages from Heather, one on his mobile and the other on his home phone, both pleading with him to contact her as soon as he could. In the cold light of day, she sounded quite desperate, far more than he faintly remembered from the murky depths of the night before.

Merlin uncoiled himself from his foetal sleeping position, rubbed his eyes and outstretched his arms, yawning. "You should call her, my friend, without delay. You assured me last night that you were going to make that call, but others were keen to distract you from the task. You must call her, Sir George. Now."

George composed himself and addressed Merlin in his formal barristerial voice.

"Listen, Merlin, I don't know how you ended up here last night, but the trial is over, the party is over, we're over. It's time to leave, my friend. I have personal matters to sort out. Sorry, but that's the way it is." George looked at Merlin and saw the telltale tears forming in his weary old eyes, like a dog being sent into the garden.

"But, Sir George, do you not remember the words you spoke to me last night? Would you really cast me to the wind after all the plans we shared, the dreams we had, the songs we sang?"

Before George could respond the doorbell rang throughout the tiny apartment, continuously.

George's basement flat had its own front door, which he opened, knowing who would be there. Heather looked worn out, as if she had not slept for some time. Her eyes were puffy, betraying long hours spent crying, and her hands were visibly shaking. As soon as George had opened the door, Heather fell into his arms, crying without inhibition.

"Oh, George, why didn't you ring? I needed you so badly last night, I really did."

"I believe the correct thing to do in such circumstances is make a cup of tea," said Merlin. "Making a fine cup of tea was one of the many skills taught to me in Brickstonia. Now, milk, sugar?"

"Who on earth is he?" enquired Heather, drying her eyes.

"I am Merlin, my good lady, and you are sweet Lady Heather, the love of my dearest friend, the great Sir George. My, you are indeed a beautiful creature. I congratulate you, Sir George."

Heather looked at George and asked as diplomatically as she could, under the circumstances, "What's going on, George? This is the Merlin guy who's been in the papers the last week, your case, isn't it? Shit, what on earth are you doing? The Bar Council would go nuts if they found out."

"No fear, my friend," said Merlin happily. "We discussed such matters last night and your good friend is leaving the Bar to become my personal representative on this Earth. He has been highly recommended to me by the good St. Yves, who knows all lawyers, past and present. I am so happy. Perhaps you could join forces with us. We'd have such fun."

"Oh, shit," said George.

Heather began to lighten up when the situation became clearer in her mind.

"I think Merlin's right. Let's have a cup of tea and a chat. It seems we've all got a lot to talk about. Milk, no sugar, Merlin, same for 'Sir George'."

Merlin confidently retreated into the kitchen to make some tea while George and Heather sat down on George's sofa bed after he had performed its one-minute transition from bed to sofa and stuffed the duvet in a cupboard.

Heather sat next to George, holding his hands. "Listen, George, I've been to hell and back over the last day. Yesterday afternoon I was called in to see my boss at Pentheus. I thought I was going to get another bonus or something. But sitting with him was the sadist from HR – did I tell you about her? Well, never mind, believe me, she's a complete female bastard of the worst kind. Wouldn't know the truth if it slapped her in the face. Anyway, it turns out that the head company has imposed a five percent headcount reduction across all its subsidiaries worldwide. What that means is that they're kicking people out to reduce their cost base. So, my boss starts to explain all this and I'm wondering, you know, what's it got to do with me, when he says, 'So, I'm sorry, Heather, but we're having to let you go.' The bastards, George. Because I've only been there for a couple of months I'm still in the probationary period, which means they can sack me for no reason and give me one month's pay. One fucking month! I thought I'd be there until hell freezes over – or at least until I had some money in the bank. I was so confident that I was onto a good thing I maxed out on three credit cards. Jesus, I'm in such debt you wouldn't believe."

George placed his hand around Heather's head and pulled her towards him, stroking her hair.

"I'm sorry, Heather, I really am. But it's not the end of the world...."

"And it got worse, much worse," Heather said as Merlin appeared with two cups of tea.

"Two cups of tea, milk, no sugar, as requested. I do hope you find the flavour to your satisfaction," he said.

"Merlin, that's very kind of you, but we do need to talk, you know, privately, if you don't mind," said George with a slight edge of irritation in his voice.

"I shall be as quiet as a mouse. I shall close my ears, my friends," Merlin replied before retreating to a corner and sitting upright in a sleeping warrior pose, eyes closed, cross-legged, against the wall.

Heather sighed. "Never mind him, George, it doesn't bother me, honestly. Look, the sacking was only the beginning. I thought I was going to faint or be sick. I went to the toilet and there was blood everywhere. I thought...I thought I was going to lose the baby, George, I really did." At which point Heather burst into tears again.

"The child, the child! Is it safe? Please, I must know, dearest Heather, is the child well?" shouted Merlin, rousing from his supposed trance.

Heather seemed not to mind Merlin's involvement in such an intimate conversation, but George was less agreeable.

"Merlin, just butt out, please, there's a good fellow."

"If you wish, my good knight, but your words this day are far removed from our exchanges in the tavern yesterday," said Merlin, obviously put out.

"That was yesterday, Merlin, look—" George said, his voice rising, before Heather intervened.

"George, listen to me, I really don't mind. He's here, OK, and the flat is too small for him not to listen. You're not going to throw him out, are you? It's freezing out there."

"OK, OK." George resigned himself to the situation and picked up the beer instead of the tea.

"Oh, thank you, Sir George, thank you. We are practically family now, you know. I can help, of that I am sure, and as sure as I know you have been my salvation, perhaps I can help you. But please, let the good lady finish her tale."

George stared at Merlin, wondering how he had gotten himself into this position, but Heather was as keen as Merlin was for her to finish the story.

"Anyway," she continued, "I totally freaked and they got an ambulance to take me to Southwark Hospital. I suppose they were worried that my reaction might have been stress-induced and I might sue them."

"Now that's a good idea," interjected George.

"So, I wait for what feels like an eternity in the accident and emergency ward and eventually I'm seen by a nurse who's been on her feet for nearly eighteen hours. It was while I was waiting that I tried to phone you."

"Oh Jesus, I'm sorry, Heather, I really am," said George, tears forming in his eyes. Merlin had already let go completely and was sobbing.

"They examined me, and it turned out that I had septicemia in my urinary tract, which had burst. It was localised; they gave me some antibiotics to help clear it up."

"So, you're OK, and the baby's OK, yes?" asked George eagerly.

"Yes, George. I'm OK, the baby is OK. I was just really frightened, that's all. I went home and crashed out and came around as soon as I felt ready to face the world. So here I am, just a bit shocked and jobless with a mountain of unpaid bills. Apart from that I'm absolutely fine."

George held Heather close to him while they both cried, gently.

"We'll be OK, Heather, I promise you we will," he said. "I do love you, you know that, don't you?"

"I know, George, and I love you too." This made Merlin cry

even louder than before. "Listen, George," continued Heather, "there is something I need to tell you, something I was never going to tell you, but I must tell you now." She paused and composed herself. "Do you remember the day you were made a tenant? You remember that I slipped out to go to the toilet, and while I was away you got the call to chambers to be told that you'd got the tenancy? Well, what happened was that I had a tip-off from Paul Styles. He told me to make sure that I had my mobile with me. The phone was on, but in the silent mode, which makes it shake without making a noise. I felt the phone go off in my pocket and went outside. It was Paul, who asked me to go over to chambers. Listen George, I didn't really expect to be made an offer; I always presumed it would be you. But Paul said to me, 'We want you to join us,' but I had – the same day – already accepted the job at Pentheus. I should have told them earlier, I know that. But maybe I was just, you know, curious, flattered. Anyway I told Paul there and then that I had made my mind up and they all reconvened and decided to offer the tenancy to you. Maybe it doesn't matter now, but I had to tell you." She paused again. "Are you angry with me, George? I will understand if you are. I just felt that you should know."

George placed his head in his hands, letting the story sink in.

"The sly bastards. I would never, ever, have guessed that one, Heather, never in a million years. The whole lot of them lied through their teeth. They didn't really want me at all. Jesus, I feel sick." George paused to try and bring himself out of the newest shocker of the day. "Heather, all that matters to me now is that you're safe, the baby's safe, and we're together. That's all that matters."

"The saints be praised," exclaimed Merlin. "There is so much love in this abode of yours I can hardly breathe. We are so fortunate; many gods bless us. Now, you must tell me what we need to achieve, and we will plot and scheme and think and think some more. If we know what we have to do, by the gods we will do it. Tell me, what does your heart desire, my dearest Lady Heather?"

"Er, you couldn't just wave that wand of yours and produce a million pounds out of thin air, could you?" she asked.

"Or at least tell us the numbers of tonight's lottery draw," joked George.

Merlin approached George and Heather, who were sitting tightly together on the sofa, and shuffled them apart to allow him to sit between them. Taking one of George's hands and one of Heather's, he told them both solemnly, "Listen, my friends. You are my family. I will fight for you and I would gladly die for you. I cannot produce money out of thin air. I cannot see into the future well enough to see numbers. But I feel such a powerful force, which we together can harness and bring about our fortunes. I need you, both of you. Sir George has the purest heart of any lawyer known to St. Yves, and the fire that burns within your heart, dearest Heather, will be much needed in the days to come. If you can see the possibilities, together we can achieve our dreams."

George lowered his head, while Heather smiled.

"So, I give up my glorious practice at the Bar?" said George.

"And together we start a new life," Merlin said. "As we agreed last night."

"Tell me this is all a bad dream, George, please," Heather said in disbelief. "Yesterday I was a high-flying executive at a leading publishing house and you had just won an incredible courtroom trial. Today I'm out of a job and you're thinking about jacking it all in to represent this, this...old boy who thinks he's Merlin. I mean, is it just me or have you lost your marbles?

"OK, Merlin, or whoever you are," said Heather, squaring up to the challenge, "why on earth would George give up a promising practice at the Bar – a position that he has worked hard for many years to achieve – in order to become the agent of a lost soul who has been found guilty of assault, someone who has no clear past and an even murkier future? I don't get it. I need some help on this one."

"That is a very good question, my dearest Heather, but one I cannot answer. It is a matter for Sir George to resolve. He must look into his heart and ask where his future lies. He must—"

"OK, Merlin, I can answer for myself," George said, asserting himself. "Perhaps I'm confusing my career at the Bar with my feelings for Three Harcourt Square."

"Perhaps you are, George," said Heather sarcastically, fearing the worst.

"But I don't know how to explain it. I just feel that my future does not lie any more at the Bar. I mean, can I see myself sitting on the bench like Judge Watts, presiding over petty criminal trials and that being the highlight of my career? I've only just got off the blocks and I've already pissed off M.B., who might end up as Chair of the Bar Council. I've practically told one of the most respected clerks in the Temple to fuck off and—"

"But wait a minute, George," said Heather. "You've pulled off a spectacular victory, your first ever trial, under the media spotlight. You could walk into another set of chambers and start afresh, if that's what you wanted. You and Sam Leggitt, from what I understand, came out of the trial as good mates, drinking buddies, for God's sake. That's all you really need, isn't it – a good relationship with a busy instructing solicitor."

"Well, that's all true. But I feel deeply unsure that a practice at the criminal Bar is what I want. The idea of staying at the Bar makes me feel physically sick, it really does. Logically you're right, of course you are. It's just how I *feel*, that's all. I don't know how I can explain; it's a great bus journey. I just don't know if I'm on the right bus. Does that make any sense?" George lowered his head, knowing that he had no real argument to put to Heather, only raw emotion.

Merlin decided that he could keep his peace no longer and looked intensely into George's worried face.

"You must follow your heart, Sir George, you must. The decision you make today will determine the course of the rest of your life. You have been chosen, my good knight, chosen by forces you don't yet understand, but you will, I assure you, understand a great deal more in the days ahead. It is all part of the plan. But you must choose, freely and with the blessing of your good lady. The role of your Lady Heather has already been decided."

Heather felt herself reach new heights of anger and righteous indignation. "My role has already been decided! By whom, may I ask?"

"Oh," said Merlin politely, "by the Great Council and St. Yves."

"By the Great Council and St. Yves? George, get a grip, for fuck's sake. Give the old boy his bus fare home and let's pick up where we left off."

Merlin lowered his head, tears welling in his eyes. George looked at Heather and then at Merlin, and took a deep breath.

"Heather, listen. Maybe I have lost my marbles, but maybe not. I simply, at this point in time, cannot stomach the idea of turning up at chambers on Monday and picking up where I left off yesterday. I'll phone Paul Styles at home later today and tell him that I need some time to recover from all the excitement, you know, buy some time. In the meantime, I want to take my chances and act for Merlin – you know, as his agent or manager, whatever. It just feels like the right thing to do."

"The right thing to do?" responded Heather angrily. "And what of the Bar Council? Surely you haven't forgotten the rules that forbid you from, what is it again? ...oh, yes, 'undertaking the general conduct of a client's affairs', 'dealing with a client's financial affairs', 'acting as a legal representative without the instructions of a solicitor' etc., etc. George, listen to me, if you go ahead with this you'll be committing professional suicide, and if it all falls through, which it will, you'll be left with nothing except a very red face and financial ruin."

Before George could collect his thoughts, Merlin interjected, looking quite pleased with himself.

"Oh, there won't be any financial ruin, my good friends. No, no, quite the contrary. There is a great deal of money involved, I can assure you. A king's ransom has been set aside by the Great Council."

Heather looked at George, her curiosity having been aroused.

"A king's ransom, Merlin? What do you mean?" she asked in a decidedly softer tone. George noticed with slight concern an unfamiliar look in her eyes.

"We are to make a great deal of money before my departure, which is not long away. The money is to be put to a good cause, of course, but I know St. Yves is a fair man and will not begrudge you an equity."

Heather paused and thought for a moment, trying hard to prevent a rift with George that she understood could be everlasting.

"George, maybe there is a way through this. You, as you said, buy some time from chambers. There's no need to burn your bridges right now. As far as the Bar Council is concerned, we get around that one quite easily."

Merlin smiled, but George looked slightly puzzled.

"Enlighten me, Heather, go on," he said.

"Well, it's quite simple. I don't give a toss about the Bar. As far as they are concerned I've already left. So, I'll handle the money and front the negotiations, and keep you clean. I mean you trust me, don't you?"

George did not allow himself time to pause. "Of course, I trust you, of course I do. OK, let me think this through."

"We've already thought this through, George." Heather suddenly looked quite perky and excited. "It's time for action."

George looked lovingly at Heather, mightily relieved at the turn of events.

"OK, action it is. But first we go out for a glorious lunch, have a good drink, and get some sleep. How does that sound?"

"Splendid, it sounds absolutely splendid. I am so pleased," said Merlin, excited as a young child.

CHAPTER SEVENTEEN
Press

5 a.m., Sunday, 24th December 2000, office of the Editor-in-Chief,
News on Sunday, *South London.*

Simon Hall had been the editor-in-chief of the *News on Sunday* for over two years, a record-breaking stint. Pressure from WorldCorp, the corporate owner of the *News*, imposed such aggressive sales targets that no editor survived more than a year or so before they were deemed to have failed and were forced to 'move on'. But Simon was doing well, and the weekly figures were touching their targets, so on paper at least, Simon was safe. Advertising revenue was in free fall, as it had been for over two years, so the sales figures meant life or death to Simon. He had worked himself up from the ranks, starting as a cub reporter for a local newspaper in Liverpool twenty years previously, aged fifteen. He knew what the public wanted: sex, scandal, exposure of hypocrisy, bums and tits, football, and an old-fashioned tragedy if space permitted. If the public had heard of an individual, then the public wanted to know what that person did, in private, in detail. It was their right, as Simon saw it. And if one of the many prostitutes on the invisible payroll of the *News* managed to bed a well-known figure, come away with a compromising picture or two, or better still an incriminating tape recording, so much the better. In fact, Simon had come to the view that there were no rules, except the meta-rules of how to avoid being caught, which could arise in a number of ways: infringing the voluntary code of ethics of the Press Complaints Commission (annoying but not life-threatening); libel (potentially expensive and therefore serious); contempt of court (very dangerous if the in-house legal team did not take the rap); breach of confidentiality (potentially serious but with possible long-term gains); invasion of privacy (legal minefield, but worth the hassle if sensational enough); and indiscretion (naming and shaming a friend of the boss, total disaster).

Simon had given up pretending to have any life outside the *News*. He was happily divorced with no children, so thirty-five-year-old Simon's entire energy was devoted to his work, whether it was five in the morning or five in the evening, no matter where he was, at work, in his office, in the back seat of his chauffeur-driven car, in a restaurant, asleep in bed, asleep in his office, or lying in his enormous bath, next to which was installed a hands-free waterproof wireless telephone system.

Ralph Crossley, Simon's chain-smoking deputy, was fifteen years older than his boss, but what he lacked in ambition and talent was more than compensated for in bucketloads of loyalty and deviousness. Ralph knew every dirty trick in the book, partly because he had written it. His ability to turn around a difficult situation was legendary, although sometimes very expensive. Ralph was really an old-fashioned hack who believed, without exception, that everyone had a price. "We're all tarts," he would say, parodying Oscar Wilde. "It's just that some of us are more expensive than others."

Simon and Ralph practically lived in Simon's office, which was designed to look grubby and well-worn, a look that was just as costly as that of some of the other, more salubrious, executive offices scattered around the vast complex in Battersea, South London. His office looked like a bomb had hit it, and that suited Simon fine. No one knew where anything was except Simon personally, not even his personal assistant, who was useless at typing but had other qualities more in demand by the Neanderthal-types than identifying typos and literals.

Simon looked across his large, tatty, untidy desk at Ralph, who was puffing heavily on his cigarette. Scattered around were the final editions of every Sunday newspaper, copies of which had already been in circulation for several hours. Both Simon and Ralph enjoyed this weekly ritual more than any other: the phones were normally quiet, there were few people in the building, and they could quietly reflect on the competition.

"I reckon we'll storm it today," suggested Ralph, looking among the papers on the desk.

Simon picked up a single piece of paper, which contained the most important information to hand, being the snapshot of 'consumer interest issues', commissioned on a weekly basis – a document that informed Ralph what was of the most interest to a cross section of the public, taken by phone on Friday afternoons, always referred to as 'the weeklies' by Simon and Ralph.

"The weeklies have the Merlin story ahead by a mile. We've got quality dirt on three MPs – coke, sex, and lies, and all the fucking public want to hear about is the old boy who walks out of court saying he's Merlin. Let's build the silly fucker up before we pull him down. Works every time, eh Ralph?"

"Sure does, boss. Like you say, it's all a matter of timing. Remember with that pop star – what's her name again? – the one we knew was a lesbian. We built her up for three weeks before we lit the fuse paper, and got the inside story on the suicide. Fucking work of art, that was."

Simon smiled and licked his lips. *Yes, that was a glorious result*, he thought. *We even bought the suicide story from the sister and got change out of fifteen grand.* "Did the world a favour with that one," he commented. "Silly dyke couldn't sing a fucking note."

Simon and Ralph continued to flick through the mounds of papers in front of them.

"What I don't get," said Ralph, "is why no one's come forward to identify the old boy. I mean, his face has been in the papers for nearly a week. Surely someone knows him. That would be a good angle to take, don't you reckon, boss?"

"I've been onto all the pariahs, and no one's heard a whisper," Simon said. "It may happen, it may not. In the meantime, let's roll with it."

Simon picked up the *News on Sunday* and reread the story that started on the front page with the teaser: *Merlin Walks Free. Sensational Story pages 3, 4, 32 and 33.* "What we have to ask ourselves, Ralph, is what do the public want to hear next. He's obviously got no money to sue, so let's free fall. Let's see what we've got."

"We haven't really got much further than the court trial – Jesus, what a farce that was. Perhaps if he can do a Uri Geller trick of some kind, you know, a bit of magic?"

"A bit of magic, like what? Bending spoons hasn't been newsworthy for fucking years. Your granny could bend a spoon and stick one end up her arse and the other up her crack and nobody would give a fuck. We can do better than that. Think."

Simon and Ralph paused for a moment before Simon had one of his eureka moments.

"Ralph, find out where the old boy is hiding. Everyone wants to talk to him. Offer him a truckload of dough – you can go up to twenty-five grand. We want an exclusive, you know, how he conned the jury and so on. Tell him that if he spills the beans we'll pay the money into an offshore account and fix him up with a little pad where he can't be extradited. What do you think, worth a try?"

"Twenty-five grand? The problem is what the other rags are thinking. From what I've heard, the bidding is going to start a lot higher, boss."

Simon winced. He knew he was trying his luck with one of the most experienced scumbags in the business.

"I'll go higher, Ralph, a lot higher, but it better be worth it. The other papers are all looking in the same direction – backward – look."

Simon pointed out the broadsheet coverage of the Merlin story, much of it devoted to the historical basis for Merlin, King Arthur, Knights of the Round Table, Camelot, Stonehenge, Druidism, and Paganism.

"*The Times* has even commissioned Simon Shama to do a full-page spread quoting everyone from the Venerable fucking Bede to some ninth-century monk. The *Observer*'s got David Starkey and the *Independent* those young archaeologists from the TV giving it the Scottish angle on the Picts and whatnot. I've heard even the highbrows are going to offer silly money to give the staff thing a scientific going over. Yeah, you're right as always, this is going to cost."

"What about a DNA sample, boss? It might not be great news

now, but if he keeps climbing higher, and I think this story's got legs for another couple of weeks at least, then we can break the news that he's actually only fifty years old or whatever."

Simon paused again, thinking hard. "You can do that no matter what, Ralph, and let's use that as best we can, when the time is right. Good idea. Now, I'm sure we can think of something else before we leave."

"Well," said Ralph, "it won't do any harm to have the lowdown on his habits. You know, the usual."

"Sure, I thought you were already onto that one. Hopefully young boys. There's not going to be much interest if he's straight. Just run with it, Ralph, I'm not giving you a blank check, but whatever resources you need, I'll roll with them. Let's say three young 'uns, doing a twenty-four hour surveillance, as a starter. OK?"

"Sure thing, boss, you got it."

"And give me a ring as soon as anything turns up, I mean anything, OK? Listen, if you can't get any quality shit on the old boy, try that lawyer of his or the judge, or the prosecution. Maybe one of the witnesses. But make sure the lawyers sign off on that one. Could be a good fallback, you never know."

*　　*　　*

George and Heather had taken Merlin's advice. They had slept soundly for some hours after returning from a long and indulgent lunch. This time the hangover had disappeared, and at six in the morning, George felt unusually refreshed and alert. Heather, likewise, was waking up, and turned around to give George an early morning cuddle, knowing they would soon be up and about.

"Hope Merlin had a good night's sleep in the bath," she said, half awake.

George giggled lightly. "Well, there's nowhere else for him to get some peace and quiet, is there? I mean, the kitchen floor is hardly big enough for a cat, let alone the great and mysterious Merlin. I'll get dressed and see if the corner shop is open, and get the papers, see if my name's in print. I think you'll be safe with Merlin, don't you?"

Heather, by now, was quite alert and brushed back her red hair, looking at George.

"I think you can trust me with Merlin, George. Get me some prawn cocktail crisps, can you? Three packets, thanks."

George put on his weekend gear of a fleecy top, blue jeans and well-worn trainers and closed the door quietly behind him, leaving Heather to dress quickly and see if Merlin was awake.

Heather knocked gently on the bathroom door and peeked inside. Merlin was curled up in the bath with a couple of pillows and a spare duvet, looking deeply contented, his arms wrapped firmly around his staff.

"Er, we're up, Merlin, cup of tea?"

"That would be wonderful," said Merlin, fully awake.

Heather made tea for three and before she reached the single room where she and George had slept, George was coming back through the front door, carrying an armful of Sunday newspapers.

"Shit, you won't believe what's in all the papers. And I mean *all* the papers," he said, placing the wads of newsprint on the floor.

George and Heather scoured the voluminous papers, taking turns to squeal in surprise and amazement at the extent of the coverage, although George was more interested in finding his own name than Merlin's.

"You know," said Heather breathlessly, her wide green eyes shining with disarming brightness, as if possessed by some unseen force, "we really could milk this, George, for a lot of money. I think Merlin's right about that one. I might have been at Pentheus for only a few months, but I understand how this can be turned to our advantage. And I kept the names and numbers of all the press contacts in my personal diary."

"They made a big mistake getting rid of you," George said.

Merlin strolled into the room and sat against the wall.

"You enjoy reading. That is a good thing, my friends. I was never too keen on the idea. What are they saying?" he asked.

"What they're saying is that you're famous, Merlin. Look, your picture is in practically every newspaper," said George, almost proudly.

"And pray, what does that mean? Is fame a good thing?" Merlin asked innocently.

"Good?" said Heather. "It's bloody brilliant. If we can't make a few quid out of this, then we should be shot."

"What do you suggest, Heather? I mean, you contact the papers, say you're acting for Merlin, and then what?"

Merlin sat quietly, listening intently.

"I can ring everyone I know and say I'm acting for Merlin," Heather said, waiting for a challenge from either George or Merlin, but none came. "I'll say that Merlin's willing to give an exclusive interview, and we'd like to know, say within three hours, what the offer is. We then tell everyone their offer is well below what everyone else has offered and give them another chance to place their best and final bids. You know, create an auction. That will take another couple of hours. By late afternoon we'll be able to decide who's really going to put up or not, and take it from there. What do you think?"

"Sounds great. What do you reckon, Merlin?" asked George.

"Am I to understand that we negotiate with these journals and ascertain the amount of money they would be willing to pay me to speak with them?"

"Got it in one, Merlin," George said.

"And that's it?" enquired Merlin.

"Oh no," Heather said. "I'll also work on the television companies and the radio stations and see if I can do the same with them."

"But I thought you said you'd sell the papers the exclusive story, Heather," said George, looking puzzled.

"Jesus, you're dumb for a lawyer, George. We sell exclusivity as many times as we can: the exclusive interview in print, the exclusive interview for television, the exclusive interview for radio. I'll even set up an exclusive internet deal, you watch. That's how it works."

"And what do I do while you're wheeling and dealing like crazy?" George asked.

"You look after Merlin. Buy him some Merlin clothes. Make him look the part. Look at him. He looks like a fucking bank manager who's been on a weekend bender, for Christ's sake. He's got to look like Merlin, you know, the robe, the funny hat, some moccasins—"

Merlin felt he had to interject. "Not a white beard, not that, please. And no funny hat, I was never keen on funny hats."

"OK, no white beard, otherwise you'll be taken for Santa Claus, and that's not our game, is it, George?"

Perhaps it was the mention of the words 'Santa Claus,' or perhaps George had noticed the date on all the newspapers, but the penny suddenly dropped that Christmas was only two days away.

"Oh God, it's Christmas on Monday," he exclaimed.

"And like, so what, it's Christmas on Monday," said Heather, not wanting the subject to change. "Unless you've got some hidden family story to tell me, George, there's only your mother in Scotland for you to worry about. My folks don't expect me home this year. Christmas is just Christmas. Just send some checks out in the post. What's the problem?"

Merlin could see that something was troubling George and asked him softly, "Christmas is a religious festival remembering the life and death of Jesus Christ, the earthly son of the Christian god, is it not?"

"Well, of course it is, but it's turned into something a bit more than that, Merlin. It's a time for families and presents and—"

"And getting drunk and eating tangerines, cold turkey, and all the crap that goes with it. Listen, George, if it's your mum you're worried about, the best thing to do is to make sure you give her a phone call on Christmas day and send her a nice check once we've made a few quid, OK?"

"Yeah, OK, Heather, but I don't know, you know, it's Christmas," George said sadly.

"Listen, my good friend," said Merlin, looking deep into George's eyes. "We paid no homage to the Christian god. Well, not until those Romans started to invade our shores. At this time of year we celebrated the longest night in the lunar calendar, with drink and songs, storytelling and dancing. It was a time to celebrate the beginning of a new year. That is the real time to celebrate, George, the beginning of the new year, as it has been in Scotland for aeons. Forget about Christmas, but remember your mother, and then we celebrate the new year in great spirit, with style. What do you say, my friend, what do you say?"

George quickly recovered from his momentary lapse and agreed that Christmas would come and go, but they would make up for it the following week.

"I don't know how to explain it, really. This will be the first time I've ever missed Christmas, so to speak. It's new ground for me."

"George," said Heather, "I promise you we'll have a slap-up meal on Christmas day. We'll eat turkey, wear stupid paper hats, and buy loads of tangerines and nuts, if that will make you happy. OK?"

George smiled and took a deep breath. "Thanks, Heather, yes, that would make me feel happy. And sing songs together after a few drinks."

"And sing some songs. Would that be 'Holy Night' or 'Last Christmas'?" said Heather, smiling.

"Oh, I'm so excited, George," said Merlin mischievously. "Songs, drinking. That is life. And if we are to go and buy me new attire, can we walk over Hampstead Heath while the sun rises?"

George laughed nervously and looked at his watch. "The sun rises at about eight o'clock, Merlin. Sure, let's have a walk over the Heath. We've got some distance to cover before we get there, but we'll make sunrise."

"Sir George, please remember I have been incarcerated in Brickstonia since the autumn equinox, and before that...well, forever. I have prayed for the day I could walk as a free man among trees, over hills and uncut grass, watching the miracle of dawn. I have told you friends are important and Nature is my best friend. I would walk many an hour to see such a sight. I am ready when you are."

"OK, Merlin. You're on. Heather, are you going to get cracking now or will you wait until tomorrow morning? I mean, who's going to answer the phone this early on a Sunday?"

Heather smiled and replied, "Lawyers may sleep late on

Sundays, but journalists do not, I can assure you. You and Merlin have your walk, buy some clothes, and I'll surprise you when you get back. OK?"

George kissed Heather gently on the lips and said his goodbyes.

"Come on, Merlin, put my old coat onto keep you warm. Anything you want me to bring you back, Heather?"

"Yes, George, another few packets of prawn cocktail crisps, that's all."

CHAPTER EIGHTEEN
Mnemosyne

Dawn, Sunday, 24th December 2000, Kite Hill, Hampstead Heath.

At the summit of Kite Hill, on Hampstead Heath, looking due south over the vast London metropolis, the naked eye on a clear day can see for nearly thirty miles. Some landmarks give bearings: St. Paul's Cathedral, the London Eye, the skyscrapers of the City, the Millennium Dome next to the 'second City' around Canary Wharf, and the high telecommunication transmitters in Croydon and Crystal Palace over twenty miles south, that mark the beginning of the rolling hills of the South Downs.

Several benches are scattered around the top of Kite Hill, on which, at nearly every hour of every day, somebody is sitting watching the peaceful view, the silence of which belies the frantic activity of over five million people living and working within a few square miles.

But there is more to see than just London: when the sun rises slowly from the west, casting its light over a vast historic theatre, when the moon glides across the sky casting its bluey-grey aura over the millions of lights of the city, when ever-moving clouds pass overhead, then the mind can rest and simply gaze vacuously at the wonders of nature. That is the time when the connoisseurs will take their seats and watch in awe of the raw majestic expanse of a slowly changing work of art: the rising of the sun over the horizon.

George and Merlin had walked without conversation through the virtual darkness of the tree-lined residential back streets of Tufnell Park, Dartmouth Park, past Highgate Cemetery, through the private Holly Lodge Estate, along Millfield Lane onto Hampstead Heath itself, and up a steep hill to the top of Kite Hill.

They finally sat down on a bench, looking south, as the sun was rising into a clear star-studded sky, and the near-full moon was setting in the west. Having walked at a good pace for over an hour, neither Merlin nor George felt the bitter cold of a late December morning. Merlin placed his staff to one side and took a deep breath.

"This is a sight for a king," said Merlin, astounded at the beauty before him. "We must do this every day."

George was relieved just to be sitting down. He was surprised that he appeared to be more out of breath than his companion, and waited a while before responding.

"Merlin, tell me, now we're past the trial and all of that is over, tell me, who you are, please?"

Merlin closed his eyes and took deep breaths of the fresh cold air as if he was savouring a rare and beautiful perfume.

"Who am I? Who am I?" he said eventually, eyes still closed. "You know who I am. I am Merlin."

George closed his eyes. "OK, if you don't want to talk, I won't push it."

Merlin, however, was not finished. "I have wondered many times since the day I was detained, who I am. I have considered many possibilities. Perhaps I am indeed just a silly old man who has lost his memory and has awoken without knowledge of his past and somehow came to believe he was Merlin." He took in a few more deep breaths. "But I think that is unlikely. If that was the truth of the matter, then why has no one come forward to declare my true name? And why would St. Yves talk to me so often, as he does?"

"Perhaps, no one who knows you has seen you on the television or in the papers yet. Maybe it's just a matter of time. And St. Yves. You've mentioned his name more than once. Who is he?"

Merlin turned towards George and looked into his eyes. "You make fun of me, my good knight. I cannot believe you are ignorant of the only saintly lawyer to walk this earth, the only true-hearted patron saint of lawyers, the lawyer who defied his king to protect the poor from the crippling taxes extracted by all manner of foul means to pay for the crusades against the followers of Islam. You should go on a pilgrimage to Treguier to atone for your lack of education, Sir George. I am disappointed, and saddened. The good saint was one of the first to persuade those who had lost their way to follow their hearts, to be true to themselves and others."

George, for no clear reason, least of all any reason based in logic, suddenly felt deeply concerned and worried. No, he had never heard of St. Yves, nor Treguier, but kept quiet, knowing that the depth of his ignorance was far more profound than Merlin realised.

Merlin spoke again, with more than a hint of anger in his voice. "Do you truly believe that I am simply a silly old man who has lost his memory? It is a strange thing to lose, is it not? I have not lost my mind, good George. Can you keep your mind but lose your memory? I have never heard of such a thing, have you?"

George was becoming slightly perplexed. "It's not unknown for people to lose their memories, Merlin, without losing their minds, particularly if they have been through a trauma of some kind. It does happen."

"Trauma? What kind of trauma?" asked Merlin with some urgency.

"Hell, I don't know. You could have got a bang on the head, fallen over, been hit by something."

"A bang on the head? No, I had no bang on the head. The doctors in Brickstonia looked, and there was no sign of any bangs, anywhere."

"Well, you might have been through something *like* a bang on the head, but not an actual bang, you know, like an event you found too much to bear, a shock of some kind," continued George, unconvincingly.

"A shock? What kind of shock?"

"I don't know, Merlin, I'm not a specialist in these things. I don't know."

Merlin paused and breathed deeply for some time.

"I do feel, my friend, that my home is far away to the north, although I did travel a great deal. I remember times past, a long time past, when I was at home. The earliest faint flickering image in my mind is the sight of a group of fine, strong men, warriors one and all, who valued my skills. I had powers, Sir George, and some tricks, yes, but real skills and powers. This life sometimes come to me in my dreams, but when I awake and struggle to keep the sounds and images in my mind, they simply vanish back to whence they came."

Merlin closed his eyes and breathed as before, slowly and consciously. "I have a feeling that St. Yves will tell me the secret of my reason for being here soon enough. I am here for a reason, you know, as we all are."

George had an idea, but waited for a few moments before deciding whether to share it with Merlin.

"Do you want to know who you really are, Merlin, do you?"

"We all, surely, want to know who we really are, my good knight, do we not?"

"I want you to consider going to a hypnotherapist. There are people who can gain access to parts of your mind that have been put out of reach for some reason. Don't say yes or no just now, just think about it."

"A hyp-no-thera-pist," said Merlin. "Interesting. Yes, I will think about it."

"And perhaps we can have your staff analysed, and see if that sheds any light on all of this."

"My staff? Analysed?" Merlin paused for thought. "Yes, that sounds like a good idea. But it must not be damaged in the process. Is that agreeable?"

"Sure is, Merlin. That would be progress. OK. Now, are you ready to venture into the big city for some shopping?"

"Shopping? That sounds fun and fun is a good thing. Yes, now the sun is up, I am ready. Lead the way, Sir George."

Just as George and Merlin were about to move off, a voice came from the distance, shouting, "Merlin, Merlin, my friend, wait, wait."

George turned around and, despite the relative darkness, could clearly make out the silhouette of a tall man and a far shorter lady with straight jet-black hair. As the figures approached, he realised that the man was Xavier Feelgood, the prosecution witness.

Xavier bounded over to Merlin and hugged him tightly while his extremely attractive longhaired lady friend stood by, her hands to her face, holding back tears of joy.

"Merlin, my dear friend, you cannot be leaving at this moment. Why, we have so much to catch up on. I see you have your lawyer friend with you. That is good. This is my lady, Zena, as fine a lady as can be found in these lands. Come. Let us sit and talk."

George resigned himself to the inevitable delay while all four sat down on the still-warm bench. Merlin and Xavier sat close to each other at one end in animated conversation, while Zena sat disarmingly close to George on the bench, staring at the sunrise, chanting quietly.

"Oh Merlin," George could hear Xavier say, pointing skywards, "can you see the white chariot of the goddess Luna, can you see Helios riding across the sky, do you hear the voices of Dagda, Belenus, Enid, why Dwyn as well, Mabon, Jarl, Aurora…can you hear them, Merlin? They are laughing with joy at your freedom, they celebrate your presence. Oh this is a glorious, glorious day, my friend."

George felt he was entitled to his say. "I'm afraid Merlin has not quite regained his full memory, Xavier, we were just discussing—"

Xavier interrupted. "Lost his memory? Why, we can't let that get in our way. Come, Merlin, let us invoke Mnemosyne. The muse of memory cannot have forgotten you, my friend."

Merlin stared hard and long at Xavier and gently touched his face with his hands. "Why, it is Xavier. Xavier, how could I ever have forgotten you, after all we went through. Xavier, Xavier," he said before placing his arms around Xavier and weeping joyfully. "I am beginning to remember. Yes, it is coming back. When you came into the courtroom I had such a strong feeling that you were already a friend. It was all a bit too much for me, my mind was in turmoil. I felt so very tired with all the memories flooding back."

Xavier simled warmly at Merlin and leaned over to take a better look at George. "Why, the last time I saw Sir George he was all dressed up with that funny wig and dark gown, but yes, I do remember, but does he?"

Merlin laughed raucously. "It is the good Sir George who

has lost his memory, not me. Sir George, this hypnotherapist of yours, he must speak with you first. You have a lot to remember."

Xavier picked up on the joke. "Why, there's no need to see a hypnotherapist. He needs a PLRS. That is a Past Life Regression Supervisor, to you, Merlin!"

"Oh, yeah," said George, "and in which box of chocolates do we find a PLRS?"

"Look no further," Xavier said. "How else would a silly old pagan like me be able to afford to live in such a wonderful neck of the woods? Let me introduce myself: Xavier Feelgood, regression supervisor to the great and good, rich and bored, at your service."

"Wonderful, wonderful," said Merlin.

"Oh shit," said George.

CHAPTER NINETEEN
Hustle

It was very late in the day by the time George and Merlin fell through the door of George's basement flat in Tufnell Park. George had tried to ring Heather on more than one occasion, but the phone was forever engaged.

"Oh, you've decided to return, have you? I was going to send out a search party for the two of you. Where on earth have you been?" asked Heather angrily.

Merlin disappeared quickly into the toilet, while George tried to placate her.

"It's a long story, Heather."

"I'm sure it is, and it better be good."

"Oh, it's good all right," said George, "and we didn't spend a penny. I mean, we didn't get as far as the shopping thing. We've been round to Xavier's."

"Xavier? Talk fast, George, I'm all ears."

George explained the meeting at the summit of Kite Hill, and the subsequent visit to Xavier's place on the borders of Hampstead Heath. He forgot to mention Zena, but managed to explain that Merlin had regained his memory.

"That Xavier guy is really something. He kind of hypnotises you, just with his voice, then gets you to remember your past lives. It's amazing, it really is, and you wouldn't believe who some of his clients are...."

Heather looked at George as if he had been drinking too much. "And I suppose you're one of the forgotten Knights of the Round Table, or maybe you did us all a favour killing that dragon, or, I know, you led the savage Scots against the English at the battle of—"

"No, no, don't be silly," George said. "I was a monk in fourth-century Brittany. The monastery was being used as a fortress for the French nobility...it was being attacked by fierce Norsemen...I was knighted on the battlefield after saving the life of a member of the royal family, my banner was trimmed by the King himself, it was so real—"

"George, fucking get a grip, OK?"

"And there's St. Yves, Heather," continued George breathlessly. "He was an ecclesiastical judge in Brittany during the time of Philip the Fourth...or was it the Third? Anyway, he's the patron saint of lawyers. We've been chosen to work with Merlin because of our noble spirit. Isn't it amazing? Xavier really wants to meet you. He thinks you're probably a daughter of Boudicca, doesn't he, Merlin?" he said as Merlin re-entered the room.

"Indeed he does. I know for sure that you are of noble blood, my good lady. Your desire to make a personal fortune is clearly driven by the wrongs you have suffered and the influence of Nemesis." Merlin lowered his head. "Your body still burns with the sting of humiliation, your heart possessed by the desire for retribution, for revenge, but that will pass, Lady Heather. Your true spirit will prevail. Nemesis will seek comfort elsewhere. St. Yves knows this."

Heather looked even more wild-eyed than before. "OK, OK, I have had enough of this, perhaps later, maybe. I get the picture. Just forget for one moment all of this past lives stuff, frigging Nemesis, patron saints and the rest of it, and let me bring you up to date with what's been going on in the real world, yes? I mean, can I have your full twenty-first-century selves in deep-shit mode for one minute, please?"

George and Merlin looked at each other and exchanged signs of relief that Heather was still on talking terms with both of them. George had tried to explain to Merlin that Heather might not be too amused with their digression.

"Right, this is how the land lies, and listen carefully," Heather said as if she was addressing a council of war just before a major battle. "The bidding's up to fifty thousand pounds, that's the

News on Sunday, but they want to meet with Merlin first, before putting their offer formally on the table. They want a response by ten o'clock tomorrow morning. The *Star* will pay twenty but that includes a photo shoot with three 'wenches'. The *Express* and the *Mail* will pay twenty, but they both want an exclusive serialisation option on any book that might be written and the *Sun* will pay fifteen for an interview, but they also want a photo shoot with one of their Page Three girls. The highbrows won't go past ten thousand. There's also some interest in examining Merlin's staff, but those interested all want a written agreement, so that's going to slow things down."

Merlin shook his head, indicating that he didn't understand a word.

George looked disappointed. "How real is the offer from the *News on Sunday*, Heather? Why do they need to meet?"

"They want to know, as they put it, how compos mentis Merlin is right now before they commit themselves. I don't know really, they might be up to something. I can't say I trust them too much; something kinda off about that lot. But what I think we should do is meet them, with Merlin, say as little as possible, and see where we end up. I think the others will be persuaded to go higher, but not by much. I checked your answer machine and there are about four other possibilities from magazines of one kind or another. They'll pay some money – a few thousand – but none of them want to pay for an exclusive."

"Sounds good," said George, not having much to add. "Anything else?"

"Well," said Heather teasingly, "there is some interest from television companies. Channel Six has a live children's programme early on Wednesday morning, Boxing Day. If we turn up at seven thirty in the morning 'ready for action' as they put it, then Merlin will be placed in the studio to take questions from the audience and with a phone-in, you know the kind of thing? It's not a great deal of money – a couple of grand – but it's great exposure."

"How do you feel about that, Merlin?" enquired George.

Merlin looked puzzled. "I answer questions from children, is that it?"

"Yes, Merlin, that's all there is to it. You'll be in a studio, lots of lights, cameras, a small live audience of young children, and they'll ask you questions, that's all."

"I can answer questions, if that is what I need to do," Merlin replied.

"OK," said Heather, "let's roll with Channel Six, meet up with the *News on Sunday* and keep the others on the boil in the meantime. I've still to get the radio side up and running, but that can wait. The important thing is to keep some momentum going and get some real cash in, quickly. I mean, we need offices, a dedicated phone, get online, a photocopier, fax, headed paper—"

"Slow down, Heather, you're making me dizzy," interrupted George. "How soon are we going to need all of this?"

"By the new year, we'll be raking it in," said Heather confidently. "We just need the first serious hit, then we'll be moving, fast. But first I need to sleep, I'm whacked."

Heather scurried to the toilet, leaving Merlin alone with George. Merlin looked relieved, pleased even, but puzzled. "Yes, sleep is a good idea. Your lady works so very hard. But we are doing this for good reasons, are we not, Sir George? I mean, we will not disappoint our good saint, will we?"

It was George's turn to look surprised. "For good reasons? There are millions of good reasons, all of them in pound notes."

Merlin looked deep into George's excited eyes. "I understand about money, my friend. Those in Brickstonia talk of little else, but what are the noble causes that we serve? I cannot have been put on this earth at this time to make a king's ransom to go shopping. There are other reasons, surely. Perhaps St. Yves will reveal to me whether we are to raise an army to free the good souls imprisoned by the forces of evil? Perhaps we are to take arms against the oppressor? Is there a ransom to be paid to liberate those who have been unjustly incarcerated? I am becoming confused, Sir George, and confusion makes me tired."

Heather returned and took a duvet from the cupboard. "OK, gentlemen, if you don't mind, I could really do with some peace."

Merlin cast a glance at George, which George interpreted

as meaning that now was not the time to question Heather's motives. Merlin had opened a moral debate, one that would not go away, and for some reason George's heart sank as he realised what they were doing, and the motto of his esteemed pupil master's ancient family resonated in his mind: '*pas de corps, pas d'ame*', which they had agreed over a bottle of port to be best translated as 'heartless bastards go to hell'.

"Get some sleep, Heather. I need to think," he said.

★　★　★

"OK, we'll see you in Starbucks in Camden Town at noon," said Heather to Ralph Crossley of the *News on Sunday*, "but no cameras and in strict confidence." Heather, even from her brief experience at Pentheus, knew that she should ask for a signed confidentiality letter before the meeting, but knew also that there was insufficient time or resources to complete such a task. It was a chance that had to be taken.

George and Heather needed to talk about money, not possible money or maybe money, but real money. Between them they calculated that they could spend about two thousand pounds before their worlds started to collapse. It was going to be close, and the immediacy of their problems somehow managed to blank out any questioning of their real motives.

George, Merlin, and Heather decided that they should meet with the *News on Sunday* together.

"Well, Merlin, we've no car, so it's a half-hour walk, two stops on the Underground, or a bus ride," George said.

Heather intervened and suggested that a bus ride would be best, to allow Merlin to see some sights of real life, albeit along the litter-strewn streets from Tufnell Park, through Kentish Town down to Camden Town.

Merlin sat on the top deck of the number 134 bus, watching everything, saying nothing, in awe of the bustling activities of the last-minute Christmas shoppers as the bus inched its way through bumper-to-bumper traffic all the way down Kentish Town Road.

George tried to study Merlin's reaction to the world before

him: the cars, buses, bikes, bright lights, the entire pre-Christmas frenzy of it all, wondering whether Merlin would be fazed by the spectacle or even lower his guard and reveal something he might not intend. But what George saw, looking intensely at Merlin's profile as he surveyed the street activity, was a look of such sadness and sorrow George felt obliged to avert his gaze elsewhere, out of respect.

"Right," said Heather as the three of them descended the stairs into the frenzy of the sprawling Camden Market. "First things first. Let's get Merlin kitted out. There are at least two fancy dress shops around here." Soon enough the three of them were standing outside a theatrical clothes shop. In the window were numerous fancy outfits. A full set of magician's robes, the closest to what they were looking for, was displayed proudly in the window.

Merlin stopped in his tracks. "There is something I must tell you, Lady Heather."

Heather feared for the worst and held her breath as she asked what it was that was so important.

"The clothes you wish me to don, such as those," Merlin said, pointing to the purple robe and tall pointed hat decorated with celestial objects of one kind and another, "were never worn by me. They are not the clothes I wish to wear. My friends in Brickstonia teased me about a funny hat. I never wore such a thing; I know some witches who liked that sort of thing. The robe is a fine garment but I don't like the colour; that colour is about wealth, status and power. But the hat? Is it really necessary? I don't like funny hats. Never did."

George and Heather looked at each other with concern. "What would you feel comfortable in, Merlin?" asked George patiently. Merlin looked around at the hundreds of people jostling along the packed pavements and noticed a successful-looking middle-aged man wearing a complete set of black clothes: leather jacket, polo-neck, corduroy trousers and trainers, all black. "That's how I'd like to dress, like that."

"Right, let's do it," George said. "He'll look like a French philosopher, but it's better than the fallen clergyman image."

Well before noon Merlin was kitted out exactly as he wanted. George was quite proud of the overall effect, although the staff that Merlin would not let go of, even in his sleep, appeared slightly incongruous.

Heather had no difficulty in spotting the representatives from the *News on Sunday*. Sitting in the small area cordoned off for smokers, Ralph Crossly and his tarty-looking companion simply oozed gutter journalism.

"Ah, the famous Merlin," said Ralph creepily. "Many congratulations on your glorious victory. You look very, er...*modern*. You must be Heather. We talked on the phone. This is my assistant, Tracy."

"And this is George Winsome," replied Heather abruptly. "Let's talk."

Ralph went on and on about how excited they all were at the *News* to be given such a wonderful opportunity to interview Merlin. "We were all rooting for you, you know," said Ralph without too much conviction. "One right up the arse of the establishment, great stuff. Tracy, get some coffees, please."

It was soon apparent that Ralph had his own agenda, as he leaned forward to Heather and said in a low voice, just above a whisper, "Listen, you don't need to keep up the act with us. If you can tell us the real story about the old boy, then we'll lay fifty on the table and give him a hideaway out of the reach of the law. Anywhere you want. It's got to be your best bet. I mean, for how long can you keep up this Merlin stuff, really?"

Heather lowered her head in disappointment. "So that's your game. I'm sorry, Mr. Crossley, but you're wasting your time – and ours. We're here to negotiate a serious interview, not confess to perjury. You've got Merlin all wrong."

Ralph's mood changed dramatically. "I don't think you understand, my dear. We've been doing our homework. I mean, look at the old boy. He's maybe in his late fifties, early sixties. You've done well to get this far, but don't push it. Our offer is the best you're going to get. Take it or leave it."

"We'll leave it, thank you," said Heather. "Come on, let's go."

As Merlin got up to leave, Tracy tried to hold onto one of the trinkets attached to Merlin's staff. Without warning or rational explanation, one of the still-hot coffees flew across the table onto Tracy's lap, making her scream out in shock and pain.

"Time to go," said George.

"You'll regret this, I promise you," Ralph said, wiping Tracy's coffee-stained dress. "If you don't want to play ball with us, you'll find out the hard way what happens when you try to take the piss out of the great British public."

"Do what you fucking want," Heather said, her voice disarmingly fierce. "The great British public will decide who's taking the piss, you hapless half-breeds."

George, Heather, and Merlin hotfooted it as far away from the café as they could. "What a balls-up," said Heather. "I didn't see that one coming. Shit, back to the drawing board."

George tried to reconcile a quickly fading image of the sweet innocent Heather he once knew with the warlike creature he had just witnessed, but was more concerned about the young girl and the incident with the coffee. "How did you do that, Merlin?"

"Do what?" replied Merlin innocently.

"You know, make the cup fly off the table. That was you, wasn't it?"

"The young lady was trying to remove one of the sacred objects from my staff. I could not allow that to happen, that is all."

"Look, forget about it, George. We need to get back to your place and get back on the case."

"We have made an enemy today, my friends. I have had many enemies. Good people always have enemies, you know," said Merlin as he shook his head.

"Let's just get home and tie up one of the others, while there's still time, OK?" Heather obviously felt responsible for the fiasco and was also concerned as to the possible repercussions of the meeting. "I'm sorry about that, Merlin. They really are the scum of the universe. How we could ever sink so low I just don't know. I'm beginning to understand what you mean, you know, about doing the right thing. That episode has just taught us what the wrong thing is. We are different from them, very different. I suppose I should thank you."

"Not at all," said Merlin. "I could sense their evil, anyone could. I wonder if Loki is up to his old tricks. We have found the right path, and not one moment too early. I feared we were losing our way, but all is well."

CHAPTER TWENTY
Luck

George sat down on his uncomfortable sofa bed, while Merlin sat cross-legged on the floor. "So, what do we do now, Heather? It's Christmas Eve, we've no money, no deals, no jobs. Any ideas?" George was not great company when depressed, as Heather was beginning to realise.

"I want to go back to my flat and get a change of clothes. I can do what I have to do from there. At least I've got a laptop, so I can exchange documents by email if needs be. I'll come back later. I'd prefer to work on my own. Be good. I'll try and ring a bit later. If not, I'll see you before midnight."

And with that, Heather was out the door into the cold ever-darkening early evening, on her way to her private little pad in Islington.

As soon as Heather was gone, an idea came into George's mind. He went into the small back room where the flotsam of his earlier years was chaotically packed away in rotting old suitcases and black bin liners, emerging after some time with a small, stiff black leather pouch neatly containing five poker dice.

"OK, Merlin, let's see what you can do. See these dice?" he said as he rolled the five dice on the floor. "They each have six sides. Look, an ace, a king, a queen, a jack, ten red diamonds and nine black diamonds. It's really a card game, but played with dice. The idea is to get the highest hand you can."

Merlin was amused and enthralled as George rolled the dice again and again, explaining all the while the rules of the game.

"So, you see, Merlin, the highest hand you can get is five of something. Five aces down to five nines. Then four of the same, followed by a full house, as I told you, three of one kind and two of another."

"This is a very amusing game. It would be useful for passing time before a battle or keeping children distracted, my friend, but I fear I don't understand how it will help us."

"Listen, Merlin. I saw what happened in the café. You made that cup fly off the table because you were angry. Your memory has returned, I know, and, I suspect, some of your powers. I think you can, you know, influence the dice, if you put your mind to it. Go on, try, please."

Merlin looked as if he would raise an objection to George's little game, but then, with a twinkle in his eye, said he would play along.

At first nothing seemed to happen. Merlin would stare and stare at the dice as they rolled along the carpet. Each time they landed randomly.

"Try harder, Merlin, I know you can do it," said George impatiently.

Merlin rolled the dice several times, until at last he rolled five aces.

"OK, let's call that luck. This time I want you to will the dice to show five aces," George said.

Merlin rolled again. This time four aces came up, the last being a ten, which eventually rolled to show the ace, as if an invisible finger had gently rolled it into place.

"No, that's not good enough. It looks too obvious. Try harder. It's got to look natural."

Merlin tried again and again. Eventually he was rolling five aces, consistently.

"We're on a winner here, Merlin."

"A winner? How do you mean?" asked Merlin.

"Get your coat on, me old mate, we're off to a casino. I'll explain about roulette on the way." George kissed Merlin's bald head.

★   ★   ★

Heather rang George's doorbell well after midnight, confident that George and Merlin would still be up and awake. She picked up a rather sombre mood in the flat as she walked through the front door.

"What's up, guys? I've got some good news. Why are you looking so glum? What's happened?"

"Er, you're not going to like this, Heather. I've blown all my money." George lowered his head in shame while Merlin sat cross-legged, leaning against the wall, his eyes firmly closed.

"OK, George, spill the beans." Heather was ready for the worst.

"Well, it's like this. Merlin's powers are coming back, believe me. He can do little things, like move a cup or a piece of paper. He can also give little objects, you know, like a ball or a dice, a bit of a push in the right direction, if you know what I mean," said George sheepishly.

"No, I'm not sure what you mean, George."

"Well, like a ball on a roulette table...."

"I think I'm getting the picture. You've lost a bundle at the casino, haven't you?" Heather was not amused. "How much, George, how much?"

There was an embarrassing silence before George blurted out, "About a thousand pounds."

It was Heather's turn to lower her head.

"Oh God, I'm sorry, Heather. We must have been about thirty grand ahead at one point. We got greedy and placed the whole lot on one number, shit or bust."

"And it was bust," Heather said.

"Sure was," replied George while Merlin sniffled loudly in the background.

Merlin broke his silence. "It was all my fault, dearest Heather. I felt I could have continued my winning ways all night, but I made a fatal error. I was not the only one with powers around the table. Three others joined our table, and they all placed their counters on a different number to the one we chose. I was not strong enough to hold the ball; their combined powers were far stronger than mine. It is not a good sign. I fear something is wrong."

"You should have seen it, Heather, the croupier couldn't believe it. The ball lands in our spot, number thirteen, then jumps up into number seven and back again about three times.

Eventually it rests on number seven, we're sitting on thirteen, and we were fucked."

Heather composed herself. "Listen, you idiots, I've been working like a Trojan, hustling like mad while you two piss away money we don't have. Before we go any further you must promise me to stay away from casinos, betting halls, and bookies. OK? No more gambling. We're going to have to do this my way, the hard way. If you can't agree to that then we call it a day."

"Fair enough," muttered George.

"More than fair, my dear lady, more than fair," echoed Merlin.

"Right, now we've got that sorted, let me tell you the good news. The *Express* will pay twenty-two grand. We throw everyone else overboard for now. We give them one week of exclusivity in the printed media, and then we can do what we like. But they expect a lot from you, Merlin. It's a two-hour interview with photographs, but they agree that it's up to us what you wear. The appearance on Channel Six is confirmed. Three thousand pounds. But you must be on the ball. If they think you're not up to it, we get sent packing and we pick up one hundred pounds expenses. I've got other irons in the fire, but most of it is on hold until the brief sober period between Christmas and New Year, which means in reality, Friday morning. Then it's parties until New Year, so we won't get any serious conversations until next Wednesday at the earliest. Jesus, why does everyone need to drink themselves silly at this time of year? It's like an alcoholics' convention that lasts for two weeks."

"Lighten up, Heather, you know what it's like. People are working twelve hours a day out there, one way or another. They need space to chill out, get drunk, and let their hair down. I mean, if we've got a few quid perhaps we could join them?"

Heather looked at George as if he was pushing his luck, which he was, having just blown the money. Heather was now firmly in charge.

"OK, George, tomorrow we have a slap-up Christmas dinner, but nothing too silly or expensive. We'll probably have to eat very early or very late to get a table."

"Don't worry about that. Merlin's still a celebrity. We'll find somewhere decent. I'll try the Ivy. Never know who we might bump into."

"That's what I'm afraid of," said Heather.

CHAPTER TWENTY-ONE
Television

5:15 a.m., Wednesday, 27th December 2000, Tufnell Park.

George, Merlin and Heather were fully dressed and wide awake as they awaited the chauffeur-driven Mercedes, promised by Channel Six, to take Merlin to their studios in Camden Town, situated next to Regent's Canal, which winds its quiet way to Little Venice.

Outside George's flat the sky was dark and overcast, and there was a slight drizzle of rain. George looked at his watch, again.

"Perhaps we should wait outside. The driver will probably think we live upstairs," he suggested impatiently.

"Just be patient, George, he'll be here in a minute. Relax while you can," said Heather. "We'll hear them come to the door, don't worry."

Sure enough, they heard the footsteps approach their door and a confident flapping of the letterbox.

"Right," said George, "we're off. If we've got time I'd like to get some papers on our way, see what's happening."

It was apparent to both George and Heather that Merlin preferred solitude and silence early in the morning. He was sitting peacefully on the floor, kitted out in his black uniform, head and face closely shaved, holding onto his staff tightly as ever.

Even Heather was impressed with the professionalism and courtesy of the driver, who made a great fuss over Merlin and opened the doors of the car for each of them.

"I'll sit in the front. I want to jump out at a newsagent and pick up a couple of papers, OK?" The driver nodded to George and within a few minutes George was frantically turning over the pages of several newspapers, looking for something relating to Merlin.

The *Express* was now feeding teasers to the public, along the lines that an exclusive interview would appear over two days, starting on Saturday. "What time is the *Express* interview again, Heather, remind me?"

"Four o'clock this afternoon, at my place. Let's get this out of the way before we get sidetracked into that one."

George continued flipping over the pages of the day's papers. "Extraordinary, isn't it, Heather? I mean, one day it's all Merlin, Merlin, Merlin, then nothing, nothing at all, as if it never happened. Frightening, really."

"Don't worry, George, it's a sleeper. We need to think long-term. It will happen. I mean, it is happening, don't worry."

The driver pulled into the basement car park of the small steel-clad building that once housed TV-AM before it lost its broadcast licence in the early nineties. He instructed George to take a lift to the ground floor and they would come out inside the building, just opposite the reception area, where someone would be waiting to greet them.

The lift door opened to the sight of a very young-looking professional lady, who introduced herself as Jane. She led the three of them to a makeup area and asked if anyone wanted tea or coffee while Merlin's makeup was done. This made Merlin panic slightly.

"It won't hurt, Merlin, it'll just make you look less, er, less shiny, that's all," said Jane, but Merlin could not be persuaded that it mattered how shiny he looked and he refused to be made-up.

"I've never heard of anything so ridiculous," he moaned.

"OK," said Jane in her bouncy, upbeat, energised tone, "let's just have a tea or coffee and wait for the producer, John Whittam. I know he wants a chat before Merlin goes on air."

"And when do you think that might be, Jane?" George asked as politely as he could.

Jane looked at her watch. "Well, it's five to six. This place will start to get pretty busy in a few minutes. The children's show starts at seven thirty and goes on till nine, and the presenters meet up with the guests, most times, between seven and seven fifteen, you know, just to say hello. John will be with us in a minute and he'll run you through the details. I have to dash. I'll see you in a few minutes. You can sit here, watching the television."

George, Merlin, and Heather quietly and nervously watched the badly dubbed Japanese cartoons that Channel Six broadcast before the live show. It was difficult not to watch the cartoon, as there were four wall-mounted televisions in the room.

Merlin leaned on his staff. "This is a strange village, my friends. Do you think they are perhaps slaves to Kronos? One minute in time means so much to them, it can't be healthy. Perhaps it is because they are all so young in years. Do they watch cartoons all day? They were very popular in Brickstonia, you know. I do like *Tom and Jerry*, although sometimes the violence brings back such bad memories."

George held his peace and waited quietly, enjoying the cartoon, and the time seemed to drift by until three people bounced into the room, all looking very smart, hyper and youthful.

John Whittam, a clean-cut lad in his late twenties, looked considerably older than the two presenters, introduced as Paula and Ali as if they were household names. The six of them sat round the small table in the centre of the room.

"I'm so glad you've come," John said to Merlin. "We're all very excited about you being here. Congratulations, by the way, on your victory. You must be very relieved."

Merlin looked surprisingly shy as the beautifully made-up Paula stroked his staff. "You won't be casting any spells today, will you Merlin?" she asked in a provocative tone. "Our audience is very young, you know."

"Now listen, Merlin," continued John. "Paula and Ali will be on air for a few minutes before they introduce you. All you have to do is sit on the sofa next to them, relax and they'll take you through it. We've got some telephone lines open to the audience and we'll be sifting through them from the control centre and we'll put them through one by one. You just chat with Paula and Ali, then answer the questions that come through. How do you feel about that?"

"I can answer questions, my friend. Yes, I can do that," replied Merlin.

John didn't seem convinced. Ali leaned towards Merlin as if to get a better, closer, look at his guest. "We'll just ask you a few friendly questions, like, 'what was King Arthur really like?', 'What sort of magic do you do?', 'What was Camelot really like?', you know, that sort of thing."

John looked intensely at Merlin, George, and Heather to gauge their reactions.

George decided he had to intervene quickly. "I think you'd better understand that Merlin is not the Merlin of the court of King Arthur and he didn't live in Camelot."

"He didn't?" replied Paula, sounding more surprised than disappointed. "Where did he live?"

"I lived in a tree for many, many years, due to a spell put upon me by a jealous witch. I was born in Scotland, you know. I explained all of this during my ordeal," said Merlin.

It was the turn of John, Paula, and Ali to exchange concerned glances between them.

"My magic takes many forms," continued Merlin, "but I am still a little rusty, as you might say."

Heather picked up that Merlin's appearance was hanging in the balance and took the initiative. "Why don't you ask Merlin about his staff? You might have read that it is thousands of years old. Look, the handle is made of human bone."

Paula failed to suppress a loud "Yuck" and her co-presenter scratched his forehead.

John was quick to keep things moving along. "OK, OK, I know what we'll do. We'll go straight to the questions and keep it short and simple. It'll work, I'm sure it will. Paula, Ali, let's have a quick word outside. Merlin, we'll see you on-air in ten."

As the door closed, George whispered to Heather, "Look, I'm not so sure about this. It's all going to go pear-shaped, I can feel it. Perhaps we should call it a day and get out of here."

"I don't think so, George. Let's stick with it. I'm sure Merlin will be all right, won't you?"

Merlin might have answered, but he was too enthralled in

watching the cartoon to take notice of Heather.

Merlin, Heather and George waited for what felt like an eternity to George before Jane bounded in to the room.

"OK, OK, we're on. Merlin, if you want to come with me. George and Heather, you can watch from the side. You'll find it quite exciting, I'm sure. Come on, Merlin, let's go."

George and Heather had never been to a television studio before and, for some reason, were expecting to see a large theatre-type arena with a huge audience, several roaming cameras, and frantic activity around the set. But as they approached the live studio, they saw only Paula and Ali sitting on one of a couple of sofas in front of a blank blue screen, heavily lit up by large lights to the side, facing two battered-looking mobile cameras. The whole setup looked as if it had taken a few moments to put together, but there was no time for any complaints. Merlin was on one of the sofas and the two presenters on the other. This was live television. Live.

Paula and Ali went through what sounded like a well-rehearsed double-act, looking into whichever camera had a red light above it, in front of which was a transparent rolling autocue, which George could make out from where he was standing: PAULA: 'YOU'VE UNWRAPPED ALL YOUR PRESENTS. YOU'VE HAD ENOUGH TURKEY. YOU COULDN'T EAT ONE MORE TANGERINE, YOU CAN'T FACE WATCHING *THE GREAT ESCAPE*, SO WHY DON'T YOU MEET MERLIN, OUR VERY OWN REAL-LIFE MAGICIAN.'

Paula turned away from the camera and looked at Merlin. "We've all followed your case closely, Merlin, and we've all been fascinated by the trial. Some of our audience would like to ask you some questions." She held her hand to her ear. "We've got Lucy on line two, from Bournemouth. Lucy, what would you like to ask Merlin?"

A little girl's voice was heard as if coming from the back of the room: "I would like to ask Merlin what he used to eat for breakfast when he was my age."

"And how old are you, Lucy?" Ali asked in a patronising voice.

"I'm six and three quarters," squeaked Lucy.

Ali and Paula looked anxiously at Merlin. "Lucy wants to know what you used to eat for breakfast, Merlin. Porridge, perhaps?"

Merlin looked around as if he was looking for the little girl and thought for a moment.

"When I was your age, the first thing I would eat in the morning might be some squirrel stew or maybe a pickled rabbit's heart, if there was any left over from the night before," he said.

"That's disgusting!" said Lucy, and Ali and Paula moved onto the next call.

"OK, we've got James from Glasgow, who's eight years old, on line one. James, what do you want to ask Merlin?"

"Hi, Merlin." There was a worrying pause while James tried to stop giggling.

"Have you ever seen a real battle, with people gettin' killed an' that?"

This time Merlin was quicker off the mark with his response.

"I saw many battles, James. Sometimes I took the form of a crow – or was it a magpie? – and watched from a high tree. But it was not easy to see what was going on, as there was so much blood and guts everywhere, and the cries of the injured were very distracting, you know. Most warriors died a slow painful death. It was only the few who were killed outright with a single blow to their neck or the back of the head. Mostly it was just legs and arms being hacked off, with blood splattering everywhere. It was worse if there were horses. The foot soldiers would try to cut the back of the legs of the horses or ram a pole up their rear. And the sound a horse makes crying out in agony still haunts me, James, truly it does."

By this time both Ali and Paula were looking horrified, holding their hands to their ears, trying to listen to instructions from the control centre.

Next up was a very educated-sounding young lady, Charlotte from St. Albans. "Hello, Merlin. We've been studying medieval history at school. I got an A star for my project." Charlotte paused for some form of applause, but none was coming, everyone being too concerned with what sweet young Charlotte was about to throw at Merlin.

"My project was to imagine what differences a person from the Dark Ages would find in the modern world. What is the biggest difference between now and when you first lived? Does it all seem like magic to you?"

Merlin looked perplexed. "There is less magic now than before, my sweet, wise Charlotte. What I see does not seem very important, princess. There is a great deal of knowledge in this new world, but little wisdom. People in this age use complicated mechanisms without any thought. It seems to make them very impatient and needy, like babies." He looked around him with sadness in his eyes. "I am more entertained staring into an open fire than a screen you call a television. People expect me to be amazed watching an airplane flying on high. Such a sight does not compare to seeing a dragon in full flight. A horse makes a better friend than a motor car, Charlotte, and friends are important."

Ali had already moved on from Charlotte, whom he feared was a tad too smart for her own good. "I think Charlotte's line has gone. Maybe we've got time for just one more question before Merlin has to go or *disappear*," quipped Ali, rather pleased with himself. "Alison, aged seven, from Watford, what question do you have?"

"I would like to know if Merlin's staff can do any magic and where can I buy one?"

Ali and Paula both sighed with relief through their rictus smiles as Merlin picked up his staff.

"Oh, I don't think you'll be able to buy one. You could make one, but you'd have to use a big bone from someone you knew well...."

"Like my granny. I could use part of my granny," suggested Alison.

"Yes, I suppose you could...." Merlin said thoughtfully.

Paula was receiving fierce instructions from the director. "Now, we wouldn't want you digging up your granny, would we, Alison. That wouldn't be very nice, would it?"

"Oh no, Paula, Gran isn't dead yet, but she's having a hip operation and I could use her old one."

"That's a good idea," said Merlin.

"Er, no it's not, Merlin," Ali said, losing his cool. "I don't think we want Granny's old hip bone being used for making walking sticks, Merlin. I don't think so."

Paula noticed a frantic floor technician to her left signaling that there were two minutes left before they would cut to the commercials, and asked Merlin if they could look at his staff.

"Perhaps you could let the camera have a closer look at your staff, Merlin."

Merlin looked around and saw a camera about ten feet away. "Well, of course I could...." he said helpfully, and suddenly the staff took to the air, apparently of its own accord, and flew up to the camera, hovered for a moment and then returned to Merlin.

"Was that close enough?" asked Merlin with a smile.

Paula and Ali noticed a light at the back of the room change from red to green, indicating that they were no longer on-air, and fell back in their chairs with relief.

"Fuck me, that was close," said Paula. "Don't ever put me through that crap again. I couldn't take it." She looked towards the director's control centre at the back of the room. "Not a bad trick at the end, Merlin, seen better, though. But all that shit about arms and legs and poles being rammed up the arses of screaming horses, I mean we really didn't need that detail."

Merlin looked at Paula as if she had been suddenly transformed into an old crone.

"Time for us to leave," said Heather sharply. "Come on, let's go."

Merlin, George, and Heather did not wait to see John, who was engaged in a furious argument with the director. They fled the building as quickly as they could and walked briskly north in the direction of Tufnell Park.

Heather was the first to break the silence.

"Oh God, what have we done? Shit, we'll really need to get our act together. What a balls-up."

"Oh, come on, Heather. It wasn't that bad."

Heather came to an abrupt halt and looked George firmly in the eye.

"Wasn't that bad? Are you off yer head? Channel Six will

be hauled over the coals by the ITC for broadcasting material offensive to children. The compliance officer at Channel Six will be fending off complaints for the next three days, and we'll be lucky if we ever see the inside of a TV studio again. Jesus, what a mess."

"She was a strange girl, that Paula. Very strange," added Merlin.

There was no stopping Heather now. "The only strange thing about all of that was your performance, Merlin. Let's get straight to my flat and work out what we're doing this afternoon. We must be more professional about this, George. We can't leave things to chance like we did, otherwise we'll be finished within days."

Merlin strode ahead with his staff, walking with a slight swagger.

"Well, I thought I was rather good, my dearest Heather. It's been a while since I could move my staff around with such ease. I am indeed regaining my strength."

"Christ," Heather said to George, "this is going to be hard work."

George increased his pace to catch up with Merlin.

"Listen, Merlin. It was your first appearance on TV. We're still standing. Now, tell me, how did you do that thing with your staff? That's the sort of stuff we need to work on."

CHAPTER TWENTY-TWO
Truth

10 a.m., Wednesday, 27th December 2000, Flat C, 24 Green Way, Islington.

Heather's flat was in stark contrast to George's. It was tidier, and more expensive-looking, a deceptive impression attributable to the fact that Heather enjoyed scouring markets and charity shops for cheap items that pleased her eye. It was, as she often referred to it, a "haven of peace – a private sanctuary." Being a second-floor apartment with neighbours upstairs, downstairs and to one side meant that peace and quiet was paramount, a rule that Heather was happy to abide by, and enforce.

George, Merlin and Heather walked up the single flight of communal stairs and rolled through her private front door, not one word having passed Heather's lips since Camden Town. George spotted the well-worn two-seated white leather sofa and settled in one corner, while Merlin sniffed around like a dog in a new home and found his patch on the floor, against the wall.

"Don't get too comfy," said Heather menacingly. "It's ten o'clock and we've got the bid interview this afternoon at four. They're coming here, remember. Let's sit in the kitchen and work out our game plan."

George and Merlin reluctantly unsettled themselves and sat around the small kitchen table, as requested, while Heather made some tea.

"OK," Heather said, "it's time for the truth. We cannot hack it out any longer. Merlin, I want to know exactly what powers you have or don't have. I want to know where you come from and I want to know now."

George was quite content for Heather to take the reins, for

this session at least, and looked at Merlin, smiling. "Lady Heather wants to know, Merlin."

Heather got into her stride. "Right, I remember the incident in Starbucks with the coffee, and I know what I saw earlier this morning. OK, Merlin, move your staff around without touching it."

George sensed danger and tried to intervene. "No, Heather, it's not going to work like that. Merlin needs to be angry or worked up, you can't just ask him to perform tricks like a dog. He's not some kind of professional illusionist, like David Copperfield."

Merlin, however, needed no baiting. His staff rose into the air, a full four feet off the ground, and remained there, motionless.

Heather grabbed the staff, pulled on it, and was surprised that she could overcome Merlin's willpower.

Merlin bowed his head. "You see, I have remembered how to control my staff, but it is a very weak force. I could do better when I was a babe in arms. You have exposed me, I am sorry."

"Not at all, Merlin," said Heather, trying to disguise her wonder. "The point is that floating sticks will get us a few bookings at children's parties, but it's not going to make you – or us – very rich. What else can you do? I mean, is that it? Can you move other objects other than your staff?"

George knew it was best to keep quiet while Merlin looked around the room before his eyes settled on a remote control for the small, wall-mounted television. Merlin looked at the object with some intensity, and it rose and circled the room. The small buttons were activated and the television sparked into life, making Merlin laugh playfully. Heather snatched the remote out of the air and placed it back on the kitchen worktop.

"OK, I've got the picture. Telekinesis." She looked around the room. "What's the heaviest object you can raise, Merlin?"

Merlin took his time and spotted an old-fashioned upright vacuum cleaner. It rose a few inches and then fell to the floor. "That machine tests my strength to its limits, my friends."

Heather tried to think rationally. "OK, if you have the mind power to move objects, what else can you do with your mind?"

Merlin looked uneasy and concerned.

"What are you thinking, Heather?" asked George. "You want him to bend some spoons?"

"Well, maybe later. Let's concentrate on what Merlin can do that we can't, apart from bending spoons, which isn't very original or interesting. I know...." She rearranged two chairs and placed Merlin and George back to back. "Don't move, give me one minute," she said excitedly.

"OK, here's a blank piece of paper for you, George, and one for you, Merlin. And one pencil each. Now George, I want you to draw something, you know, something unusual, not a boat or a plane or a house, something simple but unusual. OK?"

George quite liked the idea of the game and quickly drew a simple-looking cup.

Heather looked at it and asked Merlin if he could draw whatever George had just drawn. Merlin closed his eyes in concentration and drew an object, his eyes still closed.

Heather anxiously compared the two drawings. They were both definitely cups, but different types.

"Right, let's do that again. This time, George, try something really unusual and distinctive."

George drew a spiral, around which were three stars.

Merlin then drew a spiral, not exactly the same as George's, but undeniably a spiral. And there were three stars, but not where George had placed his.

"Now this is interesting," said Heather.

"But not very fruitful, my friend," said Merlin. "Sir George and I have a special relationship. I love him as deeply as a man loves his brother's child, you know. I could not perform such a task with anyone. There is Xavier, of course, but this is not a test of my powers, but a test of my friendship with Sir George. Surely people would presume, would they not, that we have colluded?"

"Er, they might, Merlin, but if someone else chose the object, which I then drew, then it would be more interesting," George said.

"I think Merlin's right," said Heather. "It would look too contrived. We could introduce an element of randomness, but we would need to experiment beforehand. OK, let's move on.

Merlin, you said in the television studio earlier that you watched a battle in the form of a crow. Can you do that?" She tried not to sound too excited.

"You mean turn into a crow, right now?" asked Merlin innocently.

"Right now, Merlin," said George and Heather simultaneously.

"I'll try," said Merlin as he closed his eyes and breathed deeply.

George and Heather watched and waited with bated breath. The seconds ticked by and nothing happened.

Merlin opened his eyes. "Such a process requires great skill. I am not ready, not ready," he said almost shamefully. "Xavier's very good at that one, you know."

"Xavier's another matter, Merlin. At this point in time it's you we need to concentrate upon. Now think, what can you do that would really impress a journalist? I mean, we've got a bit of telekinesis, and some localised telepathy, but there must be something else that would really freak out a journalist, surely?"

The three of them sat in silence, sipping their cups of tea.

"I know," said Merlin, "I can see people."

"What do you mean, 'see people'? Like you can see people in this room who we can't see?" George asked.

"No, no, my dear friend. I mean I can see *into* people. I can look at someone, or better still hold their hand, and their whole life flashes into my mind. It is very distracting, you know, and not very pleasant sometimes. I used to be able to see their futures as well as their pasts, but that is more difficult, and not always accurate. And many people are unaware of the influence of others in their lives, particularly desires driven by anger and a thirst for revenge." Merlin gave Heather a long look.

George and Heather looked at each other, knowing there was only one way to proceed.

"OK, Merlin, I'll go first," said George.

"No, it should be me. Merlin might just be reading your mind, as he did with the drawing. Besides, I expect he's already seen your past," said Heather, clocking a sly grin on Merlin's face. "Try it with me, Merlin."

Merlin outstretched his hand and held onto Heather's, and

closed his eyes. After a few seconds, he smiled, and then looked sorrowful, and opened his eyes, now full of tears.

Heather burst into tears. "Oh God, I didn't see that coming." She continued to sob uncontrollably.

Merlin looked at George. "Heather had a brother, called Simon, who died when he was three years old. Heather must have been about seven. He died in an accident, in water."

"OK, OK, Merlin, that's enough, please," implored Heather, trying to regain her composure. "We went on holiday when I was very young, to the Lake District. I was supposed to be looking after my younger brother. I dared him to go into the lake. I thought he would just get his shoes wet. He fell over. It wasn't my fault. It all happened so quickly. I tried to get him but he just went under. Oh God, I haven't thought about Simon for years. My little sister was only a baby. She grew up hearing that I had killed her brother."

George placed Heather's head on his shoulder. "Let's leave it there for just now, shall we? I think we've gone far enough today."

"No, George, I want to go on. I want to know all about Merlin. I want to know his past, in detail."

"Only if you're ready to go on, Heather," said George.

"I am ready, George. I really am. What's the time? Shit, half twelve. We've got a lot to get through before four."

*　*　*

Simon Hall at the *News on Sunday* was not in a great mood, but he rarely was on Wednesday, with only two days to go before hard decisions had to be made as to what was in and what was out of the forthcoming Sunday edition of the *News*. The presses had to start rolling on the features by Thursday, and the latest he could hold the printing for the main paper was Friday evening.

"OK, Ralph, what have we got on Merlin? The story will be dead by next week, so this Sunday is our last chance to stick it up him. You met up with the old boy on Monday, sounded like a fuckup all round. You didn't even get one hair to analyse," Simon said angrily.

"He's nearly fucking bald, Simon. Looks like some Left-Bank nouveau pop-philosopher." Ralph looked around with some concern, worried that he had inadvertently disclosed his guilty pleasure of French philosophy, and quickly reverted to the Ralph that Simon knew. "Was I supposed to stick my hands between his legs and steal a pube? I mean, give me a break, Simon."

Simon paused as if he was giving serious consideration to Ralph's idea. "What about the saliva from the cup? Anything come up?"

"I told you, Simon, his cup went flying all over Tracy. There was nothing left to give to forensics. Not even a print from the tea cup. We've got a good line on the judge's son, though."

"Yeah, OK, Ralph, but where does that leave us with Merlin? A story about a dope-smoking son of a judge is hardly news anymore, even if he's caught dealing bang to rights."

"Well," said Ralph, "we know where the old boy's staying, with his barrister, that George Winsome guy, who was also there on Wednesday. And there's a lady in the frame as well, Heather Armstrong. Apparently, she's also a barrister who was booted out of Pentheus Publishing and is now holding herself out as a kind of agent-manager. She was the one doing all the running when we met."

"Yeah, OK," said Simon. "But where's the story?"

"Well," said Ralph, thinking hard. "We could make enquiries from the Bar Council as to whether this sort of behaviour is consistent with the high standards we expect from barristers, you know, spin that one. I mean what the fuck is he doing representing someone in court as his learned counsel one minute and acting as his personal representative the next?"

Simon interjected, "Wait a minute, Ralph. What exactly did he say he was doing at the meeting? I mean did he actually say he was Merlin's lawyer?"

Ralph looked sheepishly in the general direction of the coffee-stained carpet, signaling to Simon, as he had on many occasions previously, that he was skating on thin ice.

"Well, I don't recall him saying much on that score, Simon. But he was there, wasn't he? I mean, he wasn't his valet or whatever. I think we're entitled to presume, let's say, that he was there in a legal capacity. He didn't say he *wasn't* his lawyer." Ralph gave his best evil grin. "Perhaps if we make a formal complaint, that'll stir things up. We can get the legal department to draft the letter. And as for Merlin, well, we didn't get a sample, but we sure as hell had the opportunity, so let's imagine we did get a little DNA from somewhere. Let's imagine a little further that the sample proved Merlin was about fifty years old and then we can ask our dear readers if anyone knows his real name. If we come up trumps we can stick it to him, if we don't, we just drop it and no one will remember in a week's time what we were going on about."

Simon paused to think for a moment. "OK, I can just about see a story. Keep digging, Ralph. We need just a little more spice to add to the pot."

"Thanks, Simon. I'll see what I can do."

★   ★   ★

Heather leaned against her front door and sighed heavily. "Well, I think we gave them their money's worth."

Merlin sat on the floor, leaned his back against the wall, clearly exhausted, closed his eyes and appeared to fall into an immediate and deep sleep.

"I'm going to be the first down the newsagent on Sunday morning. Hope the pictures look good. Heather, you're an absolute star. Without all the pain of the afternoon we would never have given them such a great story. I can't wait for the weekend. It will really turn this around, big time," said George. Any attempt at hiding his excitement had been completely thrown away.

"Look, it's still only eight o'clock. Why don't we celebrate? We get the check next week," he suggested, optimistically.

"Celebrate? Are you joking? Merlin's going to be out for the count until tomorrow," replied Heather.

"I don't think so. The old boy will be up and about within a couple of hours, I'll bet."

"And then what? I hope you're not thinking of a casino. Are you, George?"

"Well, not unless we feel like it later. Let's wait until Merlin's batteries are recharged and then go out. When was the last time you went dancing?"

"Dancing? In my delicate condition?" joked Heather.

"Yeah." George sensed that Heather was warming to the idea. "Let's have a drink down the West End, have something to eat, and then see if we've got any energy left for Stringfellows, then review the casino option. What do you say, Heather? It's been a pretty emotional day."

"It sure has. Yes, why not? I'll have a bath and then let's paint the town red."

"Like the old days, Heather, just like the old days," said George, not noticing the broad grin on Merlin's face.

CHAPTER TWENTY-THREE
Reality

10 a.m., Wednesday, 3rd January 2001, Flat C, 24 Green Way, Islington.

Heather sat at her little kitchen, enjoying the silence that she knew would not last long. George was still asleep, as he had been since the day before. In fact, Heather worked out that George had been asleep for just over twenty-four hours. Merlin had risen before dawn and had taken off on his own for the first time, to watch the dawn over Hampstead Heath. Heather sipped her coffee and smiled, trying to take in all that had happened over the previous few days and wondering just how long it would take her to get through the two hundred and eighty unread emails, which were growing in number by the minute.

George walked bleary eyed into the kitchen, wearing his jeans and an old baggy T-shirt belonging to Heather.

"What time is it? Shit, what *day* is it? Where's Merlin?"

"It's ten o'clock – in the morning. Today is Wednesday, the third of January and the year is 2001." Heather waited for the inevitable reaction.

"Wednesday! What happened to Monday? And Tuesday? Did you say 2001?"

"George, ever since we went out last Wednesday to that disco and then the casino, we've been going to parties ever since. Does the Saturday piece in the *Express* ring a bell? So, we went out to celebrate again. The New Year's party that we ended up in – don't ask me where – took us through Sunday night. You remember after the piece in the *News on Sunday* we decided to drown our sorrows, and we got home about seven in the morning, and we've slept ever since. Welcome back to reality, the party's over. It's time to take stock and get back to work. Merlin, by the way, headed off this morning, before dawn. I heard him say that he was off to catch the rising sun over Hampstead Heath. I wouldn't worry about him, he'll turn up soon enough. Let's just enjoy some quiet time together. It won't last, believe me. As I said, it's time to take stock. Why don't you have a bath? You'd look better for a shave. Drink some coffee, then we can have a serious conversation."

"Sure. You're right." George stifled a yawn, felt some serious stubble on his face, and redirected himself towards the bathroom.

★ ★ ★

George sat down opposite Heather looking, and feeling, surprisingly alert. In front of Heather was a mountain of newspapers, going back several days.

"Back in the land of the living, eh, George? Are you ready?"

"Sure, I'm ready. Fire away."

"Right, let's look at what's happened since last week. Let's start with the aftermath of the Channel Six fiasco."

"No, need for that. I remember the stink in the papers, and the on-air apology that Channel Six was forced to broadcast. Fast forward till Saturday." George was enjoying the challenge of piecing together the previous few days.

"OK, here's the *Express* piece. Take a sober look," Heather said in a very professional tone.

George reread the two-page spread in the Saturday edition of the *Express*. Yes, he remembered it, vaguely. It was great. Merlin had provided the *Express* journalist with enough material to write thousands of words, and there was hardly a negative word written. Merlin's story was pieced together in a way only a sharp journalist could manage with a long introduction covering the trial and a separate piece about the staff, promising the results of a forensic examination later. There was a whole column dedicated to Merlin's life story, going back thousands of years. Three theories were explored in little boxes under headings of 'Reincarnation', 'Genetic Memory', and 'Cosmic Synchronicity'. George tried to read the story in the cold light of day, as if he was reading it for the first time, as an objective reader.

"Still sounds a bit wacky to me," he said. "So, he's first born into a warrior clan in northern Scotland, about two or three thousand years after the last ice age. He has special spiritual powers, recognised while very young. He describes his mother as a princess from Scandinavia but he is told that his father was not of an earthly form and was thought to be an angel. Sounds good! Right, moving on...." George tried to contain himself, not knowing whether to laugh or cry. "So, then there's a bit of a gap. He's reborn, but this time it's the early fourth century. His father is a warrior and his mother a queen, but we're still in Scotland. When he's still young, he travels south and lives most of his life as a hermit in a forest, probably situated on the west coast of Scotland, near the English border. Maybe as far south as Wales. Hmm, so far so good. Another gap and he's reborn for a third time, this time in the aftermath and confusion of post-Roman occupation, during the struggle between the various factions fighting it out for control over Britain. He's on the side of the Britons, a group from Brittany who came from the south but unified the north-westerly part of France, Cornwall, and parts of the British coast as far north as Iona. There's a great battle, but he's on the losing side, with many of his closest friends whom he loved as his family being savagely slaughtered, and goes mad with grief. He returns to the forest, where he falls in love with a witch who steals his powers and imprisons him in a tree. Next episode, we know. He wakes up on Hampstead Heath and we're in the present. So, fundamentally they're saying this is Merlin's fourth life on earth. Sounds OK to me." George laughed nervously. "I see they got your email address correctly stated. Bet that helped. What's the bit about the staff again? I thought we would keep that for the broadsheet papers?"

"For a lawyer you've got a memory like a sieve, George. Remember the episode with the journalist from the *Express* after the interview was over? At that point, we thought they would slaughter us?"

"Er, vaguely, go on," said George meekly.

"You must remember, George. The young lady and the photographer were about to leave. Merlin held her hand. He peered into her eyes for some time then she burst into tears. Merlin took her into the kitchen for a quiet chat and, after she composed herself, she returned and left. Now that bit of the story I still haven't got out of Merlin. He said he had promised not to tell anyone. There's no mention of the episode in the paper."

"Oh, yes, that's right," said George. "OK, then there's Sunday." George shuffled through the papers and retrieved the Sunday edition of the *News on Sunday* and looked again at the front-page headline: *EXCLUSIVE: Merlin the Fraud: see pages 8, 9 and 13.* George reread the piece again, having managed to bury the detail in the back of his mind. "Jesus, they really went to town on him. How the hell did they get a DNA sample? Forty-eight years old? What?" George read further into the article. "They're not very nice about you, are they? Bit unfair to call you a 'failed barrister booted out of Pentheus during a minor reshuffle'. No mention of me, as far as I recall, that's a result," he said optimistically.

"You haven't got to page thirteen, yet, obviously."

George carried on reading and quickly turned over the page where his eyes fixed upon the strap-line: *George Winsome: The Facts*, and remembered the sinking feeling he first felt some days ago before he managed to blot it all out with copious amounts of alcohol.

"Oh, Christ!" blurted George. "I was rather hoping that bit was all a bad dream."

"'Fraid not, George. Take a good look and see how you feel now."

George read through the five columns of space dedicated to painting George as a third-rate lawyer, from a third-rate set of chambers, who had no practice to speak of except for Merlin, who had left the Bar to become Merlin's personal lawyer, working with his 'common-law wife', Heather Armstrong. The paper made great play on the fact that 'formal complaints have been submitted to the General Council of the Bar, who are likely to disbar the young lawyer for numerous serious breaches of the

Bar Code of Conduct'. There was a short but vicious reference to George's late father, referring to him as an 'over-ambitious door-to-door insurance salesman who couldn't take the pressures of modern-day corporate life'. The piece ended dramatically with a request to contact the 'Merlin Hot Line' if anyone could shed light on Merlin's real past.

George placed his head in his hands and wept. How could they dig up the death of his father in such a callous manner? *What sort of people are they?* he wondered. He pondered for a moment whether he could take any action against them before accepting that, although the piece was unfair in its selection of facts, it was all essentially true, except for the liberty they had taken when they described him as Merlin's personal lawyer, and Heather as his common-law wife. And, rightly or wrongly, English law provided no protection to the reputation of the dead.

"Well, what are we going to do now, Heather? At least there's no letter yet from the Bar Council. I suppose they're still counting the rules I'm supposed to have broken. I thought we had that one covered. I guess I was wrong not to see how far they would go. Looks like we're the ones in deep shit." Not for the first time in his life, George lowered his head in despair.

"Well, not that deep, George," purred Heather.

"Oh, there's some good news, is there? Please tell me before I jump out of the window." George held his head in his hands, feeling very sorry for himself.

"I renegotiated the fee from the *Express* up to thirty thousand pounds, in return for them to have the staff forensically examined. The results should be through next week sometime. The check was in the post this morning. Look, they even remembered to make the check out in my name. Don't worry, George, I'm not about to run off, I've nowhere to go. And then there's the cash from the casino, Wednesday night. Must be over ten thousand, mostly in fifties. We spent some of it, but not much. Just as well we left the casino when we did. I thought the bouncers were going to throw us out, you know, when they began to suspect Merlin was messing with the roulette ball. That trick is well and truly up. But listen, I've been looking through my emails this morning. We're in good shape. Nobody likes the *News on Sunday*, so the other papers are taking our side. It's great. We've got several leads to take and meetings to attend. My suggestion is that we think long-term from now on. It'll mean a bit of a lull, but in a few months' time, there'll be a documentary going out on the Discovery Channel and a book tie-in. Those two projects will get us about one hundred grand up-front, and more to follow if the programme gets sold overseas. The book will take some time to earn out the advance, but it might make us a bundle in the long run. We'll be all right, if we play this smart, George, believe me. And I haven't told you the best bit."

"The best bit? Please tell all, Heather."

"The best bit, George, is this," said Heather, showing George an email on her laptop. "It's an invitation from the private secretary to Prince Charles, to see him at Highgrove. Yes, our future king wants to meet Merlin. Says 'they've got a lot to talk about'."

George took a long slug of the lukewarm coffee.

"Prince Charles. Sounds interesting. But where does that take us? I mean he's not going to put his hands in his pockets, is he? What's in it for us, I mean Merlin? No I don't, I mean us. You know what I mean, Heather, where does the check come from?"

Heather looked lovingly into George's eyes. "You're hard work, George. You're right, the Prince of Wales isn't going to pay us any money, not directly. But if we get our dear Prince to maybe endorse the book, or be interviewed for the documentary, or agree to be photographed with our dear Merlin, then not only will he be more in demand, but I can charge three times as much for his appearance fee. If I accepted every invitation I received by email, Merlin would be busy for several months. There's already invitations to Christmas parties – 2001, that is!"

"So, this really is our fate together, Heather. I suppose I must contact Three Harcourt Square and let them know that I won't be coming back. I mean, they won't have noticed me going AWOL for a few days, but if I don't show my face next week, I'll have Paul Styles on the phone asking me what's going on. I didn't give him a precise date when I would turn up, but I certainly left him with the impression it would be a matter of days, not weeks."

Heather noticed that George was quite sad at the idea of formally resigning from chambers and made a suggestion. "George, I'm not sure if you're really ready to burn your bridges with the Bar. Why should you? We haven't yet received a formal complaint, and maybe it's just a wind-up. They're lying through their teeth about you acting as Merlin's lawyer, and they know it. Let's see what happens. In the meantime, why don't you write to M.B. and say that you want to take some time out – I don't know – call it paternity leave, you know, buy some time till the birth of the baby. That way you keep your options open, and you can reassess the position in June, after the birth. Enjoy some *freedom*. What do you think?"

George tried to hide the fact that he had completely forgotten about the baby, but Heather was ahead of him and smiled.

"Yes, George. That's one fact that you can't forget. I don't think the penny has quite dropped yet. Come July, you'll be a father."

"A father. That's an awesome idea. I suppose I should make an honest woman out of you, my dearest."

"I didn't expect you to get on a bended knee, George, and suppose that's the closest to romance you're going to get. So, if that was a proposal of marriage, I might have to say yes. Yes, George, I want to get married, but only if you really want to and only if you really love me."

George looked into Heather's eyes and felt such love that tears started to flow down his cheeks. "Of course I want to, and yes, I love you."

George and Heather hugged and kissed, only to be disturbed by the doorbell, causing them both to pull away, laughing.

"Bet I know who that is," said George.

"Bet I do as well," said Heather.

CHAPTER TWENTY-FOUR
Nemesis

Sunday, 7th January 2001, The Haven, Belsize Park.

Xavier's place reminded Heather of a cottage in Wales she had been to on holiday as a child. From the outside, the small, detached dwelling, tucked away in a quiet corner far away from the busy main road, looked at odds with the grander terraced houses and purpose-built flats common to the Belsize Park area of North London, down the hill from Hampstead. Standing alone, with a lovingly maintained small front garden, the house gave the impression that it had miraculously survived the widespread destruction of a long-gone age of quaint little houses dotted irregularly in isolated fields. It seemed strange to Heather that there was no street number on the outside of the front door, only a small wooden plaque with the neatly carved words 'The Haven'. There was no sign of any doorbell.

Merlin pulled open the small wooden garden gate, which made a soft little clanging sound when it was closed by Heather, who reluctantly followed Merlin and George towards the light-blue front door.

Xavier appeared, his towering figure standing at least a foot taller than the front door, and welcomed the three of them to his 'little home'.

Inside, the overwhelming smell was of wood – ancient oak beams and floorboards, pine furniture, endless rows of hardwood bookshelves, beech worktops and ash blinds. The magnificent fireplace, in which large dry logs crackled and smouldered, dominated the large front room. Heather shared George's sense of peace as she sank into a large soft easy chair near the fire.

The room felt almost crowded with the four of them –

George, Heather, Xavier, and Merlin – all sitting around the fire in an awkward semicircle, each in their own soft chair of different colours, shapes and sizes.

"Would you rather we sit on the floor?" Xavier asked Heather politely, as if to break the ice.

"No, no, I'm fine where I am, thank you, Xavier," replied Heather, feeling very self-conscious. "It's a wonderful house you have. It must be very old. All that's missing is a thatched roof."

"It did have a thatched roof until the early sixties, and then the local council declared it was a fire hazard and insisted the thatch be replaced with tiles. I preferred it as it was."

George resisted the temptation to make any stupid remark or comment, knowing full well that Heather was one wrong word away from walking out of Xavier's house. George had taken many hours to persuade her to join him and Merlin to talk with Xavier. Merlin had insisted that his 'close friend', St. Yves, needed to communicate with George and Heather, to reveal Merlin's purpose. Heather was adamant that she could do without such nonsense, but George had been equally forceful that if they didn't go along with the session, they might never see Merlin again.

Besides, George had been notified by the General Council of the Bar that a three-day disciplinary hearing would take place during the legal recess in August to decide whether he was guilty of serious professional misconduct or not. In the meantime, he was under a suspension from practising law under any circumstances. The Bar had several witnesses lined up including George's own head of chambers, who intended to give evidence that George had confessed to taking 'highly sensitive instructions without the involvement or authority of his instructing solicitor'. George had been informed that M.B. had already provided a damning statement to the tribunal, and had agreed to not accept the position of Chair of the Bar Council until the matter had been resolved.

Bearing in mind the other alleged breaches of the barristers' Code of Conduct, George felt pessimistic about defending his cause with any success. Heather had escaped the attentions of the Bar Council, partly because she was not in their eyes worthy of disciplinary attention as she was not practising from chambers and partly, Heather and George reasoned, because she had not held herself out as Merlin's lawyer, and was therefore acting outside her professional code of conduct. The twist that the *News on Sunday* had put on George's involvement was devastating. The fact was, for whatever reasons, George was the target of their professional body and not Heather.

"Do you mind if I smoke, Heather?" Xavier asked. "I will resist the temptation if the smoke annoys you."

Heather patted her still-flat stomach. "I don't expect to be here long enough for the smoke to annoy me or my baby, Xavier. Please go ahead."

Xavier took a small pipe from the mantelpiece, plucked a slender piece of wood from the fire and puffed and puffed until the pipe was well and truly lit.

"This is a very important day, my friends," Xavier said solemnly as if addressing a small committee. "Merlin has been told by St. Yves why he is here, is that not correct, Merlin?"

Merlin was staring intensely into the flames and it felt to George like some time passed before he decided to speak.

"Yes, indeed, Xavier. The last time I came here the spirit of St. Yves visited me. He was very concerned."

Heather could not hold back the urge to interrupt. "May I ask, Merlin, why this St. Yves cannot attend this meeting and tell us himself why you are here?"

"That is a fair question, my dearest Heather, very fair. You see, St. Yves left this earth nearly seven hundred years ago. He is a great and pure spirit, one of the very few who form the Great Council. He has earned the right not to come back to what he called the 'ruined palace', having been absolved from all further earthly duties. There is no reason for him to make his presence felt on this earth except to me, and others who are sufficiently pure in heart to hear him."

Xavier took another puff from the pipe and looked at George and Heather to gauge their reactions to Merlin's story.

"St. Yves is with us, Lady Heather, in spirit, but I am afraid neither you nor Sir George will be able to see him for some time." Merlin lowered his head apologetically. "You may never see him, but he may make his presence felt."

George too lowered his head, fearing he knew exactly what Merlin meant.

"OK," said George. "I get the picture. It makes sense, kind of. So, why are you here, Merlin? Is there a task you must fulfil or perhaps stop something happening? And what's it got to do with me and Heather?"

Merlin was looking at Xavier, who gave him a distinct nod.

Merlin turned towards George and said in a reverential, soft voice, "Your father was a very honourable man, George. He placed the interests of his friends before himself, before his own family, and that is a sign of noble blood. Since St. Yves left this world, with the passing of nearly seven hundred years, there have been only a handful of lawyers who have reached the attention of the Great Council. There have been many false hopes, but the temptations of power and fortune overwhelm even the most promising of those who have the potential to do truly noble and pure deeds. Many start their lives with the very best of intentions until a moment arrives when they make the wrong decision, take the wrong path and they are then forever lost. It is very saddening to witness."

By now Heather was listening very seriously to Merlin. "And so, where does George come into play?"

Merlin turned his attention to Heather. "It is about both you and George, dearest Heather. It is the will of the Great Council, as expressed through St. Yves, that I save your souls. They believe that you are both capable of great and noble actions and it sorrows them too much to witness you falling to the temptation of fame and fortune and dealing with men dedicated to evil. I was chosen to be your guide, the saviour of your souls, that much I know. But St. Yves now has his doubts as to whether you and George were the right choice. I am beginning to doubt whether I was the right guide for you. Maybe that is the fault. St. Yves now argues that because the trial has made me famous — which was not foreseen — you now see the possibility of swimming in riches gained from my name and this distraction has overcome your ancestral nobility. You have allowed Nemesis into your heart and seek only revenge, retribution, and common wealth for selfish ends. It is all too common, I'm afraid."

Heather sat upright, no longer able to contain herself. "This is a fine story, but I still don't get it. I mean, *who are you*? What has this St. Yves guy got to do with you? And *save our souls*, like for what? We're not doing anything wrong, are we? I mean, wanting to make it in life isn't a sin of some kind. You've lost me." Heather placed her arms across her chest and looked at Merlin sternly. She seemed quite angry when she realised Xavier was having a quiet giggle.

Xavier tapped out the ashen contents of his pipe by the fire and looked towards Heather.

"Merlin has not told you the whole story yet. Merlin, please, if you will."

Merlin closed his eyes and breathed deeply. "I have told you many times, I have had many lives. This is the fourth life I remember. I suspect there are more. A long time ago an evil, jealous sorceress imprisoned me in a tree. Her name was Nimue, one of the damsels of the lake to be found at the Fountain of Barenton, near the resting place of St. Yves. But as time passed the spell became weaker. I was awoken by the natural waves of the kosmos, as I have been since. Only now has my soul returned to this earthly form. I have some time left before I leave, not long, and St. Yves insists that it is my final duty to do some good on this earth before I take my place on the Great Council. Many great people started their lives in law; it was thought you and George were the right choice for me. My challenge, my purpose is to make you both see the good that you can do, and to appreciate the powers you could have. The three of you can help change the world, if you only remembered the good you intended to do at the beginning, a quality common to both of you, and is the basis of your love for each other. There are so few good people left; it is a great concern of the Council."

"The three of us?" enquired Heather.

"Yes," said Merlin, looking at Heather's tummy, smiling, "the three of you."

They sat quietly for a few moments before Heather could hold her peace no longer.

"I am afraid you have the wrong person. I don't think my soul needs saving, thank you all the same. And I could never, ever, imagine putting another human being before my child. No one. Not even George. And I see no wrong in wanting to live in a safe and warm house, a big one, in a safe area. And a child's education these days costs a fortune. If you think that I would sacrifice my child's well-being under any circumstances, for another person, fuck it, for a whole country, for an entire race, I would not, ever."

Xavier smiled while George looked somewhat saddened by Heather's outburst.

"You would be quite shocked at the amount of money I make, Heather," said Xavier. "The more I charge, the busier I become. I have a two-year waiting list of clients who wish to pay me hundreds, sometimes thousands of pounds an hour. I eat simply, but well. My greatest daily joy is to bathe in the ponds, under the moonlight. It costs nothing. I sit on the top of Kite Hill watching the sunrise, and it costs nothing. Zena and I spend time together, embracing, it costs nothing. Most of the money I make goes to worthy causes I hear about from my clients and friends, or sometimes I hear about misfortunes from the newspapers. The point is that the achievement of your dreams and the protection of your family does not mean you have to sell your integrity. You merely have to make the right decisions and live with an open heart. There is so much to learn, it is a joy to be alive."

Heather wanted to respond, to argue that the issue in her mind came down to priorities, but George's tears stopped the conversation in its tracks.

"Why, Sir George, you shed tears. What is the cause of your pain?" Merlin asked.

George looked up, making no effort to hide his sadness. "Heather, I can't believe what you just said. If you had a choice between the baby and me, you would not choose me. I suppose I can understand that, but it is very shocking to hear you say it, that's all."

It was Heather's turn to lower her head. She hadn't considered the impact her statement would make upon George, but there was no fudging the issue and she remained silent while George composed himself.

Xavier seemed pleased with the progress the small meeting was making and smiled broadly. "You are of noble blood, Heather. I have mentioned this to George and Merlin. I believe you are a direct descendant of the great Boudicca, who was also brought down by the influence of Nemesis. That is your danger, too. I could place you in a trance and you would find out for yourself who you really are. More importantly, how to avoid past mistakes."

"Thanks for the offer, Xavier, but I think I'll pass on that one. George, I'm sorry for upsetting you, I really am, but I'm only being honest with you. Most mothers, I expect, feel the same. I do love you, George, I really do." She got out of her chair, and hugged and kissed George and wiped away his tears. "I don't know what to make of this, but I do know there is an element of truth in what they're saying. I always wanted to do the right thing, and to use my knowledge and training for good. That's why I was so keen to work with children, particularly those who found themselves in trouble. They either pull through or end up wreaking havoc for the rest of their lives, and the consequences reverberate for generations. It felt like such an important role in life. But I simply couldn't afford to continue what was beginning to feel like unpaid charity work. I can't, no, I won't, make that sacrifice."

Xavier let Heather's words sink in before standing up.

"Heather, you can have it both ways. It can be made to work. Imagine what strength you would have if you could continue your work with children if you had enough money not to worry about such niggling matters."

The thought entered Heather's mind that perhaps she would resume her career at the Bar if she already had money, and yes, she thought to herself, she would be better, more confident and stronger. Completely fearless. A better lawyer all round.

Merlin surveyed the faces around him. "We have made such progress today, I am so happy. Now I can see the way forward.

I can see that my good Sir George and the noble Lady Heather have understood the problems that we were facing and recognised the moral corruption that was threatening their nobility."

George, now composed, felt he had missed something. "Well, excuse me, but now it's my turn to admit that I don't quite get this. We make a bundle of money, in a good way, somehow, Heather resumes her practice and everything's OK. But, first of all, I don't know how we're going to make this money – and what about me? In a few weeks' time I'm likely to be disbarred, a thought that turns my stomach – I mean being disbarred is just so *dishonourable* – and nothing that's been said today is going to change that fact."

"You are quite right, George, your future is another matter," said Xavier. "You must enquire into your heart for the answer. You have some time to consider your future. It does not need to be decided today."

"But the money question does, Merlin," said Heather. "We're going along to visit the Prince of Wales pretty soon. I can imagine ways of making a lot of money out of that trip, but I'm not sure it would accord with these high principles I've suddenly acquired. I want to trick Prince Charles, somehow, into helping us make a fortune. I suppose I have to go back to the drawing board, otherwise this St. Yves is going to find some other souls to save."

Merlin was quick to answer. "My dearest Heather, it can be done, and I'm sure, with the blessing of St. Yves, whose lifelong struggle was against the tyranny of those who thought themselves superior to others because of their royal blood. There is no end to the wrongdoings of royalty. They may try to appear to do good but it is too little too late. Why, even the would-be queen, Camilla, has a price to pay. There is much anger among members of the Great Council at the way the Princess Diana was driven to madness and despair. She was rescued from further torment just in time. The child she was carrying would have come under the influence of men whose hearts have turned to stone. If your trick does no harm to the children, I am sure St. Yves would approve. He is by no means prone to vindictiveness, but his sense of humour has not deserted him. And, my good lady, you will find that St. Yves is a tough but fair negotiator. He ran rings around three kings, you know. He understands your heart and that will be his strength to help you find your true path. His voice will be more persuasive to you than mine. He is better at that sort of thing than I."

Heather smiled and looked relieved. "Well, I can almost feel the presence of St. Yves," she joked, looking around nervously.

"Yes, St. Yves is pleased, I can tell," said Merlin. "It is too early for you to feel his spirit, but that, I am sure, will come."

"Yes, a very satisfactory day, all in all, my friends," Xavier said. "Once the future of George is resolved, everything will fall into place, as it should. Kosmos always prevails over chaos."

CHAPTER TWENTY-FIVE
Royalty

6:30 a.m., Friday, 30th March 2001.

"Well, exactly how long will it take to get from North London to Highgrove?" George asked impatiently. "I wish you'd let me drive, Heather, I really do."

Heather wrapped the seatbelt around her 'bump' as she called it, and turned on the engine of the chic black 5 Series BMW, otherwise known to Heather, George, and Merlin as the 'Merlinmobile'. There had been considerable debate as to whether such an expensive-looking vehicle was really necessary, but once the car had been test-driven, Heather refused to back down and persuaded George and Merlin it was really an investment, and an important part of their professional image. Besides, it was secondhand and had been bought for less than ten thousand pounds. Heather argued that the car would not compromise her ideals and would be given to a charity in due course. "We can't turn up at important functions and events in a bloody banger, can we? Appearances are very important, are they not?" Heather asked rhetorically, sure that Merlin would agree with her. George had gotten over the purchase, and now moaned about Heather taking the wheel instead of him.

Merlin sat in the back, ignoring the front-seat squabbles. "I hope this does not continue all the way to the castle. I have matters I wish to concentrate upon. You talk to each other as if you have already exchanged sacred vows. Perhaps it is the speed at which you travel that causes such disharmony; it is very distracting, you know."

George and Heather maintained a discreet silence, realising that Merlin was quite right.

"OK, it will take at least three hours, depending on the traffic. I'll take the M4 past Swindon, through Wootton Bassett and then pick up the B4042 towards Malmesbury and then onto Tetbury. I've got directions from there," said Heather, but neither George nor Merlin were interested in such detail. The fact was that they were on their way to have a cup of tea with Prince Charles, and the nerves were beginning to set in.

"Can you remind me, my dearest Heather," asked Merlin mischievously, "of the religious beliefs of this prince?"

George looked at Heather and smiled. Clearly Merlin was in a playful mood.

"The religious beliefs of Prince Charles are very confused. He is the future head of the Church of England, but he is also a pagan at heart. Perhaps he will appoint you as his favoured advisor on all spiritual matters," Heather suggested, "just like the old days."

"Not a pagan, surely. He represents the highest religious authority, does he not, in the Christian tradition," said Merlin, sounding unsure of himself. "But I am afraid I still do not fully understand the recent history of the complex world of the Windsors, and I certainly do not understand a future king who told the world that his vows before his god could be broken at his own discretion. It is very confusing to my mind. I have a lot of questions for him."

"Listen, Merlin," Heather said. "You won't get very far if you think he's going to sit down and answer your questions. He is obviously curious about you. I'm sure he'll want to know about Stonehenge and all of that stuff. You just have to keep him busy, and remember our plan."

Merlin sighed. "Ah, yes. I told the story about those stones in Brickstonia so many times but nobody listens. Until the bones of the giants who carried the stones are found, they will never believe me. I suppose I will need to explain it all again to this prince. And, yes, the plan. I have not forgotten the plan."

A long silence followed. Heather concentrated on her driving and Merlin closed his eyes while the world sped past his darkened window.

"Listen, George," said Heather quietly, as if unseen ears might hear her words. "I've brought that camera, just in case, you know, the opportunity arises."

"Have you tried it out yet?" George asked eagerly.

"Bet your life I have. It's amazing, I mean for its size. Look." Heather pulled from her pocket the smallest-looking camera George had ever seen, about the size of a credit card and not much thicker.

"It's digital so there's no film. It's powered by one of those incredibly small rechargeable batteries. It uses a self-adjusting infrared light instead of the usual flash. You can either take three hundred stills or it will work as a camcorder but only for ten seconds. You plug it into your laptop and print up immediately and send the images as an email attachment anywhere in the world. Brilliant, isn't it?" enthused Heather.

"It is a very powerful machine, Heather, and must be used wisely and carefully, as we agreed," Merlin advised from the back seat, his eyes still closed.

"Of course, Merlin, of course. You've always told me to be prepared for the unexpected, and so I am."

"We're only popping in for a cup of tea, for Christ's sake. The two of you sound as if we're off for an orgy," George said.

"An orgy?" exclaimed Merlin, rattling his staff. "Maybe they will invoke the spirit of Dionysus; I fear this gathering could last for several days."

"Please," said Heather, "I asked you never to use that name again, after what happened at Stringfellows that time. You remember, when everyone started to take their clothes off on the dance floor."

"That was one hell of a night," George said nostalgically, "and another place we've been barred from. On second thought, maybe not, Merlin. I mean not at Highgrove, for God's sake."

"I told you two before, those days are over. Let's just relax before we get there, please?" asked Heather. "It won't be long now."

*　　*　　*

The massive security gates opened automatically as the BMW cruised off the public road and crunched its way towards the main entrance to the vast complex of Highgrove.

"They have stronger powers than I, I fear," said Merlin as Heather gently steered the car along the gravel path leading to the main house, past acre upon acre of exquisitely manicured gardens and fields of rye, wheat, oats, beans, and peas.

Heather and George were too preoccupied staring in wonder at the sheer size of the estate to explain the workings of the state-of-the-art security system and the CCTV that had already checked out the number plate of the car.

"This is almost as nerve-wracking as a jury trial," quipped George. "I'll be glad when it's over."

At the front door of the surprisingly small mock neo-Classical house resplendent with balustrades and Romanesque pillars, Heather, Merlin, and George were greeted like celebrities by a very professional lady named Alison. She ushered them into a quiet, homey room scattered with pastel-coloured seats and sofas. No one dared to make a comment of any kind while they waited for the Prince, for fear of being overheard.

Prince Charles suddenly entered the room, on his own, dressed casually in a country fashion, and introduced himself, taking care to avoid any physical contact. It was obvious who the Prince wanted to talk to, as Heather and George were left with Alison while Prince Charles insisted on giving Merlin a personal tour around his 'organic oasis'. Before Prince Charles and Merlin had left the room, the tour had already begun: "And so after the property was purchased by the Duchy of Cornwall from Maurice Macmillan – you know, the son of Harold – in 1980, we've transformed the estate...." The words trailed off as Merlin and Prince Charles headed out of the room.

Alison, a natural blonde, ponytailed, sprightly young lady dressed in full Sloane Ranger uniform, right down to the upturned collar of the white-and-blue striped shirt and blue sweater and matching pearl earrings and necklace, tried her best to entertain Heather and George, ignoring the obvious disappointment on their faces as a result of being left out.

"The Prince wants to show Merlin around on his own. He'll be back shortly, I'm sure. The first stop is always the Orchard Room, where the main entertaining takes place. The stone ceiling is simply amazing – have a look," said Alison, handing Heather a well-worn copy of a coffee table book entitled: *Highgrove: Portrait of an Estate.*

"Why, thank you so much, Alison," said Heather with a hint of sarcasm. "It's funny how you never really notice that scar on his face until you see him close up."

Alison had heard it all before, and worse. "Yes, people often make that comment. The result of a kick in the face by a pony during a polo match. It was many years ago now, but the scar is still very prominent. Prince Charles was *so* brave, you know."

Alison's emphasis on the word 'so' made her sound childish, and Heather tried to make a small, polite smile, but the resulting look was more one of half-hidden contempt.

George could take no more, either. "Any chance of a tea or coffee, Alison? We've been driving for hours."

"Of course, George, I should have mentioned, refreshments are on their way." Sure enough, right on cue, a maid entered, wearing the type of outfit George had only ever seen in a pub strip show, pushing a trolley bursting on two levels with silverware and plates of biscuits.

"You simply must try the biscuits. They're made from the oats grown on the estate, everything is completely organic," enthused Alison.

George tried to keep his eyes off the legs of the maid, his gaze wandering recklessly up her skirt in search of a garter.

He and Heather sat quietly, looking around the expensively decorated room, staring at each item from the chandeliers to the soft cream carpet and over to the obviously never-used Italian marble fireplace, wondering how much it all cost. Then a high-pitched voice was heard from outside: "Where the fuck is he? I've been saddled up for two hours waiting for that arsehole. It's not the Merlin day today, is it? He'll be sticking it up the old boy all day. I thought April Fool's Day wasn't until Sunday." The lady popped her head round the door, cigarette in hand, and saw a bright red Alison sitting in silence with Heather and George.

"Oh sorry, Ally," said the lady in a completely different, softer voice, "I didn't know you were entertaining."

"Not to worry, Camilla. Chuck, I mean Prince Charles, is giving Merlin a tour. He shouldn't be long."

As the door closed Heather and George looked towards the floor in deep embarrassment.

"More tea?" asked Alison. "Perhaps another biscuit?"

"No thanks," Heather said, "but perhaps you could point me in the right direction for the ladies?"

"Oh, of course. Come with me." Alison was clearly grateful to be given something to do.

Within a minute or two, Alison returned on her own and sat opposite George.

"Tell me about Merlin, George. Is he mad?" she enquired in a matter-of-fact manner.

"Oh yes, Alison, completely off his head. I mean, he is Merlin, of course, you know, the real Merlin, but he's totally mad. I've seen him take over a dance floor, take all his clothes off and shake his booty all night, like real crazy. And when he's full of booze or whatever, he's a real danger. I hope the Prince doesn't intend to offer him anything stronger than tea. Know what I mean, Ally?"

Alison looked at George wryly, indicating that she knew his game and was quite enjoying it. "I read that you and your lady, Heather, intend to wed soon. Will that be before or after the birth?" she asked, deciding it was her turn to be naughty.

"Oh, I don't know," said George casually. "We might wait until afterwards, in which case the baby can be known by its formal legal title."

"And what might that be, George?"

"Well, a baby whose parents marry after birth are called, in law, 'special bastards'."

"Special bastards, eh? Well, I know a few of them," said Alison, holding back a giggle. "Heather has been gone for some time, George, do you think I should send out a search party for her?"

"No need for that, Ally. Heather always takes her time. I wouldn't worry. Give her another few minutes. Tell me about the rose garden. I've heard *so* much about it."

George and Alison chatted uncomfortably for another ten minutes before a smiling Heather returned as if she had just left a moment before.

"Oh, the toilets are simply divine," she said, knowing that she sounded completely insincere. "I could spend all day in that little room."

Another uncomfortable hour passed by before Prince Charles entered the room, Merlin in tow.

"Fascinating, absolutely fascinating. I have so enjoyed our little chat, Merlin. Could you leave your details with Alison? I must have you round again, soon." Prince Charles approached Heather and Geroge, shook their hands and thanked them warmly for bringing Merlin along and muttered something about wishing he had more time to spend with them.

"Alison will show you to the gift shop. I am sure you'll find many things of interest," said Prince Charles, as if he was an official from National Heritage urging package tourists to spend some money before getting back on a tour bus.

"Merlin," he continued, "it's been a real pleasure. Thank you so much for your time." Prince Charles held out his hand, which Merlin squeezed tightly. There was an embarrassing moment when it was quite clear that Prince Charles wanted to retrieve his hand, but Merlin held on firmly. Prince Charles pulled his hand away sharply, looking Merlin in the eye with some fear, and walked away brusquely.

Merlin appeared quite upset and said in a loud voice, "My dear friends, it is time for us to leave." He headed for the front door, ahead of Alison, who looked quite flustered as George, Heather, and Merlin headed straight for their car without any mention of a visit to the shop.

Before the car had even left the estate, Merlin began one of his familiar rants, usually reserved for the 'ruffians, villains, and scoundrels' he had encountered in public places.

"That man, if I can call him such, is a fraud," suggested Merlin angrily.

"A fraud?" George said as Heather sped out of the security gates. "You mean he's not a real prince?"

"No, no, he is a real prince. His German ancestors were present at the great battle when I lost so many of my soul brothers. How my heart rages at that family. No, I mean he is an emotional fraud. He breathes insincerity; he is not the person he wishes others to believe he is. His riches and status allow him to hide from his guilt and sorrow. He still mourns the death of his uncle and the friend he lost while playing in the snow. His first wife haunts him. It is not guilt that burdens him but simply regret for the years he did not share his life with his true love. He wishes to be respected as a worthy king and for his lady to be queen, but that will never be. Never. His son William will take the throne before he has served ten summers, after a decade of calamity and humiliation. This is his punishment for the many wrongs committed by his ancestors against the poor and defenceless and the cruel acts committed in the name of religion. The worst part of the tragedy is that he is fully aware of his destiny and knows his weakness is hubris. I remembered our plan, but the Prince was ahead of me. He only seemed interested in watering his plants. I fear I have failed you, my friends."

Heather kept quiet, biting her lip, enjoying the few moments during which she knew something Merlin and George did not.

Merlin sat back in the leather seat of the BMW and closed his eyes as if to find some peace of mind.

"Well," said George, turning around towards Merlin, "it looks like we've burned our bridges with the royal family. That didn't take long. We lasted longer in Stringfellows. What a poor showing." George turned to Heather. "Well, we've blown that one. No sensational pictures of the estate, then?"

Heather smiled and patted one of her pockets. "Don't talk so fast, George, we've got all we need in here."

"Got what, exactly?" George asked.

Before Heather could answer, Merlin interjected, "He asked me to water his herbs, you know. It wasn't my idea."

"What's wrong with that, Merlin? Many people would be *so* delighted to be asked to water the Prince's bushes," George said, emphasising the word 'so' for the last time.

"What's wrong with that?" exclaimed Merlin indignantly.

"Well, I didn't expect him to pull out his royal member and invite me to water the poor flowers, did I?"

"I did," said Heather, hardly able to contain her excitement. "In fact, that was the plan, Merlin."

Merlin looked slightly confused. "But I thought the plan was to take some interesting pictures of the estate, as you said, Heather, 'some unusual shots'."

George turned around to face Heather, hardly able to keep a straight face. "You didn't, did you?"

"Oh yes I did," Heather replied with a smile. "For at least ten seconds. Both of them, like two firemen. Clear view from the side French window."

"I didn't think it was that long. Never heard of such a thing," added Merlin, still sounding dazed.

George looked at Heather. "You don't mean it, do you?"

Heather handed George the camera. "Look after this. It's worth more than the crown jewels. I've never seen such a small willy. It might need some digitised enhancing."

The journey back to North London seemed to take a lot less time than the outward trip, mainly because Merlin, Heather, and George spent so much time in raucous laughter together.

"I knew some opportunity would arise, in some shape or form. St. Yves promised me." Heather practically screamed with laughter, wiping tears from her eyes. "I can hear St. Yves laughing out loud. He's got a great sense of humour for a saint, Merlin. He seems strangely keen for a saint to want to humiliate royalty but, you know, I get it now."

"I might have guessed St. Yves would have something up his sleeve. How a man can spend his life studying and practising canon law without going mad is beyond me. I think his humour keeps him sane. Time to celebrate, I think," suggested Merlin.

"I'm not sure I could take any more celebrations, Merlin, and I think Heather needs some rest," said George warmly, looking at her bump.

"Oh, I don't mean that type of celebration, my friends. I mean a real celebration of universal oneness and unconditional love. Whilst we are on this journey, can we not pass by the Stones?

Once there I can conduct the bonding ceremony. I was very good at that, you know. You have given me such joy, it is the least I can do."

"What are you going on about, Merlin, you've lost me," said George, feeling worried.

Heather was quicker on the uptake.

"What he means, George, is that we take the A346 at Swindon and head south," she said, looking at Merlin's reflection in the rear mirror. "Head for Stonehenge, wait until dark when there's nobody around, and then Merlin will perform a ten-thousand-year-old marriage ceremony within the inner circle of stones."

"Oh shit," said George, taken aback. "Is that what you meant, Merlin?"

"Indeed it is," Merlin answered gleefully, "but the ceremony is better at dawn, unless we are blessed tonight with a full moon, in which case I recommend the lunar ceremony. We might even do both, if the gods permit."

"Sounds good to me, Merlin," Heather said.

"And me," added George, gently rubbing Heather's protruding tummy.

CHAPTER TWENTY-SIX
Jackpot

10 p.m., Saturday, 31st March 2001, Flat C, 24 Green Way, Islington.

Heather's eyes opened slowly, her mind unsure as to whether it was day or night. One eye peered out of the duvet and focussed upon the alarm clock: '10 p.m' it read in unequivocal bright red. Simultaneously, George stirred beside her.

"What time is it, Heather?" asked George.

"Ten o'clock."

"Morning or evening?"

"Evening. And it's Saturday." Heather felt increasingly alert as each moment passed. George rolled back over to continue his sleep, taking most of the duvet with him. Heather decided that it was time to get up.

"Come on, George, we must have been asleep for nearly eight hours. We need to talk about what we're going to do."

George curled up into an even smaller ball, while Heather headed for the kitchen to make some coffee. He heard the toilet flush, indicating that Merlin was also up and about.

Within a few minutes, Merlin, Heather, and George had reconvened around the kitchen table, the camera sitting in the middle of the table as the focus of attention. The kitchen had become the nerve centre for what was now a thriving little business, keeping Merlin busy with talks and low-key appearances. At the heart of this enterprise was Heather's personal laptop computer.

"OK, George, I take it you're awake now?" Heather asked impatiently.

"Yeah, sure am," said George, stifling a yawn.

After the three of them had returned to Heather's flat following the pagan wedding ceremony conducted by Merlin in the middle of Stonehenge, they had decided not to view the contents of the camera until they had all slept. Heather carefully plugged the camera into the computer and pressed several keys in quick succession till she came across the request to open and display the images contained in the small object.

She pressed the return key and the machine whirred into action. In a few seconds a series of flashing small blue markers indicated that the downloading process was counting up to one hundred percent.

Merlin, Heather, and George watched the laptop monitor, transfixed, while the clear images of the Prince of Wales in the foreground and Merlin behind him but also in full shot, stood in close proximity to one another, in what looked like a greenhouse. Both were holding their members, pissing onto two separate pots of plants. The Prince was obviously talking. The lighting was not brilliant, but sufficient to see everything very clearly.

The image ran perfectly for about ten seconds, then Heather pressed a couple of keys and it played again. Merlin looked at the screen in disbelief, gently touching it as if he might feel real flesh.

"Sometimes you give yourself away, Merlin. You just don't get this new world, do you?" Heather smiled and quickly copied the contents of the camera onto the hard drive of her computer. "I'll also copy it onto a CD, just in case," she said. "Right, we need to work out how to milk this one without losing control. We've only one shot at this, and if the money is to be put to good use, it might as well be as much as we can get. Any suggestions, George?"

George looked lost and concerned. "Hell, this is beyond me. If we send it to anyone that'll be the end of it, I guess."

"That's what I think," said Heather. "We can't let go of this or transmit the images to anyone, it's too risky. We'll need to draw up a list of journalists, perhaps even senior editors, meet them individually in a secure location, and let them view this and take it from there. I'll ask them to sign a confidentiality agreement beforehand, which won't be bulletproof, but if I word it strongly enough, it might put them off doing the dirty on us."

"Sounds good," George said. "But why newspapers? Perhaps we should start with television companies, you know, and then release it to the papers."

"Maybe you're thinking in the right direction, George. If we approach a mega company, you know, like WorldMedia, NewsCorp, Bertelsmann, Turner, or Pearson, we could do a one-stop deal for an exclusive for both television and newsprint. I'll avoid the big boys whose links are too close to St James's Palace, so the BBC's out for a start. We'll offer, say, a twenty-four-hour moratorium, and then do a blanket non-exclusive with a number of syndicates."

George knew he was out of his depth but could no longer contain his excitement. "So, what sort of figures are we looking at? I mean, I wouldn't know where to start. WorldMedia? Don't they own Pentheus?"

"They sure do, George, but this is well above the level I used to operate at. Even my old boss wouldn't get to hear about this until the deal was done and dusted. It would involve the most senior personnel of the senior board of WorldMedia, based in California. They're seven or eight hours behind us, so it's the middle of the afternoon in LA and about five in the afternoon in New York, where their other US operations are based. We need at least three bidders, and set one of them up as a patsy, you know, just to keep the ball rolling. Listen, why don't you two disappear next door for a few hours? I'll need some space to get this going."

Merlin and George looked at each other and smiled, then they retreated to the small room next door in search of one of a number of videos that George had brought round from his flat, to keep them occupied.

"OK, Merlin, it's either *Spartacus*, *Joan of Arc*, *Braveheart*, *Henry the Fifth*, *The Vikings*, *Seven Brides for Seven Brothers*, or *Gladiator*. Hell, let's do them all. You choose the first."

"Ooh," said Merlin, "I like the sound of *Seven Brides for Seven Brothers*."

"Merlin, for a dippy pagan druid, you've got great taste."

"'Pagan' I can live with, but I care not for that word, 'druid', my friend, I am more of an antinomian."

"Whatever," said George casually, not knowing what Merlin was going on about.

★   ★   ★

"And is that your best and final offer?" Heather asked in her hard-nosed executive lawyer tone of voice. "OK, I'll get back to you on this number within the hour."

George walked in to make another cup of tea for himself and Merlin.

"Jesus, Heather. Where do you get your stamina from? You've been going solid for nine hours."

"George, I'm so excited I don't think I'll ever sleep again. I'll have this wrapped up in a couple of hours. Look, the shops should be open by now. Can't you go out and get some fresh croissants or something?"

"Sure, I'll leave you alone until say ten o'clock, but this hanging around is a killer, I can't wait. It wouldn't be so bad if Merlin would watch another video, but all he wants to do is see Seven Brides for Seven Brothers over and over again. There's only such much Howard Keel one can take, I mean, please, before he commits to memory all the words to 'Bless Your Beautiful Hide' at least."

"Ten o'clock is fine with me, George," said Heather abruptly. Then the phone rang again, as it had done incessantly for the last six hours. This time it was from Heather's 'front runner' as she had planned: WorldMedia.

"Look, Heather," said Carl Senator, the thirty-year-old Senior Vice-President of Corporate Affairs from Los Angeles, "how can you expect me to bid any higher when you won't even show me the goods. There's only so far we can take a blind auction. If you're selling, honey, you gotta put the goods on the table."

Heather was in no mood to take bullshit, especially from the boss's son. "Listen, Carl, I'm fighting them off. Everyone knows I'm for real. I've told you what to do. You've got five hundred workers in the UK and you use four high-powered law firms all based in London. You choose one person, and one person only, and give them my mobile telephone number; you then immediately email me to confirm from whom I should expect the call. When they ring I will agree to meet them somewhere nearby within the hour. I will show them the footage on my PC. They must be naked from the waist up while it's on. No, I'm not joking. They call you once they've seen the images, you then call me, we cut the deal, I email you with confirmation of the terms, you email me back with a secure electronic signature, your guy gives me an irrevocable banker's draft and then I hand over the disc to your guy, and I'll print off and countersign the contract and post you a fully executed hard copy. That's the only way I see it working, given it's Sunday morning and tomorrow's a bank holiday. And don't call me honey."

"OK, Heather, I'll roll with you. I know the guy to send. What was the name of the guy who sacked you again?"

"Don't worry about that just now, Carl, I'll send you a list of idiots once this is over." Heather was surprised at her own vindictiveness, hoping in a bizarre manner that St. Yves wasn't listening in. The only cure for the sin of revenge, she thought, was success, and she wasn't there yet. In fact, she could practically taste blood in her mouth as the pain and humiliation of her sacking came back to mind.

Heather stared at her email inbox as if hypnotised. Within three minutes, the communication from LA had arrived stating that Andrew Furlong, the senior partner of Furlong & Furlong, a City law firm that Heather knew well, would be contacting her shortly. Heather did not have time to close the email before the phone rang, and it was only two minutes later that she and Andrew had agreed to meet in Café Uno in Islington High Street, only five minutes away. Within seconds Heather was outdoors, heading for the rendezvous.

"I'll see you in a few minutes, Merlin. Tell George I'll be back very soon." Heather ignored the fact that Merlin was pretending to ride a horse-drawn sleigh, whipping the imaginary horses wildly, being chased by a gun-waving posse galloping after the seven brothers who had just kidnapped the town's finest virgins. Merlin liked that bit.

A few moments later George reappeared with some not-so-hot croissants, having walked a good mile to find a shop that made hot croissants early on a Sunday morning.

He missed Heather by seconds.

"Where's Heather, Merlin?" he asked, but Merlin hardly noticed, being so enthralled with the video.

"Not, now, my friend. Look, the snow's going to fall; the brothers are safe, until the spring, that is. Sit down, Sir George, please, they are about to start singing again."

George sat down and started to nibble on one of the croissants, content to wait for Heather's return.

Merlin continued looking at the video, but leaned over George and whispered, "It is Heather's day, my good friend. Fear not, she will show you the fruits of her labour later. You must have faith, this is Heather's day."

George sat back and tried to bring himself to watch the rest of the video again. He looked at his watch practically every minute, until it was nearly eleven o'clock.

By then George could take no more and went into the kitchen to ring Heather on her mobile from their land-based phone.

"Heather, is that you? Where are you? Are you all right?"

"I'm coming through the door now, George," she said, and George walked through to the front door to see Heather triumphantly walking through it, holding a piece of paper.

"Right," said Heather, "turn that crap off, Merlin. You can watch the rest later."

Merlin reluctantly pulled himself away from the television and followed Heather and George into the kitchen.

"OK, I've done the deal with WorldMedia. They've given us a banker's draft that I have in my hand. There'll be more to follow from the news syndicates over the next few days, weeks even, but here's the first installment."

Heather placed the small piece of paper facedown on the table; it was slightly larger than a normal check.

"Well, don't you want to have a look?"

Merlin stared hard at the piece of paper, and smiled as if he knew the answer.

George's hand trembled slightly as he picked up the banker's draft and read the front.

"Oh yes!" said George, placing it back down immediately as

if he had seen a vision. George picked it up again and read the figure: "Two million, five hundred thousand pounds, sterling."

Merlin smiled again. "That is a lot of money in today's world, is it not?"

George leaned over and hugged and kissed Heather.

"I like the sound of that. Two million, five hundred thousand pounds, sterling. Oh yes, I like the sound of that, very much. Heather, you're a genius!"

"Well," said Heather, trying halfheartedly to sound modest, "it makes up for the first check, which nearly got eaten up by my overdraft."

"It certainly does, Heather. Two and a half big ones. What are we going to do with it? It's like winning the lottery. I can't believe it." George stared at the check and shook his head in disbelief, kissing the piece of paper before placing it back on the table. "We can do a lot of good with this, and sort out our lives at the same time. It's a different day. I just wish I knew what to do with it, it all seems a bit unreal just now."

"I'll tell you what we're going to do, George: nothing at all. At least for a few days until our minds are clearer. First off, I want to go home and see my mum and dad, and my sister if she's around. We can meet my folks together at some later stage, but I really want to see them on my own, so I intend to go away for two or three days. All I want you to do is stay out of trouble and bank the money first thing Tuesday morning. I'm ready for that croissant now. Are there any left? And I suggest that you keep the television tuned to CNN. I reckon the fireworks will start pretty soon."

"Why CNN? Does WorldMedia own CNN?" George asked meekly.

"They don't own CNN, there's just a close relationship between the two companies. There's a lot you don't know, George," said Heather coyly.

Merlin, Heather, and George watched CNN, intensely waiting for the news to break. They didn't have to wait long, as indicated by the rarely used device of a flashing red on-screen message: *Major news flash coming up: STAY TUNED.*

The anchor lady could hardly contain herself.

"News has just come in from London that the king-in-waiting, Prince Charles, has been caught on camera watering his cannabis plants. The method used to water the plants is, well, quite unusual. A statement is expected from the Palace shortly," explained the presenter, obviously reading from notes, and not the autocue.

"Watering his *cannabis* plants? What on earth is this?" exclaimed Heather in disbelief.

The now-familiar series of images filled the television screen, Prince Charles and Merlin fully exposed.

The footage zoomed in unexpectedly onto the herbal recipient of the royal pee, avoiding very carefully explicit exposure. The plant, once magnified, clearly showed the distinctive shape and colour of the hemp plant, otherwise known as grass to the dope-smoking members of the public, as evidenced by the very clear on-screen comparisons.

"Holy shit!" George exclaimed. "I didn't notice that. He's pissing on his fucking grass, that's why he wanted Merlin, to piss on his fucking organic grass! Our bonnie Prince thought he was tricking us." George could contain himself no longer and fell to the floor in hysterical convulsions, kicking his legs in the air and clutching his stomach. "Jesus, talking to your plants is one thing. Fair enough. Guess he thinks Merlin's pee is the best fertiliser ever made."

Merlin was not so excited about it all, but appeared to be closely examining the moving images, as if his real concern was something to do with size.

"OK, George," Heather said. "This will run and run and run some more. Jesus, no wonder they were so keen. Bastards, I should have held out for more. Anyway, I shouldn't complain. They spotted it, we didn't. Listen, I'm going to pack and head off to Scotland. I'll take the train; I should be back by Tuesday night. I'll put an auto-response on my email system and we let the answering machine take messages, and come out guns blazing with some sort of PR statement next week. Why don't you hide the check, and enjoy yourself for a couple of days? Go round to Xavier's or whatever. I trust you, George, I do. Just enjoy yourselves."

Merlin and George exchanged glances and smiled.

"Xavier? Why, he would be mightily pleased to see us," said Merlin. "We must take round *Seven Brides*, I am sure Xavier will enjoy it as much as I. Oh, happy days, my friends. Happy days."

CHAPTER TWENTY-SEVEN
Proceedings

2 p.m., Sunday, 1st April 2001, South End Green, Hampstead.

George and Merlin had been wandering the streets of Hampstead and Belsize Park for nearly two hours, searching in vain for Xavier's house, having started their search from the top of Kite Hill.

"Can't you remember any street names or landmarks, Merlin? We've been going around in circles forever," George asked, feeling tired and impatient. He realised that he was being unfair blaming Merlin when he should have been able to remember himself where Xavier lived. "Let's sit and have a drink and try to work this one out. Hold on, I'll get some money out the cash point."

George placed the card into a hole in the wall and checked the balance: £309.11. "OK," he said, "I'll swipe three hundred pounds; it's only until Tuesday. Right, Merlin, let's have a beer. We haven't had a good drink since that night with Heather weeks ago. She won't mind."

George and Merlin found a quiet café and sat outside in the light sunshine, sipping continental-sized glasses of lager. George realised that they were in the lower part of Hampstead, near the overland railway, South End Green to the locals, a small village-like community situated on the west side of Hampstead Heath.

They sat in silence until they noticed how many people were staring at Merlin and giggling, particularly the women. A small group of council workmen, digging up the pavement on the other side of the road to the café, adjacent to a small but busy open-air bus depot, began pointing in Merlin's direction.

"Show us your knob, Merlin, go on!" shouted one of the

young lads, much to the amusement of his fellow labourers, his rough voice carrying across the traffic.

Merlin ignored them and turned to George. "There are so many names for the male member, I am surprised you can remember them all. It is a strange obsession, you know. If the organ was displayed more often, then perhaps people would take less notice."

George sat quietly enjoying the continental scene, sipping his beer rapidly. "Just keep your prick to yourself, Merlin. If you expose yourself in this environment, we'll get arrested and you'll be back in Brickstonia before you know it."

Merlin paused for a few moments. "So, my good friend Sir George, what is the plan? We have tried very hard to locate Xavier's abode, but the location has escaped us. What are we to do?"

"Well, I suggest we have another beer and think about it."

"A very sound idea, my good knight, but this ale makes me leak too often, and is too, too...fizzy for my liking. I think it is a drink for children. Perhaps they sell whiskybae, you know, the water of life?"

"Whisky? I should have remembered, Merlin, of course. Which type?" asked George teasingly.

"There are different types?" Merlin sounded like a child who's discovered sherbet for the first time.

"I think," said George, "that we're better off going to a pub, and then you can try out as many types of 'whiskybae' as you wish, but don't expect me to carry you home, all right?"

"Never fear, Sir George, I have supped with some of the finest men on earth, and never lost my legs, or my mind. Some considered me to be quite skillful in the art of drinking, you know." Merlin was obviously already feeling the effects of a small lager.

George looked at him with some concern. "Look, I'll take you to one or two pubs and see how we get on. But when I ask you to stop, you stop. Is that fair enough?" George finished his beer with a single gulp. "I know, the Sir Richard Steele on Haverstock Hill. There's always an interesting crowd in there. Bet someone knows Xavier, so we might kill two birds with one stone. OK, Merlin me old mate, let's try the Sir Richard Steele, it's only a few minutes' walk away."

"Today is going to be a grand day, my friend. Did you count the magpies on the way?"

"Magpies? No, I didn't count any magpies. Why do you ask?"

"Well, I counted seven in a single grouping," said Merlin. "A secret will be out before the moon sets. You should always count magpies, Sir George."

"OK, Merlin, will do," replied George halfheartedly. "Come on, let's go."

★　　★　　★

It had been at least two years since George had set foot in the Sir Richard Steele public house, but the décor was unchanged: the wooden floors looked the same and the walls were still covered with all manner of artistic memorabilia: old street signs, faded posters, oil paintings, books, and oddments that might be found in a bric-a-brac store in a small coastal town. There was a lit candle on every table. George looked up at the ceiling and smiled as he feasted his eyes on the irreverent, bawdy imitation of the Sistine Chapel. The smoke-filled rooms were all buzzing with an eclectic assortment of humanity from the very old to the very young, some poor, many well off and well-known from the world of sport, television, and the theatre. The queue to buy drinks was three deep, and the noise was so loud that it was difficult to make out what music was being played.

George smiled broadly. "This is more like it. Reminds me of *Star Wars* every time," he said, knowing that such a comment would fly right over Merlin's head. George was not quite expecting the roar that went up when everyone noticed Merlin, and within minutes a sizable crowd had gathered around him while George fought his way towards the bar. From a far corner someone was trying their hand at the beer-stained upright piano, and soon the atmosphere became quite raucous, but immensely friendly. Before long Merlin and George had become separated and time drifted by as they engaged in quick-fire banter with people from every walk of life. Occasionally there was another roar when Merlin retold one of a hundred stories to a core of nearly ten people. And so it continued until the barmen started to shout, "Time, gentlemen, please!"

George pushed his way through a tight crowd surrounding Merlin and said, "Come on, it's time to find Xavier's again. We've been here for hours, Merlin."

"Xavier's, did you say?" said a voice amidst the crowd. "Did you hear that? We're all off to The Haven!"

George and Merlin fought their way out of the pub into the cold, fresh night air. Merlin took in a deep breath and suddenly buckled, falling into George's arms, triggering another roar of laughter from the crowd now spilling onto the pavement. George held firmly onto Merlin's staff. "Oh shit, what am I supposed to do now? Anyone know the number of a cab?"

"Don't be silly," said a well-presented suited and booted middle-aged man who George recognised from the pub. He was either an accountant or television presenter; George had drunk too much to remember. "We'll carry him to Xavier's. It's not far. Come on, lads, grab a leg, can't you?"

Before George could counter the suggestion with a better one, four men grabbed a Merlin limb each, laughing and joking as they staggered recklessly up the hill back towards Hampstead. Before long they were standing outside a small-looking cottage off the main road. When George knocked on the front door, a loud noise came from the inside as if a party was in full swing, which it was.

Xavier came to the door, looking down with obvious amusement at the inebriated Merlin being carried by four strangers, George at the rear.

"Come in, my friends, come in. I knew you were coming. Welcome back, my dear friend George. It's been too long. Very good of you to bring some company. Yes, yes, all according to plan," said the towering Xavier as he ushered the crowd into his little bohemian cottage. George had drunk too much to notice much detail but the smell of incense and grass was impossible to ignore.

"Just put Merlin over there, please," Xavier said authoritatively, pointing towards an empty armchair, as if a new sofa was being delivered. "Now, George, how do you like your smoke? Pipe? Cigarette? In tea, or perhaps a biscuit?"

George did not want to own up to the fact that he had never partaken of any form of cannabis in his whole life. But such willpower as was required to refuse such an offer had long since evaporated into the night.

"Pipe. A pipe, please, Xavier," he said casually.

Xavier peered over the heads of the crowd of people, who were variously laughing, talking, singing, flirting, and dancing until he caught the eye of Zena, who was puffing away on a small pipe. He nodded her over and she approached George and handed him the innocent-looking object. George took a very small puff, trying unsuccessfully not to inhale and coughed loudly, causing Zena to giggle.

"No, George. Like this," she said. She inhaled slowly, held her breath for a few seconds then exhaled even more slowly through her nose.

George copied Zena and managed only the most token smile before he felt his lights go out as if he had been hit over the head with a very heavy object, insufficiently conscious to notice that he had been skillfully caught by a complete stranger, who placed him in a quiet corner, near Merlin.

★   ★   ★

George woke up to the unmistakable sounds and smell of fried eggs and bacon. Feeling surprisingly bereft of a serious hangover, he surveyed his immediate environment and vaguely remembered walking the Hampstead streets after closing time, and being welcomed by Xavier.

He rubbed his eyes and looked around the expansive room. The hearth of the beautifully carved oak fireplace was still glowing with warm embers of a sweet-smelling fire.

The furnishings were soft and oriental, and George noticed numerous stones of a multitude of shapes, colours, and sizes, most of which he could not identify other than some emerald quartz and moonstones. A few candles had been lit above the fireplace and George realised that there was complete silence other than the increasing crackling of bacon and the spitting of fried eggs, at which point George remembered he was hungry, very hungry.

"This is a very special time, George," Zena said as she came into the room, wooden spatula in hand. "Merlin and Xavier have gone to welcome the sun. They will be back later."

George looked around the room, trying to find any clue as to what time it was. There was some light coming through a wooden Venetian blind, but it was difficult to tell whether it was very late or very early.

"It's about six o'clock on Monday morning," said Zena, as if she understood his immediate concern. "You are hungry, yes?"

George felt a frisson of sexual tension in the air and noticed that the barefooted Zena was wearing what looked like a paper-thin cotton dress over her svelte, petite body, leaving little to the imagination.

George let the question hang in the air and smiled broadly. "Don't worry," Zena said in an unnervingly sexy voice, "I'm not going to bite you. Not unless you want me to, that is."

George's mind assessed the immediate possibilities as he looked intensely into Zena's flirtatious eyes. "It's a nice thought, Zena, a very nice thought, but the only thing I'd like to eat is the breakfast you're cooking."

Zena returned George's smile as if he had passed some sort of test. "Of course, please come into the kitchen and let's eat."

George followed Zena into an enormous country-style kitchen, in the centre of which was a large wooden table big enough for at least eight people, and the two of them sat down to the eggs and bacon, fruit, and freshly squeezed orange juice.

"Do you follow the pagan traditions, George? Being so close to Merlin, you must have learnt a lot about the festival of Ostara?"

Zena quickly picked up the vacuous look in George's eyes. "You must know of Eostre, or perhaps you know her as Eastre?" George remained silent and obviously embarrassed.

Zena continued. "On the first Sunday that follows the first full

moon that follows the Vernal Equinox we always celebrate the
goddess of spring. It matters not what name you give her. Shortly
before the end of the first millennium the Roman Christians
adopted the date to mark the death of Jesus. It brought the pagans
and the Christians together. Rather sweet, really."

George was still at a loss as to what Zena was going on about,
but felt relaxed enough not to try and change the subject.

"So, you and Xavier are practising pagans, if that's the right
way of putting it?" he asked politely.

"Yes, you could put it that way, George. We have reached a
position of harmony between our way of life and the Christian
tradition. It wasn't always so. Xavier specialises in helping people
to find out who they really are. What he practices is not so much
a religion, more a way of life. Xavier teaches about Heh, the
ancient god of Eternity, about achieving the balance between
the opposing tensions of chaos and kosmos, and finding a path
through the natural order of things. Have you ever read any of
von Humboldt's work? Foucault? We are students, you might say,
of nature, of the order of things. You know, the *natural* order of
things, the logic of the universe."

"I like that, Zena. 'Students of nature'…'the natural order
of things'…'logic of the universe'. Sounds good to me," said
George, tucking into his breakfast, which tasted divine. "Er, can't
say I've read von…von…"

"Alexander von Humboldt. You must know of his German
works on kosmos?"

George shook his head to signify to Zena that she may as well
have been talking a foreign language, and wiped the plate clean
with the last piece of chunky bread. He placed the gooey mass
into his mouth and sighed with pleasure.

Zena stared at George as though he were a small boy and
smiled. Edging a little closer to George, she whispered, "It is
nearly time for Merlin to *return*, has he told you that?"

"Return? Return where? What do you mean?" asked George
with some concern.

"Perhaps I shouldn't have said anything. It is for Merlin to
explain. He'll be back soon, now the sun is up. Come, let's go next

door and listen to some music while we await their return. Why don't you relax? Maybe a dream will help you to see your future more clearly. Many people come here just to dream, you know."

George did not take Zena's comments about dreaming too seriously, but did feel tired and found a comfy spot on a cushion while Zena placed a CD onto a very expensive-looking but discreetly hidden compact disc player. The music was unlike anything George had heard before, being neither classical nor country. *Perhaps it's early Scottish folk music,* he thought, as he listened to the soothing sounds of a lady gently singing a quiet lament in a language he could not follow, accompanied only by a single string instrument, the identity of which George could not pinpoint. He closed his eyes and felt a warm glow spread from his legs upwards until he quietly fell into the deepest of sleeps.

★　★　★

George woke up to Merlin's loud, excited voice, a familiar sound. "What a glorious sunrise you have missed, my good knight, absolutely glorious," said Merlin, brandishing his staff wildly.

George quickly regained his faculties while Merlin and Xavier found places to sit.

"Has Zena been looking after you, my friend?" Xavier asked mischievously.

Zena spoke without opening her eyes. "George is a true knight, Xavier, as you know. He's been a perfect gentleman."

Merlin looked pleasantly surprised and relieved. "I told you his heart was pure. There was never any doubt, in my mind, my noble knight." He patted George's leg with a wink, smiling wryly at Zena. "It's always the same at this time of year, Xavier. I wouldn't trust Zena with anything that's got a heartbeat and tongue during the festivities of Ostara." He laughed loud and long while Zena kept her eyes closed, clearly blushing.

"I hear your good lady is with her folks, George, and will return tomorrow. We don't have much time, so I would like to start," said Xavier.

"Start what?" asked George.

"As you say in your world, Sir George, the proceedings," Xavier replied wryly, pulling back the chairs and straightening the rug while Merlin took off his jacket.

"But first, George, we need to loosen up, with some exercises. Stay with me on this one," said Xavier in a formal, professional tone, "I normally charge five hundred pounds an hour for the deluxe routine."

Merlin and Zena silently followed Xavier's gentle exercises, which were a strange combination of yoga and martial art warm-ups that reminded George of his one and only judo lesson attended at university. George did his best to follow suit, but was clearly a long way behind Zena, who was as supple as a natural ballerina, Xavier, who was surprisingly strong and loose, and even Merlin, who was gamely doing his best, moaning loudly with every stretch.

"It helps enormously if you breathe," Xavier told George as he tried to lie back on his folded legs, arms outstretched behind him. George managed to laugh nervously and tried to breathe consciously and relax.

After about twenty minutes, Xavier finally sat cross-legged, eyes closed, placing the palms of his hands together and raising his fingertips ever higher until he was fully stretched, and then slowly lowered his hands, breathed in deeply, exhaled and opened his eyes, and smiled at George.

"Feel better, George?" he asked.

"Yes, I do, Xavier. And my headache's gone, thanks." George was pleasantly surprised at the immediate rewards for what felt like a fair trade-off for one source of pain to another.

Zena left the group, purposefully. "And put some undergarments on, please, Zena," said Xavier. "Otherwise George will be distracted throughout. It is not fair to tease such a healthy young man." Merlin laughed his raucous best, and it was George's turn to blush.

Zena returned with a fully loaded pipe, lit it, and handed it to Xavier, who drew so deeply on it that George wondered whether there would be anything left. Xavier held his breath for some considerable time, and exhaled with impressive patience, then he passed the pipe to George. "Do not fear, George," said Xavier, "you will not pass out this time."

George felt like he was in a fifties American movie, smoking the peace pipe inside the tepee sitting next to the Big Chief. He started to giggle nervously before taking the plunge and inhaling lightly and emulating Xavier as best he could. Then he passed the pipe to Merlin, feeling pride in not having fainted or spluttered. Once the pipe had done the first round, Xavier spoke in a deep solemn voice.

"Merlin must return, Sir George, at the time of the summer solstice," he said. "His journey will be complete before the honey moon is full."

George looked over towards Merlin, whose eyes were filling with tears. "I will miss you and Heather terribly, Sir George, but it has been decided long ago, and so it shall be."

Zena reloaded the pipe with some grass from a small leather pouch, lit it, and the pipe was suddenly doing another round. This time George was slightly more confident and inhaled as deeply as he could, by now feeling not dizzy, but surprisingly alert, albeit in a state of mind he found unworldly.

"Now," said Xavier, "let us go back to the beginning." George felt as if he were among very old friends, in a simple, warm and safe place, which felt simultaneously alien and familiar. "There are many questions which need to be answered, the first of which is how this money which I understand you have acquired will be put to good use in accordance with the wishes of the Great Council. You, George, must look long and hard into your heart and decide how to live your life in a noble way that is consistent with your past and the demands of the future. Your addiction to the material will pass, my good knight. Zena has told me you slept well. Did you dream?"

George was unaccustomed to talking about his dreams, which if he had he rarely remembered. To him, dreams fell into the same category as a rash on his privates; it was just personal detail that should remain personal. However, this time there was a difference, as those around him had no such inhibitions and he felt no sense of embarrassment.

"Yeah, come to think if it, I did have a dream," he said meekly.

"And do you remember any part of it?" enquired Xavier patiently.

"Well…." George took his time. "It sounds a bit funny, but I was swimming underwater, in an ocean, I suppose, and felt, you know, quite happy, breathing without thinking about it."

"And then?" prodded Xavier gently.

"And then I was suddenly flying high above the ground. It was a great feeling."

"And were you looking up or below, while you were flying?" asked Xavier.

George had to think about the answer. "I'm not sure. I wasn't really looking up or below, just flying."

"Was there anyone else in this dream?" Xavier asked, sounding very serious.

"Anyone else? Let me think. That's a strange question. There was someone else, yes. I was flying with someone. But there was no voice or face, I just felt as if someone was with me."

"Who was it, do you think?" Xavier asked.

George again took his time. "I don't know. I really don't. Just someone."

"Well, it wasn't St. Yves," suggested Merlin. "You would have known if it was him."

Xavier looked at George with a stare that George found quite unsettling. "George. When was the last time you visited your mother? A long time ago, I would bet. Why don't you go and see her?"

George was trying hard to connect his dream to Xavier's suggestion, but as the thought sunk in, he realised that a long time had passed since he'd spent any time with his mother.

"It's funny you should say that. Heather's with her parents just now. Maybe you're right. I'll think about it. Yeah, thanks."

"And think about the money, as well, George," said Xavier.

"No problem there, Xavier, it's difficult to think about anything else."

CHAPTER TWENTY-EIGHT
Secrets

Tuesday, 3rd April 2001, Tufnell Park.

George and Merlin surveyed the chaos that was his flat and realised instantly that the place had been ransacked. Clothes and papers were strewn everywhere.

"Jesus, what a mess. Looks like they've really gone to town," said George in despair. "What a God Almighty mess."

While Merlin walked around shaking his head, George tried to work out what was of value that might be missing and soon concluded that nothing had been stolen, indicating that whoever was responsible had searched in vain for something specific. A thought suddenly came into George's mind and he told Merlin to wait there while he hotfooted around to Heather's flat, running down Tufnell Park Road in hope of coming across a cab.

It was some time before George returned to his own flat, looking completely white and shaken.

"Oh God, Merlin, Heather's place has been turned over as well. They've taken the fucking check. I'm in deep shit, like you wouldn't believe. The money's probably already in some Swiss bank account. We'll never get it back. Oh shit, what am I going to say to Heather?" George sank to his knees, crying like a baby, but Merlin seemed unperturbed, his eyes still glued to George's small television and video machine, watching *Seven Brides for Seven Brothers*.

"Oh, I have missed this film, it brings me such joy," said Merlin as if all was well.

"I can't believe you can sit and watch that video, while my world crumbles around me. What are we going to do?" George asked, sinking deeper and deeper into despair as the moments passed.

"What are we going to do?" enquired Merlin. "I think we should watch the end of the film."

"But the check, the banker's draft for two and a half million pounds is missing. Haven't you got the point, Merlin? I'm totally fucked, I really am."

"You cannot find the piece of paper with the numbers on it?" asked Merlin casually. "You should have said. Look in the box for the video."

George practically ripped the box apart and found, slipped into the inside back cover, the piece of paper that he had been searching for.

"Oh, praise the gods, hallelujah, may the saints be praised!" shouted George as he hugged and kissed Merlin, who tried to fend him off so as not to have his view of the film interrupted.

"You should have asked before you flew out of the door, my friend. I knew that to keep the sacred scroll safe, it was necessary for you to lose it, so to speak. Your hiding place at the other abode was woefully inadequate, so I took the liberty of placing it in the video box, as I intended to keep the box with me at all times. I'm sorry if I have disturbed you, I thought it was for the best."

George did not answer due to his excited but mightily relieved state. "No, I don't mind. Not at all. Oh, thank God. Listen, bring the video with you and you can watch it to your heart's content. We need to go to Heather's and clean up before she gets back. Her place is in an absolute state. Just as well she took her laptop with her. Listen, we'll put this into the bank on the way and sort out Heather's place before she gets back." George rushed out of the door once again, clutching the draft tightly, Merlin in tow, staff in hand.

"Let's think of a present for Heather," said George. "We've arranged to meet at her flat. We can buy something on the way."

★   ★   ★

George and Merlin tidied up Heather's flat, a feat that took them nearly two hours.

"I don't know why you couldn't just snap your fingers like Mary fucking Poppins, Merlin. I mean if you've got powers like yours, you could use them to help clear up, couldn't you?"

Merlin was strolling around using the upright old Hoover, having enormous fun.

Merlin raised his voice above the noise of the Hoover. "I have decided not to use my powers again until they have been fully restored. I will know when the time is right. You should rejoice in this activity, my friend, it is good exercise and is strangely satisfying. Perhaps you should do it more often."

"More often? I'm getting worried about you, Merlin, you're getting a bit too domesticated for my liking," replied George as he straightened up a print on the wall.

George and Merlin sat exhausted on the sofa, waiting the door to open, which it did, eventually, revealing a relaxed-looking Heather.

"I'm impressed. I can see you two have been busy. What a transformation. Feeling guilty, were you? Great job." Heather placed her laptop on the kitchen table. "Not got into any trouble, then?"

George calmly told Heather about the break-ins, and managed to mention, casually, that they had had a quiet time chilling out with Xavier.

"That's great, George. Tell me all about it. So, the money's in the bank, and they didn't take anything, nothing at all?" asked Heather with some concern.

"The money's safe, Heather," George said, looking at Merlin sheepishly. "Nothing's been taken from my place. I knew you had taken your laptop, I don't know if any papers have been removed. You'll have to check that one."

Heather quickly ruffled through the papers that George had hastily stacked together and shook her head.

"Nope, nothing at all. Maybe they were looking just for the money. I'm not sure if we should tell the police. Given that nothing's been taken, I'm not sure what they can do. I think I'd rather leave them out of this, what do you think, George?"

"I think you're right," said George, "seems more trouble than it's worth getting the police involved. Let's just get the locks sorted out and put it down to experience. Now, when you're ready, I've some news I have to tell you. By the way, how are your parents? And your sister?"

"My dad is doing well, old age seems to suit university professors, my sister and I are best of mates, and my mum is fine." Heather paused for a moment. "And so is yours."

"My mother? You went to see my mother?" asked George incredulously.

"We're practically married, George, in a Stone Age sort of way," Heather said teasingly. "There aren't that many Winsomes in Glasgow, you know, only one in fact. I got the number from the phone book, rang up and said, 'You're George's mother, aren't you?' She told me you had just left. Quite a coincidence, really. But that was only the beginning. My family lived in Glasgow for a year; it was shortly after my brother died. A one-year lectureship came up at the university and it was a good excuse to make a break with the past and a lucky break for my dad at the time. I had completely forgotten about it. Did you know that we both went to the same primary school for one term? Seems we've known each other for longer than I thought, Georgie-porgie."

George ignored Heather's revelation and looked at her with unusual intensity. "So, you sat and chatted with my mum?"

"Oh, I certainly did, George, for a long time," said Heather mischievously.

"And what exactly did you talk about, with my mum, my dearest Heather?" George asked almost breathlessly.

Merlin looked at Heather with a knowing smile. "Why, your father, of course," said Heather. "Seems like you've been holding some secrets back from me, haven't you, George Winsome? I didn't know you wanted to be a writer and documentary producer. I mean, you were writing film scripts when you were thirteen years old. Your mother showed me one. She's kept everything."

George lowered his head and sat down, placing his head in his hands. "Well, that's another secret out the bag. How much did she tell you?"

"Time for the tea ceremony, won't be a minute," said Merlin, hardly able to contain himself as he scurried off to the kitchen. "I do like it when the truth comes out, it's such fun."

George and Heather sat down together on the sofa, holding hands.

"So, what exactly did my mother tell you, then?" George asked.

"The lot, George, I mean everything. From an early age you showed great potential in your writing. I saw your English textbooks from school. You wrote an essay when you were twelve about what you wanted to do when you were older. You wanted to write books and produce documentaries about real life. Your mother was joking that everyone else had written that they wanted to be footballers or fighter pilots or sailors, but not you. No, you wanted to write and make documentaries. Quite precocious for a twelve-year-old. And then...."

"And then my father died," said George softly, a flood of memories coming back to him. "My father died. I stopped writing, and later decided that I wanted to be a lawyer. I suppose when my father died I blotted out my past. I don't remember changing my mind about writing; I just seemed to forget about it, as if it was part of a past life. I felt such anger – and shame – at the way my dad had been treated. I suppose I felt that by becoming a lawyer I could help fight such injustices. But that's not the way it seemed at the time. I just wanted to forget the past, forget the pain, and change direction."

Merlin was lurking in the doorway, unseen by George or Heather, his presence being given away by the sound of his chuckles. "At least you didn't wake up on Hampstead Heath after spending hundreds of years imprisoned in a tree. You should think yourself quite lucky, really. No harm done."

George gave Merlin a threatening look, but then broke out in a broad smile. "You're right, Merlin. No harm done. Listen, if you don't mind, that's enough bloody therapy for one day. I've got a lot to think about. I owe you a present," said George, changing the subject quickly onto safer ground, while passing to Heather a small box carefully wrapped in thick red wrapping paper, which Heather lovingly opened to reveal an exquisite diamond-encrusted ring.

"Don't think of it as a wedding ring, Heather, that's another matter. Think of it as an engagement ring or just a symbol of our love, whatever. It's just a present, from me to you," said George, and he kissed her.

"It was my choice as well, you know," said Merlin, pursing his lips for a kiss from Heather, who gently pecked him on the cheek.

"Thank you, both of you, it's gorgeous. I will treasure it forever, George. Now is that it, or are there more revelations to come?" Heather joked as she placed the diamond on her ring finger and held it up to the light, looking immensely satisfied.

George looked at Merlin, and they both nodded as if they knew the time was ripe for Heather to be told the next instalment.

"Merlin must leave us before the summer solstice, Heather. I don't know how it's going to happen, and I don't think Merlin does either," said George, looking at Merlin, who was shaking his head. "But the fact is that one way or another, Merlin will be gone before the last week of July, isn't that right, Merlin? Looks like you'll miss out on my case with the Bar Council."

Merlin looked deeply sad and lowered his head. "Yes, that is the truth, my dear friends, that's the way it is. I will not see the harvest moon."

Heather suddenly took on the look of the hard-nosed clear-thinking corporate terrorist that George found quite frightening. "So, we need to think of the endgame, don't we, if we've got less than three months of Merlin's company. I mean, we don't have legal careers right now, George, we've got Merlin."

"Heather, if my career as a barrister is over, that closes one door. I will still have other options to pursue; there's a big wide world outside the English Bar but the door is still open for you to return to the Bar, if that's what you want. We've got several truckloads of money, and that's just the beginning. If what you've said is right, checks are going to be raining on us for some time from all the newspaper syndicates. Maybe I'll get back into my writing; I'll need to think about it. My head hurts at the moment. It's not money we need any more, it's a purpose in life. And besides, Merlin is not only going to disappear before the end of July, but he wants to go on his own pilgrimage to Scotland before he leaves. On foot, mostly. We'll probably see Merlin for one more day, and then it's all over. We have to move on. He's not a lifetime meal ticket, or a passport to heaven, Heather. We've got freedom money, now we need to get a life. A life that has a good effect on others."

"Well, you've changed, George, you really have," said Heather, suddenly feeling and looking very saddened. She turned towards Merlin.

"You're going on a journey, Merlin, to see Scotland before you leave. I see. When *do* you leave?" she asked.

"The sooner the better, my dearest Heather. People already mock me. It is time to move on. There are places I want to see, and people I need to talk with. I am not for this city life, it is too removed from nature. It is not right, for me. I feel at home under the stars, I like to be awakened by the warmth of the sun, I feel lost without it. I enjoy the simple pleasure of walking, but not when in fear of being slain by a soulless machine. I will be back, I promise you. Xavier will contact you. I will leave in time to say goodbye at the place you call Kite Hill at dawn, then I will return before the equinox. Let us enjoy this time together, quietly without distraction."

"OK, Merlin," said George, trying to hide his tears. "You put on *Seven Brides for Seven Brothers* and I'll get a Chinese takeaway. And maybe some champagne, unless you want some whiskybae?"

"Whiskybae?" said Heather. "I haven't heard that word for a long time. Tempting, but better not right now, maybe after the birth."

"Chinese food, with whisky. OK, sounds good. I'll be back in a bit," said George.

"OK," Heather said. "No more business tonight, but tomorrow it's full steam ahead. I bet my email inbox is bursting at the seams. Have you seen the papers today?"

CHAPTER TWENTY-NINE
Metanoia

Saturday, 16th June 2001, 1 Makebourne Avenue, Highgate.

Heather sank into the newly acquired secondhand midnight-blue Liberty sofa, rubbing her large tummy, munching on her tenth packet of prawn cocktail crisps of the day, wondering whether the forthcoming baby's nursery would be better painted a light yellow instead of sky blue with white clouds, which seemed like a good idea at the time. George fidgeted at a modest pine desk next door, buried in his own mid-range laptop computer, wrestling with his first attempt at writing up his story of Merlin, not sure whether he was writing a stage play, screen play, biography, novel, or reportage, but he was writing and contented.

For the first time in her life Heather had found uninhibited joy and a profound peace of mind. The baby was due in a few days and all was well. Moreover, the issue of the money had been finally resolved. This had not been a straightforward matter, as Heather had failed to understand initially that a saintly lawyer such as St. Yves was capable of tough and prolonged negotiations. Soon enough Heather learnt not to fear the quiet, cultured voice that came to her in moments of solitude, an ancient voice that resonated with such a beautiful and distinctive French accent. Heather conversed with the saint as if she was concluding a good-faith business deal with an old, trusted friend.

Heather had come to understand that the humiliation she felt at the way she had been treated at Pentheus was her motivation to acquire wealth and achieve success. Merlin was right: some force was at work driving and feeding her need for revenge and retribution. Once that penny had dropped, Heather realised what she really wanted out of life and was now completely clear in her mind that her future lay at the Bar, working with disadvantaged, emotionally abandoned children. The money would be pitiful to modest, but that was no longer the issue. She would live a simple and uncomplicated life, but her own children would receive the best education available. That was the deal, an authentic deal Heather had made with St. Yves, or more accurately, with herself.

St. Yves had even insisted on the creation of a trust fund in favour of her children – present and future – leaving Heather and George with little real cash to spend. All of that was easy enough; the difficult part was St. Yves coming to the view that Heather's change of heart was utterly and completely genuine, an issue that was only resolved on the first occasion that Heather felt the presence that she knew instinctively to be the spirit of St. Yves. Heather did not see a shadowy, ghostlike figure but conversed internally with a voice that felt as real as a lucid dream. What surprised Heather was that the experience of St. Yves felt so heartwarming and peaceful.

'Ivo', as she had learnt to call St. Yves, had explained it all: about the reign of Louis, which had been a good time, about how the next French King – the third Philip – had imposed punitive taxes to fund a long fight with the English, which made Ivo take sides with the poor and the abandoned, and how the next King Philip eventually made peace with the English and why that moment marked Ivo's time to leave the world on the 19th of May 1303, the day before the Treaty of Paris was signed. They shared a delight in detail, 'to confront the devil' as Ivo put it. That made a lot of sense to Heather: the devil was indeed in the details.

At one point, Heather told St. Yves to keep the money – "every fucking penny" – leave her alone and let her get on with her life. That had been the turning point, the moment Ivo knew Heather had ripped herself loose from the forces of revenge and rediscovered her kind and charitable heart.

*   *   *

George surveyed the large, bay-windowed front room that had been converted into a tasteful office, overlooking a quiet, private road, and decided to place another log on the smouldering hearth in the marbled fireplace, feeling as he did so another wave of relief and satisfaction at being the joint freehold owner of a large, albeit somewhat shabby and neglected, house in a prime Highgate location. His ambition to write and produce had returned, not overnight but gradually, as he realised that he had to pick up where he left off over ten years ago and regain the pleasure and satisfaction he used to experience when writing as a young boy.

But George and Heather were acutely aware that the sands of time were running out, and that there was less than a week to go before Merlin's anticipated disappearance.

There was no need for George or Heather to be concerned about Merlin's whereabouts, as he was now being followed by a disparate crowd numbering at any given time between two and nearly two hundred devotees, followers, and well-wishers in addition to the occasional journalist and television or radio crew. At first, Merlin tried to avoid the spotlight, but as his journey became more widely talked about, so the crowd and interest grew, and Merlin became increasingly relaxed about the company around him. Motorists might stop and offer him a lift, farmers would invite him to sleep in their fields, hoteliers would seek him out hoping he would grace their hotel with a night's sleep (and a signed photograph with the smiling owner), passing cars would toot their horns, and children would confidently come up to converse with the famous Merlin and ask for his autograph. Merlin had tried hard not to walk the path of the celebrity, living meagrely from day to day, relying entirely on the generosity of those whose lives he walked through, giving time to whomever wished to share his company while he made his way through Scotland and back.

Newspapers followed his path with interest, and one Scottish newspaper carried a daily update, with a map indicating the route Merlin had taken along the west coast of Scotland, through Ayrshire, from where he had taken a boat to the southern Hebrides, passing by the island of Arran, over Kintyre to Islay and then Jura, further north to Iona (the only place Merlin stayed for more than one night) and northwards again up to Skye, all the way across the very northern part of the Scottish wilderness to Dunnet Head; and onwards to the Orkney Islands before commencing the southward journey through the outskirts of Inverness, finding an easterly path around the Cairngorm Mountains, through Fife and then Edinburgh. Merlin had been travelling for the most part by foot and boat, but there had been occasions when he would even accept a lift in a car or tractor if the driver was persuasive enough, or on the back of a horse, a bicycle, piggy back, skateboard, improvised rickshaw, even a homemade chariot, and was now in Peebles in Tweeddale, sitting in quiet reflection by an ancient thorn tree on the banks of the River Tweed at the point where it is joined by the Powsail Burn.

Heather pressed a remote-control button and the enormous digital surround-sound television, rescued from a recycling plant and repaired for pennies, sparked into life. Speed flicking through over one hundred channels, Heather came to Channel 687, a new venture called the 'Celtic Channel' that seemed to appear on spare digital channels at will, funded by the Scottish Tourist Board, and listened carefully to the local red-haired presenter sitting on a Scottish hillside, Merlin in the background, leaning on his ever-present staff, as if he was a wild animal in the savannah. Heather settled in even deeper into the soft cushions, and shouted, "He's on again, George, come and have a look." An announcement running across the bottom of the screen promised an hour-length documentary to follow the programme, revealing the results of the scientific examination of Merlin's staff.

George was quite relieved to abandon his monitor, and bounded into the living room to watch the television.

"God knows where he got that old hooded gown from," commented Heather. "Goes well with his wee white beard, though."

The Scottish presenter talked almost in a whisper as if he might disturb a solitary lion. "As we sit and gaze at this wonderful, soft, and extraordinary man we ask oorsel, 'Is this the very same spot where Merlin the Wylte or Merlin Caledonius was murdered by the treacherous shepherds of Meldred? Is the reason the famous Merlin is here to look upon his own grave?'" The camera pulled back to focus upon Merlin before the presenter continued: "Was it not prophesied that 'when Tweed and Powsail meet at Merlin's grave, England and Scotland shall one monarch have?' and did they no meet the very day oor ane King James took the throne?"

George and Heather watched transfixed as the camera focused tightly on Merlin, who stood up, pulled out his prick, and let loose a long steaming stream of piss.

"Oh shit," said George, "you just never know what the old bugger's going to do next. Can't be many people who piss on their own graves. Oh dear, God knows what they'll make of that," he said as Merlin put back his member and moved on, an enormous cheering crowd in tow, emerging from behind the camera.

"They'll be taking samples and selling the water for generations to come," Heather suggested. "Everyone wants a piece of him, George."

"Well, I hope he makes it back here in time, Heather. It's not going to be much fun if he disappears in a puff of smoke in Watford. I mean, he's got a bit of style, surely he won't let us down."

"Just relax, I'm sure he'll be back. He could make it in one day if he wanted to. He's not due to disappear for a week, stop fretting."

"Well, maybe I just miss him, Heather, that's all. It's not very exciting any more; even the *News on Sunday* can't be bothered putting the boot in now the public is behind him. Nothing much has happened since that trainee solicitor at Furlong's was sent to prison for fraud. Seems he was destined to get caught for something, sooner or later. Bet it was him who tried to steal the check. Ironic really that it was the *News on Sunday* who finally nailed him."

"Well," said Heather, "they got a good story out of it. Mind you, not as good as the exposé by Simon Hall's ex-wife of his secret life as a cross-dresser. I was surprised he didn't die of embarrassment. Those photographs were quite spectacular."

"What goes around, comes around. We know that from our own experience, Heather. There are no exceptions, none. I bet the government's review of the future of the monarchy will put an end to Prince Charles's ambitions, especially when those who bought his organic grass succumb to the temptations of the check book." George sat down next to Heather, placing his head gently on her tummy, listening intensely. "I can hear the baby, Heather, can you?"

"Oh yeah, and what's he saying?"

"He's saying, 'Why can't you let me out of here so my daddy can make me a little brother.'"

Heather whacked him with one of the large soft matching cushions.

"One boy's enough, George. The next one will be a girl," she said, sounding unnervingly confident. "But let's get this one over with first. They reckon the baby will arrive before the weekend."

CHAPTER THIRTY
Farewell

5 p.m., Friday, 22nd June 2001, maternity ward, Whittington Hospital, Highgate, North London.

George looked around the small functional clean hospital room on the top floor of the Whittington Hospital where mothers were dispatched to have their babies. The smell of antiseptic wash lingered in every corner, but both Heather and George felt reassured to be in a hospital environment, notwithstanding the off-white clinical surroundings and stainless-steel décor. The room was private and clean, and the duty midwife, Marsha, a fifty-year-old Jamaican mother of eight, was a birthing veteran of the old school. Unknown to George, Marsha had an elder sister called Martha, who had sat on the jury that tried Merlin. But those dots were not to be connected by George or Marsha. There were more immediate issues at stake.

"You just take your time, young lady. The baby will come when it's ready. Just press that button when you need me, I'm one minute away," Marsha said as she disappeared into the corridor.

Heather lay on the heavy iron hospital bed, naked except for a thin white cotton gown, by now unable to see her own heavily swollen ankles.

"Sit down, George, you're making me nervous. Why can't you just relax?" she said, holding her enormous stomach as if to hold in the baby.

"Relax? Relax! Are you joking? You're about to have a baby, there's no word from Merlin, England are playing Greece in less than three hours, and you're asking me to relax. If they lose today they won't even qualify for the World Cup finals." George paced around the room, which was feeling smaller by the minute.

"Well, I'm glad you've got your priorities right, George. I

don't know why you're so excited about the football; Scotland's not even playing. In the meantime, we've got a baby on the way." Heather breathed in and out, trying to ride the waves of pain that were coming increasingly frequently.

George ran over to the panic button. "I'll get the midwife, shall I? Sounds imminent," he said in a mild panic.

"No, not yet. Oh God, the pain! All right, get the midwife," gasped Heather.

Within seconds Marsha appeared. "How y'doin', honey? How frequent are the contractions?" she asked as she put on a rubber glove and felt inside Heather to gauge the width of the birth canal while George turned away, embarrassed.

"I don't know. Maybe about every ten minutes now. How long can I take this? Nobody tells you about the pain, oh God."

"Listen, Heather," said Marsha, as if George wasn't present, "if you don't want to feel no pain, that's the way we can do it. It's up to you, you just say when, OK, my dear?"

Heather grimaced. "No, I don't want to take anything; I want this to happen on its own. I can take it. It's OK."

George stood at the window, looking at his watch, wondering if it was such a good idea for him to be around, but that's what he and Heather had always agreed. The midwife was, in her heart, very anti men being present during childbirth despite the trend towards fathers being there during labour.

Marsha left the room again, having satisfied herself that Heather was a long way from giving birth, several hours at the earliest.

"Listen Heather, I'm just going to pop down to the café. Hell, it should be open by now. Do you want anything?"

"I don't want anything, George, just be quick, OK?"

"Five minutes, Heather, I promise you, five minutes. Press call on your mobile and I'll come running." George breathed a sigh of relief and headed towards the downstairs café.

He reappeared after a full twenty minutes, looking sheepish, as Heather lay in bed, counting aloud and breathing in a heavy but controlled manner.

"You OK? I mean how long do you reckon?" asked George.

"Hell, George, I don't know. I really don't know. Could be several hours at this rate."

"Several hours?" George looked at his watch. "You wouldn't mind if I turned on the television? It'll help drown out the screaming from next door."

"George, if you think I'm giving birth to the chanting of 'Come on, England' you're off yer fucking head. I don't think so." Heather gritted her teeth with the onslaught of another painful contraction.

George was frantically trying to figure a way out of his predicament when the door burst open.

"Oh, Heather, thank God I've found you. You've no idea what I've been through trying to find you. I thought you might be in the Royal Free. I'm so glad I've found you. I just needed to be with you, Heather." Heather's mother looked as anxious as George felt as she hugged and kissed her daughter. Then she took off her jacket and obviously settled in for the duration.

"And you must be George," she said. "My, you are a good-looking lad. Please, call me Karen. Now, what on earth are you doing here? This is no place for a father-to-be, haven't you got friends to spend time with?"

George could only manage a halfhearted "Hi" while he tried to get over the extraordinary similarity between Heather and her mum. Looking at Karen, he felt he was seeing the face of his beloved as she would look in thirty years' time. It was an eerie sensation, but pleasantly reassuring.

"Oh, Mum, for God's sake. This is all I need. George and I agreed a long time ago that he would be present at the birth, it's the way we wanted it to be."

Marsha heard the raised voices and popped her head round the door. "Everything OK in here? My, what a crowd. Any more expected or is the show sold out? Perhaps the father would like to leave?"

Heather looked around the faces and smiled at George.

"OK, George, I've got the message. Go and watch the bloody football. I'm clearly in a minority of one, go on. I've got my mobile. Just keep yours on, OK?" Another intense contraction caused Heather to yell out in pain, and George knew that was his cue.

"Well, only if you want me to go," he said before the three ladies shouted in unison, "Please, just go!"

★   ★   ★

George took in a deep breath of a cool spring evening and closed his eyes, asking himself where he should go. After a few seconds, the answer was obvious: Xavier's. But first he needed a drink, and therefore the plan was: one pint in the Sir Richard Steele, then onto Xavier's.

George set off towards Chalk Farm, the route map that he had set himself involving a thirty-minute stroll through the Holly Lodge Estate, avoiding his own house, which posed too great a temptation to pop into, over the Heath and cutting slightly south to end up at the Sir Richard Steele.

George could hear the chanting from the large crowd that had assembled in and around the pub well before he could see the pub entrance. It was just past six o'clock and the country was rapidly coming to a standstill in anticipation of an easy victory over Greece, to take them into the World Cup finals. England had already thrashed Germany laying to rest many painful defeats of the past. George dared imagine England in the finals of the World Cup – all they had to do was win this next game and glory was theirs for the taking. *Yes*, thought George, *it's all beginning to make sense, the natural order of things, I get it.*

Inside the Sir Richard Steele was a tightly packed mob, mostly dressed to varying degrees in the red and white colours of the English football kit. The presence of a few fully kitted-out supporters of Greece added to the convivial, almost party-like atmosphere. George fought his way to the bar and eventually found himself a tiny space from where he could just about see one of the three television screens. It was seven thirty and time for kick-off. Half an hour later a goal for Greece silenced the England supporters but sending the few Greeks into raptures of delight. Half-time came all too soon creating a scramble for orders at the bar. A Greek supporter squeezed his way back from the bar, brushed his way past George spilling some beer and apologised. George wondered why the face seemed familiar but let the moment pass.

"Hello, Sir George, now why did I think I'd find you here?"

George turned around to see the enormous figure of Xavier.

"Xavier!" exclaimed George. "I was just on my way to see you. Where's Merlin?"

Xavier looked at George solemnly. "It is time we went, my friend. Merlin will be joining us soon."

George looked sadly at the television screen and back at Xavier.

"Do not worry about this game, George. You will hear of this match for many years to come. England will not win today but all will be well. A soul is to be redeemed. It is a good time to go."

The Greek supporter who had spilt the beer over George shouted towards Xavier, "They'll need the powers of Merlin to save them this time!"

Xavier smiled and looked at George. "It is time to go, my friend. We shall pass by my house to prepare, and then we must go to the meeting place."

George looked forlornly around him, realising that his time was well and truly up and sighed as England equalised. He reluctantly followed Xavier out of the door and into the abandoned street outside, pausing when he heard loud collective groans from inside the pub as Greece scored again, taking the lead.

*   *   *

Some hours later, George was following Xavier over the now-dark, almost misty green fields of Hampstead Heath, lightened only by a near-full moon.

Xavier stood still for a moment, as if unsure of his destination. "Now, I know where we will not be meeting, but the other half of the question is slightly more involved," he mumbled as George pulled his jacket in a little tighter against the evening chill.

Xavier passed by a close-knit mound of fir trees, the location of Merlin's arrest. "We are not far. We will meet at a grove of young oak trees; these are mature firs," he said confidently as he bounded off in a northerly direction towards Kenwood House.

"Yes, it is here," he shouted after a spirited ten-minute walk, as he came across an almost perfect circle of young oaks, next to which was a wooden bench, on which George could see the silhouetted figure of a dreadlocked man. On hearing Xavier and George approach, the man jumped to his feet.

"Xavier, the man himself. Hey brother, thanks for the invite. I owe you, man."

As George approached the man he could just about make out his dark features and recognised him to be the Rastafarian jury member, Rufus Christian.

"Rufus, dear Rufus," said Xavier in a theatrical tone. "How nice of you to come."

Rufus and Xavier embraced like two long-lost brothers, joking and patting each other wildly.

"You remember Mr. Winsome, don't you?" asked Xavier, almost beside himself with glee.

"Man, how could I forget? Hey, how's it going? You can represent me any time, brother," said Rufus, holding up his hand for a high five. George did his awkward best to high five Rufus, trying to contain his astonishment at meeting a juror in such a bizarre context.

"Where are the others?" asked Rufus innocently.

"Others?" George said incredulously. "Others? What others?"

"Hi! Hi! Is that you, Xavier?" a young man cried from a few yards away, coming from over the rising, which eventually led to the top of Kite Hill, accompanied by another large male figure.

Within a few moments the two new faces were sufficiently proximate for George to make out clearly the large round face of Mobo, walking next to a young scruffy-looking lad who George immediately recognised as his drinking companion on the day of Merlin's release: the judge's son, Sihairly.

It was clear from the long friendly exchanges that Xavier held the answers to many of George's questions, but the time did not seem appropriate to start quizzing him about how the group came to be in the same place at the same time.

Mobo and George stood to the side of the others. "What on earth are you doing here, Mobo? I mean, in a thousand years I wouldn't have expected to see you, I mean not here and now."

Mobo faced up to George, bypassing completely any sense of embarrassment. "There's a lot we don't know about each other, George. I've known Xavier for many, many years." Mobo let loose one of his uninhibited chuckles. "He's taught me a lot, you know, about myself, that is. An awful lot. I thought our double-act in court was worthy of an Oscar. Stroke of genius for Xavier to change his story, worked a treat all round. I was mightily concerned when I first saw Xavier's witness statement but I knew all would work out in the end. Let's just say I've been around a bit longer than you, George, to understand these things. You might call it serendipity, we call it cosmic synchronicity. Anyway, my friend – no harm done – truth and justice prevailed, in the end."

Xavier and Mobo shared a hug and smiled at each other like long-lost friends.

"So," said Xavier turning towards the other guests, "you have all arrived. My heartfelt congratulations to you all. It is a miracle. Now we can take our places." He led the group into the centre of the circle of oak trees.

George was the first to notice a small figure sitting upright, wrapped up in a dark gown, squatting on the grass within the circle of trees.

The figure threw back his hood and smiled. "What took you so long? I was beginning to wonder whether I had been abandoned and forgotten," said Merlin, laughing. "Please, all of you take a seat. George next to me, here, please. And Sihairly, you can sit here, on my other side. Please, Rufus, Mobo, Xavier, sit down. If it wasn't for that silly football match, I might never have lost my crowd." This triggered a round of nervous laughter.

The group soon settled into a little circle, protected by the ring of young oaks, while Xavier quickly collected some twigs and dead branches and started to make a small fire, fanned by the light evening breeze. The fire gave off little heat but allowed those present to see each other without difficulty.

Sihairly, Rufus, and Mobo simultaneously fumbled with wafer-thin Rizla papers, busying themselves by rolling enormous reefers. Xavier followed suit once the fire was under way, and within minutes there were four joints being passed around the group of six, not a word being spoken during the process.

Eventually Merlin broke the silence. "I have Xavier to thank for bringing us together on this solemn night. I must depart before the sun rises, this I think you all know. I have achieved all I wished to achieve during my time here but there are one or two matters to be settled." Without warning, Merlin delivered a severe blow across Sihairly's face with his staff. The distinct sickening cracking sound and flood of blood indicated an expertly broken nose.

Sihairly placed his hands on his face, writhing backward and forward in excruciating pain. "What da fuck was that for, you bastard?" was all Sihairly managed to blurt out before the tears took over.

The others remained quiet but concerned, as Merlin explained his actions.

"That was a message from your father, Sihairly. You have much to learn. You will not force your will over your father again, I think. Now," said Merlin, casually handing Sihairly what looked like a handkerchief, "you must make a decision whether to leave this company right now, sit down and keep quiet, or challenge me to fight. Well?"

All eyes were on Sihairly, who, judging by the heavy sobbing, was not about to seek revenge on Merlin.

"I'll stay," he said through the tears that showed no signs of abating. "I'll stay."

"And be quiet?" added Merlin.

"And be quiet," added Sihairly meekly.

Another round of smoking continued in silence before Merlin looked at Mobo.

"My lord Ojukwu Ibo Moboto," said Merlin firmly, causing Mobo to keep a close eye on Merlin's staff, "it is a rare pleasure to meet someone who knows who they are. Xavier has told me of the progress you have made. I congratulate you."

Mobo looked more relieved than complimented and nodded towards Merlin out of respect. "I thank you, Merlin. It is a great pleasure to share this occasion with you."

"I wanted you to be here, my friend, because you are destined for the highest judicial office in the land, a rare feat for any man and a great honour for your noble ancestors," said Merlin while Mobo listened intensely.

"You are to become a Law Lord, and your wisdom will be captured in your judgements for generations. You are one of a very select people who truly understand human rights, and human dignity. I have a present for you."

Merlin shuffled around the inside of his cloak and produced a beautifully decorated jade amulet, which he handed to George, who passed it to Xavier and finally to Mobo, who handled the object with great reverence, eventually placing the thin leather necklace around his neck proudly.

"Thank you, Merlin," he said, "I will treasure this object."

"I am sure you will, Mobo," said Merlin affectionately. "It has no power, my friend, other than to remind you of your duty to others. However, if you lose your compassion, the object will desert you."

Mobo twiddled with the amulet before deciding that he would have time enough to examine it in greater detail soon enough, on his own.

Merlin turned towards Xavier, whose eyes seemed to become clearer and clearer the more he smoked.

"Xavier, my friend, my old friend. We know each other too well for words to serve much purpose. I will return again one day, and I know that you will be present, somewhere. As the kosmos will dictate. I made you a solemn promise a long, long time ago, after a ferocious battle, that I would forever keep the spirit of your brother Haki alive, who fought and died so bravely on that day."

Xavier lowered his head as if a flood of memories had resurfaced after many years.

"On my travels, Xavier, I searched around the outskirts of our village on the island of Hoy, where you and Haki played as children. I came across this." He handed to George to hand to Xavier a stone, which, to George, appeared to be nothing more than a large pebble.

Xavier examined it carefully, closed his eyes and rubbed the surface. "I cannot thank you enough, Merlin. This writing," said Xavier, showing George what looked to him like random scratch marks on a common large pebble, "was made by my brother. It was how he wrote his name when he was a boy." Xavier proudly placed the object into an inside pocket. "His spirit is still strong, Merlin. I cannot thank you enough."

The group descended into another long period of silence, while the fire gently crackled and sparked and the warm southerly wind gently swayed the branches of the young supple oak trees.

Merlin eventually opened his eyes again and turned towards Rufus.

"Christian Rufus, my Lion from Zion, you must be the purest antinomian I have ever met." A comment which only Xavier and Rufus seemed to find amusing. "I have heard of your wily ways. Perhaps if you had not taken such a stance during the Great Deliberations, the jury might not have taken quite the same route. It is a strange art you practise, but understandable nonetheless. I have need for a Keeper of the Staff after my departure. Are you willing to accept such a responsibility?"

"Right on," said Rufus, leaning over to take the staff from Merlin's outstretched hand. "Nice one, Merlin." He placed the staff over the top of his crossed legs, indicating that it wasn't going anywhere.

Merlin turned sideways to look at George. "My great and noble knight, Sir George. How I have enjoyed witnessing your journey into manhood. There is perhaps only one greater gift than a healthy, strong, and spirited child. You are a father, Sir George, my friend."

George tried to hold back tears of pride as the words sunk in, and how he longed at that moment to be in the arms of Heather.

"It was not my intention to return to these earthly shores at this time, Sir George, and I have suffered considerable confusion as a result. Maybe I shall return again, perhaps if the Ancient Order of Great Council who have asked me to join them so permits. I have felt enough human emotion to last me for quite a while. I am very grateful to you and your dear Lady Heather for reminding me of Sjöfn's great power, which is purer and stronger than that of Eros himself."

Merlin again closed his eyes while the reefers were passed around. "I am mightily relieved to hear news that the prospect of great riches did not corrupt your soul. I was, my friend, very worried, I must confess. You and Heather can now pursue your rightful paths in life, although you must be patient for your labours to bear fruit. You know in that true and courageous heart of yours that your future lies in the written word and the exposure of evil and corruption. The trial by your elders will not result in dishonour. You will be given advice as to how to conduct yourself, no more. Reflect on their wisdom and connect with the order of things, the kosmos. You have been given the one gift that cannot be surpassed: an open heart and a pure soul."

George lowered his head, knowing that Merlin was right.

"Let these men bear witness to my blessing to you and Lady Heather, who faces many battles in the years ahead," continued Merlin. "Your children will receive the very best education and training you can find, but you must teach them to never lose sight of their obligations to others. Xavier and Mobo are the godparents of your child, and you must take advice from them when the need arises."

Mobo and Xavier spontaneously leant over to shake George's hand.

"You have been my saviour, Merlin. I will never forget what you've taught me, and I freely give my promise to you, as you request," said George feeling many years older. "Perhaps you will pay us a visit sometime? You know, drop in for a cup of tea?"

Merlin laughed softly before closing his eyes and breathing deeply, and once again a compelling, meditative silence overcame the group.

With their eyes closed, neither George, Sihairly, Xavier, or Mobo witnessed the precise moment the transformation occurred, but something did happen while they sat in the semi-darkness around the fire. Perhaps it was the sound of a bird's feet scratching beneath Merlin's gown that caused George to open his eyes and turn towards Merlin, who had simply disappeared into thin air, his clothes lying in a crumpled heap where he had, only moments before, been sitting.

The group collectively stared at where Merlin had been, only to see a bird appear from under the hood of Merlin's cloak. It was a strange-looking creature, very similar to a crow, but with white markings on the tips of its wings, which were long and pointed in shape, like a magpie's. The bird shuffled forward on its clawed feet, let loose the hoarse-throated cawing sound of a magpie, looked around at its white-tipped wings, and flew off towards the moon.

"I don't think I would have believed it even if I had seen it with my own eyes," said Mobo in disbelief, as the bird became harder and harder to see against the dark sky.

Sihairly stood up, and without saying a word to anyone, walked off into the distance.

"A very skillful piece of work," suggested Xavier. "Merlin always found that one tricky." He laughed. "Now who's for a swim? The reward will be a fine breakfast prepared by Zena, and a taste of my finest grass before the celebrations begin in earnest. Today we shall live in the present, not the past."

Mobo looked at Xavier. "Sounds like a mighty fine idea to me, Xavier, count me in. George? Rufus?"

Rufus looked lost in the detail of the staff that he now had to himself. "Swim? Are you crazy? Well, maybe later. Smoke sounds good."

All present knew that George felt an overwhelming desire to be elsewhere. "I've got to say hello to my son. It's time for me to go." George embraced Xavier, Rufus, and then Mobo and disappeared into the rapidly lifting darkness, heading west toward Whittington Hospital.

"Goodbye my friends, goodbye," he said, raising his arm without turning around. "Goodbye."

★   ★   ★

Heather and Karen were sound asleep, as was the baby, wrapped tightly in Heather's arms, all seven pounds of him. The birth had been a long time coming, with mother and grandmother completely exhausted, too deeply asleep in bed and chair to notice the half crow, half magpie finding its way through the narrowly opened window in the room where the three of them lay.

Once inside the maternity room, Merlin transformed into human form, completely naked, and peered into the sleeping face of the baby that was embraced in its mother's loving arms. He gently stroked its still-moist and soft unblemished face.

"Have a great life, my friend, you have the finest parents any child could wish for. Stay well and never surrender your nobility. Learn from your parents, they are pure in heart." Merlin saw Heather stirring slightly and re-transformed into the white-tipped bird and flew back out of the window, just as George walked through the door.

George felt a tingling sensation as he looked around the room. He looked for the first time at the face of his newly born child, who appeared to be fast asleep but smiling a beautiful baby smile. George looked towards the window and peered out into the red dawn. "Farewell, Merlin, farewell."

George stroked the baby's thin locks of pure blond baby hair, tears streaming down his cheeks, and looked over to Heather, who was beginning to stir.

Without saying a word, George quietly took off his shoes and jacket and crept into Heather's bed, gently stroking her hair before cuddling up as tightly as he could. Stirring slightly, Heather held onto George's arm and sank back into a deep sleep.

"Good night, Heather. Sleep well, my love."

FLAME TREE PRESS
FICTION WITHOUT FRONTIERS
Award-Winners & Original Voices

Flame Tree Press is the trade fiction imprint of Flame Tree
Publishing, focusing on excellent writing in horror and the
supernatural, crime and mystery, science fiction and fantasy.
Our aim is to explore beyond the boundaries of the everyday,
with tales from both award-winning authors and original voices.

•

Other titles available include:

Thirteen Days by Sunset Beach by Ramsey Campbell
Think Yourself Lucky by Ramsey Campbell
The House by the Cemetery by John Everson
The Toy Thief by D.W. Gillespie
The Siren and the Spectre by Jonathan Janz
The Sorrows by Jonathan Janz
The Sky Woman by J.D. Moyer
Creature by Hunter Shea
The Bad Neighbour by David Tallerman
Ten Thousand Thunders by Brian Trent
Night Shift by Robin Triggs
The Mouth of the Dark by Tim Waggoner

•

Join our mailing list for free short stories, new release details,
news about our authors and special promotions:

flametreepress.com